"THERE IS NOTHING IN MY HEART THAT I COULD NOT SAY TO YOU."

"NOR IS THERE IN MINE."

"I love you," said the Prince of Antioch. "You are the most exciting woman I ever met. I would that I had been the King of France. You and I would have been as one. What have you to say to that, my Queen? Will you be equally frank with me?"

"You are the most exciting man I ever met. I would that you had been the King of France."

"Eleonore, why then should we deny ourselves what so clearly belongs to us?"

"Because . . ."

"Because of this close relationship."

"Raymond, you are in truth my uncle."

"Eleonore, you are in truth my love. . . ."

Fawcett Crest Books
by Jean Plaidy:

☐ THE LION OF JUSTICE   24318 $2.50

☐ THE PASSIONATE ENEMIES   24390 $2.50

☐ THE PLANTAGENET PRELUDE   24422 $2.75

☐ THE QUEEN'S HUSBAND   23896 $1.95

THE PLANTAGENET PRELUDE

Jean Plaidy

FAWCETT CREST • NEW YORK

THE PLANTAGENET PRELUDE

Published by Fawcett Crest Books, a unit of CBS Publications,
the Consumer Publishing Division of CBS Inc., by arrangement with G. P. Putnam's Sons

ISBN: 0-449-24422-9

Printed in the United States of America

First Fawcett Crest Printing: July 1981

10   9   8   7   6   5   4   3   2   1

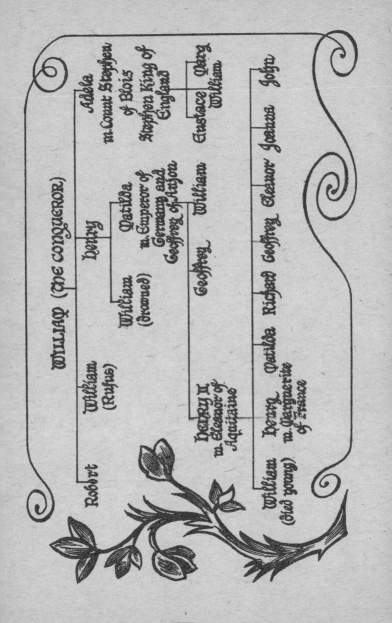

WILLIAM (THE CONQUEROR.)

- Robert
- William (Rufus)
- Henry
  - William (drowned)
  - Matilda m. Emperor of Germany and Geoffrey of Anjou
    - Henry II m. Eleanor of Aquitaine
      - William (died young)
      - Henry m. Marguerite of France
      - Matilda
      - Richard
      - Geoffrey
      - Eleanor
      - Joanna
      - John
    - Geoffrey
    - William
- Adela m. Count Stephen of Blois
  - Stephen King of England
    - Eustace
    - Mary
    - William

ELEONORE
& HENRY

Duchess and Queen

From a window of the Château de l'Ombrière the Duke of Aquitaine looked down on the scene in the shaded rose garden. It was one to enchant him. His two daughters—charming creatures both of them though the elder of the two, Eleonore, surpassed in beauty her sister Petronelle—were surrounded by members of the Court, young men and women, decorative and elegant, listening now to the minstrel who was singing his song of love.

The Duke's eyes rested on Eleonore, for she was at the centre of the group. Some quality in her set her apart from the rest of the company. It was not only her beauty, nor was it her rank. She was after all the heiress of Aquitaine until its Duke begot a son and, widowed as he was, he must bestir himself if he were to do so, for although he was but thirty-eight years of age, he had lost two wives and the only outcome of those marriages was his two girls Eleonore and Petronelle. Eleonore was tall and she was handsome; there was something commanding about her; she had the air of one born to rule. There was also a sensuality. He sighed thinking of his father whose life had been dominated by his devotion to the opposite sex and wondering whether his attractive daughter would follow her grandfather in that respect.

She was fourteen years of age, Petronelle three years

younger. Yet there was a ripeness about them both, even little Petronelle. As for Eleonore she was ready for marriage. And if anything should happen to him before this event took place, who would protect her? He imagined her in her rose garden surrounded by her minstrels and the ladies of her court; and some suitor riding into the castle. There would not only be Eleonore's vast lands and fortune to attract him but the fascinating Eleonore herself. And if she refused to marry? He knew the manners of the day. The lovely maiden would be abducted, held prisoner, deflowered if she would not yield willingly and placed in such a position that her family would be eager to marry her to her ravisher.

It was hard to imagine such a fate for Eleonore. Yet even she would be forced to submit.

He thanked God that it had not come to that. Here he was a man of thirty-eight with two attractive daughters. He must marry and beget a son. Yet what if he were to marry and there was no son? It was a logical assumption as so far there had been only daughters. How often were royal male heirs elusive. Why should he have been given only daughters? As was customary with men of his times he asked himself whether God was punishing him for his sins or perhaps the sins of his forbears.

His father had been one of the most renowned sinners of his age. Women had been his downfall. He had left his wife and set up his mistress in great state even having an image of her engraved on his shield. William the ninth Duke of Aquitaine had cared nothing for convention, and although the greatest motive in his life had been the pursuit of women, this was a common enough quality—or failing depending on the way one looked upon it—and he was renowned rather for his love of poetry and song. This Duke's ideal state had been to lie with his mistress of the moment and listen to the strumming of the harp, and the songs which were often of his own composing, sung by his minstrels. He was called the Father of the Troubadours and Eleonore had inherited his talent in this; she could compose a poem, set it to music, play it, sing it and attracted to her the finest songsters in the Duchy. What else had she inherited from her grandfather? Having noted the expression in those big languorous eyes as they rested on various comely gentlemen, the Duke wondered.

What he should do was get a son quickly and find a husband for Eleonore. But neither of these projects could be achieved without a great deal of thought. A husband for Eleonore now when she was the heiress could easily be found but it would be remembered that she could be displaced if her father had a son. And to have a son he must first find a wife! Not that that presented any great difficulty. What he must have was a *fruitful* wife. And there was the gist of the matter. Who could say until a man was married whether his wife would give him a son? What if he married to find the lady barren or capable only of giving him daughters?

So this was his dilemma. Should he marry again and try for a son? Or should he accept Eleonore as the heiress of Aquitaine? What of her husband if she married? Quite clearly, if she were to remain heiress of Aquitaine there was only one husband who would be worthy of her and that was the son of the King of France. So he was torn by doubts as he looked down on the scene in the garden.

* * *

He sent for Eleonore. Because she was clever and could read and write—a rare accomplishment—because she already seemed to regard herself as the potential ruler of Aquitaine, because her mind was agile and to be admired as much as her beauty, he had talked to her for some time as he would have talked with some of his ministers.

She came in from the warm sun into the comparative chill of the castle, wrinkling her nose a little for the smell of rushes after the rose garden was none too pleasant. She would order the serving-man to sweeten the place. It should have been done a week ago. Rushes quickly became unpleasantly odorous.

Her father would be in his apartment which was reached by a staircase at the end of the great hall. This hall itself was the main room of the castle. It stretched from one end to the other and it reached up to the rafters. The ducal apartments were small in comparison for it was in the hall with its thick stone walls and narrow slits of windows that the court spent most of its time. Here courtiers danced and played the harp and sang; here the ladies sat and embroidered as they told tales and sang their songs; and because the castle could not accommodate them all they lived in houses close by where they could be within reach of the Court.

Eleonore mounted the stairs to her father's apartment.

He stood up as she entered and, placing his hands on her shoulders, drew her to him and kissed her forehead.

"My daughter," he said, "I would speak with you."

"I guessed it, Father, since you asked me to come to you."

Some might have said commanded. Eleonore must be asked, never commanded, and graciously she granted the request.

Her father smiled at her. He would not have had her otherwise.

"You know, Eleonore, my dear daughter, that I am deeply concerned."

"For what reason?"

"I have no male heir."

She lifted her head proudly. "And why should you need a male heir when you have a daughter?"

"Aye, a fine daughter. Mistake me not. I am aware of your qualities. But men seem to follow men."

"They will be made to see that there are times when for their good they must follow a woman."

He smiled at her. "I doubt not that you would make them understand that."

"Then, Father, you have no problem. Come to the gardens and you shall hear my minstrels sing my latest song."

"A treat I shall enjoy, my dear daughter. But it is suggested to me by my ministers that my duty lies in marriage."

Eleonore's eyes blazed in sudden anger. Another marriage! A half-brother to displace her! That was something she would do everything in her power to prevent. She loved this fair land of Aquitaine. The people adored her. When she rode out they came out of their cottages to see her, to give many a heartfelt cheer. She believed that they would never feel so warmly towards any but herself. Oh, she was a woman and it may be that her sex was against her; but her grandfather, Duke William IX, had loved women, idealized women; he had instituted the Courts of the Love; he had composed poetry and songs in favour of love, and women had been the most important factor in his life. So why should not the next ruler of Aquitaine be a Duchess instead of a Duke? It was what the people wanted. She herself wanted it; and Eleonore had already made up her mind that what she wanted she would have.

"And if you married," she cried, "how could you be sure that you would get this male heir by which you set such store?"

"I am content with my daughters." He quailed before her fury which was in itself ridiculous. He, a father and a Duke, to be overawed by a girl, and his daughter at that! Why should he feel this need to placate her? "It is my ministers . . ." he began feebly.

"Then your ministers must needs mind their own affairs."

"Dear daughter, this is an affair of the Duchy."

"Very well then, marry, and I'll swear you will soon be making a pilgrimage to some saint's shrine asking for a fruitful marriage."

"A pilgrimage?"

" 'Tis the custom. But I wonder at you. You have sins to answer for, Father. You need redemption even as my grandfather did."

"I never lived the life he did."

"His sins were committed in the Courts of Love. There are others which have to be answered for. You have offended many, Father. It may be that the prayers of your enemies would be answered, prayers for retribution and not yours for forgiveness of your sins."

"Daughter, you turn all to your advantage."

"Mayhap I uphold the truth. I was ever one who liked plain speaking and always shall."

"So then let us have plain speaking. You are the heiress of Aquitaine and are determined to remain so."

"It is my wish and natural in me. A poor ruler I should be if I did not view the loss of my inheritance with abhorrence. If you marry and there is male issue I should be displaced. The people would regret it."

"Nay, they would not regret my giving them a Duke."

"First you have to get your little Duke, and God has shown you in two marriages that it is daughters for you."

"If you believe this you will not be disturbed at the prospect of my marrying."

"I shall be disturbed by your disappointment, Father."

He laughed at her. "My dear Eleonore, you are a diplomatist already. And you but fourteen years of age!"

"I have made full use of my fourteen years, sir, and something tells me that God will never give you a male child."

"Have you become a prophet then?"

"Nay. So many royal lords marry for sons. There was the King of England, think how he strove for a son. And what happened? His marriage was barren. There was a man who had scattered his bastards throughout the realms of England and Normandy, but he had one legitimate son who was drowned at sea and never could beget another. God denied his dearest wish, as he may well deny you yours. I believe that Henry of England regretted his second marriage. Of what good was it? It did not bring him the very thing he married for. Sons."

"He was a man who had led a life of great immorality."

"He and your father were alike in that. Perhaps he did not repent enough and so Heaven turned a deaf ear on his entreaties."

"I am no Henry I of England."

"Nay, Father, you are not. But you stood out against the Pope. It may be that *he* is asking Heaven not to grant your wishes for that very reason."

The Duke was silent. He had wondered the same himself. Was Heaven against him for supporting Anacletus II against Innocent II when almost the entire world agreed that Innocent was the true Pope? He had been forced to give in in time, but it would be remembered against him. When Henry of England had died and Stephen of Blois had proclaimed himself King, the Duke had joined forces with Geoffrey of Anjou and sought to subdue Normandy and bring that disturbed dukedom to Geoffrey, the husband of Matilda, Henry's daughter who many said had more right to England—and Normandy—than the upstart Stephen. And what had followed? Bitter defeat!

He, like his father, had never been a man to indulge in warfare. Aquitaine had been secure for generations and its people enjoyed a peaceful life. The Duke had hated war. He could not forget the sight of men dying around him; the heartrending wailing of women and children driven from their homes.

Could it be that he *had* offended God and that until he received absolution he could not hope for a son?

He wanted to explain to this vital girl of his why he wanted a male heir. He wanted her to understand the difficulties that could befall a woman. She never would because she saw no difficulties. Yet they were there.

He wanted to see a son growing to manhood, a son who would take the reins of government in his hands before his father died. That would give continued peace to Aquitaine.

Then the idea came to him which had come to so many before him. He must placate his God and the one way to do this was to go on a pilgrimage to offer homage to the shrines of the Saints. The most ardent sinners gained absolution in

13

this way. He, the tenth Duke William of Aquitaine, would follow their example.

"What I must do," he said, "is go on a pilgrimage. I will visit the shrine of a saint and there I shall gain forgiveness of my sins. When I haave done this I shall come back and marry, and God will grant me the blessing of a son."

Eleonore narrowed her eyes.

The pilgrimage would not be achieved in a few weeks; then there would have to be the matter of selecting a suitable bride.

It was always best to put off evil for as long as possible. There was a good deal to be done before her father could marry and beget a son.

Something told Eleonore he never would.

* * *

There was the bustle of preparations. Having made his decision Duke William felt serene in his mind. He was to travel to the shrine of Saint James at Compostella and there he would pray for a fruitful marriage. His daughter watched his preparations with a certain cynical satisfaction as though she knew his prayers would remain unanswered.

He felt contrite in a way, for he loved her dearly. He admired her, as did most people who were aware of her dominant personality. If only she had been of the male sex he would have asked nothing more. He wanted her to understand that only in being female had she failed. And not for him; like his father, he had the utmost admiration for her sex, but it was others he must consider.

At the moment she was the heiress of vast possessions. Rich Aquitaine could be hers and thereby put her in command of as much territory as that possessed by the King of France. It was true that they were the vassals of the King of France but in name only. The Kings of France knew that the Dukes of Aquitaine wielded as much—perhaps more—power than they did. It was a matter of form that the Dukes bowed to the King.

"It is a hazardous journey to Compostella," said the Duke one day to his daughter. "It is that which makes it certain that any who reach it by the very arduous nature of their journey will have their prayers answered."

"You are a fool to undertake such hazards."

"I feel it to be a duty."

"Duty! Bah! But make the journey if you wish it. And see what comes of it."

"Would to God it were not necessary, Eleonore. I think of you constantly. I find it hard to leave you."

"'Tis of your choosing," she told him coldly.

"Not mine, but those to whom I owe a duty. I shall take few men with me."

"'Twould not be fitting to travel in great state on such an errand," she agreed.

"And I would leave my bravest behind to protect you."

"I can protect myself."

"There is no harm in having a stalwart guard. And I shall confer with the King of France for he will be eager to come to your aid if I should ask him."

"You would trust him?"

"Yes, if his son were mine also and my daughter his."

"You mean a marriage!"

"Yes. A marriage between you and the son of the King of France."

She smiled quietly. Well, it was not a bad prospect. If she were going to give up Aquitaine she would be Queen of France.

Louis VI was so large that he was known as Louis the Fat. He could not possibly live much longer. Rumours filtered into Aquitaine that he was confined to his bed and because of his immense size no one could lift him from it. He had been overfond of food and this was the result. His son was a boy a year or so older than Eleonore. She liked what she had heard of young Louis. He should be easily governed by a dominating wife. And she must marry soon. Only she knew how close she had come to submitting to the ardours of some of her admirers. There were members of her sex who were women at the age of fourteen. Eleonore of Aquitaine was one of them. It was a mercy that she was ambitious and proud; this saved her from being carried away by her intense physical desires.

She, more than any, knew that for her marriage should not be long delayed.

"When I return," said her father, "I must marry; and then there must be a double wedding. When my bride comes to Aquitaine you must go to the Court of France."

"But would the King of France wish his son to marry me if I were not your heiress?"

"The King of France will rejoice in an alliance with rich Aquitaine. He is astute enough to know its worth. And there

15

are no alliances to compare with those forged by marriage bonds."

She nodded gravely.

It was a bright prospect, but she was unsure. If she could bring Aquitaine to her husband she would be warmly welcomed. But otherwise?

*   *   *

It was a cold January day when the Duke set out for Compostella.

His daughters were in the courtyard wrapped in their sable-lined cloaks, to wish him godspeed.

"Farewell," said the Duke embracing first Eleonore and then Petronelle. "God guard you."

"Rather let us ask Him to guard you, Father," said Eleonore.

"He will smile on my mission, rest assured of that," replied the Duke, "and when I return I shall be free of my burden of sin."

Eleonore was silent; she had suggested he postpone his journey for it was foolish to set off in winter. She had believed that it was always good to postpone that which one hoped would never take place. But the Duke was assured of the urgency of the undertaking and would not consider delay.

"He will suffer for his foolishness," Eleonore confided to Petronelle, who agreed with her sister. For Petronelle, like many others, adored her dazzling elder sister.

When the cavalcade had clattered out of the courtyard Eleonore and her sister went up to the topmost turret there to watch its progress.

One would never have guessed that it was the Duke of Aquitaine who rode at its head. He was humbly dressed as a pilgrim should be, and he had taken so few of his followers with him.

The castle was well fortified and Eleonore was its mistress. If any dared come against her there would be stalwart knights to protect her. And none would dare for was she not half promised to the son of the King of France?

This was a waiting time, a time when the great fire in the centre of the hall sent its smoke up to the vaulted ceiling and the smell of roasting venison filled the castle. It was too cold to frolic in the beautiful gardens; they must perforce make do with the castle hall; and there they feasted and danced; they

16

sang their ballads; they strummed their harps and the sweet notes of the lute were heard throughout the castle.

Over the entertainments reigned the bold and beautiful Eleonore. Many of the gallants sighed for her favours and she often thought of granting them; but they must for the time content themselves with singing of love.

So while Duke William traversed the icy roads on his way to Compostella, Eleonore reigned supreme surrounded by her troubadours. She might be destined to become the Queen of France but she was the first Queen of the Troubadours.

* * *

Duke William quickly realized how unwise he had been to set out in the winter. The rough roads were icy; the wind biting. Valiantly the horses endeavoured to make their way but the going was slow. Yet, said the Duke to his little band of pilgrims, the very fact that we suffer these hardships means that our sins will be the more readily forgiven. What object would there be in travelling in comfort? How could we hope for our sins to be forgiven if we did not suffer for our redemption?

When darkness fell they rested wherever they found themselves. Sometimes it would be in a castle, sometimes in a peasant's humble home.

The Duke thought much of the castle of Ombrière and pictured Eleonore in the great hall, the firelight flickering on her proud handsome face; the young men at her feet watching her with yearning in their eyes. That power in her would attract men to her until she died. It was yet another inheritance of this richly endowed young woman. She could take care of herself. That was his great comfort. Eleonore would lead others; no one would force her to do what she did not wish. He thought of her—those large eyes which could be speculative when she considered her future and soulful when she listened to the songs of her troubadours, that thick hair which fell to her waist, the oval face and the strong line of the jaw. His great comfort was: Eleonore will take care of herself no matter what happens.

When he came back with the blessing of Saint James, when he married and his son was born, Eleonore would still be a desirable *parti*. Would the King of France consider her worthy of his son without the rich lands of Aquitaine?

That was a matter to be thought of when the time came.

First he must get his son. Nay, he thought, first he must get to Compostella.

He had coughed a great deal through the night and the icy winds had affected his limbs; they felt stiff and unwieldy. It would pass when he returned to the comfort of his home. One did not expect a pilgrimage to be a comfortable holiday. The saint would be gratified that he had endured such hardship to pay homage at his shrine. And when the weather changed and he could live comfortably again, his cough would go and the stiffness leave his limbs.

The party had crossed into Spain, but here the going was rougher than ever. The countryside was sparsely populated and because it was so difficult to get along they often found no shelter when night fell. The Duke was now so weak that his followers decided that they must at the earliest opportunity construct a litter that he might be carried.

Wishing to endure the utmost hardship, the Duke protested at first. Only if he suffered would the saint intercede with such fervour for him that his sins be forgiven and he gain his goal. But it was useless; he had become too ill to sit his horse; he must submit.

There was no comfort in being carried over those rough roads. He was soon in great pain and it suddenly occurred to him that he might never reach the shrine, that there would never be the marriage which would give him the male heir for Aquitaine.

Morosely he contemplated the future as he was jolted along.

Eleonore the richest heiress in Europe and a girl of fourteen. He should have been content with what he had been given. Not a son but a girl who was as good as any boy, a girl who failed only in her sex. And because he had not been content with what God had given him, he had ventured on this pilgrimage from which he was beginning to wonder whether he would ever emerge.

Each day his dismal thoughts went back to Ombrière. What would happen if he died? As soon as that fact became known the fortune hunters would be unleashed. A young, desirable and, above all, rich girl was unprotected, and she was ripe for marriage. Adventurers would come from all directions; he could see some bold ambitious man storming the castle capturing proud Eleonore and forcing her to submit. Could anyone force Eleonore? Yes, if he had henchmen to help him in his evil designs. The thought maddened him.

18

Who was there to protect her? His brother Raymond was far away in Antioch. If only Raymond was at hand. He was something of a hero and the Duke had often thought that his father would have preferred Raymond to have inherited Aquitaine. Very tall, fastidious in his appearance, possessed of a natural elegance, Raymond of Poitiers was born to command. He had been the ideal crusader and was now Prince of Antioch, for he had married Constance, the granddaughter of the great Bohemond of the first crusade. But it was no use thinking of Raymond in far-off Antioch as a protector.

Could it be that he was going to die? As each day passed his conviction became stronger. He was finding it more and more difficult to breathe; there were times when he was not sure whether he was on the road to Compostella or fighting for possession of Normandy with the Duke of Anjou.

In his moments of lucidity he knew that he must abandon hope of reaching Compostella. His sins would be forgiven but he must pay for forgiveness with his life. And his affairs must be in order. He must be sure that Eleonore was protected.

There was one way to do this. He must ask for the help of the most powerful man in France: its King.

He would offer his Eleonore to the King's son. He had no qualms about the offer being joyously accepted. Louis had long coveted the rich lands of Aquitaine and this marriage would bring them to the crown of France.

He called to his litter two of the men he most trusted.

"Make with all speed to Paris," he said. "Let it be known that you come from the Duke of Aquitaine. Then the King himself will see you. Take this letter to him. If the letter should be lost before you reach him, tell him that I wish a marriage between his son and my daughter without delay, for I fear my days are numbered and if the marriage is not arranged others may step in before him."

Having despatched the messengers the Duke felt easier in his mind. If he were to die, Eleonore would be in good hands, her future assured.

*　　*　　*

King Louis VI of France, known as The Fat, lay on his bed breathing with difficulty. He deplored his condition and it gave him no comfort to realize that he should never have allowed himself to reach such bulk. He had enjoyed good food and had never restrained his appetite for it was an age when men were admired for their size. If one was rich one could eat to one's fill; it was only peasants who went hungry. It therefore behoved a king to show his subjects that he was in a position to consume as much food as his body could take. But what a toll it took of a man's strength!

He longed for the days of his youth, when he had sat his horse effortlessly; now there was no horse strong enough to carry him.

It was too late to repine. The end was in sight in any case.

He often said to his ministers that if only he had had the knowledge in his youth and the strength in his old age he would have conquered many kingdoms and left France richer than when he had come to the throne.

But was it not a well-known maxim: If Youth but knew and Age could do.

Now he must plan for the future and he thanked God that he had a good heir to leave to his country.

God had been good to him when he had given him young Louis. He was known throughout the kingdom as Louis the Young, as he himself was known as Louis the Fat. He had not always been the Fat of course, any more than his son would always be the Young; suffice that those were the soubriquets by which they were known at this time.

Young Louis was sixteen years old—a serious boy, inclined to religion. Not a bad thing in a King, mused Louis. Young Louis had been destined for the Church and not to rule at all for he had had an elder brother. He had spent his early years at Notre-Dame and he had taken well to the life. But it was not to be. Fate had ordained otherwise.

Bernard, that rather uncomfortable Abbot of Clairvaux, who was inclined to fulminate against all those who did not fall into line with his beliefs—and none knew more than rulers how irritating such prelates could be, for had there not always been certain friction between church and state?—had prophesied that the King's eldest son would not take the crown but that it would fall to his brother Louis the Young.

The King had been uneasy, for Bernard had a reputation for making prophecies which came true; and sure enough this one had.

One day Philippe the heir, after hunting in the forest came into Paris where a pig, running suddenly across the road, tripped his horse. Philippe fell and struck his head against a stone and died almost immediately.

By this time Bernard had become revered as a holy man who could see into the future, and young Louis much to his dismay was taken from Notre-Dame to study the craft of kingship.

The boy had always hankered after the religious life. Perhaps it was not a bad thing. A certain amount of religion was good for a king provided it did not interfere with duties. He would be called upon now and then to defend his kingdom and his father hoped that when such occasion arose he would not be squeamish about punishing those who rebelled against him. Young Louis was too gentle. Also he must get an heir. Louis had never frolicked with women. So many young men of his age had fathered a few bastards by this time. Not Louis.

Now the King sent for his son.

He sighed a little as the boy stood before him.

"Ah," he said, "you see me prostrate. Never indulge your appetite as I have done. It is not worth it."

"I see that, Sire."

"Be seated, my son. I have news for you."

Louis sat down.

"My friend and ally, the Duke of Aquitaine, is in the same sad state as that in which I find myself. It would seem neither of us is long for this world."

The King saw the lights of fear spring up in his son's eyes. They did not mean so much that he could not endure to lose his father as that he feared the heavy responsibility which that death would place on his shoulders. A King should never be afraid of his crown, thought Louis the Fat. A pity indeed that he had brought him up in religion. But how could he have known that heaven had already signed Philippe's death-warrant and sent a paltry pig to be his executioner?

Louis would forget that he had loved the ceremonies of the Church when those of State were forced upon him. It was merely the contemplation of great power that frightened him.

"Therefore," went on the King, "I think it well that you should marry and that without delay."

Now the boy was really frightened. This would never do. A pity he had never dallied with a girl in some secluded part of the hunting forests. It was all very well to be as he was if he remained the second son. But he would change when he was married to a young and beautiful girl and by all accounts Eleonore was this.

21

"You cannot get an heir too soon, my son. I have a bride for you. I could not have chosen one who pleased me more. The Duke of Aquitaine is dying, so his messengers tell me. He has suffered much hardship on the road to Compostella. His heiress is his eldest daughter. She is fourteen years of age and very desirable. There is to be a match between you two."

"Marriage," stammered young Louis, "so soon . . ."

"Without delay. It is what the Duke wishes. He has placed his daughter under my protection. This is the finest thing that could happen to France. Eleonore is heiress to all the Duke's dominions, Poitou, Saintonge, Gascony and the Basque country. I could not have chosen a more suitable bride for you."

"Father I am as yet unprepared . . ."

"Nonsense, my son. Little preparation is needed to get an heir. We shall put you to bed with this desirable and very rich girl and you will know what to do. Think of the good she can bring to France. The more lands under our protection the less likelihood of wars. The more powerful we are the more we can work for the good of France."

"The possession of lands often leads to strife. They must be protected."

"They must indeed be protected and good wise laws be made for them. It will be your duty to give a happy life to your people."

Young Louis closed his eyes. Why had this had to happen to him? Why had that miserable pig ruined his life? Philippe would have been a good king; he had been trained for it. And he, Louis, would have spent his life in the rarefied atmosphere of the Church. He would have been the Prince of the Church; how he loved the sonorous chanting, the beautiful music, the hallowed atmosphere. And he had lost this because God had called on him to do his duty in a different sphere from that for which he had been trained.

"I am sending word to the Duke of Aquitaine that I shall cherish his daughter and that I am losing no time in arranging a marriage between her and my son."

"Father, is there no help for it?"

"No help, my son. This marriage must take place without delay."

* * *

"How far to the shrine?" whispered the dying Duke.

"But a mile or so now, my good lord."

"Thank God then, I shall reach Compostella."

Just a little more pain to endure and salvation would be his. Who would have thought that he should come so far and endure so much to ask for a male heir and to find instead death.

"There are messengers, my lord Duke," said one of his bearers. "They come from the King of France."

"Thank God then. Thank God again. What news?"

"The King, my lord, sends his greetings. He will care for your daughter as he would his own for indeed he says ere you receive this message she will be almost that. For he is betrothing his son to her and the marriage of France and Aquitaine will take place without delay."

"I shall die happy," said the Duke.

So this was the answer. Eleonore would be safe. She would be Queen of France and what more could he ask for her than that? She was born to rule—not only because of her inheritance but because of her nature. She had the innate power to inspire respect and love.

It was said that the King's son was a serious boy, destined for the Church as he had been. He had proved himself to be a great churchman in the making, and would have been such had not a wayward pig made him a future King of France and husband of Eleonore of Aquitaine.

"Lift me," he said, "that I may see the shrine of St James's."

They did so and he was content.

* * *

Since her father's absence Eleonore had been the undisputed mistress of the château. During the cold winter's evenings she and her court would range themselves about the great fire in the centre of the hall; there would be singing and music and she would judge the merits of the literary compositions and perhaps sing one of her own.

This she enjoyed; to sit among them, more elegantly attired than any of the other ladies, more brilliantly witty, while at her feet sat the knights gazing at her with adoration. The first lesson in chivalry was the adoration of women. Romance was the greatest adventure of the day. It was not so much the culmination as the dalliance on the way, although Eleonore herself knew that that climax must inevitably be reached. She thrilled to the ardent glances; she allowed herself to dream of fulfilment, but in her heart she knew there must be some delay.

Sometimes she played a game of chess with an admirer, for it was part of the court education that any who aspired to gracious living must first master the game; she always found an element of excitement in the conflict over the board; because she was fighting a battle and from this she invariably emerged the victor.

In the privacy of her bedchamber she talked with her sister. Petronelle believed that everything Eleonore did was right. She imitated her elder sister in all things. Now their conversation centred round their father. They wondered constantly what was happening to him on the dangerous roads.

Petronelle turned to Eleonore and said: "Do you think he will come back?"

There was a far away look in Eleonore's eyes; she was gazing into the future. "It was foolish of him," she said, "to attempt such a journey at such a time of the year."

"Why did he not wait until the summer?"

"It would have been too easy a journey. It had to be hazardous that he might earn forgiveness for his sins."

"Had he so many?"

Eleonore laughed. "He thought he had. He was obsessed by his sins, as our grandfather was."

"What about you, Eleonore? Have you committed any sins?"

She shrugged her elegant shoulders. "I am too young to be concerned with sins. It is only when you are of an age to fear death that repentance is necessary."

"So we need not concern ourselves with repentance yet, sister. We may sin to our heart's content."

"What a pleasant prospect," cried Eleonore.

"Everyone in the castle respects you," said Petronelle adoringly. "I think they love you more than they did our father. But if he marries again and we have a brother . . ."

Petronelle looked fearfully up at Eleonore who was scowling.

"It won't happen, sister," went on Petronelle quickly. "If he married he wouldn't get a boy."

"It maddens me," cried Eleonore. "Why this reverence for the male sex? Are not women more beautiful, more subtle, often more clever than men?"

"You are, Eleonore, cleverer than any man."

24

"Yet because they go into battle, because they have greater physical strength, they regard themselves so superior that a puny son would come before a fine daughter."

"No son our father got would ever equal you, Eleonore."

"Yet he must undertake this pilgrimage in the hope that Saint James will plead for him and he come safely back, marry and get a son."

"The saints will never listen to him. They will call him ungrateful. God has given him you, Eleonore, and he is not satisfied!"

Eleonore laughed and blew a kiss to her sister.

"At least you appreciate me," she said with a smile.

She went to the narrow window and looked out on the bleak road.

"One day," she said, "we shall see a party of horsemen on that road. It will either be my father coming back triumphant or . . ."

"Or what, Eleonore?" asked Petronelle who had come to stand beside her.

But Eleonore shook her head. She would say no more.

It was but a few days later when a messenger did come to the castle.

Eleonore, who had been warned that he was sighted, was in the courtyard to greet him; she herself held the cup of hot wine for him.

"I bring ill tidings, my lady," he said before he would take the cup. "The Duke is dead. The journey was too much for him. I have a sorry tale to tell."

"Drink," said Eleonore. "Then come into the castle."

She took him into the hall and sat with him beside the fire. She ordered that food be brought to him, for he had ridden far and was exhausted. But first she must hear the news.

"He suffered towards the end, my lady, but never wavered from his purpose. We carried him right to the shrine and that made him happy. He died there in his litter but not before he had received the blessing. It was his wish that he be buried before the main altar in the Church of Saint James."

"And this was done?"

"It was done, my lady."

"Praise be to God that he died in peace."

"His one concern was for your welfare."

"Then he will be happy in Heaven for when he looks down on me he will know I can take care of myself."

25

"Before he died he received an assurance from the King of France, my lady."

Eleonore lowered her eyes.

There would be a wedding. Her own. And to the son of the King of France. Louis the Fat would not have been so eager to ally his son with her had she not been the heiress of Aquitaine.

How could she grieve? How could she mourn? Her father, who had planned to get an heir who would displace her, was no more. His plans were as nothing.

There was one heir to Aquitaine. It was Duchess Eleonore.

*   *   *

Young Louis was very apprehensive. He was to travel to Aquitaine, there to present himself to his bride and ask her hand in marriage. That was a formality. His father and hers had already decided that there should be a match between them.

What would she be like—this girl they had chosen for him? At least she was a year younger than he was. Many royal princes were married to women older than themselves. That would have terrified him.

How he wished that he had remained in Notre-Dame. He longed for the ceremonies in which he had taken part, the sonorous chanting of priests, the smell of incense, the hypnotic murmur of voices in prayer. And instead there must be feasting and celebration and he must be initiated into the mysteries of marriage.

He wished that he were like so many youths; they lived for their dalliance with women; he had heard them boasting of their adventures, laughing together, comparing their brave deeds. He could never be like that. He was too serious; he longed for a life of meditation and prayer. He wanted to be good. It was not easy for rulers to shut themselves away from life; they had to be at the heart of it. They were said to govern, but often they were governed by ministers. They had to go to war. The thought of war terrified him even more than that of love.

The King lay at Béthizy and thither had come the most influential of his ministers, among them the Abbé Suger. The marriage between young Louis and Eleonore of Aquitaine had won their immediate approval. It could only be to the good of the country that the rich lands of the south should come to the crown of France. The King could be assured that his ministers would do all in their power to expedite the marriage.

The Abbé Suger would himself arrange the journey and remain beside the Prince as his chief adviser.

The King who knew that death could not be far off was anxious that the progress from Béthizy to Aquitaine should be absolutely peaceful. There must be no pillaging of towns and villages as the cavalcade passed through. The people of the kingdom of France and the dukedom of Aquitaine must know that this was a peaceful mission which could bring nothing but good to all concerned.

"He could rest assured that his wishes would be carried out," the Abbé told him.

He sent for his son. Poor Louis! So obviously destined for the Church. And he had heard accounts of Eleonore. A voluptuous girl ripe for marriage, young as she was. She would know how to win Louis, he was sure of that. Perhaps, when he saw this girl who by all accounts was one of the most desirable in the country—and not only for her possessions—he would realize his good fortune.

He told him this when he came to his bedside. "Good fortune," he said, "not only for you, my son, but for your country, and a king's first duty is to his country."

"I am not a king yet," said Louis in a trembling voice.

"Nay, but the signs are, my son, that you will be ere long. Govern well. Make wise laws. Remember that you came to the Crown through God's will and serve Him well. Oh, my dear son, may all-powerful God protect you. If I had the misfortune to lose you and those I send with you, I should care nothing whatever either for my person or my kingdom."

Young Louis knelt by his father's bed and received his blessing.

Then he left with his party and took the road to Bordeaux.

*   *   *

The town of Bordeaux glittered in the sunshine; the river Garonne was like a silver snake and the towers of the Château de l'Ombrière stretched up to a cloudless sky.

The Prince stood on the banks of the river gazing across. The moment when he was brought face to face with his bride could not long be delayed.

He was afraid. What should he say to her? She would

27

despise him. If only he could turn and go back to Paris. Oh, the peace of Notre-Dame! The Abbé Suger had little sympathy for him. As a churchman, he might have been expected to, but all he could think of—all anyone could think of—was how good this marriage was for France.

"My lord, we should take to the boats and cross to Bordeaux. The Lady Eleonore will have heard that we are here. She will not expect delay."

He braced himself. It was no use hanging back. What was not done today must be done tomorrow.

"Let us go now," he said.

He was riding to the castle at the head of the small party he had taken with him. His standard bearer held proudly the banner of the golden lilies. He looked up at the turret and wondered whether she watched him.

She was there, exultantly gazing at the golden lilies, the emblem of power. Aquitaine might be rich but a king was necessarily of higher rank than a duke or duchess and even if the acknowledgement of suzerainty was merely a form yet it was there, and Aquitaine was in truth a vassal of France.

And I shall be Queen of France, Eleonore told herself.

She came to the courtyard. She had taken even greater care than usual with her appearance. Her natural elegance was enhanced by the light blue gown she was wearing; this was caught in at her tiny waist with a belt glittering with jewels. She was not wearing the fashionable wimple as she wanted to show off her luxuriant hair which she wore hanging over her shoulders with a jewelled band on her forehead.

She looked up at the boy on his horse as she held the cup of welcome to him.

Young, she thought, malleable. And her heart leaped in triumph.

He was looking at her as though bemused. He had never imagined such a beautiful creature; her serene eyes smiled into his calmly; the diadem on her broad high brow gave her dignity. He thought she was exquisite.

He leaped from his horse and, bowing, kissed her hand.

"Welcome to Aquitaine," she said. "Pray come into the castle."

Side by side they entered.

*   *   *

She told Petronelle when her sister came to her chamber that night: "My French Prince is not without charm. They have grace, these Franks. They make some of our knights seem gauche. His manners are perfect. At first though I sensed a reluctance."

"That passed when he saw you," said the ever-adoring Petronelle.

"I think it did," replied Eleonore judiciously. "There is something gentle about him. They brought him up as a priest."

"I can't imagine you with a priest for a husband."

"Nay, we shall soon leave the priest behind. I wish we need not wait for the ceremony. I would like to take him for my lover right away."

"You always wanted a lover, Eleonore. Father knew it and feared it."

"It is natural enough. You too, Petronelle."

Petronelle sighed and raised her eyes to the ceiling. "Alas, I have longer to wait."

Then they talked intimately about the men of the Court, their virtues and their potentialities as lovers.

Eleonore remembered some of the exploits of their grandfather.

"He was the greatest lover of his age."

"You will excel even him," Petronelle suggested.

"That would be most shocking in a woman," laughed Eleonore.

"But you will be equal to men in all things."

"I look forward to starting," said Eleonore with a laugh.

* * *

The Prince loved to listen to her singing and watch her long white fingers plucking at the lute and the harp; she said, "I will sing you one of my own songs."

And she sang of longing for love and that the only true happiness in love was through the satisfaction this could bring.

"How can you know?" he asked.

"Some instinct tells me." Her brilliant eyes were full of promise; even he found a certain desire stirring in him. He no longer thought so constantly of the solemn atmosphere of the Church; he began to wonder what mysteries he and his bride would discover together.

29

She played chess with him and beat him. Perhaps she had had more practice. When he was learning to be a priest she had been brought up in court accomplishments. It was a light-hearted battle between them. When she had checkmated him she laughed and was delighted; it was like a symbol to her.

They walked in the gardens of the castle together. She showed him the flowers and the herbs which grew in the south. She told him how it was possible to make cures and ointments, lotions to beautify the skin and make the eyes shine, a draught to stir a reluctant lover.

"Dost think that I shall need to make one for you——"

He caught her hand and looked into her face.

"No," he said, vehemently. "That will not be necessary."

"Then you find my charms enough for you, my lord?"

"Enough indeed."

"So that you long for our marriage?"

"I yearn for the day," he told her.

She drew back, laughing at him.

Not bad for my monk, she confided afterwards to Petronelle.

The Abbé Suger, seeing how their relationship was ripening, believed there should be no delaying the marriage. It was true Eleonore was in mourning for her father's recent death but this was a State marriage and the sooner it was solemnized the better for everyone concerned.

He mentioned this to the Prince and was amazed by the alacrity with which he—once so reluctant—agreed.

"The Duchess of Aquitaine is an enchantress," said the Abbé.

It was July when the wedding took place.

Eleonore's women dressed her in her glittering wedding gown and she wore her long hair flowing. She sat on her glittering caparisoned horse and rode through the streets of Bordeaux to Saint Andrew's Church where the ceremony was to be performed by the Archbishop of Bordeaux. What a day of triumph for the bride! Only a year ago she had wondered whether she would be robbed of her inheritance by a half-brother. But Fate had intervened. No one could come between her and her ambition now.

She was exultant and only a little sad that she had had to come to her triumph through the death of a father who, in her way, she had loved well enough. But there was no doubt of her success.

Duchess of Aquitaine with none to dispute her claim and soon—she believed very soon and so did everyone else—Queen of France.

* * *

Eleonore blossomed. Sensual in the extreme she found marriage to her taste. Poor Louis was a little less ardent—although there was no doubt that he loved her with a deeper emotion than she could muster for him. Eleonore loved love; she had known she would when as a very young girl she had sung of it in the gardens. There, love had been glorified—romantic love. She wanted that, but she wanted physical love as well. She it was who led the way in passion. She might have been experienced in such arts; this was not the case; he was her first lover; but with her there was a natural knowledge and understanding.

They were glorious summer days, spent in watching the celebrations for their wedding and nights spent in making love.

There was music and singing and Eleonore was initiating him into an appreciation for the chansons and poems at which she excelled. It was a delightful existence but of course it could not continue. The contests and tournaments in the castle grounds must come to an end, for the Prince must return to Paris with his bride.

She had through him become the Princess of France; through her he must become the Duke of Aquitaine.

Everywhere they went they were met by rejoicing crowds. Such an alliance all knew could bring nothing but good. The people of Aquitaine could shelter beneath the golden lilies of France and the kingdom of France had gathered a powerful neighbour into its eager embrace.

This could only mean more hopes of peace and as what was more dreaded than anything by the humble people were armies invading their homes and carrying off their goods and women, this was a desirable state of affairs.

They had reached Poitiers and were enjoying a great welcome there, when the Abbé Suger came to their apartment in the castle where they had been given hospitality, and it was clear from his expression that he was the bearer of ill news.

He was not a man to break bad news gently.

He bowed low. "Long live the King!" he said.

31

And Louis knew that his fears were realized and Eleonore that her ambition was achieved.

Her husband was now the King and she was the Queen of France.

"So my father has gone," said Louis blankly.

"He passed away in great discomfort of body," said the Abbé. "But his pains are past. If you would obey his wishes you will rule as he would have wished—that is wisely and well."

"That I shall endeavour to do with all my heart and mind," replied Louis fervently.

The carefree honeymoon was over though. There were too many warring elements in the country for the young Louis to be accepted without opposition.

It was not that the people of France wished to put up another King in Louis's place. Louis the Fat had kept them in order but he had not always given them what they considered their due. Now that a young and inexperienced boy was on the throne was the time to demand those rights.

A few days after the news of Louis VI's death reached the wedding party there was further news. This time of a rising in Orleans.

Abbé Suger told the new King that now was the time to assert his authority. How he acted now was of the utmost importance. He must show his people that while he would be a benevolent ruler he would be a firm one. He must say *au revoir* to his bride and go with all speed to Orleans and from there to Paris. Eleonore and her court should follow him at a more leisurely pace.

Louis, less disturbed by events than a short while before he would have believed possible, rode with his army to Orleans. He must act in a kingly fashion; he would not wish Eleonore to despise him for he knew that she, who was so strong and forceful herself, would indeed despise weakness. So he must not be weak.

He prayed earnestly for wisdom to make the right decision and the strength to put it into execution.

He would carry a flower Eleonore had given him—a rose from the gardens at Ombrière. She herself had plucked it and pressed it. He must carry it near his heart she had told him; he had been enchanted with the mixture of romanticism and sensuality which made up his wife's character, and her insistence that the laws of chivalry should be obeyed. She fascinated him, she who was so determined to be treated as a tender woman and at the same time so eager to be obeyed. She would expect him to come through this new ordeal with honour.

So he rode at the head of his troops, and how delighted he was that the citizens of Orleans, seeing him come with his army, quailed before his might, and instead of insisting on their dues craved pardon for their insolence in making demands to their liege lord.

An easy conquest and he had no desire to be harsh; his advisers insisted that one or two leaders of the rebellion were executed but he would not allow others to be punished. He even granted some of the reforms for which they had originally asked.

The people of Orleans cheered him. In the very streets where they had banded together and sought to plot against him they now called: *"Vive le Roi."*

That matter was settled. Louis rode on to Paris and there he was joined by Eleonore. The reuinion was tender; they had missed each other sadly.

"Now we must think of the coronation," declared Eleonore.

By December of that year the celebrations had been planned and the great event took place.

What a long way she had come in one short year! thought Eleonore with gratification.

Petronelle and the Count

She was briefly content. She was Queen of France, the leader of the Court, adored by the King, worshipped by those whom she gathered together that she might instruct them in the rules of chivalry. She surrounded herself with poets and troubadours. To win her favour a man must be possessed of exquisite manners; he must know the rules of the Courts of Love; he must be able to express himself with grace and if he had a good singing voice so much the better.

She was the judge of the literary efforts; she applauded or derided. During the summer days she would sit in the grounds of the castle surrounded by young men and women, and she would impart to them her philosophy of life.

The girls must obey her, admire her and emulate her as best they could so that they were pale shadows of herself, and she might shine the more because of this. The young men must all be in love with her, yearn for her favours and be ready to die for them, and she would be gracious or remote; and never must their passion waver. They must write their verses, sing their songs to her; they must mingle talent with desire. She was determined that the Court of France must be the most elegant in the world.

There was Petronelle growing up very quickly like a forced flower in this over-heated atmosphere. Men made verses and sang their songs to her for after all she was almost as beautiful as Eleonore, and was her sister.

How much more exciting it was to live at the Court of France than that of Aquitaine, to be a Queen instead of the heiress of a Duke, providing he did not get himself a son.

It had worked out very well.

Petronelle, following Eleonore in all things, was growing more and more impatient of her youth.

"We should find a husband for Petronelle," said Eleonore to the King.

"Why, she is a child yet," said Louis. Poor blind Louis, thought Eleonore, the King who knew so little!

"Some reach maturity earlier than others. Methinks Petronelle has reached hers."

"Think you so then? Mayhap you should talk to her, prepare her. She should be awakened gradually to what taking a husband would mean. It could be a shock for an innocent girl."

Eleonore smiled but she did not tell him of the conversations she and Petronelle had together, and had had for many years. Petronelle was no innocent. A virgin perhaps but how long would she remain so if they did not get her married?

Louis judged others by himself. His innocence was attractive to her ... at this time ... though she had begun to wonder whether it would pall. Sometimes her gaze would stray to older men, men experienced, with many an amorous adventure behind them, and she was just a little impatient with the naïvety of her husband. But it still amused her to be the leader in their relationship, to lure him to passion of which he would never have believed himself capable.

So she did not enlighten him about Petronelle. At the same time she believed it was time to find a husband for her sister.

*   *   *

Petronelle was not of a nature to wait for others to arrange her affairs.

Like her sister she loved the sensuous strumming of the musical instruments and the languorous words hinting at love.

To be young was frustrating. It always had been. And having a fascinating sister such as Eleonore did not help her to bear her lot more easily.

Eleonore had promised her that she would find a husband for her, but the King thought she was too young as yet.

"Too young," groaned Petronelle. "The King believes everyone to be as cold-blooded as himself."

"Have patience, little sister," cautioned Eleonore. "I am not of that opinion. I know that if we do not give you a husband soon you will take a lover. But have a care. It is always wiser to have a husband first. That would seem to entitle you to lovers. But a lover first . . . I believe that might be a little shocking."

"You are always singing of love," cried Petronelle. "What is the use of that?"

Eleonore could only repeat her caution, adding: "Have patience."

She herself had little of that useful virtue. She wanted excitement. Was she growing tired of holding court, of spending her nights with her serious young husband?

While she was pondering on how soon she could find a suitable husband for Petronelle and get the girl safely married, there were signs of unrest in the country. She had always been interested in increasing her power and the elevation from Duchess to Queen had enthralled her. It had been the dream of many a King of France to extend his territory throughout the entire country. Normandy, of course, was firmly in the hands of the King of England—well, perhaps not firmly, for the Count of Anjou would never accept the fact that it did not belong to his wife, Matilda, and as they had a son, naturally they would wish to restore it to him.

At this time Stephen of Blois had taken the crown of England, and it seemed very likely that he would hold it although England was not in a very happy state. Matilda, whom many believed was the true heiress, for she was the daughter of the late King Henry I, whereas Stephen was merely his nephew, would never cease to urge her husband and son to bestir themselves to get back their dues.

Suffice it then that Eleonore and Louis leave Normandy out of their calculations. But what of Toulouse? The fact that the Counts of Toulouse asserted that they were the true rulers of that province had always rankled with Eleonore. Her grandfather had married Philippa of Toulouse, and Eleonore maintained that through this marriage Toulouse had passed to Aquitaine.

Eleonore discussed this with Louis. He saw the point.

"Mind you," he temporized, "I doubt whether the Count would agree with us."

"It is not a matter for him to agree or disagree about. The fact is I have a right to Toulouse through my grandfather's marriage and I see no reason why I should waive it."

"Why did your grandfather and father never take it?" asked Louis.

Eleonore shrugged impatiently. She did not wish to recall that neither her father nor her grandfather had been noted for their success in battle. Her father had been somewhat inept politically and her grandfather had been more interested in the conquest of women than territory.

She however was more ambitious. Within her there still burned the resentment engendered by her father's desire to displace a forceful young woman, possessed of all the attributes a ruler should have, for the sake of an unborn child merely because he might be a boy.

"The fact that they allowed others to take that which was theirs does not mean that we should."

Louis was uneasy. She could have shaken him.

"But Toulouse has been independent for many years."

"I know, I know! When my grandfather went crusading he put it into the care of Raymond Saint-Gilles. It was to be a temporary measure."

"But it has remained in his family ever since."

How impatient he made her! She frowned and then allowed her smile to become tenderly exasperating. "My dear dear Louis, you are so gentle, always ready to defend your enemies. I love you for it, of course, but it is no way to rule."

He could not endure her disappointment in him. She had ensnared him completely. Sometimes he wondered whether she had given him one of those potions she had once mentioned. He could not bear that she should not admire him. It was true that he needed to be war-like. His father had warned him that he must be strong and that it might be doubly hard for him, brought up as he had been to be a priest.

"What do you suggest we do, Eleonore?"

Her smile was radiant.

"First you will summon all your vassals to Court. There you will tell them that you intend to wage war on Toulouse for what belongs to the Crown through your marriage shall be brought to it. You will tell them that you expect—nay demand—their support. It is your due and their duty. Are they not your vassals?"

37

"Eleonore, I confess the thought of going to war disturbs me."

"That is a feeling you will have to overcome, my King."

"Of course I have you always at my side."

She took his hand and smiled dazzlingly.

"Always," she assured him, "to help and comfort you."

He certainly felt much comforted.

* * *

In the gardens were gathered about Eleonore the ladies and gentlemen of the Court. There were young girls whose families had sent them to the Queen to be schooled in all the graces and accomplishments they could find nowhere else. Eleonore delighted in these young people. Her love of power was, even in this small way, satisfied. These young people regarded her as their teacher. Under her guidance they made their gowns; they sang, they composed music and songs; and they learned to play chess. Eleonore could not bear the illiterate near her. She herself had been taught to read and write and she believed it to be an important part of every girl's education—as well as that of boys. She was determined that there should be no discrimination against her sex. Never would she forget that she could have been diverted from a very brilliant future merely because she was female.

These hours when she ruled over her own little court were her relaxation. Anyone who composed a poem or a song would submit it for her approval; she would then have it read aloud or sung as the case might be, and deliver judgement.

She was determined to uphold chivalry and this meant the adoration of the female. A man must be prepared to woo the lady of his choice; he must be grateful for her smiles; he must be prepared to wait for the fulfilment of love. He must fight for his lady and die for her if need be. This was the essence of romantic love.

Eleonore was sensuous in the extreme but her sensuality was tinged with romance. She was as deeply aware of the virile men of her little court as they were of her. Often she allowed herself to imagine taking them as lovers. That would have given her immense satisfaction. How sad that a queen could not indulge in such romantic attachments. The duty of a queen was to provide the heir to the throne and even she—law unto herself that she might be—was aware that there must be no doubt as to the paternity of the heir of France.

There was one man who attracted her very much and this was Louis's cousin Raoul, the Count of Vermandois. He was not exactly young; but he had a powerful personality and a reputation for his conquests not only in war but in love.

Often he would sit at Eleonore's feet and woo her with his eyes, his gestures and the longing in his voice. There was no doubt that Raoul was inviting her to throw aside her scruples. He did not actually say so; he was wise enough to know that in Eleonore's courts of love there must be no crudity. Hints were far more exciting than bald words; and he had made his feelings clear through those.

Eleonore liked him to sit at her feet while his eyes glittered with passion. She liked to imagine herself indulging in lovemaking with such a partner; how different he would be from Louis! Poor Louis! He was not an imaginative lover; she must always be the leading spirit. All very well at times, but it would be amusing, intriguing and quite thrilling on some occasions to feel herself mastered.

Alas, she must remember that she had to bear the heir of France.

Raoul continued to adore her with his eyes; his low-pitched voice continued to lure her to indiscretion. She resisted. He was a little impatient. He enjoyed wooing the Queen but he was beginning to realize that he would never do so with success . . . not at least until she was pregnant by Louis and could safely take a lover. Such a matter could not of course be mentioned in the romantic atmosphere of Eleonore's court; though it was in his mind and perhaps hers, but he could not be sure of that.

Poor Louis, thought Raoul. It may be that he is incapable of begetting children. Perhaps one day she would be willing to let him be supplanted for that reason. Eleonore was a shrewd woman; she had few scruples he was sure, or at least if she had some now they would be eliminated given the appropriate circumstances. But he was an impatient man. Although he continued to worship at Eleonore's feet his eyes often strayed and thus it was that they alighted on Petronelle, Eleonore's young sister. What an enchanting creature she was! thought Raoul. Almost as beautiful as Eleonore herself, and he'd swear as desirous. The more he thought of Petronelle the more enchanted he was.

Petronelle might be inexperienced but she was certainly

not without knowledge; she knew the meaning of the ardent glances he sent in her direction. As she was not the Queen of France she need not entertain a queen's scruples; she was very young; she was unmarried, possibly a virgin—he, the connoisseur, believed this might well be so, although it was a state from which the girl was longing to escape. A little dangerous in view of her relationship with the Queen, and the fact of course that she had no husband. He was a bold man; he had been frustrated too long by Petronelle's sister. He would see how far he could go.

He waylaid Petronelle in the alleyways of the garden.

"What a delightful surprise," he cried as he came towards her.

"Is it such a surprise, my lord?" asked Petronelle, her head on one side, gaily provocative.

"Well I will admit to a little strategy."

"It is always wise to admit that which is already known." She had no doubted learned her repartee from her sister.

"What joy to see you alone."

"Why? Do I appear different alone than when in the company of others?"

"Yes. Do I to you?"

"Naturally I must feel some alarm remembering your reputation."

"Ah, reputation! How cruel it can be! How false! How unfair!"

"Have people been unfair to you, my lord?"

"So much would depend on what they said of me."

"They say you have known many conquests."

"I have committed myself with honour in battle I believe."

"And in the battle of love?"

"I do not regard love as a battle."

"Yet people talk of conquests."

"Perhaps I myself am in danger of being conquered?"

"By your lady wife no doubt. And I believe my sister the Queen to have had some effect on you."

"Sometimes it is not as it appears."

"I understand you not."

He took a step nearer to her and grasped her hand. "Sometimes one does not look in the direction of the sun. It is too dazzling. One averts the eyes."

"Are you looking at the sun now, my lord Count?"

"Right in its face."

"I trust you are blinded by it."

40

"Blinded to indiscretion. Made mad by it." He seized her suddenly and kissed her.

Petronelle gave an exclamation of what she meant to sound like dismay, and breaking away from him ran through the alley to a more public place in the gardens.

This was a beginning.

* * *

Count Theobald of Champagne had arrived at the Court of France. He was a man who had a reputation for governing his province with wisdom; he was a good soldier and Louis had counted on his help for carrying on the campaign against Toulouse.

Eleonore was with the King when he received the Count. She made a point of being present at such meetings for she wanted the world to know that France had a Queen as well as a King.

"Welcome to Paris," said Louis. "I trust you are in good health."

"Never better, Sire."

"And in good fettle for the fight."

"If you are referring to this matter of Toulouse, Sire, I could not aid you in this. I do not think it would have the blessing of God."

Eleonore was frowning. "Perhaps you will explain," she said coldly.

The Count bowed. "Indeed, Madame. I would not ally myself with it because I would consider it unjust to the Count of Toulouse."

"Unjust to wrest from a man that to which he clings when he has no right to do so!"

"It would seem that he has the rights of ownership, my lady."

"Do you know that Toulouse came to my grandfather through marriage and that he set up Saint-Gilles as a custodian during his absence on a crusade?"

"If that were so I cannot understand why it was not reclaimed ere this, my lady."

"Because the matter has not been resolved until now, but that is no reason why it never should be."

"I see many reasons, my lady."

"You forget that you risk the displeasure of your King and Queen."

41

The Count bowed and begged leave to retire.

When he had gone Eleonore burst out in fury: "The insolent dog! How dare he tell us what our duty is!"

"He has a right to express an opinion," Louis mildly told her.

"Are you a king? Am I a queen? Shall we be insulted in our own castle? I tell you, my lord Count of Champagne will be sorry for this."

Louis tried to soothe her, but she would not be placated.

*   *   *

Theobald went to his sister's apartments. She was the wife of Raoul, the Count of Vermandois, and he found her melancholy.

Theobald felt equally so. He had not liked the tone of the Queen's voice when she had expressed her disappointment in his refusal to support the campaign against Toulouse.

"Well, Eleonore," he said, for his sister bore the same name as the Queen, "you look a little sad. Is Raoul unfaithful again?"

His sister Eleonore shrugged her shoulders. "It is not an unusual occurrence."

"I regret that marriage," said the Count, "even though he is Louis's cousin. Who is Raoul's latest inamorata?"

"I don't know. I have not tried to find out. Sometimes I think it better to remain in ignorance."

"He should not treat you so."

"Of course he should not, but that does not prevent him. I know that he is indulging in a love affair which gives him great pleasure. It is conducted in secrecy of course. Some woman who is deceiving her husband I doubt not, as Raoul is deceiving me."

"You will never change his nature, Eleonore."

"I fear not. He will chase women as long as he has legs to carry him."

"I will have a word with him."

She shook her head. "Better not. Perhaps it is the fate of people such as we are to have unfaithful husbands. Sometimes I think it would be better if we were more humbly born. Think how our family is scattered. Childhood seems so short and if one is the youngest of a big family the older ones have left home before one is aware of them. I often think of Stephen."

"Ah, the King of England," said Theobald. "Yes, think of him often and pray for him. As King of England he needs your prayers."

"I remember the rejoicing there was within the family when he took the Crown."

"Yes," mused Theobald. "And the lamenting when it seemed that Matilda would snatch it from him."

"I would we could see more of him. It is only when he visits Normandy that I have that opportunity."

"Poor Stephen, perhaps a crown is a mixed blessing."

"You thought that, Theobald. You had more right to the Crown of England than Stephen. You were the elder son of our mother and the Conqueror was your grandfather just as much as he was Stephen's."

"Stephen had been brought up in England. There was clearly a time when King Henry thought of making him his heir."

"There would not have been those distressing wars in England if Matilda's husband had not died and she had remained in Germany."

"Yet she was the King's daughter and many would say the true heir. Stephen is our brother and I would support him with all I have, but Matilda was in fact the King's daughter and in direct line of succession. One cannot get away from that."

"Poor Stephen. I hope he is happy. What burdens he has to bear!"

"He has a good wife. No man could have a better."

"Yet he is not faithful to her. Are any men faithful?"

Theobald pressed her hand. "Do not take Raoul's infidelity too much to heart. That is his way. Stephen's queen must perforce accept this. Try to forget it."

"It is something which is always with me, Theobald, but I like not that you should have displeased the Queen."

"The King too, I fear."

"Oh, it is the Queen who counts. She rules the Court; she wishes to enlarge the kingdom of France that she may become more and more powerful. I think she might be a revengeful woman."

"I shall know how to protect myself and my lands, Eleonore. The King is young and inexperienced. It is a pity they married him to such a forceful woman. Abbé Suger is a wise man and Louis the Fat left his son in good hands . . . apart from those of his wife. But who would have expected a girl in her teens to take so much interest in affairs."

"The Queen is a woman who intends to rule. Shall you go back to Champagne now?"

"Yes. I felt I must come and put my case before the King. It is always wise when one disagrees to state one's reasons in person."

"Then I will wish you farewell, brother. It has done me good to see you. I would I could see Stephen."

"Do not wish that. It would mean trouble doubtless in Normandy if he were here."

"There is constant trouble in Normandy."

"And will be for years to come, I fear. Anjou is quiet at the moment, but his son is growing up. They say young Henry Plantagenet is quite a warrior already and that he will not only want Normandy, but England as well."

"More wars . . . more troubles!"

"So must it be when there are too many claimants to a throne. Look at this trouble now . . . with Toulouse. But never fear, Eleonore. The King, I am convinced, has little stomach for war. Doubtless this affair of Toulouse will blow over. I do not think I shall be the only one who does not wish to follow him to war."

The brother and sister took farewell of each other.

The Queen watched the Count of Champagne ride off at the head of his cavalcade.

"Curse him," said Eleonore. "How dare he flout the Queen. He shall suffer for this."

*　　*　　*

Darkness had fallen over the castle. Petronelle wrapped a cloak round her and slipped out into the fresh night air.

No one would recognize her if they saw her. They would think she was some lady of the house bent on an assignation which would be the truth, but they would never suspect she was the Queen's young sister.

Petronelle knew she was being bold and wayward; she was inviting dishonour. But what could she do? When Raoul embraced her she was weak and yielding; she had already half promised and drawn back. She had cried: "I cannot and I dare not."

And he had tenderly bitten her ear and whispered into it: "But you can and you dare."

44

She had known that there would be eventual surrender. Was that not what the songs were about? They were about wooing and romance and knights who died for their ladies, but it was so much more inviting to love than to die. Death was horrible with its blood and pain. Love was beautiful; there was desire and passion and the intense satisfaction of fulfilment which she had yet to experience.

And she would experience that before long. They would marry her soon. Suppose they married her to some impotent old man just because it would be good for State reasons. They had married Eleonore to Louis. True he was the King but he was not really very attractive. He was what they called a laggard in all that mattered. Eleonore had as much as said so. If they married her to someone she did not fancy she would have lovers. She would select someone like Raoul . . .

Raoul! She was going to meet him now, and this time there would be no holding back. He would not allow that. He had said half angrily last time: "I have waited too long." And she had thrilled to that angry note in his voice.

This time there would be no holding back.

He was waiting for her in the shrubbery.

His arms were round her, holding her firmly.

"Raoul, I dare not . . ."

"I know the place. Come."

"I must go back."

But he was laughing at her.

She said: "My sister will be furious. Do you not care for the Queen's anger?"

"Tonight I care for nothing but this," he answered.

She pretended to pull back but she knew and he knew that it was mere pretence.

They found a secluded part of the shrubbery.

"Others may come here," she protested.

"Nay, we shall be undisturbed."

"I must go back."

"You must stay here."

He was drawing her down to the earth.

She said: "I have no help but to submit."

*　　*　　*

Eleonore was quickly aware of the change in her sister and guessed the cause.

45

She summoned her to her bedchamber, and making sure that they were alone she said, "You had better tell me."

Petronelle opened her eyes very wide, assuming innocence.

Eleonore took her by the shoulders and shook her. "Do not feign innocence with me, my child. Who is the man?"

"Eleonore, I . . ."

"And I know," said Eleonore. "You could not hide it from me. It is clear. If you shouted from the turret, I have a lover, you could not say it more clearly."

"I don't see why . . ."

"No, you are a child. You are also foolish. You should have waited for marriage."

"As you did . . ."

"As I did. You know I was a virgin when I married Louis. It was necessary that I should be. Now we shall have to find a husband for you. Who is your lover? Perhaps we can marry you to him without delay. I will speak to the King."

Petronelle stammered: "That's impossible."

"Why so?"

"He . . . he is married already."

"You little fool!"

"I couldn't help it, Eleonore. I didn't mean to. At first it was only a kind of play-acting . . . like singing the songs and talking of love . . . and then . . ."

"I know. You cannot tell me anything I don't know about such matters. You should have consulted me about it. You should have told me he was making advances. Who is he?"

"Raoul . . ."

"The Count of Vermandois!"

Petronelle nodded.

Eleonore felt a wave of fury. Raoul who had pretended to admire her, who had implied that only she could satisfy him, that all other women were of no moment to him! And all the time he was making love to her sister!

"I don't believe it. Why he is old . . ."

"He is ten years older than you are. That is not much in a man."

"And you submitted to him."

Petronelle held her head high. "I did and I don't care. I'd do it again. So would you if you weren't married to the King."

Eleonore shook her sister angrily. "Don't forget you are talking to the Queen. I am mindful of my duty. You have behaved like a slut of a serving-girl."

"Then many ladies of the Court do the same. They sit with

46

you and talk in a high-minded way about love, and then by night they are with their lovers. Poetry and songs are no substitute for lovemaking, and you know it."

"So you would instruct us! But let us not waste time in recriminations. You could not wait for marriage. That is what we must consider."

"I love Raoul," said Petronelle firmly.

"And he loves you, I suppose you'll tell me."

"Oh yes, oh yes."

"But not enough to save you from his lust."

"It was love," said Petronelle ecstatically.

"And he knew to what disaster he was leading you. He knew he was married and so did you. He is married . . ." She stopped suddenly and a slow smile spread across her face.

". . . he is married," she went on slowly, "to that woman who shares my name. She is the sister of our haughty Theobald of Champagne."

"He does not love her," said Petronelle quickly. "Theirs has been a marriage which is no marriage. It is years since they were lovers. She does not understand him at all."

"So he told you, sister. A common complaint of the wayward husband. All she cannot understand is why she should be expected to be faithful while he philanders where he will. It is something I do not understand either. Suffice it you are no longer a virgin. And that is deplorable. I will speak to the King. We must get you married without delay."

"If you married me to someone else I would never give up Raoul."

"And what if it were possible to marry Raoul?"

Petronelle clasped her hands ecstatically.

"Oh, if it but were!"

"I will explore the matter."

*   *   *

The Queen received Raoul, Count of Vermandois, very coldly.

She did not give him permission to sit.

"I am displeased," she said.

"Not with me, I trust, my lady."

"With whom else! I know about you and my sister. She has confessed to me that you have seduced her. What have you to say?"

47

"That a man dazzled by the sun turns for consolation to the moon."

"There have been too many metaphors concerning the sun and moon. I have had enough of them. Are you implying that finding me unobtainable you turned to my sister?"

He bowed his head.

"My sister will not be pleased if I tell her that."

"Your magnanimity and discretion would not allow you to."

"I never allow anyone or anything to prevent my doing what I wish."

"You are the law and it is our will to obey you. What would you have me do, my Queen? Say it and I will do it or die in the attempt."

"It is not exactly one of the labours of Hercules."

"I would it were that I might show my devotion."

"You should take care. I might set you some impossible task one day."

"Nothing could strain me more than to be near you and not allowed to love you."

"You do not speak like the prospective bridegroom of another woman."

"Bridegroom!" He was alert. "My lady, alas I am married."

"To a lady of whom I gather you are not desperately enamoured."

"She is my wife. When I am in the presence of the irresistible I must perforce succumb."

"Are you referring to me or to my sister?"

"You know my feeling. I am not alone in my adoration."

"And Petronelle? You are in love with her?"

"She resembles you. What more can I say?"

"That if you were free you would agree to marry her?"

"With all my heart."

"I do not ask if you would be a faithful husband to her. I know the futility of that. She has a fancy for you."

"I would I were free."

"You could be if there were a blood tie between you and your wife."

"I know not . . ."

"You are obtuse, Count. There are always blood ties between families of our blood. So much inter-marrying through the centuries means that if we search back far enough we can find the connection."

"If this could be found . . ."

"If! It can be found. It must be found. You have seduced my sister. For all I know she may already be with child. You are responsible. Forget not that she is the sister of the Queen. Would you marry her?"

"If just cause could be found that I am not already married."

"Then found it shall be," said the Queen firmly. She was smiling to herself. Certainly Petronelle must marry her seducer; and how amusing that Raoul's wife was the sister of her enemy Theobald. This would teach that family to flout the King and Queen.

*   *   *

It was disconcerting. Count Theobald was not the only baron who ignored the King's summons. It should have been clear that the country was in no mood to go to war over Toulouse. The only enthusiasm came from the Queen and that which she imparted to her docile husband.

Eleonore rode out of Paris beside her husband ready for the siege which would bring Toulouse into their hands. Eleonore was busy with plans; she had already traced the relation between Raoul and his wife. If one went back far enough there were always blood ties. She had set the bishops working on it and they knew that if they did not find what she wished them to they would incur her displeasure.

Louis had really very little heart for war. He hated death, nor did he wish to punish his people. When he had been victorious at Orleans he had granted his rebellious subjects what they had asked for, and had stopped what he considered the cruel law of cutting off people's fingers if they did not pay their debts. Of what use was that, he had demanded, when they need their hands intact to work to pay off their debts?

The thought of innocent people's suffering worried him; but what could he do? Eleonore insisted that Toulouse was hers and therefore his, and she could not forget the insolence of Theobald of Champagne.

"Are we going to allow our subjects to treat us thus?" she had demanded. "If so we are no rulers."

He had had to agree with her; he always had to agree with her. So here he was marching on Toulouse.

Into the rich country they went. Louis's spirits were revived. Of course he would like to add these fertile provinces to his kingdom. Eleonore's eyes glowed. He wondered whether it was the sight of the land which made them so bright and eager, or the fulfilment of revenge. She was so sure that ere long Toulouse would be theirs.She would have subdued not only the Count of Toulouse who had refused to hand back that to which he had no right, but also the insolent Theobald. And when he heard that his sister was to be divorced from the Count of Vermandois he would be doubly humiliated!

He would see what it meant to defy the Queen of France—and so would others. It would be a lesson.

Alas, for Louis and Eleonore. Toulouse was well defended, and it soon became clear to Louis that even those who had rallied to his banner had no heart for the fight.

As he encamped outside the castle occupied by Raymond Saint-Gilles, group after group of his followers reminded him that they had agreed to fight with him for only a specified time. Time was running out and they must return to their estates.

Louis was disturbed.

"Command them to stay!" cried Eleonore.

But Louis had given his word. He was not a man to break that. He must stand out against Eleonore for the sake of his honour.

Thus it was the King found himself before the castle with scarcely any supporters, and it was either a case of retreat or ignominious defeat. As it was he must retire in humiliation.

There was nothing for it but to return to Paris and shelve the conquest of Toulouse, until the King and Queen could find some means of bringing it to the crown.

Such a situation was galling to the Queen. She imagined Saint-Gilles and Theobald of Champagne sneering at the royal ineptitude.

She must be revenged and the first blow should be struck through Theobald's sister. Her bishops had found that there was a blood relationship between Raoul and his wife. Therefore the marriage was no true marriage and Raoul was free to marry again.

"It is a good thing," said the Queen to the King, "that your cousin should marry with my sister."

*   *   *

The Count of Champagne was amazed one day to see his sister with a few of her attendants ride into the courtyard of his castle. He hastened down to meet her.

"Why Eleonore," he cried, "what brings you here?"

For a moment she could not answer him. She threw herself into his arms and clung to him.

"I did not know where to go."

"Where is your husband?"

"I have no husband."

"Come into the castle," said Theobald. "Tell me what this means. Raoul is dead?"

"Nay," she answered. "It is simply that he is no longer my husband."

"But this makes nonsense. You were married to him. I myself attended the ceremony. Come, sister, you must calm yourself."

He took her to his private chamber and she poured out her story. A blood tie had been discovered that meant her marriage to Raoul was not valid. She was not married to Raoul; had never been married and the ceremony she had gone through with Raoul was no true one at all. Moreover Raoul had married someone else. There had been a grand wedding and the King and Queen had attended.

"Who was the bride?" asked Theobald blankly.

"The lady Petronelle."

"What! The Queen's sister."

"Indeed yes, the Queen's sister."

"This is monstrous. It is a plot."

Eleonore nodded sadly.

Theobald was furious. It was not only the dishonour to his sister that he raged against; it was an insult to his family. The Queen had arranged this he knew. She had insisted that the bishops prove the marriage invalid and they had done so on pain of her displeasure. And why had she contrived this? To be revenged on him. Because he had refused to support her and the King over the annexation of Toulouse, she had arranged for his sister's dishonour.

"I will not endure this," he said. "This day I will send a messenger to Rome. I shall put my case before the Pope and it will be proved that this was a plot to discredit me through you, sister."

"And you think the Pope will not agree to the dissolution of the marriage?"

"How can he? The reasons put forward are groundless. I will make Raoul take you back. I will prove that his marriage to Petronelle was no marriage. She will be the one to suffer dishonour, not you, my sister."

"Raoul was eager to go to his new wife, I know."

"He will be begging to come back to you when I have the Pope's word."

Theobald was not a man to delay when action was necessary. He asked the advice of Bernard of Clairvaux who suggested that he take his case immediately to Rome with an account of the wrong done to his sister.

* * *

Petronelle was content with her marriage. She glowed with satisfaction. Watching her Eleonore felt a little discontented with her own. True it had brought her the Crown of France and she would not have missed that for anything, but she did wish it had brought her a man like Raoul instead of a monk like Louis.

She must get an heir. The country needed an heir and so did she. The purpose of marriage for such as herself was the procreation of children. She could not endure that she should fail in anything.

She was in a mood of discontent when the messenger arrived from Rome.

He brought letters for the King and the Count of Vermandois.

Eleonore made a point of being with Louis when he read his. They were very much to the point. The Pope found that there had been a miscarriage of justice. The Count of Vermandois had put away his true wife on the instigation of the Queen and the Bishops and married the Queen's sister. The Pope could find no just cause why the marriage of the Count of Vermandois and the sister of the Count of Champagne was not legal. The Count of Vermandois was excommunicated and ordered to put away the woman with whom he was now living and return to his wife.

Eleonore was furious.

"This is an insult to my sister," she cried. "Does His Holiness realize that. The sister of the Queen of France . . . !"

Louis said mildly, "My dearest, we should never have allowed Raoul to put away his wife."

"His wife! That was no true marriage. They are too closely related."

The King looked at her sadly.

"You have allowed your love for your sister to blind you," he said. "Petronelle should have looked elsewhere for a husband."

"He *is* her husband. She has lived openly with him. Do you realize what this means? Who will want to marry her now?"

"Many I think would wish for an alliance with the sister of the Queen of France."

"I'll not endure this insolence."

"This is the edict of the Pope, my love."

"You know who has done this. It is Theobald. He was determined to flout us. I'll not rest until I have driven him from Champagne."

"Champagne is his, my dear. It is independent of France."

The Queen narrowed her eyes. "Louis, sometimes I think you do not love me."

"You cannot doubt that I do."

"Yet you allow me to be insulted."

"Theobald has done only what any brother would have done. He has tried to preserve his sister's honour."

"And what of *my* sister's honour?"

"It was unwise to marry her to my cousin."

"Unwise! He had no wife, his marriage to Theobald's sister being invalid. Why shouldn't they, who had been lovers, sanctify their union!"

"Because he already had a wife."

"He had not, I tell you. The marriage was illegal. He is married to Petronelle and we are going to teach Theobald a lesson."

"How so?"

"We shall invade his lands. We shall raze his castles to the ground. I tell you we will be revenged on Theobald."

"We should have no support."

"Then we will do it without support. I have my loyal subjects of Aquitaine. They would follow me wherever I wished to go."

"Nay, Eleonore, let us not go rashly into war."

Her eyes blazed at him. He was a weakling, a monk, and they had married him to her! He had little to give her but her crown.

And he was going to obey her.

* * *

She was determined they were going to war. They were going to ravage the lands of Champagne and teach its disobedient Count a lesson. She was frustrated, married to a man who could not satisfy her intense longings. She had her

53

crown from him but had grown accustomed to that now, and she wanted a strong man whom she could find some pleasure in subduing. Louis was too easily managed although in this matter of war he was proving obstinate. It would not be for long; she would make him agree shortly and there was a certain stimulation in urging him. She enjoyed the battle with him while his repulsion to war infuriated her.

Petronelle and Raoul were smugly content with each other; and she was determined that they should remain together. She was not going to give way.

Meanwhile she badgered Louis. Was he a coward? Was he going to allow little rulers of small provinces to outwit him? Would he stand by and see the sister of his wife dishonoured? It was tantamount to dishonouring his wife.

Louis implored her to be patient, and then another matter arose which demanded his attention.

The Archbishopric of Bourges had fallen vacant and Eleonore and Louis had chosen the man who was to fill the post. He was ideal, being a friend of theirs. Then to their consternation a message came from the Pope that he had chosen Pierre de la Châtre for the office.

"How dare he interfere in matters which concern us and us only!" demanded the Queen.

Louis supported her. He was the King. It was for him to say who should be his Archbishop.

"Not so," retorted the Pope. "I have appointed Pierre de la Châtre and none other shall have it."

Louis, prompted by Eleonore, replied that as long as he lived de la Châtre should not enter Bourges.

Then the Pope made a remark which when reported to Louis raised his anger.

"The King of France is a child," said the Pope. "He must get schooling and be kept from bad habits."

"You see," cried Eleonore when this was reported, "they have no respect for you. It is because you allow people to insult you. You have been over-lenient. Look at Theobald of Champagne. If you had marched into his country and laid it waste the Pope would not have spoken to you as though you were a schoolboy."

Louis was silent for a few moments then he burst out: "It would have meant war. I hate war. Killing brings such suffering to innocent people."

"A fine way for a king to talk," commented Eleonore scornfully.

Theobald played right into her hands by supporting the Pope's choice and letting it be known.

Eleonore was furious. "What now?" she cried. "Will you stand by and allow this?"

Louis knew that he could not, and when the Pope excommunicated him he knew that he had to take action.

He prepared to march on Champagne in order to subdue the Count who had dared take sides against his King.

*   *   *

Eleonore rode out to Paris beside her reluctant husband. There was to be war with Champagne and Louis knew that such conflicts enriched no one but the soldiers who plundered and pillaged while innocent people suffered.

The Queen however was adamant and he had after much persuasion agreed that Theobald must be taught a lesson.

It was not a very impressive army that marched into Champagne. Many wandering adventurers joined it, and because it was not very large the King was glad to welcome any who followed him, even though he knew they were out for the spoils which would come their way.

As they marched deeper into the terrain of the man the Queen detested, the rougher elements of the army plundered the villages against the King's order. Louis heard the cries of protesting villagers who sought to protect their crops, their houses and their family. He saw his rough soldiery ordering the villagers from their houses, illtreating the women, raping, feasting, drinking and acting in a manner of which he had heard much and which had made him hate the thought of war.

He endeavoured to stop their cruelties; they did not heed him.

Eleonore regarded him with contempt. What sort of a king was he whom men would not obey and who shuddered at the prospect of war? She could only remember that this was the enemy's country. She exulted over the burning land. This would teach Theobald what it meant to flout his King because if that King was weak his Queen was not.

They had reached the walled city of Vitry.

There was little defence offered and in a short time the King's men were in the streets killing, pillaging, shedding the blood of its inhabitants. The old and the maimed and the

55

women and the children ran screaming before the soldiers and barricaded themselves into the wooden church.

"Enough, enough," cried Louis. But his command was not heeded.

His followers had come to pillage and murder and they could not be restrained. There then occurred a terrible incident which was to haunt the King for the rest of his days.

Inside the church the children clung to their mothers, and mothers begged for the safety of their little ones. The King's men knew no pity. They did not attempt to break into the church. They merely set it on fire.

As the flames enveloped it and the thick black smoke filled the air the cries of the innocent could be heard calling curses on their murderers and screaming for mercy.

"Have done. Have done," pleaded Louis but they would not listen to him. In any case it was too late. In that burning church were thirteen hundred innocent people and they were all burned to death.

*   *   *

In his tent Louis lay staring blankly before him. Eleonore lay beside him.

"I can hear their screaming," he said.

She answered: "There is no sound now. They are all dead."

"All dead!" he cried. "Those innocent people. Holy Mother of God help me! I shall never be able to escape from the sound of their cries."

"They should have denounced their lord. They should have sworn allegiance to you."

"They were innocent people. What did they know of our quarrel?"

"You must try to sleep."

"To sleep. If I do, I dream. I can smell the smoke. I shall never be free of it. How the wood crackled!"

"It was old and dry," she said.

"And little children . . . They called curses on us. Imagine a mother . . . with her little ones."

"It is war," said Eleonore. "It is not wise to brood on these things."

But Louis could not stop brooding.

He could not go on, he declared.

"To give in now would be victory for Theobald," Eleonore reminded him.

"I can't help it," cried Louis. "I am sick of war and killing."

"You should never have been a king."

"You speak truth. My heart is in the Church."

"Which is no place for a king's heart to be."

"Sometimes I think I should have refused to take the Crown."

"How could you, the King's son, have done that?"

"Sometimes I think God is not pleased with me. We have been six years married and have no child."

"It is a long time to wait," agreed Eleonore.

"Is there something we have done . . . or not done? Have I displeased God in some way?" The King shivered. "I feel in my heart that whatever we did before the burning of Vitry was nothing compared with that great sin."

"Stop thinking of it."

"I can't, I can't," moaned the King.

She knew that he would be useless to command an army in his present state.

"We should return to Paris," she said.

He was eager to agree. "Yes," he answered. "Disband the army. Go back. Call off the war."

"That would be folly. The army will stay here. We shall return. State duties call you to Paris. There you will rest and forget Vitry. You will learn that it is what must be expected in war."

*   *   *

The war continued. Louis was heartily sick of it but Eleonore would not allow Theobald to have the chance to say the King had been forced to retire from the field.

The King's ministers begged him to consider what good there was in continuing. Louis would have agreed but he dared not face Elconore's wrath.

He could not understand his feeling for her. It was as though he were under a spell. Whatever he might promise to do, when she showed her contempt for his weakness he always gave way to her.

The Abbot of Clairvaux who had prophesied the death of Louis's brother Philippe had become known as a worker of miracles. He had ranged himself against Louis and Eleonore, and came to the Court to ask the King to agree to a peace.

Eleonore would not hear of this.

She faced the Abbot and explained to him that to agree to a peace would be to dishonour her own sister, and although

57

this was but one of the causes which had made it necessary for Louis to make war, it was a very important one.

"Such a war," the Abbot told her, "is displeasing to God. Has that not been made clear? God has turned his face from your endeavours. The King suffers deep remorse. He had done so since the burning of Vitry."

"And before that," said Eleonore bitterly. "He has rendered me childless. You, who are said to have the power to make miracles, could perhaps work this one for me if you would."

The Abbot was thoughtful.

"Whether you should have the blessing of a child is in the hands of God."

"So is all that happens. Yet you have worked miracles, they say. Why do you not work one now?"

"I could do nothing in this matter."

"You mean you will not help me?"

"If you had a child you would doubtless change your life. Perhaps you need a child."

"I need a child," said Eleonore. "Not only because my son will be the heir to France, but because I long for a child of my own."

The Abbot nodded.

She caught his arm. "You will do this for me."

"My lady, I cannot. It is in the hands of God."

"If I persuaded the King to stop the war, to call a truce . . ."

"If you did that it might be that God would be more ready to listen to your prayers."

"I would do anything to get a child."

"Then pray with me, but first humble yourself before God. You cannot do that with the sin of war upon you."

"If there was peace you would work the miracle?"

"If there were peace I should be able to ask God to grant your request."

"I will speak to the King," she said.

She did and the result was that there was peace between Theobald and Louis.

*　　*　　*

To Eleonore's great joy she was pregnant. She was sure that Bernard had worked the miracle. All these years and no sign of a child, and now the union would be fruitful.

She had softened a little. She was planning for the child as a humble mother might have done. The songs she sang were of a different nature.

The members of the Court marvelled.

In due course the child was born. A girl.

She was not disappointed. Like all rulers Louis had hoped for a son; yet, she demanded of her ladies, why should there be this overwhelming adoration of the male? "I was my father's heiress although I was a woman," she reminded them. "Why should the King and I be sad because we have a daughter?"

The salic law prevailed in France. This meant that no woman could rule. The crown would go to the next male heir. This law was all against Eleonore's principles and she promised herself that she would not allow it to persist. Her daughter was but a baby yet and there was time enough to think of her future.

She was christened Marie and for more than a year after her birth Eleonore was content to play the devoted mother.

* * *

Life had become monotonous. Little Marie was past two years old. Eleonore was devoted to her but naturally the child was often in the company of her nurses. Eleonore continued to hold court. The songs had become more voluptuous again; they stressed the sorrows of unrequited passion and the joys of shared love.

Petronelle was her constant companion; Eleonore watched with smouldering eyes her sister and her husband together. What a passionate affair that had been! Something, sighed Eleonore, which was denied me.

She had at first been fond of Louis. He had been so overcome at the sight of her and was so devoted to her that she had developed quite an affection for him. It was not in her passionate nature to be contented with that. Louis might be her slave and it pleased her that he should be, but his piety bored her, and what was hardest of all to endure was his remorse.

He took a great interest in the Church and was constantly taking part in some ritual. He would return from such occasions glowing with satisfaction but it would not be long before he was sunk in melancholy.

He could not forget the sound of crackling flames and the screams of the aged and innocent as they had burned to death. The town itself had now become known as Vitry-the-Burned.

He would pace up and down their bedchamber while Eleonore watched him from their bed.

She knew that he would not be seeing her, seductively inviting with her long hair loose about her naked shoulders as she might be. He would be seeing the pitiless faces of men intent on murder; and when she spoke to him he would hear instead those cries for mercy.

How many times had she told him: "It was an act of war and best forgotten."

And he declared: "To my dying day I shall never forget. Remember, Eleonore, all that was done was done in my name."

"You did your best to stop it. They heeded you not." Her lips curled. What a weakling he was! His men intent on murder did not obey him! And he permitted this.

He should have been a monk.

She was weary of him. She wished they had married her to a *man*.

Yet he was the King of France and marriage to him made her a queen. But she was also Eleonore of Aquitaine. She was never going to forget that.

So she listened to him wandering on in his maudlin way and she knew that she would not go on for ever living as she was at this time. Her adventurous spirits were in revolt.

She had made a brilliant marriage; she was a mother. But for her that was not enough. She was reaching for adventure.

*　　*　　*

The opportunity came from an unexpected quarter.

For many years men had sought to expiate their sins by making pilgrimages to Jerusalem. They had believed that by undertaking an arduous journey, which often resulted in death, they showed their complete acceptance of the Christian faith and their desire for repentance. They believed that in this way they could be forgiven a life of wickedness. There had been many examples of men who had undertaken this pilgrimage. Robert the Magnificent, father of William the Conqueror, had been one. He had died during the journey leaving his son but a child, unprotected to his enemies, but it was believed that he had expiated a lifetime's sins by this gesture.

But while it was considered a Christian act to make a pilgrimage, how much greater grace could be won by taking part in a Holy War to drive the Infidel from Jerusalem.

Ever since the seventh century Jerusalem had been in the possession of the Mussulmans, khalifs of Egypt or Persia. There was conflict between Christianity and Islamism, and at the beginning of the eleventh century the persecution of Christians in the Holy Land was at its most intense. All Christians living in Jerusalem were commanded to wear a wooden cross about their necks. As these weighed five pounds they were a considerable encumbrance. Christians were not allowed to ride on horses; they might only travel on mules and asses. For the smallest disobedience they were put to death often in the cruellest manner. Their leader had suffered crucifixion; therefore that seemed a suitable punishment for those who followed him.

Pilgrims who made the journey to and from Jerusalem came back with stories of the terrible degradation that Christians were being made to suffer. Indignation came to a head when a certain French monk returned from a visit to Jerusalem. He became known as Peter the Hermit. Of small stature and almost fragile frame, his glowing spirit of determination was apparent to all who beheld him. It was his mission, he believed, to bring the Holy City into Christian hands. He travelled all over Europe, barefooted, clad in an old woollen tunic and serge cloak; living on what he could find by the wayside and what was given him; and he roused the indignation of the whole of Europe over the need to free Jerusalem from the Infidel.

It happened that in the year 1095 Pope Urban II was at Clermont in Auvergne residing over a gathering of Archbishops, Bishops, Abbots and other members of the clergy. People from all over Europe had come to hear him speak; Urban had been very impressed by the mission which Peter the Hermit had been carrying out and asked him to come to him. On the steps of the church, in the presence of the Pope, Peter told the assembly of the fate meted out to Christians in the Holy Land by the ruthless infidels who were eager to eliminate Christianity.

Peter, his dedication burning fiercely for now he saw the fulfilment of his dream, talked of the insults heaped on Christians, of the hideous deaths they were made to suffer and that he believed God had inspired him with a mission which was to bring back Jerusalem to Christianity.

61

The crowd was silent for a few seconds after he had finished speaking and then broke into loud cries of "Save Jerusalem. Save the Holy Land."

Then Pope Urban raised his hand to ask for silence.

"That royal city," he said, "which the Redeemer of the human race honoured and made illustrious by his coming and hallowed by his passion, demands deliverance. It looks to you, men of France, men from beyond the mountains, nations chosen and beloved by God, you the heirs of Charlemagne, from you, above all, Jerusalem asks for help. God will give glory to your arms. Take then the road to Jerusalem for the remission of your sins, and depart assured of the imperishable glory which awaits you in the Kingdom of Heaven."

Again that hushed silence; then from a thousand throats there had risen the cry: "God wills it."

"Aye," the Pope had cried, "God wills it. If God was not in your souls you would not have answered as one man thus. Let this be your battle cry as you go forth against the Infidel. 'God Wills It.'"

The air had been filled with people's shouting as with one voice: "God wills it."

The Pope had held up his hands for silence.

"Whosoever has a wish to enter in this pilgrimage, must wear upon his crown or on his chest the cross of the Lord."

Peter the Hermit watched with glowing eyes. His mission was accomplished. The Crusades had begun.

Since that memorable occasion there had been many a battle between Christians and Mussulmans; and it was at this time, when Louis was so troubled by his conscience and could not get the cries from Vitry-the-Burned out of his mind, and the Queen had realized that her vitality was being frustrated, that there was a great revival of anger against the Mussulmans and a desire to win back Jerusalem to Christianity.

Bernard of Clairvaux was deeply concerned by what was happening in Jerusalem. He came to the King and talked with him.

"Here is a sorry state of affairs," he said. "God will be both sorrowful and angry. It is many years since the first crusade and we are no nearer to our purpose. Atrocities are being committed on our pilgrims. It is time the Christian world revolted against its enemies."

Louis was immediately interested. He was burdened with

sin; he longed to expiate those sins and to have an opportunity to show his repentance.

Bernard nodded. "Vitry-the-Burned hangs heavy on your conscience, my lord. It should never have happened. There should never have been a campaign against Theobald of Champagne."

"I know it now."

"In the first place," said Bernard, who was determined not to let the King escape lightly, "you should not have opposed Pierre de la Châtre. You should have recognized the authority of the Pope."

It was Eleonore who had been the prime mover in this affair as in all other matters. Bernard knew it but he did not mention it. The King was in a penitent mood. Let him take the blame.

"It was wrong to insist on the Comte de Vermandois's putting away his wife and marrying the Queen's sister. It was wrong to take the war into Champagne. For these you have been punished for you will never be able to forget the burning of the church of Vitry."

"It's true," groaned the King.

"You need to sue for mercy. You need to make one great gesture. Why should you not lead a campaign to the Holy City?"

"I! What of my kingdom?"

"There are those who could care for it while you are away."

"Leave my kingdom! Lead a crusade!"

"Others have done this before you. So they have appeased God and won forgiveness."

The King stared before him. More war! He hated war. And yet his sins lay heavy on him.

Bernard raised his fanatical eyes to heaven. "I, my lord, will not turn my back on my duty. I would I were a young man and I would lead the crusade. God has declined to give me that honour. It is my duty to set before others where their duties lie. I want there to be three great assemblies, one at Bourges, another at Vézelai and another at Estampes. You will be there to give them your support. Think on this matter seriously. Only by pleasing God in this way will he forgive you for what happened at Vitry-the-Burned."

*   *   *

He did not tell Eleonore immediately. He feared her derision.

He went to his good friend and adviser the Abbé Suger.

The Abbé was appalled. "To leave France, leave your kingdom. But your duty lies here!"

"Not as I see it. I have sinned."

"You think of Vitry. You will not be blamed entirely for that. Your soldiers were undisciplined. You tried to make them desist."

"And failed in my duty. I was not strong enough to prevent them."

"Give your support to the crusade. Help those who wish to go to go. But your duty lies here in governing your kingdom."

"Bernard wishes me to go."

"Bernard is a fanatic. My lord, a King cannot be that. God would not wish you to fail in your duty."

As usual Louis was torn between two courses. He knew that his duty lay in France; yet the thought of expiating his sins in this dramatic way appealed to him.

It was not long before Eleonore was aware of the conflict in his mind.

"You are closeted for long periods with Bernard," she said, "and with Suger. What are they putting before you?"

He hesitated. Then he blurted out: "Bernard wants me to lead a crusade. Suger is against it."

"To lead a crusade. You! And what of France?"

"That is what I tell Bernard. My duty lies here."

"Lead a crusade!" murmured Eleonore. And she was thinking that she would be Regent of France. Or would she? They would set up Bernard or Suger or someone to govern with her. She would be expected to lead a cloistered life during the King's absence.

But to go on a crusade! To ride to the Holy Land. What adventures she would have! Life would hardly be dull and monotonous then.

Then she knew that this was the answer This was exactly what she had wanted.

"You must go," she said firmly. "You will throw away your burden of guilt. It is the only way if we are ever to have any peace from Vitry. And, Louis, I shall come with you."

He looked at her in amazement; but she did not see him;

64

she saw herself riding at the head of the women she would select to accompany her.

She could not wait to start.

*　　*　　*

In the market square of Vézelai Bernard was rallying men to his banner. Beside him were the King and Queen.

"If you were told," he thundered, "that an enemy had attacked your castles, your towns and your lands, had ravished your wives and your daughters, profaned your temples, would you not fly to arms? All these evils and evils still greater have come upon your brethren in the family of Christ. Why do you wait to avenge these wrongs, Christian warriors? He who gave His life for you now demands yours."

Once again a cry rose up from the throats of thousands: "God wills it."

And from none more fervently than that of the Queen of France.

The King then knelt and Bernard put the cross in his hands. Louis kissed it. Then the Queen knelt and did likewise.

She was exultant. The great adventure was about to begin.

The Lovers of Antioch

Eleonore was afire with enthusiasm as she rode back to Paris. This was going to be the greatest adventure of her life. She would ride at the head of the ladies whom she would select to take with her. She would immediately set about designing what costumes they should wear. They would be more than an inspiration to the men; they would be crusaders in very truth.

How exhilarating to be setting out on an enterprise which had the blessing of the Church, and to plan exciting adventures in the knowledge that in carrying them out one would be gaining redemption for one's past sins. This was the second occasion when she must be grateful to Bernard. He had wrought the miracle of childbirth for her and now he had presented her with this wonderful way of expiating her sins and having an exciting adventure at the same time.

She summoned her ladies to her. They should be mounted on gaily caparisoned horses, she told them; she was arranging that there should be countless pack mules to carry their baggage. Eleonore could not tolerate the idea of travelling without the beautiful gowns and all that which was necessary in order for a lady to lead a gracious life.

The minstrels now sang of war—holy war. Eleonore listened with outward attention but her thoughts were far away in the Holy Land where she saw herself riding at the head of her troupe of ladies. They should be dressed as Amazons for they were going into battle. She started an equestrian school where her ladies were taught to practise marching into war. Trumpets were sounded in their horses' ears that they might grow accustomed to the noise of battle; they were forced to jump over high barriers.

Eleonore spent excited hours preparing the boxes of dresses, perfumes, unguents and all that was needed for ladies of elegance.

Petronelle joined her and gave way to loud lamentations when she heard she was not included in the plan. At first she had believed she would be with her sister; she had practised her skill on horseback; she had found great pleasure in planning the clothes she would need.

Then it was decided that Raoul, Comte de Vermandois, should act with Abbé Suger whom the Pope had chosen to be Regent of France during the King's absence. Petronelle was overcome with grief. She wept and implored but was told she must either leave her husband or stay in France.

"I should not advise you to leave Raoul," said Eleonore with a smile. "He is a husband who would find it very easy to be unfaithful as you discovered before you married him."

So Petronelle decided she must stay behind.

"Well," said Eleonore, "one cannot have everything. You have an attractive virile husband, sister, and you must needs be content with that."

So Eleonore went on with her preparations and talked so glowingly of the Crusade to all whom she met that many more were gathered to the banner.

With her usual singlemindedness Eleonore despised all those who did not wish to join in. She told her ladies that if any man did not wish to come with them that he must be a coward. "Some of them are of the opinion that women are useless except for the domestic duties they perform and for submitting to their pleasure and their need to see themselves reproduced in their children, but I have never accepted this view," she cried. "I believe that my sex is in every sense equal to that of its opposite. And now that we are going into battle, now that we have shown France that women can and will help to carry on this holy war, why should not those men who stay at home weave and spin and look after the children of their households?"

How she laughed to scorn those who made excuses not to join in the crusade.

"Come," she cried, "we will send them our distaffs and ask them if they will make good use of them as they do not wish to do what they call men's work."

Eleonore was amused when she learned how many of them who had received the distaffs changed their minds and joined the expedition.

The day of departure grew near. It had been arranged that all the French joining in the Crusade should meet at Metz where King Louis would be ready to lead them; and the Germans should gather at Ratisbonne where the Emperor Conrad would be waiting to put himself at their head.

Both armies should then make their way to Constantinople where Manuel Comnenus, who was the grandson of Alexis Comnenus, would assist them.

Eleonore said *au revoir to* her little three-year-old daughter and set out at the head of a party of Amazons while Louis led the men. It was a brilliant cavalcade which crossed Europe, the golden lilies flying side by side with the red cross of Christianity.

*   *   *

As they made their way across Europe, men eager to join in the Crusade fell in behind the King so that his army numbered one hundred thousand men. Eleonore was in her element. They rested at the castles of noblemen who delighted to receive them and, eager to help any engaged on such an enterprise, entertained the company lavishly. Eleonore and her ladies sang and played; and there were tournaments and entertainments to enliven the company.

Louis was uncertain whether they should have enjoyed so much luxury for, he pointed out, it was not a pleasure jaunt; but Eleonore laughed this to scorn and the more magnificent the spectacle the more delighted she was.

When they reached Constantinople which was ruled by Manuel Comnenus, they found that the Emperor Conrad had arrived before them. The Greeks gave them a great welcome and there was much rejoicing.

Manuel declared that he would give them guides to conduct them into Asia Minor and would do everything in his power to aid them in their campaign against the Infidel. He was charmed by Eleonore and her party of ladies and she was in no hurry to leave such a pleasant haven.

At the beginning of October the Emperor Conrad was ready to leave Constantinople, and Manuel, true to his promise, provided guides who would conduct him through the hostile Turkish territory. The French army had not at that time completed its preparations, and as Conrad had been the first to arrive at Constantinople he was the first to leave.

It was an unpleasant shock when news reached Louis and his advisers that Conrad had been set upon by the Turks and completely routed at Iconium. Conrad himself had been wounded; his army was in disorder and it was by no means certain what further action he could take.

There was great consternation among Louis's advisers, and the King was prevailed upon to hold a secret conference in his apartments. Several of the Bishops who were accompanying the party begged the King not to include the Queen in this meeting. She was on great terms of friendship with Manuel and it would be difficult, they said, for them to voice their suspicions in her presence.

Louis, who had begun to feel that Eleonore was displaying a levity which was not always seemly, agreed, and in the quiet of his apartments the Bishop of Langres announced that he did not trust the Greeks.

"It appears to me," went on the Bishop, "that Conrad could have been led into an ambush. Who were his guides? The answer is Greeks who had been supplied by Manuel. What if Manuel is in league with the Turks?"

"They are Infidels!" cried Louis.

"They are rich. Perhaps they offered Manuel a bribe to betray Conrad."

"I cannot believe it. They would have to answer for such a deed in Heaven."

"There are some, my lord, who allow treasures on Earth to blind them to those in Heaven."

"Yet Manuel has been so gracious to us."

"Too gracious!" retorted the Bishop. "Too friendly. Fawning in fact at times. I don't trust him and now that Conrad's army has been routed I fear for ours."

"What must we do then?" asked the King. "We are pledged to take the road to Jerusalem."

"But we should not trust the Greeks. How do we know that they may not be listening to our plans and warning the Turks of them."

"I cannot believe that of Christians."

"My lord, you judge others by yourself. Alas, they lack your piety and honour. I have every reason to believe that the Greeks, under Manuel, are traitors to our cause."

"Then we will regard their advice with suspicion."

"That is not enough, my lord. They may have their spies. They may send warning to the Turks. We should take Constantinople. Let the enemy know that we will not suffer traitors."

"I would never agree to that!" cried the King. "We did not set out to punish the Greeks, but to expiate our own sins. When we took up the cross, God did not put into our hands the sword of his justice. We have come forth to fight the Infidel to restore the Holy City to Christians. I shall not engage in any other war."

The knights rallied to the King. They were eager to press forward. They wanted to continue with the march to the Holy Land and had no desire or intention to engage in a war against the Greeks.

"Then beware," said the Bishop of Langres.

"We shall take every care, fear not," said Louis. "And now we must proceed."

* · * *

When Louis and his army left Constantinople and landed in Asia Minor, they caught up with the remains of Conrad's. Louis was disturbed to find the German ruler wounded and despondent. The Turks were fierce fighters he told Louis and he was certain that they had been warned of his plans.

He was in no state to march with Louis and had decided he would return to Constantinople and perhaps go by sea to Palestine.

A mood of fierce determination swept over the French army. Each man assured himself that what had happened to the Germans should not happen to the French. They would be prepared and ready for the Turk if he should attempt to ambush them.

And so it happened that when at Phrygia on the River Maeander the armies met, the French achieved a brilliant victory over the Turks. Eleonore and her ladies watched the battle from some distance and when victory was certain they came forward, dressed the wounds of those who had suffered and celebrated the success with songs written for the occasion.

"Such an army," said the Bishop of Langres, "could if it had the mind, have taken Constantinople."

"It would not have had the heart," said Louis. "It has been gathered together to fight a holy war and nothing else will satisfy it."

Now there was high hope among the soldiers. They had succeeded where the Germans had failed. Full of optimism they planned the next march forward.

The Queen and her party were considerably encumbered by the pack-horses which carried their baggage; and it was decided that the army should be divided into two parts. The Queen and her ladies should set up their camp on the heights over the Valley of Laodicea. There they would be able to see the approach of any enemy forces. They would overlook the fertile valley and miles of surrounding country. The King would follow them and there should be a rendezvous on the heights.

The ladies must of course be well protected and Louis chose his best troops to accompany them, while he with the ladies' baggage and the remains of his army followed behind to fight off any of the enemy who might be following.

Eleonore rode at the head of her troops and beside her was her Constable, Saldebreuil of Sanzay, a man in whose conversation she delighted. He was elegant, handsome, cultured. Often she had wished that the King was a little more like him. But then more and more often she was beginning to compare poor Louis with other men, to his disadvantage.

They laughed and sang as they went along, and at length they came to the heights where the King and his commanders had decided they should rest. Eleonore looked up at the plateau. It appeared to be a grim spot and very different from the beautiful valley of Laodicea. There the grass was fresh green and clear waterfalls gushed from the hillside while wild flowers grew in profusion.

"What an enchanting spot!" cried Eleonore.

"It is indeed," Saldebreuil agreed, "and sad that we must not tarry here.".

"But we *shall* tarry here," said Eleonore. "It is too beautiful for us to ignore. It's an enchanting spot. I want to rest here. Imagine it in moonlight."

"The King's orders were that we were to encamp on the plateau," her Constable reminded her.

71

"Leave the King to me. He will understand that having discovered such a spot we cannot be so blind to the beauties of nature as to pass through it. We shall sing tonight of the glories of nature. We shall thank God for leading us to this beautiful spot."

"And the King . . ."

"The King will understand that it was my wish," said Eleonore.

So they camped in the valley and darkness fell.

* * *

The King coming along behind with the loads of baggage was aware that the Arabs were swarming for the attack.

"Thank God," he said, "that the Queen has gone on ahead and will be safe on the plateau."

By this time there were Arabs on all sides of them.

"On!" cried the King. "We must reach the plateau. There our soldiers will be waiting for us. Once we are on it we shall be able to face the enemy in all our strength."

Fiercely battling his way forward, harassed on all sides by the attacking Arabs, the French army approached the valley. To their consternation they saw that the heights above were not occupied by their troops as they had expected.

"What of the Queen?" cried Louis. "Where is she?"

It occurred to him that since she was not with his troops on the heights she must be in the valley and the horror of the situation alarmed him. He had to place himself between the Arabs and the advance troops among whom were the Queen and her ladies. He pictured what could happen to Eleonore and her women if they fell into those infidel hands. They could be sold into slavery; they could be submitted to a thousand indignities. At all costs he must reach Eleonore. But the Arabs were upon him. They had discovered the rich baggage and there were shouts of triumph as they dragged the bales from the pack-horses. Eleonore's beautiful robes, her jewels, all that which had delighted her and made the journey so far such an exciting adventure would be lost. Worse still, what would become of her and the women? What would become of his men?

All about him his soldiers were falling and there were very few left between him and the enemy. Vitry and all its horror came into his mind, and with it the terrible knowledge of the danger the Queen would be in if he were killed.

It seemed as if by a miracle that he noticed a nearby tree and above it an enormous boulder. Acting on impulse he seized the branch of this tree and swung himself up to the top of the rock. He was then out of reach of those cruel scimitars.

There was another point in his favour for it had grown suddenly dark, and the Arabs who had been attacking those who surrounded him, fearing that others would take the best of the spoils from the pack-horses, shouting to each other, hurried off to make sure of their share of the plunder.

He caught at the branch of the tree on which he had swung to the rock and descended. Then he climbed the tree. He believed he had been saved by a miracle. The tree had been put there by God for it had undoubtedly saved his life.

There he was temporarily safe. The leaves completely hid him. Peering through them he could in the moonlight make out something of the horrible carnage and he knew that this was a defeat as certain as that which had befallen Conrad of Germany.

And Eleonore? What of her? Was she safe in the valley? He thought she must be and she was in any case protected by the best of men.

Had she gone to the heights as he had commanded this would not have happened. She should never have come on this crusade. Women did occasionally follow the men, but they had to obey orders strictly and they came rather as camp followers than crusader commanders. But Eleonore would never be anything but a ruler. She would always impose her will on those about her. He wondered what his life would have been like if he had married a less forceful woman.

And even now with this horror all about him he could not regret his marriage. There was about her a quality which no other woman would ever have for him. He would never forget the first time they had met when he had thought her more beautiful than any creature he had ever seen. And he who had thought he would never wish to live with a woman had wanted Eleonore with him day and night.

He was bound to her. Whatever she did he would love her; he would never regret his marriage. And he could think thus while overlooking this carnage for which to a great degree her headstrong ways were to blame, he could still feel love for her, still be anxious for her, still never regret the day he had seen her and known she was to be his wife.

The dawn showed that the enemy had retired. The
73

packhorses minus their burdens wandered aimlessly among the bodies of fallen men.

The King descended the tree. What was left of his army rallied round him. They could not bury the dead but they could succour the wounded.

Then sadly they made their way into the valley where the Queen and her protectors received them with great sorrow.

Seven thousand fine soldiers had been slain and the army was without means of continuing the fight. The brief success at Phrygia was as though it had never been.

Louis and the French army were in as unhappy a state as Conrad and his Germans had been.

*　　*　　*

By the cooling streams of the Orontes they made fresh plans.

"We dare not stay here," said Louis. "The enemy will return. They know our weak state. They will finish us completely."

Eleonore was despondent. All those handsome men lost and with them the beautiful gowns and jewels which were her delight. She had no desire for this kind of adventure if she must appear dishevelled in a dirty gown. The adventure had been spoilt.

"And can we travel in our present state?" asked the Bishop of Langres. "What of our wounded?"

"We must somehow manage to take them with us," said the King. "And to delay here is dangerous. We must march on and hope for succour. If we can get to Pamphilia we might make our way to Antioch."

"My uncle Raymond is the Governor of Antioch as you know," said the Queen. "We must reach Antioch and there we can nurse the wounded back to health and reform the army."

"There is a chance," said Louis, "if we can get there before we are overtaken by the Arabs who will certainly pursue us. If they did, in our present sorry state we should stand little chance of survival."

"We shall do it," said Eleonore.

"And if we fail," said the King, "we shall have died in Christ, for in battle with the Infidel we have done His work and we shall know that it is His will."

It was the Queen's example rather than the King's expression of acceptance of any fate which awaited him which spurred the survivors of that disastrous campaign to continue their march.

On they went to be harassed continually by marauding bands of Arabs. On one of these skirmishes Saldebreuil de Sanzay was captured. The Queen was desolate. The thought of her handsome Constable in the hands of the Infidel was unbearable. What would they do to him! It would doubtless be better for him if he had been killed. She could not wish it otherwise if the Infidel should submit him to torture. She was more than a little in love with him as she was with several of the gallant men who surrounded her and was constantly comparing them with the monk-like Louis.

But the situation was too desperate for her to brood too long on the fate of others. They must make their way to Antioch without delay. At length famished, wretched, denuded of most of their baggage they reached Pamphilia.

* * *

The Governor of that city gave them shelter.

"We will not encroach on your goodness," said the King. "We shall stay only until we can find transport to Antioch."

The Governor told the King that Antioch was forty days march from Satalia, the port close by, but by sea it would take only three days.

"My army is in no fit state to march," said Louis. "If you can provide us with boats to take us to Antioch we will repay you well as soon as this can be arranged."

The Governor said he would do what he could.

Impatiently Eleonore awaited the arrival of the vessels. She had heard her father talk of his brother Raymond who had become the Prince of Antioch through his marriage with the grand-daughter of Bohemund. "Raymond," her father had said, "was the handsomest man I ever saw. Women always found him irresistible." So it seemed had Constance, Bohemund's grand-daughter, and so she had brought him Antioch. Eleonore was eager to see this man. As her uncle he would surely make them welcome. In Antioch she could acquire some beautiful clothes. She was deeply grieved at the loss of the baggage, for to appear romantic and beautiful was necessary to her enjoyment of life.

Each day she awaited the arrival of the vessels which would carry them to Antioch, and when at last they came there was bitter disappointment. Seaworthy they undoubtedly were, but there were so few of them that they could not carry the army and all its adherents.

Louis was nonplussed. This could only mean that some of them would have to do the hazardous land march which would take forty days.

"I cannot subject any to that," he cried to his Bishops. "We must try to carry everyone in the ships."

"They would sink," was the terse reply.

"Yet I cannot leave them to march across the land. The Arabs will attack them. They would suffer hardship, hunger . . . No, I cannot do it."

"Yet we cannot stay here, Sire."

He spent long hours on his knees begging Heaven to show him what he must do. Time was passing; he must act quickly. Finally he made his decision.

He embarked on the ships with the Queen, her ladies, the best of his army and some of the Bishops.

And so Louis and Eleonore left for Antioch. The King had lost more than three-quarters of his army.

*   *   *

The journey which was to have taken three days had stretched out to three weeks. The weather had been good however and it seemed as though fortune was smiling on them at last.

Ahead lay the green and fertile land, and Raymond, Prince of Antioch, uncle to Eleonore, having been advised of their coming had prepared special honours for them.

As soon as the ships were sighted he personally set out to greet them, and he had ordered his subjects of Antioch to gather and line the route the visitors would take that they might be given a welcome.

Thus it was that Eleonore and her uncle met.

She looked up at him for although she was by no means small he towered above her. Rumour had been true when it had said that he was the handsomest prince in Christendom. There was the faintest resemblance between them; they were both gay and adventurous; they were both ambitious; they were both eager to live their lives to the full and take the utmost advantage from it. They recognized each other as two of a kind and there was immediate rapport between them.

He took her hand and kissed it. "What pleasure this gives me," he said.

"I am very happy to be here," replied Eleonore.

He had turned to Louis. The King of France! This poor creature! Noble-looking in a saintly kind of way, of course, but no husband for his fiery Queen. It was going to be an amusing and exciting situation.

"Welcome to Antioch, Sire," said Raymond bowing.

"Our gratitude to you, kinsman. We have had an arduous journey."

"I heard with dismay of what had happened to your army. But let us not despair. Here you may rest among friends and make fresh plans. But come. Let me conduct you to the palace I have prepared for you, and there I hope you will be furnished with all you need."

There were horses for them to ride—for Eleonore a beautiful white palfrey.

"I somehow knew that this should be yours," said Raymond warmly, and he would allow no one but himself to help her into the saddle.

He rode between the King and Queen into Antioch. "What a beautiful city!" cried Eleonore enchanted by the olive groves, the palms, and the people who shouted greetings and waved leaves as they passed.

From time to time Raymond glanced at her. His niece was not only spirited but beautiful. A worthy heiress of Aquitaine. The most interesting phase of this development would be his growing acquaintance with his niece, and the possibility, perhaps through her, of bringing to fruition plans which had long been in his mind.

"If the palace I have had made ready is not to your liking," he told Eleonore, "you must tell me. Another shall be made ready for you."

"How good you are!"

He leaned towards her. "Are we not bound by kinship? And were we not I would wish to do everything in my power for you."

His eyes glowed in a manner which was something more than avuncular. Eleonore was delighted by such conversation; it was the essence of that romance of which she sang. If he were attracted by her, so was she by him. Never before had Louis seemed so insignificant. As she rode into Antioch she asked herself how different her life would have been if

77

the King of France had had the bearing, the manners and the vitality of the Prince of Antioch.

Into the courtyard of the palace they rode. There bloomed brilliant flowers and the spring sunshine glinted on the waters of the fountains and the feathery leaves of the cypress trees. From the balconies of her apartments Eleonore could look out on the olive groves and vineyards of the fertile land, and she was enchanted by it.

How Raymond understood her. He had heard of the loss of her baggage and sent to her beautiful cloths that she might choose from them, and with these came seamstresses that they might immediately provide her with the garments she needed. He gave her presents of costly jewels.

Eleonore exulted for she realized that Raymond was wooing her far more insistently than he was her husband.

There were entertainments for her pleasure. After a banquet Raymond would beg her to sing for him, and she sang some of her songs of love while he watched her with glowing eyes.

Raymond's wife Constance, through whom he had inherited Antioch, was less pleased with the visitors. She was well aware of the disturbing presence of the Queen of France, and she rejoiced in the Queen's close relationship to Raymond for a man could hardly make his niece his mistress. Raymond was the most handsome and charming man Constance had ever known and she was proud to be his wife, but she did realize that her opinions were shared by many and this of course meant that temptation was constantly offered to her attractive husband.

She preferred not to know of his infidelities. She was his wife. He could not put away the grand-daughter of great Bohemund. She was safe enough. But she would be pleased when the French party left to get on with their crusade.

Eleonore had no wish to leave. Crusading had turned out to be not quite the joyous adventure she had dreamed of. There was more to it than riding at the head of her ladies, beguiling the crusaders with her songs and enchanting them with her presence. The recent débâcle had taught her that. It had been utter misery in the boats which had brought them here, and when she thought of her baggage being rifled by those Infidels, she grew so angry that in her rage, her ladies feared, she might do herself some injury.

All that was behind her. Here she was in Antioch with the most adorable of hosts and between them a very exciting relationship was springing up.

"You must completely recover from your ordeals before you think of departing," insisted Raymond.

"You are good," replied Louis, "but I think we should not delay too long."

"You should be guided by my uncle," Eleonore warned him. "Remember how many men you have lost."

Louis might have said, Yes, through your folly. If you had obeyed my orders and gone to the plateau we could have been defended as we made our way to you. But he said no such thing. He was glad that her good spirits were restored and that she so obviously revelled in the comforts Antioch had to offer.

He did remind her gently that they had after all come to fight the Infidel and restore the Holy City to Christianity.

"Nevertheless," said Eleonore sharply, "it would be folly to go on with the enterprise until we are equipped to do so. Our men have suffered greatly. They need time to regain their health."

"And where better than here," said Raymond, "where they can rest secure among friends?"

Eleonore and Raymond exchanged smiles, and Louis agreed that they must indeed rest for a while. He turned to Raymond. "Although I thank you for your hospitality and am indeed grateful for it, you will understand me, I know, when I tell you that I am impatient to conclude my mission."

"I understand, of course," replied Raymond, "but I think the Queen is right when she says you should tarry awhile."

"God will bless you for your goodness to us," answered Louis.

*　　*　　*

There was a walled garden in the palace. In it was a beautiful fountain in the centre of which was a statue depicting lovers embracing. Eleonore often went to this garden. Raymond knew it and it had become a meeting place.

They walked in it together arm in arm. She liked to feel the pressure of his fingers on her arm.

"I live in fear," he told her, "that you will leave us soon."

"I will do my utmost to stay."

"The King grows restive."

"The King!" There was a note of impatient contempt in her voice which he was quick to notice. It merely confirmed the assessment he had made of their relationship.

"*You* should have been the commander," he ventured.

"A woman?" she asked.

"A goddess rather."

"You say delightful things, Prince Raymond. I wonder if you mean them."

He turned to face her. "Do you really doubt that?"

"I am not sure."

"I would I could convince you."

"Perhaps one day you will."

"I would that you could stay here . . . for ever."

"For ever? That is a long time."

"When two people are in such accord as I believe you and I are it does not seem long."

"Yes, we are in accord, are we not? I sensed it from the moment we met."

"You and I," he said. And he bent forward and laid his lips on her forehead. She trembled with a pleasure she had never before experienced.

"That was a very pleasant uncle's kiss," she said as though reminding him of their relationship.

"Is it because of the nearness of our kinship that we understand each other so well?"

"That may be so and we must not forget that kinship."

"Why should we remember it?" he asked.

She was faintly embarrassed and said: "Perhaps I have misunderstood."

"Nay," he cried passionately. "You have misunderstood nothing. You know the state of my feelings for you. I lie awake at night wondering about yours for me."

She said: "You are the Prince of Antioch married to Bohemund's grand-daughter. I am the heiress of Aquitaine married to the King of France."

"What of that?"

"And you are my uncle."

"I never set much store by laws, did you?"

"No," she admitted.

"Shall we be frank?"

"Let us be."

"There is nothing in my heart that I could not say to you."

"Nor is there in mine."

"I love you," said the Prince of Antioch. "You are the most exciting woman I ever met. I would that I had been the King of France. You and I would have been as one. What have you to say to that, my Queen? Will you be equally frank with me?"

"You are the most exciting man I ever met. I would that you had been the King of France."

"Eleonore, then why should we deny ourselves what so clearly belongs to us?"

"Because . . ."

"Because of this close relationship."

"Raymond, you are in truth my uncle."

"Eleonore, you are in truth my love."

He embraced her and her resistance fled. She laughed at him. Was she a woman to be bound by laws? She had sung of love, had written of love. Should she be afraid of it when she confronted it in its living form? This was the greatest adventure of her life. Raymond was the hero of romantic songs; Raymond was the lover she had always wanted. She despised the King of France. She loved the Prince of Antioch.

Neither was of a nature to hesitate. All barriers were swept away. That day Eleonore and the Prince of Antioch became lovers in truth.

* * *

He rode with her often; now and then they endeavoured to evade the party that they might repair to some secret place which he knew. They made of it a rendezvous. A bower—a small summer house in the grounds of one of his palaces. His servants knew better than to interrupt him when he was there. Perhaps he had used it many times before with other women. Eleonore did not care. She believed that there was something in their relationship which set it apart from anything else either of them had experienced.

She was twenty-six years of age and he was forty-nine; yet to her he seemed the perfect lover. His experience delighted her; his charm overwhelmed her; constantly she compared him with Louis and deplored a fate which had given her to him.

She was passionately in love, recklessly so. Perhaps one or two people were aware of their relationship, but she did not care.

What if his wife discovered? Eleonore shrugged her shoulders. She knew that this was not the first time Raymond had broken his marriage vows. How could he have known that Eleonore was the one woman in the world for him if he had not had experience with many others? And if Louis discovered what was happening? She snapped her fingers. Let him discover; let him learn that there were real men in the world.

So they met and Eleonore assured herself that everything she had suffered on the road to Antioch had been worth while.

He told her he adored her; he could not imagine what his life had been without her. Dull, uninspired, scarcely worth the effort of living.

As they lay in the arbour guarded by Raymond's servants, the Prince talked to her of his plans to keep her beside him.

"Louis must be persuaded to stay here," he said.

"He will never do that. He is quite stubborn. He has a fixed idea that he must go to the Holy Land to redeem his sins. He still dreams about Vitry-the-Burned. He will never give up the idea."

"Let me tell you of my plans. You will understand readily, I know. I would rather talk to you before I attempt to put my ideas before the King. Perhaps you will be able to make him see reason. We are harassed here continually. We are surrounded by the Infidel. The French settlement here is so small that although it consists of brave men it is not enough to hold the land. If we are not stronger, in time we will be overrun by the Saracens. Aleppo is but a short distance from Antioch and here the enemy has his headquarters. Only by strengthening our holdings here and taking these menacing cities can we assure the Christian influence on this territory, and if we were to lose the one way to the Holy Land it would be closed to Christians."

"And you suggest that Louis stays here, that you and he march on the Saracens in Aleppo?"

"That would be wise. Louis should have taken Constantinople. He could have done it and I believe some of your bishops advised it."

"But that was in the hands of Manuel."

"The treacherous Greek! He is no friend to us."

"You think that he gave false information to Conrad?"

"I am sure of it. Thus the Germans were almost destroyed."

"Then your enemy is as much Manuel the Greek Emperor as the Saracens."

"I would like to see him destroyed. You know that the rulers of Antioch are his vassals. I must accept him as my suzerain or he could bring forces superior to anything I could raise and take Antioch out of my hands. I want that man destroyed. I want to make this strip of Mediterranean coast safe for Christians, and free passage to the Holy Land assured for Christian pilgrims."

"And you think Louis could help you succeed in this?"

"He has an army."

"Very much depleted."

"But fine soldiers. The fact that there is a French army on this soil has put heart into Christians throughout the territory and fear into the Infidels. Louis was ambushed but he had before that won a great victory. If he had tried to take Constantinople he could have done so."

"And what can I do?"

"Louis sets great store by you. Everyone talks of his devotion. If you could persuade him to join with me, to postpone his journey to the Holy City, to do the work which is at hand, he would be doing greater service to God than in any other way."

"And to us," said Eleonore, "for we should be together. I would ride with the army. I would be in camp with you."

Raymond was not sure of that but he remained silent.

"Speak to Louis," he said. "Sound him. But do not let him know that I have confided in you."

She would do it, she promised. She was ready to do anything Raymond suggested; and since the project meant that they would not have to part, she could throw herself wholeheartedly into the project.

* * *

She could scarcely endure to have Louis near her. She was constantly comparing him with Raymond. There could not have been two men more unlike. Why did Louis the Fat, King of France, have such a son? Any of his brothers would have been more worthy to be King. One of his brothers, Robert, Count of Dreux, had great ambitions, she had heard. Henry, the next in age to Louis, was the Archbishop of Rheims so he would no doubt be content with his lot. There was another Philip to replace the one who had been killed by the pig, and Peter. Any of those would have made a better king than Louis. A king whose heart was in the Church was no man to rule a country. Louis had nothing but his piety to recommend him and what a bore that was!

She had held herself aloof from him and was glad that when he was occupied in State affairs he had little desire for physical contact. What a man to have married such a woman as she was! Although she had always known how unsuited they were, she had realized this more fully since her liaison with Raymond. There was a man who was indeed a man. Ruler, lover, everything that she could desire.

She was going to work for him with all her power.

Louis came to their apartment in the beautiful palace which Raymond had put at their disposal, his brow furrowed, clearly thoughtful.

What was disturbing him she wondered? Some ritual in one of the church processions? He could be enthusiastic enough about them. He was becoming obsessed by religion.

"Louis," she said, "how beautiful it is here! How peaceful! Yet at any moment this lovely country could be overrun by Infidels."

He was silent and she went on: "It is a pity that such a spot cannot be made safe for Christians."

"There is no safety on the road to Jerusalem. That is why a crusade such as ours is fraught with danger."

"Then we should make that road safe, Louis."

"No," said Louis, "we should go on to Jerusalem."

"But what if this coast were to fall into the hands of the Infidel?"

"The glory would be great for those who tried to wrest it from his hands."

"Should not a Christian do the work that is at hand?"

"He should indeed and our duty is to march on to Jerusalem." Louis's eyes were fanatical. "I see us driving the Saracen from the Holy City and making it a stronghold for Christianity for evermore."

"That would come later," said Eleonore. "First should you not make it possible for armies and pilgrims to come this way?"

"We were brought here by the grace of God."

"And given refuge by the grace of the Prince of Antioch."

"Whatever has happened, whatever will happen in the future, our duty lies clear before us. We must march on to Jerusalem."

*   *   *

Having gleaned through Eleonore that Louis was disinclined to accept his schemes, Raymond had no alternative but to call together an assembly to which he invited Louis and his chief advisers.

He laid his schemes before them and spoke passionately of the need to establish a firmer stronghold on the road to the Holy City. He pointed out the proximity of Aleppo, of the numerous Infidels who lurked on the route. The way must be made safe and the Holy City must be restored to Christianity, and until that could be done war must be made on the Saracen. Christians must band together.

The very thought of aggressive war roused a passionate revulsion in Louis. Never as long as he lived would he forget the screams of those dying in the burning church of Vitry.

He would not, he declared, make war until war was made on him.

In vain did Raymond put his case. He could see that he was swaying the priests and the nobles; but Louis remained adamant and the King's consent was essential to the plan.

In the summer house Raymond discussed the position with Eleonore. "Louis is no soldier," he said. "It is disastrous that he should command an army. He does not understand that it is far more important to make this land Christian, to strengthen our hold on it, than to make a futile pilgrimage to the Holy City."

"He is concerned only with obtaining forgiveness of his sins."

"What sins could such a man have committed?"

Eleonore laughed. "He is a monk in his outlook. He should never have been taken from the Church. And to think that they gave me to such a man."

"I wonder he wished to marry."

"I think he did not, but when he saw me he was reconciled."

"I can understand how you charmed even him. But reconciled! What shame! And you . . . the Queen of love and song."

"As I say he should have been a monk. Reluctantly he went to war and there was this unfortunate incident at Vitry. As if such things do not occur in every war. I would I were free of him. Since you and I became lovers I have realized more and more how distasteful he is to me."

Raymond embraced her, but his mind was busy.

Louis had married her because even he had seen that union with Aquitaine was desirable for France. Eleonore must have been the richest heiress in Europe. And although Louis had been given the title of Duke of Aquitaine, Eleonore was still the ruler of that rich land.

Suppose she were free of Louis? Suppose she remained in Antioch? What if he could arrange another marriage for her? Whom could she marry? It was impossible. But why not a divorce from Louis? Some excuse could be found. A close blood tie! That was the usual grounds and so easy to find because the families of most people in their position had been connected with each other at some time if one went back far enough.

His mind was busy as he made love with Eleonore.

* * *

It was essential for Raymond to fight this war. He must subdue the Infidel; he must escape from the intolerable position of remaining a vassal of the Greek Emperor. Here was his great hope and Louis . . . ineffectual, monk-like Louis stood in his way. How delighted he was that Louis's wife was unfaithful to him and with himself—her uncle. How easy it was to understand the simple fellow. A man who hated war and thought little of the profit it could bring his crown! A man who could reproach himself because his soldiers had killed a few women and children! A man who found little pleasure in the act of love and who had only been induced to indulge in it because he hoped to get children and because he had a voluptuous temptress of a wife!

Raymond laughed and set about planning how he could get the better of this king whose refusal to fall in with his plans made it impossible for him to carry them out.

They talked earnestly together . . . he and Eleonore. They must find a means of keeping her in Antioch.

He understood her far better than she understood him. He knew that her passion for him was as superficial as his for her. She did not know this. Eleonore, the romantic Queen of the Troubadours, was enamoured of love itself and she saw it as supreme. He did not tell her that since he had been the means of freeing her from irksome convention, she would break away from an accepted mode of behaviour, and nothing would restrain her. But he knew this to be so.

It would not be long before she took another lover.

They parted tenderly. They would not emerge from the arbour together. She should go first.

As she did so she saw a figure detach itself from the bushes. She pretended not to notice but walked on. The man who had emerged from the shadow followed her.

Before she reached the palace she turned and came face to face with him. She laughed derisively.

"You!" It was a man she had always despised, Thierry Galeran, a eunuch of immense stature. He was clever and had made his name at the Court of Louis the Fat, who had singled him out and made use of his statescraft. It was this King who had recommended Thierry Galeran to his son and Louis had as deep a respect for him as his father had had.

"For one moment," said Eleonore, "I had thought you might have planned to seize me for a certain purpose. What a joke! That would have been quite outside your range."

Galeran bowed. He said: "I saw you in the gardens and recognized you, my lady. I thought to offer my service should you need protection."

"I need nothing from you," she answered shortly.

She hurried into the palace and briefly wondered whether he had seen her enter the arbour. If so would he guess what she had been doing there?

She laughed to herself. "Something, my poor eunuch, which you could not understand," she murmured.

Galeran retraced his steps to the arbour; it was thus that he came face to face with the Prince of Antioch and he knew at once that the Prince had been the companion of the Queen of France.

Smarting under the Queen's insult, he debated with himself whether he should inform the King of France of what he had seen. Perhaps it was a little premature. No, he would do nothing as yet, but he would keep a close watch on the Queen.

*   *   *

Since she had broken her marriage vows with Raymond, Eleonore thought often of some of the handsome men who had made advances to her and whom she had rejected. There was Raoul, Count of Vermandois who had turned in desperation to Petronelle, and was now with the Abbé Suger helping to govern France. She had had a great fancy for him; there was Saldebreuil who was in the hands of the Infidel. She thought of him a good deal.

She mentioned to Raymond the fact that many of the best soldiers in Louis's army had fallen captive to the enemy and how she often wondered what had befallen them.

Obsessed by his great scheme Raymond constantly sought

methods of bringing it to fruition. And an idea had occurred to him which on immediate consideration seemed hopeless but on closer consideration less so.

"There is a Saracen named Saladin who is a prince of some power," he told her. "He is a man of good looks and a certain culture. I think he might even become a Christian one day."

"A Saracen become a Christian! It is unheard of."

"Not so, my love. Saracens have become Christians and Christians Saracens for certain considerations. It is not unheard of. But this Saladin is an interesting man. Do you know, I believe if you sent a message to him to the effect that you wished to make a request he would at least listen."

"This is what I wish more than anything. I could then make an offer of a ransom and see if I can bring about the return of my good Saldebreuil. Will you help me?"

"With all my heart. Leave the matter to me."

The result was that in a very short time there was a message from Saladin. He had heard a great deal about the beauty and charm of the Queen of Troubadours. She wished to make a request to him. He would grant this and ask only one favour in return which she might feel it in her heart to grant him. Would she receive him that he might have the great pleasure of hearing her request from her own lips and of seeing for himself the lady who was so renowned for her grace and beauty.

Such a reply delighted Eleonore. The incident was worthy of one of her own ballads.

If he could come to her she would be delighted to receive him, was her reply.

She told Raymond of the matter.

"He will have to make his way through a hostile army. How can he do this?" asked Raymond.

"He says it is what he will do."

"He will risk his life for a glimpse of you and the pleasure of saying a few words to you!"

Yes indeed. This was the kind of romance of which her troubadours sang. She was delighted to find that it existed in real life.

"He will never reach here," said Raymond sadly.

"He will. I know he will."

"I will do all I can to help him. I will send out an escort, and he shall be disguised in such a fashion that no one will recognize him."

Eleonore was delighted. "My dearest Raymond, how good you are to me!"

"Why should I not be to the one I love?"

Life was exciting, thought Eleonore. This was how it should be lived. Alas, from one day to the next she did not know how long she would stay here. Louis was restive. Never had she seen him so determined as he was now to go on with his plan. He would not listen to reason. Every day she grew more incensed with him and passionately wised she could end their marriage.

But she would not think of Louis. She would think of this romantic Infidel who was going to risk his life to come and see her.

*   *   *

How his dark eyes flashed as he contemplated her! How tall he was! What a warrior!

He spoke a little French, not much, but enough to convey his admiration of her and the effect she had on him.

She was no less impressed by him. He was different from any man she had ever known and the alien quality was irresistible.

She wished to ask a favour of him, he believed. She told him that a man for whom she had some regard was a prisoner in his hands. His name was Saldebreuil de Sanzay. She was ready to offer a substantial ransom for his return. Saladin declared that he would accept no ransom. It was enough that she had made a request. His greatest pleasure would be to grant what she wished.

A messenger should be disguised and sent to the castle where the Frenchman was incarcerated. He should be immediately released and given safe conduct.

"What a charming gesture," cried the Queen. "How can I thank you enough."

She set out to please him. She sang songs of her own composition, songs of love. He listened entranced.

Raymond joined them and seemed delighted that they found such pleasure in each other's company. How very cultivated her uncle was, thought Eleonore. How different from poor gauche Louis! She and Raymond were lovers, but he saw at once that there could not fail to be a strong physical attraction between herself and the fascinating Infidel.

89

The very fact that he *was* an Infidel added to his attraction. She could not help feeling completely excited in his presence.

Raymond said that he must not attempt to leave the palace for a while. He had travelled far and risked much. He and Eleonore should have more delightful interviews before he returned to his armies. Raymond would make sure that he was well guarded and that his identity was kept secret. They could rely on Raymond.

When he was alone with Eleonore—Prince Saladin having returned to the secret apartments Raymond had found for him—Raymond said to Eleonore: "I have a plan. You may think that it is impossible. If so, do not hesitate to say so. You know I think of nothing but your good."

"I know it," said Eleonore.

"You are weary of Louis."

"Utterly so."

"You would be glad to be free of him."

"Nothing could please me more."

"Why should you not be free of him? There must be a blood connection between you two. It would not be difficult to trace it. A divorce—and you would be free from Louis."

"And then?"

"Why you could marry someone else."

"*You* are married, my dearest Raymond."

"Oh, I had not hoped for that ultimate bliss. What if you found another bridegroom?"

"Are you suggesting one?"

"You are greatly taken with our handsome Saladin."

"Raymond! You know a marriage between us would be impossible."

"I see no reason why."

"Saladin . . . a Saracen!"

"A remarkably handsome one. A man of power and great wealth. There is no reason why he should not become a Christian."

Eleonore stared at her uncle. She was thinking of the attractive Saladin and a wild excitement possessed her. He would be so different, so alien and therefore fascinating.

"If it were possible . . ." began Raymond. "Imagine if it were possible . . ."

"Yes, Raymond."

"You would stay here . . . for a while. You would be ruler with him of great lands."

"An Infidel!"

"He would have to become a Christian."

"Would he?"

"For you . . . I know he would. What great glory would come to you. With your incomparable charms you would achieve what armies cannot do. You can bring Christianity to these Infidels. For if Saladin became a Christian so would his people."

"And Aquitaine?"

"My dearest Eleonore, you and he could travel to your dominions now and then. You could spend your lives travelling from place to place which is always a more entertaining way than to stay in one place."

"It does not seem impossible."

"You do not find him repulsive?"

"Not entirely so."

Raymond hid a smile. His voluptuous niece desired the man, and their own relationship had lost the first flush of novelty. He was visualizing the outcome of this daring scheme. If she married Saladin who would look after her estates in Aquitaine? Who better than her uncle who after all might have inherited them if he had been the elder brother. Eleonore could enjoy her Saracen and he would go to Aquitaine, for his position in Antioch was very insecure. And in time Aquitaine would be his. It would suit him very well, for if he were not going to get French help to subdue the Greek Emperor he would need to make other plans.

"Think about it," he said, "and you will see it is not as impossible as you at first believed."

* * *

She did think about it. Her mind was full of images. The Saracen was such a handsome man—so tall, dark-skinned with enormous expressive eyes.

Saldebreuil de Sanzay arrived back. She was delighted to see him not because he was a man whom she found charming so much as because his return was a symbol of Saladin's desire to please her.

Comparing the Saracen with Louis she despised her husband more than ever. So much meditation, so many prayers irritated her and she had no doubt whatsoever that she wished to escape from him.

She loved her uncle but he *was* after all her uncle and he was getting old. Saladin was young.

The prospect of having a new husband excited her. She would not wish to make the same mistake again. She would not want a half man as she was beginning to think Louis was. What had Louis but his dominions? Strip Louis of his Crown and there was not a man at his Court whom she would not have preferred.

But Saladin! A Saracen!

Why not? There had been marriages between Christians and Saracens before this.

She would test herself. She would see how she felt about marriage with a Saracen. She must be sure that there should be a perfect union between them.

Her manner had changed towards him. She was warmer, more inviting.

Saladin was not the man to be blind to her veiled suggestions. At their next meeting they became lovers.

A most exhilarating experience for Eleonore.

They lay together afterwards and talked of the possibilities of a marriage. First of course she must rid herself of that tiresome encumbrance, the King of France.

Saladin was dubious of this possibility, but he did not say so. He was eager to please his new and exciting mistress and was ready to indulge in any fantasy she suggested.

*   *   *

Louis was becoming restive. He had tarried long enough in Antioch; he had profited from the respite; he had refitted his army and he was now ready to march on to the Holy City.

This was something Eleonore would not tolerate. She was now deeply absorbed in her love affair with Saladin. She believed that she could happily marry him and remain in this area not far from her beloved uncle.

Louis paced up and down in their bedchamber. Eleonore lay in bed watching him, noting his lack of physical charm, comparing him with Saladin and Raymond.

"Within a week I intend to move on," Louis was saying. "I have delayed here long enough."

"You were glad enough to get here."

"Indeed I was after all our troubles, but we have tarried long enough and must move on now."

"You are wrong. You should stay here."

"For what purpose?"

"My uncle has explained the need to fight the Infidel here."

Louis looked wary. "It is something I have decided against."

"Why? Because you are afraid to fight? Because you are only half a man?"

He looked at her sadly. She had shown so often—and particularly of late—that she despised him.

"You know the reason," he said. "I have come on a crusade. I do not intend to use my armies in other wars."

Her eyes flashed. "Are you a king in truth?"

"You know I am the King of France and you the Queen. It would become you to behave as such."

Was this an implication that he knew of her adventures? She would rather boldly confess to her indiscretions than that he should discover and think she had sought to hide them.

"It is clear to me," she said, "that you and I should never have married."

"Never have married! Ours was a marriage which was highly approved both in France and Aquitaine."

"I have much to bring you. You had something to give me. That in itself was not displeasing. But as man and woman, Louis, you must know that we are quite unsuited."

"As King and Queen we must agree to suit each other."

"Why so?"

He looked astonished. "How could it be otherwise?"

"There is such a thing as divorce."

"Divorce! You cannot be serious. The King and Queen of France divorced!"

"I see no reason why a marriage which is unsuitable and distasteful should be continued."

"Distasteful?"

"To me . . . yes! I want a man for a husband not a monk. Let us have a divorce. I will marry again and you can go back to the Church. That is an admirable solution for us both."

"I do not think you can be speaking seriously."

"I am deadly serious. I have had enough of this, Louis. I want my freedom."

"You would give up the Crown of France?"

"It does not mean so much to me, and you, Louis, will have to give up Aquitaine."

"I would not have believed this possible."

"No, you would not. You are only half alive. Your heart is in the Church. Go back to the Church and give me my freedom."

He was silent. He sat on a stool and stared blankly ahead of him.

"Well?" said Eleonore impatiently.

"This is a matter of State," replied Louis. "I must talk of it with my ministers."

"Talk with whom you will, but give me my freedom. I repeat, Louis, I have had enough. It is time you and I parted."

She lay down and closed her eyes.

Louis continued to sit staring into space.

*   *   *

The next day Louis summoned his counsellors and confronted them with the Queen's proposal.

It was impossible, he was told by some. There could not possibly be a divorce.

Others thought that the Queen's behaviour was not that expected of a Queen. It had never been. The Queen came from the South and all knew that morals in the South were less strict than those in the North. The Queen's grandfather had been a notorious roué, and the Queen continued his practice of keeping a court of songsters and some of the songs they sang were not in the best taste.

Aquitaine was to be considered. There would be trouble there. If the King could retain the Queen's territory then divorce might be an admirable solution. The King could then marry a docile princess, get a son and there would be no more trouble in the royal domestic circle.

Louis was distraught. She despised him but he loved her. Strange that he who had never been interested in women should have felt so strongly about one, and she his wife. When he had first seen her, young, vital, beautiful and clever, her quick mind putting his to shame, he had adored her. She had reconciled him to marriage and kingship. But he knew that lately she had despised him. She had refused to make love with him. Not that he wished to indulge in this occupation with any great frequency. But there was the need to get an heir for so far they only had little Marie. Yet she had repulsed him, and that was strange, for Eleonore in the past had revelled in the act and had often lured him to perform it more often than he would have thought of doing.

She really did despise him. There was no doubt of it and he was uncertain how to act.

Thierry Galeran, the eunuch, asked for a private interview

with him, and when Louis granted it Galeran said he had come to talk of a delicate matter, and before he began, he craved the King's indulgence if he should say anything to offend him.

Louis, who was the most tolerant of men, was surprised and asked Galeran to say what he had to without fear of giving offence.

"It concerns the Queen, Sire."

Louis looked distressed and Galeran hurried on. "It is with great grief that I must tell you this, but the Queen has not been faithful to you."

Louis shook his head but in his heart he had known.

"You must not make such accusations, Galeran, unless you have proof of what you say."

"I have proof, Sire. The Queen has behaved criminally with two men. Her uncle Raymond and the Prince Saladin."

"That is impossible. The Queen's own uncle and an Infidel!"

"It has happened," said Galeran. "I can bring witnesses to support my story."

Louis was stunned. That the Queen should have been unfaithful perhaps did not surprise him so much, but that she should have chosen to play him false with two such people was unthinkable. Her uncle and a Saracen! Had she no feeling for the proprieties of life! Her own uncle. That was incest. A Saracen—a man not of her own creed and colour!

He knew that Galeran would not have made the accusation if he could not support it. He knew too that his father had been right when he had said that Galeran was a man whom he could trust to serve him. It was true that Eleonore hated Galeran. She had made caustic comments about him. She despised eunuchs, and being headstrong and impulsive had made no effort to hide her contempt. Galeran would have no warm feelings towards her, yet there must be some truth in his accusations.

"It would seem, Sire, that there is only one course open to you. To rid yourself of such a Queen."

"You heard the findings of the Council."

"If some means could be found to keep her lands under the Crown of France . . ."

The King shook his head. "Imagine the wars, Galeran. The people of Aquitaine would take up arms against us. They are loyal to Eleonore. They would accept no other ruler."

Galeran was thoughtful.

"You will not continue to stay here and allow the Queen to deceive you. It would put you into a position which must be unacceptable to any man and doubly so to the King of France."

"You are right, Galeran. We must leave here without delay. But the Queen will not agree to go."

Galeran said: "The Queen must be made to go."

"Short of carrying her by force I see no way of getting her to leave."

"Then, Sire, we must needs carry her by force, for you will see and so will your counsellors, that the present state of affairs is one not to be tolerated by the King of France."

Louis bowed his head. He was deeply wounded and bitterly humiliated. He kept thinking of the first time he had seen her and been so enchanted by her beauty and intelligence.

What had gone wrong that they should come to this?

*   *   *

She was going to meet her lover. How courteous Raymond was! How gallantly he stood aside for Saladin! This was how life should be lived. She had always known it. Love was supreme, that of which they sang in their ballads was truth. Nothing else was of any importance. She was going to rid herself of Louis. She was going to marry Saladin. He would become a Christian and their marriage would be the first step towards bringing Christianity to Islam.

What a joyful manner in which to bring about that desired conclusion! She would be almost a saint for what she had done for Christendom—and at the same time bringing great joy to herself!

The summer house in the garden was their meeting place. It had proved so good for her and Raymond, and Raymond now stepped aside and left it to her and Saladin.

As she passed the bushes she heard the snap of a twig. She looked over her shoulder and as she did so was seized in a pair of strong arms.

She expected to see her lover's face, and smiling she turned. She was looking into the hated eyes of Thierry Galeran.

"What are you doing here?" she demanded.

"I have come to tell you that the King is about to leave Antioch and wishes you to go to him without delay."

She was furious. How dared this man lay hands on her! She

was about to demand her release when two soldiers appeared beside him.

"This is treason," she said. "I shall have you punished . . . severely. You shall be . . ."

"My lady," said Galeran, "we obey the orders of the King."

"The orders of the King! What of them! *I* tell you . . ."

"We are the King's men," said Galeran. "I beg you come quietly or we shall be obliged to use force."

"How dare you . . ."

But she was seized by the shoulders. The indignity was more than she could bear. Where was Saladin? Where was Raymond?

Filled with rage by her own powerlessness, she had no alternative but to allow herself to be hustled out of the gardens.

More soldiers appeared. She was wrapped in a concealing cloak and forced to go with them through the city and out of its walls.

There the French army was camped ready for immediate departure.

Furious, frustrated but powerless, Eleonore had no alternative but to go with them.

The Royal Divorce

She was a prisoner—a prisoner with her husband's army.

They were on their way to Jerusalem and although Louis was distressed by the rift with his wife he felt happier in his mind to contemplate the proximity of the Holy City.

Eleonore was furious. She would never forgive him, she declared. He had abducted her. He had treated her to the utmost indignity. He had sent her old enemy, Galeran, to arrest her as though she were a common felon; and she had been forced to leave without saying farewell to her friends.

What would they think of her? What would they think of Louis? She was humiliated and she hated the source of her humiliation.

Those were unhappy months for Louis. She never ceased railing against him; she liked to taunt him with his performance both as lover and soldier.

"Go back to the Church," she would cry. "Go to a monk's cell. But first free me so that I may marry a man who is a man."

She hoped that Raymond or Saladin would come against Louis and rescue her. But perhaps that was asking too much. It would make a beautiful ballad, but real life was not exactly like that. Raymond had his great plan to think of: making war on the Greeks. As for Saladin he would doubtless remain an Infidel and the great opportunity to bring Islam peacefully to Christianity would be lost.

She railed and stormed, but it was of no avail. They marched on, and in due course came to Jerusalem where King Baldwin warmly received them. This was Louis's destination. Now he could say his prayers and receive absolution. The sin of Vitry could drop from his shoulders. He should have felt exultant. But he did not. Constantly Eleonore made friction between them. Baldwin wished him to join in with plans for aggression against the Infidel, and the peace he craved was as far off as ever.

He would stay in Jerusalem for a while, he declared. Eleonore was restive.

"What good do you do here?" she demanded.

"Don't you feel the peace of the place? This is the Holy City. Here you and I will pray together for the strength and courage to make a new start."

"The new start I wish to make does not include you," retorted Eleonore.

She was furious. She could not get the perfections of Saladin out of her mind. She had given up hope now that he would bring an army to take her from her husband.

Of one thing she was certain. There was going to be a divorce from Louis. She would not rest until she had achieved that. And if she did not marry Saladin—which on more careful consideration seemed perhaps a reckless thing to do—there were other men in the world, young, virile rulers who would be delighted to get their hands on Eleonore . . . and Aquitaine.

She would find someone. But first she must put into effect her escape from Louis.

*   *   *

The days dragged on. Louis found great solace in the Holy City. Here, he was fond of pointing out, had trod those sacred feet. Here he was at peace. He wished that he could spend the rest of his days in the holy spot.

How he wished there need not be this continual talk of war, though he recognized the need to repel the Infidel.

His ministers pointed out to him that it was unwise to leave his kingdom too long. His brother Robert was notoriously ambitious. The people had been loyal to Louis but memories were short and he had been away so long.

Eleonore was agitating to leave. She knew that there could be no satisfactory conclusion to their affairs while they were away. They must return to France and have the matter sorted out.

Still the months passed and when they had been in Jerusalem an entire year, Louis realized that he could delay no longer. He must return to his kingdom. Vessels were procured at Saint-Jean d'Acre and as the King of Sicily was at war with Greece his country seemed a good place for them to make for, on the way back to France.

Eleonore declared that she would not travel in the King's ship but would have a ship of her own and travel with those who were her friends. The King could go with his entourage, she pointed out bitterly. Men such as the Eunuch Galeran who seemed to please him so much.

Feeling it would be good to escape from her bitter tongue for a while, Louis agreed and they set sail in the month of July in their separate vessels. After a year in Jerusalem memories of Saladin were beginning to fade, but those of Raymond remained.

Perhaps, thought Eleonore, in a way she had really loved Raymond.

*　　*　　*

That journey by sea from Saint-Jean d'Acre was one Eleonore would never forget. She had not believed there could have been such misery; as she lay in her bunk she wished that she could die. This was utter degradation and discomfort. Occasionally she thought cynically of the days in Paris when she had planned this trip; of the beautiful garments she had accumulated and the dreams that had come to her. How different was the reality! Yet she tried to remind herself there had been the wonderful experiences with Raymond and Saladin. Alas they seemed as remote as her childhood now.

She cursed Louis. He was the one who had had the idea that they should set out for the Holy Land. He was the one who had forced her to leave Antioch. But for him she would be there now in blissful comfort and exhilarating company. Of one thing she was determined. She was going to divorce Louis.

On and on went the ship. Would the journey never end?

Often she believed that the vessel would sink and they all be drowned. Sometimes she thought they might be taken by pirates and half hoped they would. Anything would be better than these days when there was nothing around them but the eternal sea.

She became ill and for days was delirious. At least, she thought afterwards, at those times I did not know where I was.

Her attendants despaired of her life, and when miraculously they finally reached Naples in safety she had to be carried ashore, so weak was she.

Louis had already arrived. He had passed through several adventures.

He sat by her couch in the palace which had been put at their disposal, and she could see that he was hoping she had changed her mind.

"I feared you were lost at sea," he told her.

She smiled wanly and thought: I hoped you were. But she was too weak to indulge in vituperation.

"I thought my end had come," he said, "when one of Manuel's ships overtook us, boarded us, and I became a prisoner of the Greek Emperor."

"If you had joined with my uncle against him that would not have happened," she reminded him.

"God was with me," went on Louis. "He made that clear when he sent the Sicilians to capture the Greek ship which was carrying me."

"So you became the prisoner of the Sicilians instead of the Greeks," she said coldly.

"Indeed I was not. The King of Sicily treated me as an honoured guest."

"He had attacked the Greeks. He had seen that this was the wise thing to do . . . as Raymond did."

"Oh wars!" said Louis. "Little good ever came of them."

"Except that kings gained their crowns through them and prevented others from taking them."

"The King of Sicily gave me ships that I might come to Naples and meet you here as we had arranged. It was God's will that he should rescue me from the Greeks. Eleonore, we have suffered much, both of us. God has been good to us. Let us forget our differences."

She turned her face to the wall.

"We have a daughter," continued Louis. "We will have more children . . . sons. Eleonore, we must try to be good

101

parents to our daughter. We must get a male heir. Let us start again."

"I am determined to be free," said Eleonore. "And while we are here we must go to Rome and see the Pope."

Louis shook his head.

"I had hoped," he said, "that in view of everything that has happened we might forget our differences."

"It is because of what has happened that I remember them," said Eleonore.

And Louis knew she was adamant.

* * *

Louis was bewildered. He was torn between two emotions. His love for Eleonore was one and the other his desire for a peaceful life.

His feelings astonished him. He could not understand the power Eleonore had over him. She with her sensuous demanding body might have been repulsive to a man of his aesthetic tastes. Not so. In her presence he felt stimulated and he had come to the conclusion that unhappy as she made him he was more so without her. He knew that if she had her way and there was a divorce, duty would demand that he married elsewhere. He did not want that. What he prayed for was a reconciliation with his wife. Yet he knew that if he could have escaped from this strange power she exerted, if he could have given himself up to a life of meditation and prayer he would have been a contented man. How ironical that there were men of ambition who longed above all things for a crown, while one such as himself who had had that crown thrust on him would have given a great deal to be able to pass it on to someone else.

Suger was writing urgent letters from Paris. He had heard of the scandals surrounding the Queen and the talk that a divorce had been suggested.

Did Louis understand the full implications of this? What of his daughter? If he were wise he would seek a reconciliation with the Queen and at least do nothing until he returned to Paris and discussed the situation with Suger himself.

To shelve the matter suited Louis. He hated to make big decisions. Let it wait. There was always hope that the difficulties could be smoothed out. Eleonore was too weak now to indulge in sensational love affairs such as those she was said to have enjoyed with her uncle and Saladin. She had suffered more than he had by the sea voyage in spite of his capture and release.

"We must do nothing rash," said Louis. "We must get back to Paris and there we will see if a solution can be reached which will be satisfactory to us both."

Eleonore, her energy drained by her recent ordeals, agreed with unusual meekness.

*   *   *

Pope Eugenius III, being in exile from Rome, was in residence at Tusculum where he gave separate audiences to both Louis and Eleonore.

He had problems of his own but he was prepared to give great consideration to the dilemma of a man as powerful and as devoted to the Church as the King of France.

It was his opinion that a divorce would be disastrous, and he told Louis this. Louis was in complete agreement with him.

It was not so easy to convince Eleonore.

The Pope received her with a show of affection and told her that he deplored the nature of her problem. The Queen of France had duties to her country. She could not indulge in light and frivolous conduct, and this was what she would do if she asked for a divorce.

Why did she need a divorce? Because she no longer loved her husband? She must then pray for the return of that love. She must remember that her husband was the King of France. Could she not see that the fortune of France was bound up in the life of its King and Queen? It was her duty to love her husband; to give heirs to the country.

Eleonore pointed out that she and Louis were closely related. Louis was her fourth cousin. It was small wonder that in such circumstances there should have been only one child of the marriage.

The Pope stressed her duty. It would be sinful for her to seek a divorce from Louis. It would displease God, and in view of her recent conduct—if rumour did not lie—she was in urgent need of his clemency.

There was no doubt that Eugenius was a powerful persuader. Moreover he was the Pope and his very office put an aura about him of which even Eleonore could not be unaware.

He talked eloquently of the need to do one's duty, of the
103

eternal damnation which was awaiting those who failed in this, of the heavenly bliss which was the lot of those who succeeded. It was true that she felt ill, drained of her usual abundant energy. She found herself kneeling in prayer and promising to give her marriage another chance.

That night in the Pope's palace at Tusculum she shared Louis's bed once more; and it seemed like the blessing of Heaven when, being by this time on the way back to Paris, she discovered that she had conceived.

* * *

Pregnancy brought a certain contentment. She found re-union with little Marie a pleasure. She was surprised that she should have these strong maternal feelings. They compensated her for so much.

Her feelings towards Louis had not changed and she felt angry because she had been lured back to him. She often thought of what might have happened if she had not been persuaded by the Pope. There could have been another marriage. She had much to bring a bridegroom. Beauty, experience, sensuality and rich lands. What more could any woman offer?

Often she thought of Raymond, and wondered what would have happened if she had divorced Louis and married Saladin. He had been an exciting lover, perhaps that was due to the strangeness of him, the fact that he was an Infidel. But in her heart it was Raymond whom she had preferred—her own uncle. Well, perhaps that was why they understood each other so well. He was certainly the handsomest man she had ever seen or was ever likely to.

She had heard news of him, how disappointed he was that Louis would not help him in his fight to drive the Saracens from the land about Antioch, which was the road to Jerusalem, and that he had decided to go into battle without the allies he had hoped for. She wished him well. He had convinced her how necessary it was to make the land safe for Christians, necessary not only for pilgrims of the future but for Raymond himself if he were to hold Antioch.

For the time though she could enjoy a calm serenity while she awaited the birth of her child.

And the day came when this child was born. It was another girl! Louis was bitterly disappointed. If he had been given a son he believed that this would have been a sign of his reconciliation with God. His crusade had been a bitter disappointment both costly and purposeless. Little good had come out of it—so little that he need never have done it. The cries of those condemned to the flame at Vitry still rang in his ears; he had come near to losing his wife and had discovered an unbridled sensuality in her nature which did not stop her from acting criminally. That had been a bitter voyage of discovery. Yet he had suffered, and he hoped found favour in the sight of God, and some forgiveness of his sins. If he had been given a son he could have convinced himself that God was smiling on him.

But a daughter!

Eleonore suffered no such disappointment. As heiress of Aquitaine she would not accept the general belief that boys were superior to girls. She was content with her little girl.

The child was christened Alix.

* * *

For a short while she could give herself up to the pleasures of motherhood. She could have little Marie at her bedside and show her the baby, delighting in her children in a manner which astonished those about her.

It would not last of course. She was weak from her confinement, and fascinated by the role of motherhood. She must make a song about it. It was as beautiful as the emotions one felt for a lover.

She hoped she would have many children—boys as well as girls.

But not with Louis.

Somewhere in her mind she knew that the idea of divorce had only been set aside by her. She would return to it.

One of her women brought her the terrible news. It came through Galeran, the eunuch. He had told the woman that he thought the Queen would wish to know.

In the fighting round Antioch, Raymond had been killed and the Saracens had sent his head to the Caliph of Baghdad.

When she heard this news she listened, her eyes dilated. Raymond dead. She pictured the head she had so often caressed, held high and mocked—that beautiful head!

She had loved Raymond. He was her own flesh and blood. He had been more than a lover.

And if Louis had been a man, if he had done his duty and

105

fought side by side with Raymond, this might never have happened.

Then she fell to thinking of the humiliating manner in which she had been taken from Antioch, abducted one might say. How could she ever have believed she could live in amity with a man who had treated her so.

She was aroused from the lethargy which had possessed her since that fearful journey by sea to Naples, when she had suffered so that all her strength was sapped from her.

"Who gave you this news?" she asked.

"It was Thierry Galeran, my lady. He thought you would wish to know."

Galeran! That despised eunuch! That half man! A fit companion for Louis! He *thought* she ought to know. He was exulting in her wretchedness. He it was who had spied on her and Raymond, and carried tales to Louis.

"I will not stay here," she promised herself. "I will divorce Louis."

* * *

The more she considered the matter the more determined she became. She should never have allowed the Pope to persuade her to continue with her marriage. It had been against her judgement and she would never have agreed had she not been sick. That terrible sea voyage had upset her more than she had realized; and now here she was with two daughters and a husband whom she despised.

She was determined to bring up once more the matter of the divorce.

She did not realize that she could scarcely do this while Louis was beset by conflict on all sides. In the first place his brother Robert, a very ambitious young man who had never stopped railing against fate for bringing him into the world after his brother Louis when he would have made a much more suitable King, was roaming the country calling people to his banner. He would be able to rule France, he assured them; he was strong; his brother was a weakling who was never meant to be King. Nor had Robert for that matter. But who could have guessed that Philippe their brother should have been robbed of his crown and earthly glory by a common pig. The fact was that France must have a king and Louis was at heart a monk. Robert believed that for the good of the country Louis should be deposed, sent back to the Church and he, Robert, set up as King.

Louis was deeply distressed. Not another war, he prayed. And brother fighting against brother was distressing. He wanted no more Vitrys.

That matter was quickly settled by the people of France. They did not want ambitious Robert; they preferred Louis. Louis was a good man. Hadn't he just returned from the Holy Land? God would surely be on his side, and to wage war on him would be tantamount to waging war against God.

They would remain loyal to Louis; they would pray that he would give them a male heir soon, and then they would be sure that they were doing God's will.

So while Louis was engaged in this conflict it was not possible to talk to him of a divorce. But she was determined to.

Then there was another conflict.

Normandy had always been a source of anxiety to the Crown of France. The Dukes were too powerful, mainly because since William the Conqueror had become the King of England, while remaining Duke of Normandy, there was the might of England to contend with. Now Geoffrey Plantagenet laid claim to the dukedom.

Geoffrey at a very early age had been married to Matilda, the daughter of King Henry I of England. The marriage had been a disaster, for husband and wife had had no regard for each other from the beginning. Matilda, a stormy, passionate, arrogant woman, who believed she had a right to the throne of England—and indeed she had for she was the only legitimate issue of King Henry—was ten years older than Geoffrey and at the time of their marriage he had been only fifteen. Matilda had at first refused to live with him and had spent scarcely any time in his company. However she had later been prevailed upon to stay long enough with him to produce three sons.

The eldest of these was a youth—christened Henry—who was already making a name for himself as a soldier and one with the necessary qualities to rule. Matilda, who would never have any regard for her husband, doted on this son and had made up her mind that he would one day become King of England. This was her only consolation. She had failed to wrest the Crown from Stephen but her son should inherit what was his by right.

Louis, as King of France, was outside the quarrel between

Matilda and Stephen, but ever since the burning of the church at Vitry, Louis had shown great friendship for Theobald of Champagne and his family. Theobald's son, Henry, had joined the crusade and during that adventurous period Louis had kept the young man at his side.

Theobald was the elder brother of Stephen, King of England, and Stephen had a son Eustace. Knowing of the terrible remorse Louis had suffered through the burning of Vitry, Stephen thought it a good idea to get his brother Theobald and his nephew Henry to persuade Louis to help him secure Normandy for his son Eustace.

Thus it was that Henry of Champagne gradually began to persuade the King of France that he should favour the cause of Eustace against that of Geoffrey of Anjou and his wife Matilda.

Louis was perturbed. "I would not wish to see a war between France and Normandy," he said.

Theobald, who had come to court to add his persuasion to his son's, began to enumerate the points against Geoffrey of Anjou and his wife.

Matilda was an arrogant woman. She had a way of antagonizing everyone who came near her. If the King of France showed the people that he was against her and her husband they would stand behind Louis and King Stephen to a man.

"There must be some who would be faithful to Henry of Anjou," said the King. "I can see conflict. I don't want it. I want peace."

At the same time Louis believed that if he joined forces with Stephen he would be doing a service to Stephen's family and Stephen's brother was Theobald to whom the town of Vitry had belonged.

He must expiate his sin, for the cries of people being burned to death by his soldiers still rang in his ears.

Finally Louis decided that because of Vitry he would join forces with Stephen's brother and try to wrest Normandy from Matilda and her husband.

*   *   *

The Abbé Suger arrived in Paris. He wished to see the King on urgent business.

When they were alone together he asked Louis if he realized that by going into battle against Geoffrey and Matilda he was fighting the King of England's battle.

108

"Nay," said Louis. "I do this for Theobald of Champagne. I wronged him. By this I will right that wrong."

"My lord," said Suger, "you are deluded by Vitry. This town was sacked by your soldiers, but it was not on your orders. You have helped wage war on the Infidel. You have expiated any sin you may have incurred on that score. You owe nothing to the Count of Champagne. But you do owe something to your subjects. You should consider well before you plunge them into a war which will only be to the advantage of the King of England."

Louis wavered and Suger went on: "Yes, you will be helping King Stephen. And I ask you to consider, Is he the true heir to his throne? You know he is the nephew of the late King Henry I. Matilda is his daughter. She would be Queen of England if her nature had not been so over-bearing that the people repudiated her. Stephen rules not by right but because he is the lesser of two evils. The Crown of England by right belongs to Matilda and her son is the true heir to the throne as he is to Normandy. You should consider this well before you side with a usurper."

Louis was thoughtful. It was true he did not wish to go to war and he knew very well that that was what it would mean. Yet on the other hand he wished very much to please Theobald.

"It is too late to hold back," said Louis.

"Too late! Why should it be? I doubt Geoffrey Plantagenet wants this war. All you have to do is to withdraw your support from Prince Eustace and the matter will be settled."

"So Normandy will remain in the hands of Matilda and her husband."

"Who have more right to it than Theobald's brother Stephen. There will be a bloody war in England when Stephen dies if he does not recognize Henry Plantagenet as his heir."

"Then what can I do?" asked Louis.

"You can invite Geoffrey Plantagenet to Court. You can discuss the matter with him."

"You think he will come?"

"There is no doubt that he will. He did not take up arms against you in support of Robert. That is something to remember."

"Then I will send for him," said Louis, relieved in his heart that war might be avoided.

*   *   *

So Geoffrey Plantagenet came to the Court of France.

Geoffrey was at this time in his late thirties. He was noted for his handsome looks and his habit of wearing a sprig in his hat of the *planta genista* which had earned for him the name of Plantagenet.

He was pleased to be invited to Court. He could only believe that Louis had no heart for the fight. Geoffrey was determined to hold on to Normandy for the sake of his son Henry, who was now about seventeen.

There was one thing about which Geoffrey and his virago of a wife agreed and that was that their son Henry was not only going to keep his hold on Normandy but was going to take the Crown of England on the death of Stephen.

Eustace, Stephen's son, was not worthy of such honours—nor had he any right to them. He, Geoffrey, had no intention of going to England to settle that difference. Matilda had tried it and failed. It was not difficult to understand why. Their son Henry would succeed he was sure when the time came. The boy must win his own spurs. And he would.

Still, if he were the heir to Normandy he would be in a better position to fight for the Crown of England and it was all to the good that Louis had decided against going into battle on behalf of Stephen and his relations.

So with great confidence Geoffrey of Anjou, sporting a *planta genista* in his hat, came to Paris.

Eleonore watching from a window saw his arrival. A fine looking man, she decided; it was long since she had seen one who reminded her, although faintly, of Raymond Prince of Antioch.

She would admit that he had not Raymond's good looks, fine bearing and charm of manners. But he was not lacking in these qualities. And there was one important virtue so sadly lacking in her husband. Geoffrey Plantagenet was a man!

There was a friendly atmosphere at Court. Louis, now that he had been persuaded by Suger, was delighted that there was to be no war. Theobald and his son were disappointed. He would try to make up to them in some other way.

He had explained to young Henry of Champagne that it would be wrong to indulge in a war against the Plantagenets on such an issue.

"We must remember, my dear friend," said Louis, "that Geoffrey Plantagenet's wife is the daughter of the late King of England, Henry I, and he was the son of William, Duke of

Normandy who conquered England. Matilda has a claim to the Duchy which could never rightly be that of Eustace while Matilda has sons."

Theobald and his son were angry. Louis was like a piece of thistledown, they said to each other, blown this way and that by the wind. They would have to try to persuade him later when the Plantagenet had left Court.

But Geoffrey had no intention of leaving Court just yet. He was finding it all so diverting and more than anything was he delighted by the interest of the Queen.

Eleonore had shown from the first that he interested her. She invited him to one of her musical occasions when she herself sang songs of her own composing. They were concerned with the joy of loving and being loved.

Geoffrey was not one to ignore such gentle innuendoes. Cursed with a wife for whom he had no affection or desire, for years he had been seeking consolation elsewhere.

Matilda was now an old woman of fifty. Eleonore was some twenty years younger. She seemed very young to him, and she was one of the most beautiful and attractive women he had ever seen.

That the Queen of France was light in her morals he knew full well. There had been rumours about her adventures during the crusade. Geoffrey of Anjou was not one to refuse what was offered.

Within a few weeks of his arrival at Court he and Eleonore were lovers.

*   *   *

She liked to talk to him. He was a man of charm and easy manners. He reminded her very much of her uncle Raymond. Not that he could equal him—no one could do that, but the resemblance was there and very agreeable to her.

Not only did she enjoy their love-making but their conversation was amusing.

He told her of the wild conflicts that had ensued between himself and his wife.

"She still calls herself the Empress because before she was married to me she was married to the Emperor of Germany."

"We have all heard tales of that virago," said Eleonore. "What a time you must have had with her!"

"Think of the most difficult woman in the world and that is Matilda."

111

"And is she beautiful?"

"She was handsome enough in her youth. But I was a boy of fifteen at the time of our marriage. She was twenty-five. She seemed an old woman to me. I never took to her. And her temper . . . it is beyond description."

"But you got three sons by her."

"We were at length prevailed upon to do our duty."

"And she loves these sons?"

"Even Matilda is a mother. Our eldest is a fine boy. He's going to rule England one day."

"That would be . . . Henry."

"Ah, young Henry. What a fellow!"

"Is he as handsome as his father?"

"He is the least handsome of my sons. Not tall, but stocky and he cares not for his looks. He refuses to wear gloves in the coldest weather and his hands are chapped and red. He despises the graces of living. He will be a man, he says. He is never still. He must be here, there and everywhere! He tires out all about him. He is a boy to be proud of."

"Tell me more of him. He is very young, is he not?"

"Seventeen winters or so."

"And he is religious?"

"His religion is to live every minute of his life to the full."

"I should like to see this son of yours," she said. "What does he feel for women?"

"He likes them . . . he likes them very well."

"Like his father mayhap?"

"Well, he has already sired two bastards, I hear."

"And he but seventeen! He is not a man to waste his time. I shall see him then?"

"He will come to Paris to swear fealty to the King."

"He might have been my son-in-law. We did once think of a match between him and my daughter Marie."

"That was a match I greatly wished to see take place."

"It was Old Bernard of Clairvaux who opposed it . . . on grounds of the strong blood tie between the two."

"That was what he said. I'll dare swear he thought that such an alliance would give too much to our house. He was never a friend of ours."

"We talk much of your son."

"Yes, let us now consider ourselves."

They did, and when in due course Geoffrey's son Henry Plantagenet arrived at Court, Eleonore was completely overwhelmed by the personality of the youth. He had a vitality which she found intriguing; a virility which was undeniable.

Geoffrey was a good lover but once she saw his son, Eleonore desired no other man.

She could not understand it. This youth was by no means handsome. That he was clever there was no doubt; he had an appreciation of literature which she found exciting. But it was his overwhelming manliness which attracted her.

She thought a good deal about him. Duke of Normandy and King of England, for there was no doubt in her mind as soon as she saw him that he would succeed in his undertakings.

Stephen would die and he would claim the Crown of England and get it. Ineffectual Eustace would have no chance against him.

She wanted Henry. Not as she had wanted his father and others. This was different.

Henry was going to be a King. She wanted to marry him.

Alas, he was nearly twelve years younger than she was. As if she would allow such a trifle to stand in her way. A greater obstacle was the fact that she was married. She had asked for a divorce before, and failed to get it. She would renew her endeavours. It had been different then. Before she had been eager only to escape from Louis. Now she had the added incentive. She wanted a new husband. That husband must be Henry Plantagenet. And she made a vow that nothing was going to stand in the way of her getting him.

It did not take her long to lure him to her bed. He was sensuous in the extreme and already expert in such matters. It had been said that he took after his grandfather, that other Henry, who used to dandle him on his knee when he was a baby and had set such store by him.

That he was cuckolding the King of France meant nothing to young Henry, except that it was something of a joke; and that the beautiful elegant Queen should be so eager for him—with his careless mode of dressing and his lack of fastidiousness—amused him even more.

He was always ready to enjoy himself.

When she hinted at marriage, he was alert.

Marriage for Henry Plantagenet with the heiress of Aquitaine! Not bad! Eleonore was a rich heiress. No one could turn aside from fruitful Aquitaine without a good deal of consideration.

It was a dazzling prospect. Eleonore and Aquitaine!

"First of course I must divorce Louis," said Eleonore.

Henry agreed. He could not believe that that would be allowed. In the meantime there was no reason why he should not enjoy the hospitality of the Queen.

But Eleonore continued to think of marriage. She was determined to divorce the King of France and marry this young Henry Plantagenet for she believed there was little doubt that he would become King of England. Moreover she was passionately in love with him.

*　　*　　*

Louis paced up and down the chamber. The Abbé Suger watched him sorrowfully. His father had always feared that Louis had not the strength to make a king. He had made the Abbé Suger swear that he would stand beside him and guide him. He would need guidance. And indeed he did with such a wife. If only he had married a simple docile woman how different everything would have been! Instead of that this brilliant match had been made for him, and what had it brought him? Two girls and a wanton wife, a woman who was openly unfaithful.

And now she was demanding a divorce.

There were tears in Louis's eyes as he faced Suger.

"What can I do?" he pleaded. "What can I do?"

"You can tell the Queen that what she is asking is impossible."

"She will not let it rest there."

"The Queen must be made to do her duty."

"You do not know Eleonore."

"Not know the Queen! I know her well. She is without decency, without care that she should do her duty."

"I have never been the right husband for her. I have never been able to give her what she wanted."

"You gave her the Crown of France, Sire. Was that not enough for any woman?"

"Not for Eleonore. She wanted a lusty man."

"For shame! You gave her two children. A pity it is that they were not sons. But doubtless if you go on trying . . ."

Louis shook his head impatiently.

"She has asked me to talk to you. She is determined to get a divorce."

"On the grounds of consanguinity?"

Louis nodded. "It is true that we are fourth cousins."

"You could divorce her on the grounds of infidelity."

114

"Nay, I would not do that. Suffice it that the blood relationship is there."

"I was saying that you could divorce her for her criminal conduct but you would be unwise to do so. If you divorce her the lands of Aquitaine are lost to the French Crown. Sire, there must be no divorce."

"She wants it. She will not rest until our marriage is broken."

"Think, Sire. What if she married again? Her husband would rule with her and if he was the owner of vast possessions what a powerful neighbour you would have in Aquitaine. Nay Sire, I could never agree to a divorce for if the Queen married a powerful nobleman, there would be too much strength in the neighbourhood which would be uncomfortably close to France."

"She will give me no peace."

Suger shook his head.

"I shall oppose a divorce while there is life in me," said Suger.

Louis sighed. He knew that Suger would never allow the divorce to go through and that Eleonore would fret and fume and make life intolerable for them both.

*　　*　　*

Riding back to Normandy the young Duke Henry was thinking about Eleonore.

What a woman! He had never had a mistress such as she was before. She excited him; there was a passion about her which overwhelmed him. He was glad that she was older than he was—eleven years was it? She was so experienced. He had never denied himself his pleasures, and strangely enough, although he was far from handsome, women found him irresistible. At least many had; but they were not of the calibre of Eleonore of Aquitaine. That she—Queen of France, and woman of great experience who had been to the Holy Land and it was said had had her adventures there—should have found her need of him so great that she had lain with him in her husband's palace, was the most exciting thing that had ever happened to him.

She was heartily sick of her monk-like husband. "He is no man," she had complained bitterly. "I would be rid of him. He shall go back to his Church and I will go to the bed of a husband who will know how to treat me there."

And that husband was to be himself—he, not yet twenty years of age, a mere Duke of Normandy, had been chosen by the Queen of France. Of course he had prospects . . . oh, very great prospects; and many believed that he would fulfil their prophecies. Duke of Normandy, yes, but King of England too? Why not? His mother should be the sovereign of that country now, not that upstart Stephen.

And his Queen—Eleonore! He had to admit that it was an alluring prospect. She was beautiful; she had character; she was different from any other woman he had known; she was clever; she wrote songs and sang them charmingly. He could appreciate that.

He was glad now that his Uncle Robert—his mother's half-brother who was the bastard of King Henry I—had taken charge of his education. Uncle Robert was a man who set great store by education. He had said: "One day you will be a king and you cannot be an ignorant king." He had taken him to his castle in Bristol and there, as well as teaching him horsemanship and chivalry and how to wield a sword, he had made him study—and among his study was literature—under a man known as Master Matthew.

He had taken to learning as he took to anything that interested him. Now their knowledge of literature was a further bond between him and Eleonore, and when they were satiated with love-making they could chat idly of these matters. She said she had never known a young man so learned; he had certainly never known a woman as clever as she was.

And she could bring him Aquitaine.

The only thing that stood in the way of their marriage was that she was married already—married to the King of France.

"He shall divorce me," Eleonore had cried. "He shall. He shall!"

And in the presence of such determination he could believe that she was right.

He was sure his father would be pleased. Geoffrey was an ambitious man. He had fought hard to secure Normandy for his wife, which meant for his son, Henry himself. The thought of allying Aquitaine with Normandy, Maine and Anjou would delight him. It meant that the Duke of Normandy would be more powerful than the King of France. As for his mother she was obsessed by England and she would rejoice in any move which made the family strong enough to take it.

It was full of confidence that Henry rode into the castle of

116

Anjou to see his father. He knew that his mother would not be there and he must pay a separate visit to her. His parents were rarely together and although in their mature years there had grown up a kind of tolerance towards each other there was no affection between them.

His father was delighted to see Henry, who thought that he looked worn and unlike his usual rather jaunty self. He was handsome as Henry would never be. Yet there was something far more striking about the younger man's vitality and he had a certain charm which his father lacked.

Henry sought an early moment of being alone with his father, but before he could tell him his news Geoffrey talked to him very seriously of other matters.

He seated himself on a stool, his long legs stretched out before him, looking at his son. "Be seated, Henry," he said. "I have much to say to you."

"And I to you, Father."

Geoffrey nodded. "I have much on my mind," he said. "Have you heard what Bernard of Clairvaux has prophesied? Nay, you could not or you would not look so unconcerned. He has said that I shall be dead within the year."

"Did you offend him then?" asked Henry cynically.

"A difference of opinion. He wished me to release that trouble-maker, de Bellay. I refused and in doing so he tells me I have displeased God who will be avenged."

"Is old Bernard in God's confidence then?"

"He is a holy man, Henry."

"A plague on these holy men! They work for themselves and deceive us . . . or perhaps themselves into thinking that their will is God's. You are not disturbed by this prophecy, Father?"

"I am, Henry."

"Then cease to be. I tell you that you are as hearty as you ever were. You have not yet seen forty winters. There are many more left to you."

Geoffrey took the plant from his hat and studied it—the little *planta genista* which had given him his soubriquet. He held it out to Henry who took it wonderingly. "I shall invest you with lands and possessions without delay, Henry. You are my eldest son. You have brothers. We are surrounded by ambitious men. You are young yet . . . oh, but a man I grant you. From your mother you will have Normandy and England—from me, Anjou and Maine. To your brother Geoffrey I shall leave three castles in Anjou, but when you have
117

become King of England you must give him Maine and Anjou."

"I care not to hear you talk of death," said Henry.

"Bernard prophesied the death of the heir to the King of France and you know full well that almost immediately a wild pig entangled itself with his horse's legs and threw him, and there on the ground was a sharp flint that broke open his head and entered his brain."

"I would not allow a man to prophesy my death, Father. If he dared do so I should call it treason."

"He is not my subject, Henry." His face lightened. "It may be you are right. But at the same time I am going to make a gesture. You and I are going to Paris and there I wish you to be formally acknowledged as Duke of Normandy. You know that Stephen of England has his eyes on Normandy for his son, so I wish there to be a formal ceremony during which Louis receives you as the rightful Duke, and you swear allegiance to him as your suzerain. I fear what would happen if I were to die suddenly."

"You are not going to die, Father. I'll prophesy that, and why should you not believe your son instead of that old ghoul Bernard?"

Geoffrey smiled and taking the sprig from his son replaced it in his hat.

"All the same, Henry, I wish us to go to Paris, and we shall make preparations to depart without delay."

"Nothing would please me more although I have just left the French Court. Now listen to my news which will make you smile. The French King and Queen are not on good terms."

"I know it well. The whole world knows it." Geoffrey smiled, remembering passionate moments with Eleonore.

"There is talk of a divorce."

"Suger will never allow it. It would mean the loss of Aquitaine to the French Crown."

"The Queen is a very forceful woman."

"I know it well!"

"And she has set her heart on divorce. In fact she has decided to marry again and has chosen her husband."

"She should get her divorce first before she goes as far as that."

"I have no doubt that she will succeed. Whom do you think she has chosen for her bridegroom?"

118

Henry was smiling so complacently that his father looked at him with astonishment.

"Yes, Father. She has chosen me."

"You!" spluttered Geoffrey. "This is quite out of the question."

"I thought you would be delighted."

"Never!" cried Geoffrey vehemently.

"Have you forgotten that she would bring us Aquitaine?"

"You cannot marry that woman."

"And why indeed not?"

"She . . . she is married to the King."

"But Father, there is to be a divorce."

"There never will be."

"There will be. And if there is and she is free, you and my mother will rejoice. You must. Think of Aquitaine."

"You cannot marry Eleonore," cried Geoffrey.

"I can when she is free."

Geoffrey was silent for a few moments. "Nay," he said. "You could not . . . not if she were free and even though she brought you Aquitaine. I would never give my consent."

Henry's temper, which could be terrible, was beginning to rise.

"Should I need your consent?"

"You would need it if you would be my heir." Geoffrey looked steadily at his son. "In view of what happened between myself and the Queen of France I would never consent to the marriage."

"What mean you by that?"

"I have known her well . . . intimately. You understand?"

Henry stared at his father.

Geoffrey had risen to his feet. He strode to the door.

He looked back at his son. "For that reason," he said, "I would never give my consent to the marriage, never . . . never . . ."

*   *   *

They were on their way to Paris. Henry had raged and fumed. He had cursed his father, the old Abbé Suger and everyone who was putting an obstacle between him and his marriage with Eleonore.

So she was a woman of strong passions. He had known that. So she had adventured during the crusade she had made to the Holy Land. There were rumours about her relationship with her uncle and a Saracen, and his own father had admitted to committing adultery with her. Well, she was Eleonore and unique. The fact that she had passed through these adventures made her all the more desirable to him. Drama encircled her. Many a prince had his bride found for him and he was given a simpering virgin for whom he could have little fancy. He was not like other princes. He had always known he was unique. A great future lay before him and that future was going to be shared with Eleonore. The obstacles which people were putting in his way were going to be thrust aside. He would arrange that.

And now to Paris. He would see her there. She would watch the ceremony when he swore fealty to her erstwhile husband, and at night he would creep into her bedchamber where they would make love and plans.

So although he had raged against his father and all those who stood in his way, he was now content. He was certain of success. In the end and when it came it would be all the more enjoyable because it had not been easy to attain.

*   *   *

What a joy it was to embrace her, to indulge in that violent and compulsive love-making. There was no one like her. Eleonore was different—a tigress compared with whom all other women were tame lambs. Moreover she could bring him Aquitaine. His father was being foolish to stand out against a marriage which could bring so much to Anjou and Normandy—and in due course England, and all because Eleonore had shared his bed. Poor Eleonore! A passionate woman married to a monk. What could be expected but that she should try out men now and then? It made her all the more appreciative of him, Henry, just as his amorous adventures made him certain that there was no woman in the world to compare with her.

She was equally delighted with him. His love-making lacked the grace of that of Raymond of Antioch, but Henry's was as much to her taste. His youth was so appealing. She was sure that Henry was the man she wished to be her husband.

On the day of the ceremony she sat beside Louis on the dais and with glowing eyes watched the approach of her lover.

Henry knelt before the King of France and asked that his

120

title of Duke of Normandy might be confirmed by him. If the King would grant his permission he would swear fealty to him and remember as long as he held that title that he was the vassal of the King of France.

He unbuckled his sword and took off his spurs. He laid them at the feet of the King of France and in return the King took a handful of earth which had been brought to him for this purpose as a symbol that he accepted Henry Plantagenet as Duke of Normandy.

Then there was feasting and celebration with Geoffrey seated on one side of the King and Henry on the other, and the comforting knowledge that the powerful Count of Anjou and the King of France were allies.

The lovers found opportunities to be together. They made love and talked of the future.

His father was against a marriage; the Abbé Suger was against it; but they would find a way.

"My father must be won over," said Henry. "As for the old Abbé he can't last for ever. He looks more feeble every day."

"It must be soon," said Eleonore, "for I have sworn to be your wife and Louis is not and never has been what I want in a husband."

The fact that they were so often together was noticed of course. Courtiers smiled behind their hands. "First she tried out the father and now the son. No one can say that our Queen wastes time."

Geoffrey was powerless to prevent their meetings and in due course the King's advisers told him that the Queen and the young Duke of Normandy were causing scandal at Court.

Louis sent for Geoffrey.

"I think," he said, "that it would be advisable for you and your son to leave my Court."

Geoffrey was of the same opinion. He was angry that Eleonore and Henry should be lovers. He would have liked to resume that role with her himself. But when they met she behaved as though they had never been anything but acquaintances, and she certainly found the son preferable to his father.

"They shall never marry while I live to prevent them," he vowed.

*   *   *

It would have been pleasant riding through the country-side if he had not had to leave Eleonore behind. There were however other matters to occupy Henry's mind.

He was now undisputed Duke of Normandy and that was pleasant to contemplate. If only Eleonore could have forced Louis to divorce her he would be quite content . . . at the moment.

Geoffrey was determined not to discuss the matter of the proposed divorce. He had said it would never be granted and that put an end to the affair. He would attempt to arrange a suitable match for his son and that should not be difficult for the Dukedom of Normandy and his prospects would make young Henry a very desirable *parti*.

The day had grown very hot and they were travel-stained and weary. They were approaching Château du Loir when Geoffrey said, "Here is a pleasant spot to rest awhile. Let us stay here. Look, there is the river. I should like to bathe in it. That would be most refreshing."

Henry was willing. They called a halt and the party settled down under the trees while Geoffrey and his son and a few of their attendants took off their clothes and went for a swim in the river.

They shivered delightedly in the cold water which was so refreshing after the heat of the day. They were loath to come out and when they did they lay on the bank talking.

"Now that you are Duke of Normandy you will be ready to claim your other inheritance," said Geoffrey.

"You mean . . . England."

"I do. The people would welcome you. They rejected your mother it is true and accepted Stephen, but they only did this because she made herself objectionable to them and Stephen was there and weak as he is, he lacked your mother's arrogance. They will be ready for you, Henry."

"Yes, soon I must go to England."

"You must make Stephen understand that you are the heir. He will try of course to give everything to his son Eustace."

"Never fear, Father. He shall not do that."

"You understand what a campaign like this means?"

"There have been other campaigns, Father. You may trust me."

As they talked of England and how Eustace was a weak-ling, heavy clouds arose and obscured the sun. Before they could dress there was downpour. Wet through they returned to their camp.

That night Geoffrey rambled in his sleep. He was in a high fever.

When the news was brought to Henry he went at once to his father.

"What ails you?" he asked but Geoffrey looked at him with hopeless eyes.

"It has come, Henry," he said. "As he said it would."

"You're thinking of that man's prophecy. He should be hanged for treason. 'Tis nothing, Father. A chill, that's all. You stayed overlong by the river."

"I am shivering with fever," said Geoffrey, "and more than that there is knowledge within me that this is the last time you shall see me in the flesh."

"I refuse to listen to such talk."

"Your concern does you credit, my son. If I am not to depart with my sins on me, you had better send me a priest."

"Stop talking so. Have you not had enough of priests?"

"Methinks I need one to help me to Heaven, son."

Henry sent for a priest. The certainty that he was going to die was strong with Geoffrey. He wanted to talk to his son, explain to him the pitfalls which could entrap a young man. He himself had not enjoyed a happy married life. He did not want the same thing to befall Henry.

"It should be a blessing, Henry, and it is often a curse. You should marry a good docile woman, one who will bear you many sons. At least Matilda gave me three. But my life with her, Henry, has been one continual battle. There was never love between us. I was ten years her junior. Never marry a woman older than yourself. She will dominate you."

"I would never allow any woman to dominate me, Father."

"That is what you may think, but there is a danger. I hated Matilda and she despised me. I was a child. Fifteen and married to a virago of twenty-five who had already been the wife of the Emperor of Germany. Imagine it. My life . . . our life together was a hell."

"My mother is a very difficult woman."

"She lost England by her temper. Think of it, Henry. Had she acted differently you would not have had to fight for England. It would have been yours."

"Never fear. It shall be mine."

"I doubt it not. But your mother has led us a fine dance. Her father grew to understand her. But he was determined

123

that you should inherit the throne. He used to call you Henry the Second of England."

"That is what I shall become."

"It must be so."

"Doubt it not. No man shall put his will in the way of mine. No one." And he thought: That means you, too, Father. For I shall be King of England and Eleonore shall be my Queen.

"Beware of priests, Henry. They will seek to govern you. You stand for the State, and the State and the Church are struggling for supremacy now as they ever did."

"I know it well and will have no masters. None," declared Henry.

"I say goodbye now, my son. Bernard's prophecy is coming true. A pig killed the son of the King of France and a dip in a river killed the son of Fulk of Anjou; and both prophesied by Bernard."

"Heed not such prophecies, Father. You invite death by believing them."

"Nay, my son. Death is in this room. Can you not sense his presence? Farewell. You will rule wisely. Marry well and soon, and get fine sons. A man needs sons."

Geoffrey Plantagenet lay still and by the morning he was dead.

Bernard's prophecy had come true. Riding to his mother, Henry thought of what this would mean to him. He was master of great possessions and one obstacle to his marriage had been removed by death. He was only eighteen years of age. He could be patient a little longer.

* * *

That indomitable priest, the Abbé Suger, whom Louis the Fat had instructed to guide his son, was no longer there.

His passing was deeply mourned by the people for all knew him to have been a good man, and he was buried with great pomp at Saint-Denis.

After the funeral Eleonore knew that now nothing could stand in the way of her divorce. It was only a matter of getting agreement from Louis. He was weary of the argument. Perhaps he too was beginning to be reconciled to a parting. Perhaps he realized that he would be happier married to another woman, for marry he must, since he still had to get a male heir.

Eleonore was not the woman for him. Although he might

divorce her on grounds of consanguinity everyone knew that he could have done so for adultery. Her reputation was well known. There had been many to witness her light behaviour during the Crusade and the names of the Plantagenets, father and son, were mentioned in connection with her.

Eleonore cared nothing for this. She was still beautiful; nor was she old; she would have many childbearing days ahead; moreover she was the richest heiress in Europe.

With the opposition removed by the hand of Death, Louis's resistance did indeed crumble. It was no longer a question of whether there should be a divorce but on what grounds.

Louis's feelings for Eleonore were so mixed that he could not entirely understand them himself. He knew in his heart that had she been contrite, had she given him her word that she would abandon her immoral way of life, willingly he would have taken her back. She had fascinated him; she still did; he could easily have forgiven her lapses from virtue if she had become a loving wife. He did not care for women generally, only Eleonore. He had loved her for herself, and the rich lands of Aquitaine had not influenced his feelings. But he did want a quiet, peaceful life and he knew he would never have that with Eleonore. He must divorce her, but if only she had given one little sign of contrition how happy he would have been to meet her half way!

Again and again he would think of her with her lovers. Her own uncle! That was even more criminal than the others. Then a rare anger would arise in him. I will divorce her for adultery, he thought, and it was in such a mood that he approached his ministers.

But he was the King of France. He should not think of revenge, or his own personal feelings. He must only think of what was best for France.

If he divorced her for adultery he could not re-marry, for according to the laws of the Church, once married its members were always married. It was his duty as King to marry again. He had only two daughters and the salic laws of France would prevent their inheriting the throne.

On the other hand if the marriage was ended because of consanguinity there would be no hindrance to re-marriage because, since their close blood ties prevented their marriage being legal in the first place, they had never really been married, and either was free to marry again.

As for the little girls Marie and Alix, they could be legitimized easily enough.

It was the answer. The marriage would cease to exist because of the close blood ties of Louis and Eleonore.

It was the solution most satisfactory to all.

*   *   *

Eleonore was eagerly awaiting the outcome of the meeting of the council under the direction of the Archbishop of Bordeaux. She had taken up residence in the château close to the church of Notre-Dame de Beaugency where the decision was being made. She sat at the window, her eyes on the road. At any moment a messenger would come riding to the château and then she would know whether or not she was free.

Once she had the news she would lose no time in meeting Henry and they would be married without delay.

She would have to say goodbye to her daughters Marie and Alix. That had been her only regret. She had been surprised herself by the depth of her feelings for her children; but she knew that even they could not compensate her for the loss of Henry, and she shuddered at the thought of spending the rest of her days with Louis for the sake of girls who would in a few years time marry and leave her.

No, she was too full of vigour, too sensuous, too egotistical to devote her life to others.

Henry was the man for her. She had known it in the first few weeks of their acquaintance. Strong, egotistical himself, and a sensualist, his nature matched hers. She had known from the first that even though she had a husband and Henry was eleven years younger than she was, he was the man she would marry.

Now, in a fever of impatience, she waited for the messengers. At last she saw them. Two Bishops attended by two gentlemen were riding into the castle courtyard.

She ran down to meet them.

"My lords," she said, "your answer."

"May we enter the castle?" asked the Bishop of Langres reprovingly.

"Nay," she cried imperiously. "I will wait no longer to hear the verdict. I command you tell me instantly without delay."

The Bishop hesitated; then he looked resigned.

He said: "It is the Council's decision that on account of the close blood relationship between yourself and the King they declare the nullity of the marriage."

Eleonore waited for no more. A great joy had come to her.

"Come into the château, my friends," she said. "I would refresh you."

Free! she was thinking. At least free of Louis. No more would she have to endure the boring company of the King, no more would she fret against a restriction on her freedom. She could go to her lover now.

There should be no delay. As soon as she had listened to this tiresome deputation, she would make preparations for her journey. Her first task must be to let Henry know that she was coming to him.

"Ride with all speed," she told her messenger. "Tell the Duke of Normandy that Eleonore of Aquitaine sends greetings. Tell him she is on the way to her own town of Bordeaux, that she will look for him there, and that she is eager to waste no more time."

* * *

Oh, the joy of riding in the fresh spring air! It was Easter time, the most beautiful time of the year, and how rich and fertile were the lands of the South!

As she rode south the country people came out to greet her. They cheered her. There had been stories of the immoral life she had led while married to the King of France but to the people of the South these seemed like romantic adventures. Seated on her palfrey with her hair flowing and in her gown with the long sleeves which fell to the hem of her skirts, she was a beautiful sight. A Queen in very truth and she was back among them. She had brought colour to her father's Court. Songs had been written about her; she herself wrote songs and sang them, and they were about love and chivalry. It was small wonder in their eyes that she was not appreciated in the cold land of the North. Now she was coming back and it was an occasion for rejoicing.

One day when she was riding through the domain of the Count of Blois, a party of horsemen came riding towards them. As they approached, Eleonore saw that they were led by a young man of pleasing appearance.

He pulled up before the Queen, doffing his hat and waving it in a gesture of gallantry as he bowed before her.

"It is indeed the Queen of Queens," he said.

She inclined her head, pleased to be so addressed.

"Journeying from the Court of France to Bordeaux," he went on. "You will need to rest for the night at some worthy castle. Yet knowing mine to be unworthy I offer it to you. My Castle of Blois is close at hand. It is the finest shelter you could find in these parts. I should be honoured indeed if you would allow me to entertain you there."

"We should be delighted," replied the Queen; and added, "You are Theobald, Count of Champagne."

"I am honoured that you should know me."

"I knew your father well," said Eleonore and thought grimly: He had a great influence on our lives. It was our conflict with him over Petronelle's marriage that led to the burning of Vitry and our Crusade.

That elder Theobald had been dead for some two years. This was his son, and he was clearly not only young and good-looking but ambitious.

As they rode side by side towards the castle of Blois he was congratulating himself on the prospect of having such a notorious lady under his roof. She was a beauty too.

Eleonore was aware of his admiration but it pleased her only mildly, She longed for one man and one man only—Henry, Duke of Normandy.

When they reached the courtyard of his castle Theobald leaped from his horse and commanded that a goblet of wine be brought. He stood by her horse while the goblet was brought; then sipped it and passed it to her.

Their eyes met over the cup; his were bold, and he could not hide from her the speculative gleam in them.

Foolish man! she thought. Did he think that she was ready to accept any man, and that the only qualifications he needed to accept her favours were those of his manhood? Did he think he could compare with Raymond of Antioch, Saladin, and chief of all, Henry of Normandy? She would be delighted to teach him a lesson.

"How honoured I am that you should come to my castle," he said as he helped her to alight. "I warn you I shall do everything in my power to make your stay here a long one."

"My lord is gracious," she said. "But we are but passing on our way to my town of Bordeaux and I am in some haste to reach it."

"You will at least rest here the night."

"Indeed I will and it is good of you to play the host so kindly."

"I would give all the kindness of which I am capable to such a gracious lady."

He himself conducted her to her bedchamber.

"The finest in the castle," he said. "It is my own." She looked startled and he added: "I shall occupy one close by to make sure that you are well guarded through the night."

I must be careful of my lord of Champagne, thought Eleonore. He is too ambitious.

It was easy to see what was in the young braggart's mind. He would indeed need to be taught a lesson.

She ordered that her baggage be brought to the chamber and there her women dressed her in a gown of velvet with long hanging sleeves lined with miniver; she wore her beautiful hair loose about her shoulders and thus she sat almost in state in the hall of the castle of Blois.

Theobald had ordered that the choicest meats be prepared for the banquet; he had instructed his troubadours to make songs to celebrate the Queen's stay at his castle. Nothing that could be done to make her stay memorable was forgotten.

She sat in the great hall of the castle, enthroned as a queen, and beside her was Theobald his eyes growing more and more caressing, and more bold, as the night wore on.

She was amused and a little cynical.

Can it be that he wishes to marry me? she asked herself. She was free now. Men had courted her when she was Louis's wife because of her reputation. Now they would court her because of her fortune.

She decided to amuse herself a little with Theobald.

"This," he told her passionately, "is the finest hour my castle has ever known."

"Let us hope," she answered, "that it will know many more."

His eyes lit with pleasure. Could she really mean that she would stay here?

He answered: "That could only be if you consented to stay here."

"How could I do that, my lord, when I have my own castles beyond Blois?"

" 'Tis true you have many fine castles. I would like this castle of Blois to be one of yours."

"You are over-generous with your castles, my young lord. Is it because they have been such a short time in your possession? What would your noble father say if he looked down from heaven and heard you giving away what he has left you."

"He would be happy indeed for he would know what went with the castle."

"And what is that?"

"My heart, my hand, all that I possess."

"Is this a proposal of marriage?"

"It is."

"Ah, I doubt not you are one of many. When a woman is possessed of many rich lands it is amazing how ready men are to fall in love with her."

"You know you are the most beautiful woman in the world. The fact that you own Aquitaine is of no importance."

"I could never marry a man who was not sensible of the power of lands and riches. It seems he would be a poor helpmeet to me in the governing of my possessions."

"Nay, I am well aware of them. What I tell you is that were you the humblest serving-maid I would be willing to sacrifice all for your sake."

"What you mean is you would be ready to take me to your bed for a night, perhaps two, if I proved worthy. I could never marry a man who thought me such a fool that he must tell me blatant lies."

"I see you are too clever for me."

"You realize that then. A man should never marry a woman who is too clever for him. It is not the key to happy marriage."

"Oh, Eleonore, you are known throughout the land of France as the Queen of Love. Have done with banter. I would marry you. I beg of you consider my proposal."

"I do not need to consider it. I could not marry you. You must look elsewhere for your wife."

"I shall not give up hope."

"It is always comforting to hope," she said. "Now I would listen to your excellent minstrels."

She was amused by the young man. His wooing was almost abrupt. She had been in his castle not more than a few hours and he had asked her to marry him. Nay, my little man, she thought, you must do better than that. Do you think you could compare with my Henry?

She would tell Henry about the brash young fellow. How they would laugh together. Perhaps she would make a song about it. Oh, she could not wait to be with Henry!

She was thoughtful as her women undressed her, combed her hair and helped her to the bed which had been made ready for her.

130

"Four of you will sleep in this room tonight," she said, "and one of my esquires will sleep across my door. It has occurred to me that we may have a visitor."

Her women laughed. "Surely the Count would not be so bold."

"I am here in his castle. He has hinted and I have seen some purpose in his eyes. I think I should take these precautions."

How right she was. As she expected the young Count attempted to come to her bedchamber. Her trusted esquire who lay across her door sprang to his feet, his sword unsheathed. When commanded to stand aside he said that he acted on the orders of the Queen and any who crossed the threshold would do so only over his dead body.

"A fuss about nothing," grumbled the Count and went fuming back to his bed.

How Eleonore laughed in the morning when she heard the account of this.

She decided that she would not spend another night in the castle of Blois and secretly ordered that preparations be made to leave.

Theobald came to her. He was very suave. He begged her to stay another night for he had heard that there was a band of robbers in the neighbourhood and by the next day he could get together an escort to accompany her and her party.

A twinge of alarm came to Eleonore then. She knew what means ambitious young men adopted with heiresses. He could make her a prisoner in his castle, force her to submit to his attentions and keep her there until she agreed to marry him. She had no doubt that plans along this line were formulating in the Count's mind.

She was not really afraid and half amused. How dared he! He had been in possession of his estates only two years and he was behaving like a brigand.

She would teach him a lesson.

She pretended to believe him.

There was more feasting that night, more songs were sung. She noticed how he endeavoured to fill her goblet. Did he think she was an innocent? It was she who contrived to make him drink as much as to fuddle his mind. She knew that he spoke truth when he said he was sending for guards. They would not be to conduct her on her way but to guard her in the castle.

She had planned what she would do. She had ordered that

131

every member of her party be prepared to leave that night in secret. As soon as the castle was quiet they would creep down to the stables where everything would be in readiness. They would slip away and when the Count awoke in the morning he would find his guests had gone.

She was an intrigant by nature.

She amused herself by giving a little encouragement to the Count, implying that she might consider him, providing he behaved in a manner which she considered due to her dignity. She would be hurried into nothing and any attempt to effect this would meet with her disapproval.

She managed to instil into his somewhat fuddled mind that he must give her time and that she would be rather amused by his methods to coerce her.

Thus he decided to leave her in peace for that night and her plans were successful. Very quietly she and her party left Blois, and in the morning when the ambitious young Count awoke he cursed himself and all who served him because they had allowed this prize to slip between his fingers.

*   *   *

How she laughed as she looked back at the far distant castle of Blois in the early morning light. If he sent the fleetest riders after her he would never catch her now.

"We will make for Anjou," she said. "There we shall be safe for that is the Count of Anjou's land, and the Count of Anjou is the Duke of Normandy and were I to fall into his hands it would be with the greatest of pleasure for he is the man I am going to marry."

So they made for Anjou and as they crossed into it she was exultant.

Her complacency was short-lived. As they crossed the meadows they saw a rider in the distance, a young man who begged to speak to the Queen.

He told her he had been in the employ of Henry Plantagenet, now Duke of Normandy, and had been passed into the service of Henry's young brother, Geoffrey Plantagenet.

"My lady," he said, "I still serve the Duke of Normandy and so I come to tell you that four miles ahead lies an ambush. Geoffrey Plantagenet plans to abduct you, to take you to his castle, and to keep you there until you promise to marry him. He hates his brother because he has inherited much while he has but three castles in Anjou."

Eleonore laughed aloud.

"Take this young man," she said, "give him food and from henceforth he shall serve me. I promise you, my good fellow, that ere long you shall find yourself in the service of the Duke of Normandy for any who serves me will serve him also. We will now change course. We will leave Anjou and go south to Aquitaine. We will ride to Poitiers and I promise you it will not be long before we have reached my city."

Warily they rode. There had been two indications of what ambitious men would attempt to win the hand of an heiress.

"None shall take by force what is mine to give," said Eleonore.

They came to her city of Poitiers and she took up her lodging in the château; there she sent a messenger to Henry to tell him that she would await him there and when he came they would be married without delay.

*   *   *

How long the waiting seemed and yet she knew he came with all speed! It was necessary for them to marry quickly and that no hint of who her bridegroom was to be should reach Louis's ears. As Duchess of Aquitaine she was his vassal and he had the right to forbid her to marry a man of whom he did not approve, and it would not be only Louis who disapproved of a match between Normandy and Aquitaine.

At length he came. She was in the courtyard waiting to greet him. With great joy they embraced and eagerly discussed the arrangements for the wedding which must take place without delay. They would not wait for the ceremony of course, although each realized the importance of it. They had been lovers before and were impatient for each other.

The wedding was to take place on Whit Sunday and it would not be celebrated with the pomp which had accompanied that of Eleonore to the King of France for it was most important for it to take place before anyone could stop it.

However spies had already conveyed to Louis that Henry of Normandy had joined Eleonore in Poitiers and that arrangements were going on to celebrate their marriage.

Louis was furious. Not only was he jealous of Eleonore's obsession with young Henry, but if Aquitaine and Normandy were joined by the marriage of these two, then Henry of Normandy would be the most powerful man in the country.

He demanded that his vassal, Henry of Normandy, come to Paris immediately.

That was a summons which Henry could only ignore. Instead of obeying the King he went to the Cathedral with Eleonore and there, on that warm Whit Sunday, Eleonore of Aquitaine became the bride of Henry of Normandy.

Queen of England

Rarely had Louis's passions been so strongly aroused as when he heard of the marriage of Eleonore and Henry. In the first place he could not endure to think of her with that young virile man. Henry of Normandy was uncouth; he might be learned, but he was rough in manners and Eleonore had always been so fastidious. What was the attraction? He knew. It was that overwhelming sensuality in her which had both fascinated and yet appalled him.

There was more to it than mere jealousy. There was the political implication.

Henry of Normandy had now become the most powerful man in France. Apart from Normandy he would now be in control of Aquitaine, Maine and Anjou; which meant that he possessed more land than anyone in France, not excluding the King.

Louis's ministers deplored the divorce and its consequences. They implied that they had told him so and he should never have agreed to let Eleonore go. Only a few weeks after the separation and she had changed the face of France, geographically and politically! Henry had a touch of his great-grandfather in him which was recognized by many. He was undoubtedly a chip off the old conquering block. It was as though William the Conqueror was reborn.

If he got control of England, which seemed likely, and was in possession of so large a slice of France, what power would be his? And there could be no doubt that he would know how to exploit it.

Louis discussed the matter at length with his counsellors. Men such as Henry of Normandy had many enemies. There was his brother for one. Geoffrey of Anjou was incensed because his father had left him only three castles. It was true that there had been a proviso in his father's will that if and when Henry became King of England, Anjou was to be passed over to Geoffrey, but knowing Henry, Geoffrey rather doubted this would come to pass. Henry had always been too fond of his possessions to give anything up. If Geoffrey was ever going to gain possession of Anjou he felt he must do it now before Henry had the might of England behind him to help him hold it.

There was one other who feared Henry and that was Eustace, the son of Stephen. Because his father was the King, Eustace rather naturally believed that on his death he should take the Crown. Matilda had found it impossible to wrest that desirable object from Stephen so why should her son become King on Stephen's death? That Matilda had the first right to the throne mattered not to Eustace. He was determined to fight for it.

As Louis's ministers pointed out, here were two stalwart allies, both with grievances against Henry and much to gain.

Let there be an alliance between them and surely if they stood together against Henry they would have a fair chance of victory.

Louis called a meeting and plans were discussed. Both Eustace and Geoffrey were exultant at the thought of having their revenge on Henry. They hated him fiercely for Henry, with his careless ways, his rather crude manners and his innate knowledge that he was going to make a mark on the world, aroused their bitter envy.

In the family circle Geoffrey had always been obliged to take second place to his elder brother. It had been clear that Henry was his father's favourite, and his mother, whose tongue and tempers they all tried to escape, had a devotion for Henry which seemed alien to her fierce head-strong egotistical nature. It seemed as though she had transferred all her hopes and ambitions—and they had been monumental—to her eldest son. Geoffrey had always lived in Henry's shadow and he hated him for it.

Eustace hated Henry of Normandy with an equal fervour. If Geoffrey was a weak man, Eustace was not. He had fierce passions; he longed for power and often he despised his father for his weakness. Eustace was such that he would have stopped at nothing to reach his goal. He was violent and his desire for power was much greater than any qualities he possessed to attain and hold it.

These were the chief allies whom Louis drew to him. As a further gesture he offered his sister Constance to Eustace as a bride.

"It is fitting," said Louis, "that the sister of the King of France should in time be the Queen of England."

The strongest bonds to hold together an alliance were those of marriage and Louis could not have told the world more clearly that he was supporting Eustace's claim to the throne of England.

"There is one other matter," his ministers reminded him, "you are now free to marry and you should do so without delay. You must marry and produce a son. It is what the people are waiting for."

Somewhat reluctantly, but understanding the need for him to take this step, Louis was married to Constance, the daughter of Alfonso of Castile.

*   *   *

Both Henry and Eleonore believed their marriage to be an ideal one. They were two of a kind. Sensual in the extreme they had known themselves to be; that was what had first attracted them; but there was more than that. She delighted in his vigour and ambition. He was charmed by her ability to follow his quick mind as he explained his schemes to her.

When he talked of going to England, much as she would hate to lose him she would put no obstacle in the way of his going. Indeed, she was eager for him to go. It was his destiny to become the King of England.

What a woman she was! She could be beautiful and more seductive than any woman he had known; yet her mind was alert; she had grown in political stature because of her need to keep pace with him. The fact that she was some twelve years older than he was meant nothing to them as yet. Her body was perfect and her mind was mature.

Theirs, as they had known it would be, was the perfect union.

Therefore when he talked to her of his plans for going to England, for making an understanding with Stephen, fighting him for the crown if need be, she was with him. The parting would be agonizing for her but she knew he must go.

They were destined to be King and Queen of England, and if they must suffer to gain the prize then so be it.

She was as completely confident of his final victory as he was himself.

How pleasant to lie together in their bed which had lost none of its charm now that it was no longer illicit and when they were temporarily satiated with the force of their passion to talk of the future.

"Stephen is a strange man," mused Henry. "It is difficult for me to think of him as an enemy. My mother declared that she hated him and yet sometimes a strange look comes into her eyes when she speaks of him."

"It is natural that she should hate the usurper who took her throne."

"It seems he is a man it is difficult to hate. He has shown a kindliness to me which is strange. When I went to Scotland in order to march against him and was deceived as to the support I could count on, he gave me money and the means to return to Normandy. What do you think of such a man?"

"That he is a fool," said Eleonore.

"Yes, in a measure. But I am not sure. I cannot find it easy to think of him as my enemy."

"Oh come, my love, he has taken your mother's crown. He would set up his son Eustace in your place. Rest assured he is your enemy."

"Aye, so it would seem. Men and women have strange passions, Eleonore. I would like to know more of Stephen's."

"Do not concern yourself with his nature but his Crown. The Crown that is yours."

" 'Tis true, and ere long I must go to England to claim it."

And so they made plans during those idyllic weeks, but they knew that the honeymoon must soon be over and the arduous task of gaining a crown must begin.

* * *

They travelled to Falaise where Eleonore met the redoubtable Matilda—Countess of Anjou, daughter of Henry I of England who was still known as the Empress because of her first marriage to the Emperor of Germany.

The two women took each other's measure.

Matilda was naturally delighted with Henry's marriage to the greatest heiress in Europe. Moreover she recognized a strong woman.

She decided that she approved of the match.

Eleonore, knowing something of the history of her mother-in-law, could not help thinking that she had mismanaged her life. There she was, still handsome, a woman who had found it difficult to control her passion. She had passed on her temper to her son, Henry. Because of the amity between them Eleonore had so far seen little of that temper; she had heard rumours though that it was formidable.

It should never be aroused against her, she assured herself. And if it were? Well, was Eleonore of Aquitaine of the nature to be alarmed by a man's tantrums?

Often she wondered why Matilda had been content to give up the fight for her Crown. She had fought for it and had come near to gaining it, but her unfortunate nature had been her downfall and in due course although the people of England recognized her prior claim they preferred the mild and charming Stephen to the virago Matilda.

And so Stephen reigned in England and Henry must cross the seas and challenge his right to the Crown.

Matilda talked with them. She wished that she was younger so that she could accompany her son to England. Now and then she mentioned the past. The English were a people it was not easy to understand. They had acclaimed her in Canterbury and had been ready to do so in London, but suddenly they had turned against her and just as she and her company were going into the hall to dine, the mob had stormed the palace and she had been forced to flee.

Henry knew what had happened. He told Eleonore when they were alone. Matilda had offended the English so much that they would never accept her.

"Make sure," Matilda confided in Eleonore, "that Henry never offends the English—at least not until the crown is safe on his head."

Eleonore certainly would, although she believed that Henry would be wiser in that respect than his mother had been.

He was eager now to leave for England, he wanted to get that matter settled. If he could bring Stephen to such a pass that he swore his heir should be Henry Plantagenet, he would be content. He was going to try.

Both Matilda, his mother, and Eleonore, his wife, agreed that he should lose no time and he prepared to leave for England.

Before he was ready there was news for him. Forces were

mustering against him. Eustace was determined to take Normandy, and Henry's own brother wanted Anjou.

Henry cursed them loudly, and then he was glad that he had knowledge of his brother's treachery and Eustace's designs before he had left for England.

Naturally he could not leave for England. He must remain where he was and deal with Eustace and Geoffrey who came against him with the help and blessing of Eleonore's one-time husband, the King of France.

* * *

Henry never showed his genius for generalship so well as when he was faced with seemingly overwhelming difficulties. He immediately abandoned his plans to go after the English Crown in order to consolidate his position in Normandy. Because he was the possessor of much land he had a great deal to protect and hold, but he was full of vigour and by no means disturbed to pit his skill against that of the Queen's previous husband.

"Let Louis come against me," he declared. "I'll show him and you who is the better man."

"I at least do not need to be shown," answered Eleonore. "You will fight and win. I was never more sure of it. As for that blustering Eustace, you will soon let him know what it means to come against the true heir to England. And your brother Geoffrey is a fool. Look how he tried to trick me and failed."

The Empress Matilda also declared her faith in him. He need have no fear. With two determined women to look after his interests he would succeed.

They were right, and although several months were spent in fighting off these enemies, Henry defeated his foolish brother Geoffrey, and Eustace returned from the fight dispirited while Louis made overtures for peace.

Yet victorious as he was he did not wish to waste time. The lust for conquest was on him. He knew that now was the time to strike for England.

Like the good general he was he set about reviewing his resources.

He could safely leave his wife and mother to rule in his stead. They were both experienced women. How glad he was that he had not married a silly simpering girl. How foolish were those who shook their heads over a marriage in which
140

the wife was twelve years the senior of her husband. Eleonore had lived longer than he had, and during those years had gleaned much wisdom. It was a great comfort to know that the interests of this amazing woman were his.

His mother's temper had not improved with the years and she would never be loved, but Eleonore managed to win people to her, proud and often overbearing as she was. None but these two could better look after his affairs in his absence, for one thing they both had in common was their devotion to him.

He could turn his thoughts to England and Stephen, that strange man who was so gentle and yet such a great fighter. He had never understood Stephen. There had been long years of civil war in England—with Stephen on one side and Matilda, Henry's mother, on the other, and yet when his mother spoke of Stephen a strangely soft look would come into her eyes; and even when he had gone to England to make an attempt to take the crown Stephen had been kind to him.

There was some mystery about Stephen and his mother. So be it. Stephen held the crown and when he died—if not before—that crown must pass to Henry.

If Stephen had not had sons there might have been no war to fight, for it would be better to wait and take the crown peacefully on Stephen's death than to fight for it now. But there was ambitious Eustace who had dared to try to take Normandy, and another son William who did not by all accounts seem to be much of a fighter.

He must therefore go to England without delay, and as soon as he had gathered together a fleet to carry him there and the men-at-arms to fight for him he would set out.

To his great joy while he was making his preparations he received a message from Robert of Beaumont, the Earl of Leicester, to the effect that if he came to England he, Leicester, would be ready to support him.

This was a triumph, for Robert's father had served William the Conqueror well and prospered under him, and his son, Henry I had allowed Robert to be among those favoured young men who were brought up at his Court, and in due course he had married a rich wife. The Earl was a cautious man; he did not wish to lose anything that he had gained but he saw clearly that there could be very little prosperity under the rule of Eustace if he ever came to the throne. He had been saddened to see the country torn by civil war while Matilda and Stephen battled for the Crown and although he believed that Stephen was the better choice he was looking forward to the time when England was once more ruled by a strong king such as Henry I and his father had been. He had known Robert of Gloucester, Henry I's illegitimate son, who had supported Matilda and through him had learned of the good qualities of young Henry of Normandy. Leicester believed that the best hope of prosperity for England on Stephen's death would be the accession to the Crown of Henry Plantagenet. He knew that this was a time when he could no longer remain neutral. Stephen was a sick man; he had never recovered from the death of his wife, the gentle Matilda, who had stood firmly beside him through his many vicissitudes and had been a far greater prop to him than even he realized. Stephen had always been subject to mysterious illnesses; he was a lovable man but a weak one; he liked to be on good terms with everyone, and that was no way for a king to be. No, in Robert of Leicester's opinion England's hopes lay in Henry Plantagenet, and he wrote to the young man telling him that he was prepared to put his wealth and his experience behind his cause.

"There is not a more powerful man in England," cried Henry, his eyes gleaming. "Victory is assured."

But he was too clever to let that change his preparations which were going to be as thorough as though he were facing the most formidable army in the world.

It was a January day when he sailed for England with his fleet of thirty-six ships and landed at Bristol. There he found men of the West Country ready to rally to his cause.

*　　*　　*

Sadly Eleonore missed him. He had absorbed her life to such an extent that she asked for no other lover. She threw herself into the task of looking after his affairs and her friendship with her mother-in-law the Empress ripened. The two women admired each other and although their strong temperaments often clashed, for neither would give way in the slightest degree in her opinions to please the other, they never forgot that discord between them would be detrimental to Henry, and for both of them he was the centre of their lives.

Eleonore had her little court about her. Gallant men sang her songs and composed verses of their own. Many of them were addressed to her; and because of her reputation, which would always be with her, many of them were hopeful. But

Eleonore was devoted to her Duke. They all knew that, but could such a woman be expected to keep her sensuality smouldering, not allowing it to burst into fire before the return of her lord which might be who knew when?

But Eleonore was so enamoured of her husband that none of those about her pleased her. Moreover he had not been gone for more than a month when she knew for certain that she was pregnant and she began to think exclusively of the child.

Matilda was delighted. "You'll have sons," she declared. "You are like me. All my children were sons and there were three of them. I might have had twenty sons if I'd had a fancy for my husband, but I never did, though many women found him attractive . . ."

She looked obliquely at Eleonore who nodded gravely, remembering the charm of him who had earned for himself the name of Geoffrey the Fair.

"Yes," went on Matilda, "he had many a mistress. It never bothered me. He was my husband when he was but fifteen. I thought him a foolish boy and I never took to him. I bore a grudge against him because they'd given him to me: First they gave me an old man and then a young boy. It wasn't fair. You know they might have married me to Stephen."

"English history would have been different if they had."

"All those wretched civil wars would never have taken place." Matilda's eyes grew dreamy. "Yes, if my father had known his only legitimate son was going to be drowned at sea, he would have married me to Stephen. I'm certain of it. I would have been better for him than that meek wife of his and he would have been better for me. He was one of the handsomest men you ever saw. I think the biggest blow in my life was when I heard that he had taken the Crown. I'd always believed he would stand by me. Crowns, my daughter, what blood has been shed because of them—and more will most certainly be!"

"Not Henry's," said Eleonore firmly.

"Nay, not Henry's. But what if it should be Stephen's?"

She was silent for a while. Then she went on: "Stephen must know that that wild boy of his cannot inherit the Crown. The people would never accept Eustace. And then he has William. *That* woman's children. It always infuriated me that she had the same name as mine. If only Stephen could be made to see reason."

"Would he call it reason to give up the Crown to Henry?"

"He cannot live long. What if there was a truce? What if
143

they made an agreement? Stephen to rule as long as he lives and then Henry to be the King of England."

"Would a man pass over his own son for another?"

"If it were justice perhaps. If it would stop war. If it would give England what she always needs, what she had in the times of my father Henry I and my grandfather William the Conqueror. Those are the strong men England needs and my son and your husband is one of them."

"Stephen would never agree," said Eleonore. "I cannot believe any man would pass over his own son."

Matilda narrowed her eyes.

"You do not know Stephen," she said. "There is much that is not known of Stephen."

* * *

News came of Henry's progress. It was good news. All over England people were rallying to his banner. Eustace had made himself unpopular and people were weary of continual civil war. They recalled the good old days under King Henry, whose stern laws had brought order and prosperity to the land. He had not been called the Lion of Justice for nothing. There was something about young Henry Plantagenet that inspired their confidence. He was of the same calibre as his grandfather and great-grandfather.

There was no doubt in Eleonore's mind that he would succeed. The question was when, and how long would it be before they were united?

She had left Matilda and travelled to Rouen as she wished the birth to take place in that city and there she prepared for her confinement.

She was exultant on that hot August day to learn that she had borne a son. How delighted Henry would be. She immediately despatched messengers to him. The news would cheer him wherever he was.

She decided that his name should be William. He was after all the son of the Duchess of Aquitaine and William was the name so many of the Dukes of that country had borne. Moreover Henry's renowned great-grandfather, the mighty Conqueror, had been so called.

As she lay with her child in her arms her women marvelled at the manner in which childbirth had softened her. They had not seen her with her daughters. Now and then she thought of them—little Marie and Alix—and wondered

144

whether they ever missed their mother. She had loved them dearly for a while after their birth. There had been occasions when she would have liked to devote herself to them. She thought of the infants in her arms, tightly bound in their swaddling clothes that their limbs might grow straight. The poor little things had offended her fastidiousness. Bound thus how could it be otherwise for they were not allowed to emerge from their cocoons for days on end, disregarding the fact that the poor little things must perform their natural functions.

It should be different with her son. She would watch over him, assure herself that his limbs would grow straight without the swaddling clothes.

She loved him dearly—a living reminder of her passion for Henry—and she knew that the best news she could send him was the birth of a boy. Perhaps she should have called him Henry. Nay, she was implying that she had brought him Aquitaine and until he could offer her the Crown of England she was bringing more to the marriage than he was. It was well to remind him that they stood equal.

"The next son must be Henry," she wrote to him. "But our firstborn is named after my father and grandfather and the most illustrious member of your family, your great-grandfather whom it is said few men rivalled in his day or ever will after."

While she was lying-in the most amazing news was brought to her. She wished to rise from her bed and make a great feast not only of roast meats but of song and story to celebrate the event, for nothing could have more clearly showed that God was on the side of the Duke of Normandy.

Stephen and Henry had faced each other at Wallingford and were about to do battle when Stephen decided that instead of fighting he would like to talk to Henry. It had been difficult to persuade Henry to do this for he was certain of victory and believed that the battle might well decide the issue. However, he finally agreed and as the result of their meeting, to the astonishment of all, the battle did not take place.

Eustace, who was burning with the desire to cut off the head of the man he called the upstart Henry and send it to his wife, was so angry at what he thought was the cowardice of his father that he gave way to violent rage. He had never been very stable but even his most intimate followers had never seen his control desert him to such an extent.

He would raise money, he declared, and he would fight the battles which his father was afraid to face. Did Stephen not understand that it was his heritage which Henry was trying

145

to take from him? He, Eustace, was the heir to the throne of England and he was not going to allow his father's weakness to bestow it on Henry.

In vain did his friends try to restrain him; he reminded them that he was the commander of his armies and marched to Bury St Edmunds, where he rested at the Abbey, and when he had refreshed himself he demanded that the Abbot supply him with money that he might go into battle without his father's help against Henry of Normandy. The Abbot declared that he had nothing to give him whereupon Eustace demanded to know why the treasures of the Abbey should not be sold to provide him with what he needed.

The Abbot took the opportunity, while he pretended to consider, of locking away the treasure. Then he refused.

Calling curses on the Abbot and his Abbey, Eustace rode away, but not far. He ordered his men to take what they wanted from the countryside and every granary was plundered, every dwelling robbed, but the main object of his pillage was to be the Abbey. His soldiers returned to it and forced the monks to tell them where the treasure was hidden. When they had plundered the place, Eustace led them back to the nearest castle to make merry.

He sat at table to eat of the roasting meats which his servants had prepared, his anger still within him. He was going to make war on Henry of Normandy, he declared; he was going to drive him from the shores of England and very soon they would see him, Eustace, crowned King.

As he stood up to drink to that day, he fell to the floor in agony. He writhed for a moment and then was still, and when they bent over him they saw that he was dead.

This was the news that was brought to Eleonore while she lay awaiting the return of her strength.

She wanted to shout in triumph: This is a glorious day. Eustace is dead. How can Stephen make his son William his heir? William has already declared he has no talent for ruling and no wish to either.

It must be Henry now. God, by striking down Eustace, has shown England who is worthy to be her King.

*   *   *

Henry was sure of his destiny. The news that Eleonore had borne him a son following so soon on that of Eustace's death seemed to be an omen. He was of a nature to regard anything

146

that was to his benefit as an omen while he disregarded any sign that could be to his detriment. In this he resembled his great-grandfather William the Conqueror. In his heart he knew it was one of the qualities needed to succeed.

But the death of Eustace did seem like an act of God. The people of Suffolk who had suffered from his ill-temper declared that God had struck him down in anger and if they had had any doubts before that Henry Platagenet should be the next King they no longer had.

Victory was in sight.

He was longing for the day when he could return to Eleonore. He missed her. No other woman would do for him, he had discovered. Not that he had been faithful to her. That was too much to expect. He was too lusty a man for that. Eleonore would understand. While he was with her he would be faithful; but during long campaigns away from her she must allow him a little licence. He fell to musing about women. The best since he had arrived in England had been a woman of some experience, since making love was her living. Her name he believed was Hikenai. She was amusing; there was very little she had not experienced. He laughed to recall her. She had followed the camp and had made herself exclusively his for that time. Strangely enough he had been contented with her as she had been with him. He was a man who needed women, but if he had a good one he did not wish to be promiscuous. One satisfied him providing she was always there when he needed her.

He had watched Hikenai's figure thicken and noticed the obvious signs of pregnancy. She had been pleased.

"This one," she had said, "will be a king's son."

"You go too fast," he told her.

"Come, my lord Duke, you'll be a king before this little one has known two summers."

"It's a good and loyal statement," he told her, and expressed the hope that it would be a boy.

While he had been in England he had seen his other two boys.

"By God," he had cried, "I am a begetter of boys."

He had wondered whether their mother would still appeal to him. He had been devoted to Avice some few years before when he was in England, and the two boys she had borne him were fine little fellows. He remembered her saying she would call her firstborn Geoffrey after their grandfather, and William after their illustrious ancestor, he who was known as

147

the Conqueror. Yes, he had been deeply enamoured of Avice. How old could he have been when Geoffrey was born? He was only twenty now. Fifteen! Oh, he had been a lusty young fellow even then.

Avice was living at Stamford. It had delighted him to see the boys again. He had spent a night with Avice but the attraction was gone. After Eleonore perhaps, only such a practised harlot as Hikenai could satisfy him.

So he had taken his quick farewell of Avice and promised her that when he was King he would not forget her boys.

And now Stephen and he had called a truce. He would never understand Stephen. He liked his kinsman but Stephen was not of the stuff kings were made. There was something kind, sentimental, too emotional about him. He reminded him of Louis of France who had never been able to get out of his mind that his soldiers had pillaged a town in the church of which men, women and children had been burned to death.

Cruelty was not a kingly quality but perforce it must be committed now and then, and when this happened it was best done quickly and forgotten.

When he was King of England he would follow the lines laid down first by William the Conqueror and then by his grandfather Henry I for they were ruthless men, but never cruel for the sake of cruelty. Justice came first with them. That was the way to rule.

And now what next? What was Stephen implying?

There came a message for a meeting at Winchester. He would listen eagerly to Stephen's proposal.

*   *   *

It was clear what Stephen's intentions were. He was not so much an old man as a sick and tired one. He had lost his wife and his elder son. He was in no mood to continue the fight.

If he were allowed to rule in peace for the rest of his life he would name his successor Henry, Duke of Normandy, who unlike himself was in the direct line of succession. He was sure that the people would accept Henry. He was the son of the daughter of Henry I, himself son of the great Conqueror, whereas Stephen was the son of the Conqueror's daughter Adela. There could be no one to raise a voice against Henry's claim.

Henry was wise. He looked intently at Stephen. How long

could he live? One year. Two years. Three at most.

Let the war be called off. He was content. He would go back to Normandy but he would first have the King's assurance that it was his wish that he should follow him to the throne.

It should be done so that there was no doubt that it was Stephen's wish, and the two travelled to London where a conclave of Archbishops, Bishops, Abbots, Earls, Justiciars, Sheriffs and Barons should be called.

And to these people the declaration should be made and set out in a treaty after the signing of which, fealty should be sworn to Henry.

A triumph. He had achieved what he had come for and without much bloodshed. This was the kind of victory all wise rulers hoped for.

Before the gathering Stephen made his declaration:

"I, the King of England, Stephen, have made Henry, Duke of Normandy, the successor to the kingdom of England after me, and my heir by hereditary right and thus I have given and confirmed to him and his heirs the kingdom of England. The Duke, because of this honour and grant and confirmation made to him by me, has done homage to me and sworn by oath that he will be faithful to me . . ."

Indeed he would, for he was wise enough to know that if he waited until the death of Stephen, which could not be long, all men would honour him.

This declaration was of the greatest value. How much more important it was for Stephen to have made him his heir than for him to have won the Crown in battle. Now all men must accept him.

He wanted now to get back to Eleonore. He wanted to tell her in detail of his triumph.

First though he must go to Oxford to receive the homage of the men who would be his subjects.

Before he left for that town he heard that Hikenai had been brought to bed, and went to see her.

She smiled at him from her bed and held up her child.

"Our son, my lord," she said.

"Another boy! So I am father of another boy."

"I shall call him Geoffrey after your father," she told him, "so that you will never forget that he is a member of the family."

"I am going to be King of England, Hikenai," he said. "And that day soon. I swear to you that when I am I shall not forget our son Geoffrey."

"I'll keep you to that promise, my lord," she answered.

Then he went on to Oxford to receive the homage of those who would in time be his subjects.

* * *

Now he was torn between the desire to go back to Normandy to be with Eleonore and see their baby son, and to stay in England and consolidate his position. The important men of England had sworn fealty to him, Stephen had given him his word that he should follow him to the throne, even so, a man should be close at hand to watch his interests.

He could not make up his mind but it was not long before it was made up for him. His enemies in Normandy were attempting to take advantage of his absence. His mother wrote to him that she thought it wise for him to return. It was April when he arrived in Normandy. What joy there was in his reunion with Eleonore. This was a little tempered by a certain anxiety which the baby was arousing. He was not as lusty as they had at first hoped he would be.

There was plenty to occupy him while Eleonore cared for the little boy and it was not long before he had settled the uprisings. He took a troop of soldiers around his entire dominions and made it clear that he expected and would have obedience.

Matilda wanted to know what had happened during the parley with Stephen, and she listened intently while he told her how friendly Stephen had been to him and so anxious for peace was he that he had been ready to pass over his son William for the sake of it.

Matilda nodded. "He is an old man, I believe now."

"He carries himself well and has a pleasant countenance," answered Henry.

"He always had," said Matilda. "He knew how to charm people. I used to mock him for it. When he was young he would go out of his way to please people who could never bring any good to him. I used to say he was practising so that it would seem natural to those who could bring him good."

"One could not help but like him," said Henry, "and he was very eager to be pleasant to me."

Matilda nodded, and was quite lost in memories of the days when she and Stephen had been more than mere cousins.

They talked of the troubles in the country.

"There is Geoffrey," said Matilda. "He will not be content."

"I know it, Mother."

"He was furious when your father left almost everything to you and nothing but three castles to him. True, your father's wish was that when you gained England you should give Anjou and Maine to him."

"I doubt he would be worthy of them," said Henry.

Matilda laughed. "You like not to part with any of your possessions. You are like my father. They say my grandfather was the same. You remind me of them, Henry."

"There are no two rulers whom it would please me to resemble more."

With Eleonore there had been a return to their passion. She had missed him sorely she told him. "I devoted myself to our child and awaited your return."

"I longed for you as you longed for me," answered Henry, and thought briefly of Avice of whom he had tired and of Hikenai who had amused him. When they went to England he would have to bring her boy to Court. He wondered what Eleonore would say to that. Would she calculate the date of his birth and know that he had been unfaithful during this early stage of their marriage? Oh, but she would understand. Had she been there it would never have happened.

Eleonore was pregnant again. This delighted them both. Little William was so delicate, they both feared that they might lose him. If they could get another son—a healthy one—they could better bear losing their first-born. When Henry thought of his lusty little bastards he asked himself, as many kings had before, why it was that the illegitimate offspring were so healthy and the legitimate ones so frail.

It was fortunate that they were enjoying a period of comparative peace when the messenger arrived from England.

One of Eleonore's women had seen the approach of a rider from a turret window and hastened to inform her mistress, who looking out saw that the man was riding fast even though his horse seemed exhausted.

"It is important news," she cried. "Go and tell the Duke."

She was in the courtyard when Henry joined her there and they were both waiting when the messenger rode into the courtyard.

"I come from the Archbishop of Canterbury, my lord," he said. "He begs the Duke of Normandy ride with all speed to England. King Stephen is dead. Long live King Henry."

*   *   *

It was fortunate, said Matilda, that she was in the castle.

"My hopes have been realized," she said. "And to think it had to come about through Stephen's death. My son, we must talk at once . . . the three of us. It is very important that you take the right action now."

In the private chamber of Henry and Eleonore they sat with the Empress. Henry listened intently to what she had to say. The fact that she had once had the Crown within her grasp and lost it made Henry regard her advice with great respect. She was experienced; she knew the English; she had offended them in a manner he must never do. If she could live her life again she would not make the same mistakes. Therefore he must profit from her experience. It was wonderful to have these two people with him. Caught up as he was in the midst of family jealousies yet there were two whom he could trust absolutely . . . his wife and his mother.

He took their hands and kissed them fervently. He wanted them to know how much he relied on them. They both knew it and loved him the more because of it.

"There should be no delay," said Eleonore. "Stephen is dead. There may be some who would want to set up his young son William on the throne."

"I thank God Leicester is my man," said Henry. "And you are right. I am determined to leave for England without delay."

"When you go," said Matilda, "you must take a company with you. It would be folly to go with too small a following."

"I have already summoned my leading nobles to assemble at Barfleur preparatory to sailing for England. They are eager to come, seeing rich lands and titles awaiting them. There must be no delay."

"No more than can be helped," said Matilda. "Eleonore must go with you."

"I intend to," said Eleonore.

"And you should be crowned, the pair of you, as soon as it can be arranged. A king is not a King of England until he has been crowned. I was the Queen . . . the true Queen but my enemies in London drove me out. If I had been crowned first . . . It is all over. But remember it."

"I shall see that the coronation takes place immediately."

"And your brothers. What of Geoffrey and William? What do you think they will be at while you are in England?"

"Mischief," said Henry grimly.

"And it will be necessary for you to stay there. You cannot accept the Crown and run away. You will have to show the

152

English that England is of more moment to you than Normandy. And meanwhile Geoffrey will remember his father's will. Was he not to have Anjou and Maine when you had England?"

"He would lose it to Louis . . . or someone. You know Geoffrey could never hold anything."

" 'Tis true. And you are loath to take your hands off it. You must keep it, my son. And the only way to do this is to take your brothers with you. Make them work for you. Promise them lands . . . over there. But take them with you so that they cannot brew mischief here."

"By God, you are right," said Henry. "I shall send for them and as soon as the wind is favourable we sail."

"It is a good thing that he did not wait a month or two before dying," said Eleonore lightly. "Or I might have been too advanced in my pregnancy to enjoy a sea trip."

Henry was impatient to go. He hated delays. In a short time all who were to make the journey—including his brothers—were assembled at Barfleur. But if he could command his subjects Henry could not command the winds.

How tiresome was the weather! Stormy day followed stormy day. It was impossible to set sail in such weather.

Four weeks passed and then one day the seas were calm, the weather perfect.

And so Henry set sail for England.

*   *   *

However, the crossing was rough and it was impossible for the convoy to keep together. The ship in which Henry and Eleonore travelled landed near Southampton with a few others, but in a short time, to Henry's relief, it was discovered that all had landed safely and it would only be a matter of a few hours before everyone was accounted for.

They were not far from Winchester, and as that was the home of the country's treasure Henry decided to make for that city.

As he approached it, news of his arrival had spread, and the chief nobles of the neighbourhood came forward to greet him and give him their allegiance.

It was a triumphant entry into the city of Winchester. Remembering the oft-told account of his mother's brief successes Henry realized that he must have the recognition of the people of London, that city which because of its trade and riches had become the chief of England.

He therefore determined to leave for London without delay.

The bleak December weather was not to Eleonore's liking as she and Henry set out with their retinue for the great city. She had, it was true, grown a little accustomed to it in Paris which she had always felt so cold after her own Languedoc; but this was equally chilly and she reminded herself that it was winter and not the best time to see the place. Of course there were compensations. A crown, a country which was bigger and richer and held more prospects of power and riches than that of France. It ill-behoved her at such a prospect to object to weather.

News of their arrival had spread over the South of England and people came from their homes to cheer the new King. They promised themselves that gone were the times when people lived in terror of robbers and murderers on the highway because of the weak rule of King Stephen. Their grandparents remembered the days of King Henry I when such stern punishment was meted out that offenders were deterred from their crimes for fear of losing their hands, feet, ears, noses, or even having their eyes put out. That had made life safe for law-abiding people. During Stephen's reign many wicked barons had built castles with the sole purpose of using them as strongholds from which they might conduct their wicked plans to rob travellers and often take them to their castles to torture for their sport. That was a return of an old evil which those strong kings William the Conqueror and Henry I had put down. With the return of amiable Stephen they had begun to come back. Stephen had hated to punish offenders. If they were brought to him he would say: "Let it pass this time. Don't do it again."

So in this young man they saw new hope. He was the grandson of just Henry I and in direct line of succession. As long as he did not take after his mother Matilda but after his grandfather Henry they would welcome him wherever he went.

They had heard that he did and that when he was in England he had been admired and respected by those who had met him; everywhere there was great hope that he would bring back to England that law and order which had been instituted by the Conqueror.

He rode with his wife, one of the most beautiful women they had ever seen. A special cheer for her then. And how graciously she responded! They had never seen such grace and poise. She wore a wimple over which was a circlet of sparkling diamonds, rubies and sapphires. Her gown was fastened at the throat by a collar of jewels similar to those in the circlet. The sleeves of this were long and tight to her wrists and over this she wore a cloak which was lined with ermine, and long and wide so that the tight sleeves of her gown were visible. The English had never seen such elegance and they applauded it.

Now there would be an end to senseless civil war. They would have a just King and a beautiful Queen; there would be royal children, for there was already a son and the Queen was noticeably pregnant. They knew that this Queen had been the Queen of France and had divorced the King of that country to marry their Henry.

They liked her for it. It was always pleasant to score over the French. They had already adopted Henry as an Englishman. Was he not the grandson of their own Henry I, son of the Conqueror, born in England, educated there, and who never failed to proclaim himself an Englishman?

There had been rumours about the life the Queen had led on a Holy Crusade. It amused them that she had played false the King of France.

So the people of England were very ready to welcome their new King and Queen.

Into London they rode, there to be met by Theobald, the Archbishop of Canterbury, and the chief nobles. There was no doubt of the people's enthusiasm. Henry made himself affable, as did Eleonore. Never for one moment did he forget the disastrous impression his mother had made on the Londoners and how this had cost her the Crown.

The Archbishop was of the opinion that the coronation should take place without delay. Henry agreed with him. Until a King was crowned he was not the acknowledged ruler, his mother had warned him time and time again. Here again he had learned from her. She had never achieved the all-important coronation.

With a foresight characteristic of her, long before Stephen's death Eleonore had sent to Constantinople for the finest material known, so that on the day of her Coronation in Westminster Abbey she would be looking her most brilliant best. The materials had arrived before she left Barfleur and she had them with her.

She was therefore ready for whatever date was suggested and as Archbishop Theobald had said "No Delay," it was to be the 19th December.

The great day arrived. Eleonore was dressed in robes of silk and brocade of such magnificence as the people of England had never seen before. She was like a goddess. As for Henry, he was never very eager to dress himself up. He was a man of action and he asked that his garments should not impede him but be comfortable. However on his Coronation day he made special concessions and because of this he was able to stand beside his elegant and luxuriant Queen without making too great a contrast. His short hair, his shaven chin and moustachios appealed to the people. His dress was a doublet and short cloak of the kind which was not usual in England although it was a common feature of Angevin fashion. His dalmatica, made of fine brocade, was embroidered in gold. The pair looked startlingly majestic and the spectators were enchanted.

"Long live the King and his Queen," they cried wholeheartedly for they believed that a new era was beginning. There would be a colourful Court, such as they loved and they could take a new interest in the lives of their royal family.

Stephen's Queen had been a good woman but the good were never so interesting as the naughty ones. Stephen himself though one of the handsomest men of his times was too mild.

They liked this pair.

The Queen would cease to be known as Eleonore and would become Eleanor in the English fashion, and their King was affectionately nicknamed Courtmantle on account of the shortness of his cloak.

They were accepted.

The weather was bleak; the castle of Westminster was draughty, and the Queen missed the warmth of her southern home, but the glow of satisfaction she knew from this rich acquisition, this land of mystery, the possession and holding of which had been the greatest ambition of the greatest of all Conquerors, made up for any lack of comfort.

King Henry and Queen Eleanor were the rightful rulers of England. With what pride they rode through the streets; with what joy they listened to the loyal shouts of the people. And so to Westminster Palace, there to spend their first Christmas in their new land.

HENRY &
THOMAS

The King's Will

As soon as the Christmas festivities were over Eleanor began to consider her lying-in. Westminster Palace did not seem a suitable spot and she decided to move to the palace of Bermondsey.

This was situated in a village close to London where, a short while before, a priory had been built. It was a pleasant place and she settled into the Saxon palace with pleasure. From the long narrow glassless windows she could see the green fields surrounding the palace and was struck by their freshness; the gardens were beautiful too and she was glad that she had come here for the birth of her second child.

Henry would not be with her during those weeks when she awaited the birth. He was very much aware of the need to consolidate his position. Although he was only twenty-one he had wisdom far beyond his years; he was a born ruler and a good judge of human nature. The cheers of the people at the Coronation still rang in his ears but he was well aware how fickle the acclaim of the people could be. He would never forget that he must never relinquish his hold on the Crown.

The first thing he set about doing was to choose his chief ministers. The Earl of Leicester was an obvious choice; he had already had an indication of his friendship and he had assessed the man's character. He knew that if he was a good friend to Leicester, the Earl would be a loyal subject to him. Therefore he was his first choice. Another he chose was Richard de Luci, a man who had had some standing under Stephen. Henry did not care that he had been a supporter of Stephen. He took to the man at once and read honesty in his face, and Henry trusted his own judgement.

These two were to be his chief advisers and he told them that he intended to go into action immediately. He was going to show the people of England that he intended to restore law and order throughout the land and this meant that he must silence any who would not accept him as their King and, popular as he had been in London and Winchester, he knew he could not hope for every man in the country to acclaim him. There would for instance be all those barons who had profited by the laxity of the law and had built up riches by exploiting those weaker than themselves. He was going to make immediate war on such people and destroy their castles, and for this reason he would make a tour of the country that all might be made aware of the new King's intentions.

This suggestion was acclaimed by his ministers and all right-thinking men and women, and great optimism swept over the country.

In Bermondsey, Eleanor awaited the birth of the child while Henry began his pilgrimage. He travelled in great state as became a king and with him rode not only his army but his domestic staff with all their accoutrements. His bed with clean straw for his bedding was carried in the cavalcade, with objects of furniture, his clothes and food. There were cooks, stewards, scullions, and other members of his household staff marched with his soldiers.

People turned out in their thousands to watch the procession pass and so during those early days of his reign he began to rid the country of the brigand barons, burning down many of their fortresses much to the delight of those who had for long lived in fear of them.

There were of course many who resented this but they had little chance against the King. As the days passed he grew in strength and it was clear to many that the weak rule of Stephen was over.

Meanwhile in the village of Bermondsey Eleanor gave birth to her child.

This was a cause for great rejoicing for not only was it a boy but this time a lusty one. This was a great comfort for little

William's health had not improved and it seemed hardly likely that he would reach his manhood.

"There is only one name for this boy," declared Eleanor. "He must be called Henry after his father."

*   *   *

As soon as Eleanor had risen from child-bed she joined Henry and they went about the country together in order to show themselves to their people.

"Let us be together while we can," said Henry, "for I fear trouble either in Normandy, Aquitaine, Maine or Anjou . . . and then I shall have to leave you to govern here in my absence."

Eleanor replied that she hoped he would stay with her, but if by ill-chance he was forced to go away she would use all her skill to govern in his place and according to his wishes.

"It was a good day when we were wed," he told her. "Two sons you have already given me and it is not so long since we were married."

"I am anxious about William," she said. "He doesn't seem to have the will to live."

"He'll grow out of it."

"*You* could never have been like that."

"Oh, I would bawl for all I wanted and when my grandfather used to dandle me on his knee, he told me that *his* father grasped a handful of rushes when he was a few days old and that this was a symbol of what his life would be. He'd take land wherever he found it. And it seems I took after him. You can't expect everyone to be like us."

"I'd expect it of your son," replied Eleanor. "Henry is more like you. He has more life in him already than our poor little William."

"William'll change. He'll be a scholar most likely. Forget not he has two learned parents."

Although he was smiling he was thinking of his illegitimate son by Hikenai and of his promise to bring him to Court.

Not yet, he comforted himself. The boy would be too young for a few years.

During one of his visits to Bermondsey his brother Geoffrey came to the palace and demanded an audience.

Geoffrey's looks were sullen.

"How like you England?" asked Henry.

160

"How could I like a land in which I am a pauper depending on my brother's whims?" demanded Geoffrey.

"What an impatient fellow you are!" retorted Henry. "I have not had the Crown long enough to dispose of land and castles."

"I believe some have been favoured by you."

"Those whose support it was necessary to have, yes. I expect yours, brother, without payment."

"Perhaps you expect too much," grumbled Geoffrey.

"Be patient, brother. Great good will come to you if you will but be."

"Great good should have come to me by now. Did not my father leave me Anjou and Maine in his will, to be mine when you gained the Crown of England?"

"All in good time," parried Henry.

And he thought: "How long would this boy hold Anjou and Maine? To give them to him would be to throw them to our enemies."

"In whose good time?" demanded Geoffrey. "Mine or yours?"

"In that of the King," answered Henry; and Geoffrey went away grumbling.

Very soon afterwards Henry heard that his brother had left England and had returned to Anjou.

*   *   *

It was as he had expected. Geoffrey had gone back to raise men to his standard. He was declaring that he had right on his side. His father had left him Anjou and Maine which were to come to him when his brother secured the Crown of England and now Henry refused to hand them over. There was only one thing to do and that was fight for them.

As Henry was occupied in England there were men ready to flock to Geoffrey's banner.

Matilda, the Empress, had come to England. She wanted to see her son in the crown which she had always believed should have been hers. He was delighted to see her for her single-minded devotion to him had endeared her to him, and he believed she had never really cared for anyone but himself, and that he could rely on her advice.

He told her of Geoffrey's fury and pointed out that he could not give him the land his father had promised him. She saw the point at once. Only her eldest son was worthy to rule. All her hopes were in him. His brothers, she believed, should have been contented to serve him.

The more possessions in the hands of the King of England, the more powerful he would be and that was for the good of the House of Plantagenet.

"You will never get my brothers to see that," sighed Henry ruefully. "There is also William. How shall I satisfy him? He will soon be wanting territory to rule over. I have been talking over with Eleanor a plan for conquering Ireland and setting up William as its King."

Matilda was thoughtful. "That's well enough for later on. First you must make sure of your position here, and what of Anjou and Maine? What do you think would happen if you took a war into Ireland? Geoffrey would immediately revolt and take your possessions over there. Perhaps even Normandy. Nay! You have secured the Crown of England. Now make sure that you lose nothing that you have before you seek fresh conquests. You should go and see what mischief Geoffrey is making."

He talked this proposition over with Eleanor and she was sure that Matilda was right.

"I shall miss you bitterly," she said. "But you must go and save Anjou and Maine." She grew pale. "Perhaps even Aquitaine is in danger. Nay, you must go. You can leave me here with Leicester and Richard de Luci. You know you can trust us."

"Aye, I know," answered Henry; and he thought: They are right. This is what happened to my grandfather and my great-grandfather. Their lives were spent between England and Normandy because being in possession of one there was always the need to keep the other.

Eleanor was pregnant once more. He must leave her. She would be capable of ruling with the help of men whom he could trust.

And so he set sail for his troubled possessions across the sea.

* * *

There was much to occupy her.

She had set about making a Court in England to compare with those which had delighted her in Aquitaine and Paris. Already troubadours from Provence were coming to her Court.

They were singing their songs of love and often she was the heroine of the romantic stories they portrayed.

Whenever she rode out her clothes were admired by the people who gathered to stare at her and raise a loyal shout. She set new fashions. She was often seen with her hair loosely plaited covered by fine gauze; her gowns with their long hanging sleeves were the delight and wonder of the citizens of London, a city of which she was becoming very fond.

She delighted in the Tower of London at the east end of the city; she liked to pass under the gateway of Ludgate and enter the old Cathedral; she loved the river down which she sailed to Westminster past the Strand with the beautiful gardens running down to the river's edge. It was the power of the city that she loved for it was the richest city in England, and she liked to remind herself that these people were her subjects and that she with Henry ruled over this land.

There were times though when she sighed for the warmer breezes of Aquitaine and she longed to be there again, Henry and her troubadours beside her; but she realized that the destiny which had made him a king decreed that they would often have to be parted from each other, as now when it was her duty to watch their interests in England while he made sure that his turbulent brother did not succeed in his ambitious schemes.

Since she was pregnant she did not miss him so sorely. Her children occupied her time. It seemed that after all she was meant to be a mother for she changed when she became pregnant and when her babies were young. She often thought of Marie and Alix and wondered if they missed her. She thought too of Louis with his new wife and whether he had forgotten her.

But there was too much near at hand and in the present for her to concern herself with far-off days.

There was the new baby, the mischief which little Henry was constantly brewing and the growing weakness of little William.

That was her main concern. His nurses shook their heads over him. He grew more pale and listless every day; and very soon before the new baby was born she knew for sure that when she gained one child she would lose another.

And so it happened.

She was with him when he died. She held his little hand in hers and he gazed at her with wondering eyes as though to

163

ask her why she had borne him since his stay on earth was to be so brief. He was but three years old.

She took him into her arms and held his frail body close to hers.

"Rest my little one," she said. "It may be that you have been spared much sorrow."

And so died little William, the first born, the son of whom they had had such bright hopes.

* * *

The newly born child was a daughter. Eleanor thought it would please the Empress if this child was named after her so they called her Matilda.

It had not taken Henry long to bring Geoffrey to his knees. Of course Henry had no intention of giving him Anjou. Their father had promised it, it was true, but Henry knew that his father had not been noted for his wisdom. Henry was not going to give Anjou into his brother's feckless hands. But his father had left that fair land to Geoffrey. There were the conditions plain enough. To be Geoffrey's when Henry became King of England. So Henry compromised by promising to pay Geoffrey an income of several thousand pounds a year for possession of Anjou.

This seemed a reasonable arrangement to both brothers. To Geoffrey, because he knew he would never be able to hold it against his brother, and to Henry, because he knew Anjou would never be safe while he was not at hand to protect it. Moreover promises could always be broken, and if Geoffrey were such a fool as to believe he could be paid so much money yearly he deserved to lose it.

So the arrangement was made and then Geoffrey had an unexpected offer from Brittany. That province was in turmoil. It was the prey of robbers and needed a strong ruler. As Geoffrey was the brother of the man to whom many were beginning to show respect and who could come to his help if need be, he seemed a good candidate to take over Brittany. It was a Heaven-sent opportunity in Henry's eyes.

Geoffrey would now have a land to rule. He would be an important man. He was to get his pension for handing over Anjou—or rather for refraining from attempting to take it.

All was well for a while.

Henry decided that England could safely be left in the hands of Leicester and Richard de Luci and of his ministers, and that Eleanor who had suffered the loss of young William and had recently undergone the trials of childbirth, should spend a little time in her beloved Aquitaine. The winter would be more comfortably passed there.

Eleanor was delighted, not only to rejoin her husband but to be once more in her native land.

* * *

What a joy it was to be there! She felt young again. These were like the days when she and her sister Petronelle had sat in the gardens and played their lutes and sang their songs of the pleasures of love.

Petronelle was now at the Court of France of course. She often wondered about her marriage with Raoul de Vermandois and thought of how she had felt a little jealousy because Raoul's impassioned glances had once been directed towards her. They had two daughters now—Eleonore and Isabelle. That seemed long ago and she wondered how she could have considered the fastidious Raoul de Vermandois attractive.

Now she compared all men with Henry and they suffered in the comparison. That seemed strange for even she had to admit that he was not a handsome man—nor was he tall as Raymond of Antioch had been. Raymond had been a man whom everyone would notice not only for his handsome looks but for his outstanding stature. Henry was a man who commanded immediate attention because of his strength. He was not fastidious as the men she had previously admired had been. He was not gallant; he was too impatient to waste words. There was too much of interest in his life to give him time to rest. He slept little; he was up with the dawn; he rarely sat down; he could not endure inactivity. When his hair, which was thick and curly, was clipped square on his forehead, he resembled a lion, for his nostrils flared and his eyes could be hot with rage. He was clearly made to fit a saddle and when he sat a horse he and the animal were as one. His clothes were never fancy except for State occasions when he realized the need to appear kingly and impress the multitude. His hands were strong and their skin rough, for he scorned gloves and would ride out in biting winds without them. They impeded his progress he said, and were for ladies. He was a great huntsman, a trait he had inherited from his ancestors. It was his most popular form of relaxation. Notwithstanding all his interests he was a scholar. He never

165

forgot the training which his uncle—his mother's bastard brother—had determined he should have. Henry was a man who needed little sleep, who wished his mind to be active every moment of his waking hours as his body was.

It was small wonder, Eleanor often thought, that she had remained enamoured of him.

He was always in her thoughts. She wondered what would have happened if she could have married him when she married Louis. That made her laugh. Henry had been but a baby at that time. She had never noticed the difference in their ages. Had he? she wondered.

Their passion was as strong as ever, and after their separations which happened frequently, they were united as they had been in the first days of their marriage.

She was, of course, learning to know him. His temper was quick and violent and when it arose everyone around him was terrified. His nostrils would flare and his eyes flash; he would kick inanimate objects and sometimes lie on the floor and pummel it with his fists.

These rages were terrible and when they occurred it was as though devils possessed him.

Eleanor, capable of showing anger herself, was horrified to see the extent to which Henry's rages carried him. During the first years of their marriage she had seen little of this side of his nature because he had been so content with his marriage and his gaining of the English Crown. But when any crossed him, these fits of anger would take possession of him, and once he had decided that any man or woman was his enemy he could never see them as anything else.

Nevertheless she understood him and she loved him and he was sufficient for her. She would have liked him to have joined her on those occasions when her troubadours were gathered about her. She would have liked Henry to have sung a song of love which he had written to her.

Henry had little time for such pastimes. So she sighed and decided that she would hold her little court without him.

There were many who were ready to sing their songs to her. She felt young again. Ardent eyes glowed into hers while delicate fingers—different from Henry's blunt weather-battered ones—plucked at lutestrings.

What have I done since my marriage to Henry? she asked herself as she listened. I have borne children—three in three years. I have either been pregnant or giving birth. She laughed. The duty of a queen of course but hardly fitting for the heroine of a love song.

Henry had seemed content. The death of little William had shocked him, not so much for the loss of the child but because he was his eldest son. They had young Henry—that was good—and Matilda, but Henry wanted more sons. He was constantly speaking of the plight of his grandfather Henry I who had had one legitimate son—though many illegitimate ones—and when that son had been drowned there was only his daughter to follow him. What had happened? Civil war.

"We must get sons," said Henry. "We have my little name-sake but look what happened to William? We need more sons and we must get them while you are of an age to bear them."

He was in his early twenties—plenty of time for him. But her? The time when she would cease to be able to bear children was not so far away.

This was the first reference to the difference in their ages. It ruffled her like the faintest stirring of a rising wind.

And so she must go on bearing children. She could be a fond mother but she was a woman of too strong a personality to subdue it to that of others—husband or children.

Encroaching age, childbearing, those were matters for the future. Here she was in her beloved château surrounded by troubadours whose delight it was to sing songs to the lady of their dreams, and who could insprire them to such ecstasy as their Queen.

There was one among all those who sang to her who attracted her attention more than any other. This was a handsome young man named Bernard. He called himself Bernard de Ventadour but it was whispered that he had no right to the name. It was true that he had been born in the Château de Ventadour, but his enemies said that he was the son of one of the kitchen women and a serf. The Comte and Comtesse de Ventadour, as was the custom with so many, allowed the child to be brought up on their estate and so he would have had access to the castle.

That he was possessed of especial gifts was soon apparent, and as the Count and Countess loved song and poetry he was allowed to join their company of singers.

It soon became clear that he was a poet of no small ability and as both the Count and Countess encouraged him, his fame spread and many came to the castle to hear his verses.

The subject of these was, naturally, love, and every poet of the day selected the most beautiful and desirable lady of his circle to whom to address his words. The Countess of Ventadour was undoubtedly a beautiful woman and to whom should a member of her household address his poems but to the lady of the castle.

The songs of Bernard grew more and more daring and as he sang them he would sit at the feet of the Countess and give her the benefit of his eloquent love-hungry eyes. This was the custom; each troubadour had his lady; but most of the troubadours were of noble families and that the son of an oven girl and a serf should raise his eyes to a countess and sing of his longings was more daring than could be countenanced.

In any case the Count thought so. He told Bernard that there was no longer a place for him at the Château de Ventadour.

Bernard could do nothing but prepare to leave. He was not unduly disturbed, for he had heard that Queen Eleanor was in residence in her native land and his reputation as one of the finest poets in the land had travelled far.

He presented himself to Eleanor who received him immediately for she had long admired his poems and even set some of them to her own music.

"You are welcome," she told him. "I look forward to hearing you sing for us."

To express respectful admiration was second nature to Bernard. And now that the beauty of the Countess was removed it was replaced by a brighter luminary. Eleanor could not help but be pleased by the frank admiration, bordering on adoration, which she read in his eyes. It was comforting following on Henry's implication that they must get sons while she still had time to bear them.

Bernard, now known as Bernard de Ventadour—as fine a name as many of Eleanor's courtiers—became the favoured poet of the Queen's entourage. He was constantly at her feet. Poems and song poured from him and their subject was always Eleanor, the Queen of love.

She could not but be pleased. Bernard had such a beautiful voice. He was writing some of the best poetry in France and it was to her. Such words intoxicated her.

Henry came once upon her circle of troubadours and sat down among them. His quick eyes took in the sprawling figure of Bernard de Ventadour at her feet and he noticed the soft looks Eleanor cast in the poet's direction.

His eyes narrowed. He did not think for one moment that

this emotion which was obviously between them could possibly be the result of physical love. Eleanor would have too much sense. Any child she bore could be a King or a Queen of England and she was enough a Queen to know that child could have only one father and he the King. Even so, there was no doubt that she liked this pretty fellow with his delicate be-ringed hands. He wondered whether Eleanor had given him the rings he was wearing.

He watched and listened and he remembered that very soon he would have to bring his bastards to Court. For Avice's children that would be easy, for they had been born before he had known Eleanor. But young Geoffrey, Hikenai's son, would need a little explaining because he had been born after their marriage. For all Eleanor's lively past she had been a faithful wife, which was surprising. But she had been fully occupied with childbearing. No sooner was one child born than another was on the way and there had been little time for any extramarital adventures as far as she was concerned. He could see by her fondness for these poets who sang of a love which never seemed to reach any physical fulfilment that she was living in some romantic dream and that meant that it would be difficult for her to accept the needs of a man such as himself. He was no romantic. He was a realist. Women were important in his life and he had no intention that it should be otherwise. It was something she had to come to terms with, and she would on the day he brought young Geoffrey to Court and had him brought up in that special manner reserved for a king's bastards. His grandfather Henry I had had enough of them. William the Conqueror had not it seemed. He had never heard of a single one of his. But no one could hope to be like the Conqueror who had only lived to conquer and rule. These were good enough matters but not enough to fill a man's life. And Eleanor would have to be made to understand.

He saw in this Ventadour affair a means of making his task easier when the moment came to confront her with young Geoffrey.

He rose suddenly in the middle of one of Bernard's songs and left the company. Eleanor looked after him with amazement but she remained seated until the song was finished.

Then she said: "It seems that the King was not pleased with your little piece, Bernard."

"And my lady?"

"I thought it excellent. If the lady you sing of really is
169

possessed of so much beauty and virtue she must be a goddess."

"She is," replied Bernard fervently.

"And your recital of her virtues clearly bored the King."

"I care not for the King's boredom if I give the Queen pleasure."

"Be careful, Bernard. The King is a violent man."

He bowed his head. How graceful he was! How gallant! And how she loved his poetry!

When she was alone with Henry he decided to begin the attack.

"That oven girl's bastard will have to leave the Court," he said.

"Bernard! Why he is reckoned as one of the greatest poets in the country."

"A slut's bastard to give himself airs!"

"His talent makes him equal to an earl."

"Not in my eyes," said the King. "And I like not the insolent manner in which he regards you."

"Insolent! He is never that. He respects none as he does his Queen."

"By God," cried Henry, "it seems the fellow aspires to be your lover."

"Only in his dreams."

"Dreams! The upstart dog! Tell him that I shall send him back to the ovens where he belongs."

"No great poet belongs working at an oven. You have some learning, Henry. You have a respect for talent . . . one might say genius."

"And I say insolence," shouted the King. "I'll have his eyes put out."

"The whole of Aquitaine would rise against you. A great poet . . . one of our greatest . . . and simply because he writes a poem . . ."

"To the Queen," cried Henry, "to whom he suggests . . . what does he suggest? By my mother's blood, if words were deeds he would be in your bed. I swear it."

"But words are not deeds and I trust I know my duty."

The King seized her by her shoulders and threw her on to the bed.

"Know this," he said, "if ever I heard that you had deceived me I would kill your lover. Do you know that?"

"And rightly so. I would not blame you."

"So you would not have blamed Louis if he had killed your lovers."

"Talk to me not of Louis."

"Indeed, I am no Louis."

"Would I have loved you, borne your children if you had been?"

"You bore Louis children."

"I was younger then. I was trapped and I had not then found the way out of the trap."

"I like not this dalliance with your poet."

"Why do you fear I should prefer him to you?"

The King picked up the stool which stood in the room and threw it against the wall.

Through the castle there was hushed silence. The King was in one of his tempers. He was showing his anger and jealousy and suspicion against Bernard de Ventadour and the young poet was warned that he should slip quietly away until the storm had blown over.

Henry raged about the apartment accusing her of infidelity but there was something lacking in this bout of rage.

Finally he flung himself on to the bed where Eleanor had lain watching him.

He seized her with sudden passion and declared once more that he would run his sword through any man who dared to make love to her.

Eleanor accepted his embraces; Ventadour retired from the Court although he was to return later; and very soon after that incident Eleanor discovered that she was once more pregnant.

Since Henry's appearance in France the situation there had become more peaceful and he felt it was time that he returned to England.

He had no intention of leaving Eleanor behind in France. He decided that she and the children should travel back to England ahead of him. The new child should be born there.

*　　*　　*

She missed Aquitaine and her troubadours for although there were many poets and singers at her Court they did not seem the same as those of Provence. Often she thought of Bernard de Ventadour who had been driven from the Castle of Ventadour because of his verses to the Countess and now had displeased the King because of his devotion to Eleanor.

171

Bernard was a man who must have a lady to whom he could address his poems. No doubt that this time he had found another castle and another lady.

She shrugged aside romantic thoughts and gave herself up to the matter of preparing for another birth. My destiny, she thought! Is there to be no end of it? If I get another son I shall call a halt to this pattern.

She dreamed of a son. She wanted a son this time. She was fond of her children but young Henry was too overbearing, and already looked like his father. He bullied Matilda who did not show the spirit of the grandmother for whom she had been named.

This son would be different, she promised herself. Tall and handsome as Raymond of Antioch, as great a ruler as his father, in truth a king. But how could he be, when he had an elder brother?

It pleased her to dream of this son who had been conceived in the warmth of Aquitaine. Aquitaine should be his. She patted her body and whispered: "I shall bequeath it to you, little son."

The child moved within her and she laughed delightedly. He must have understood her. She was convinced this one was going to be no ordinary child.

She had travelled to Oxford for she had decided that in this neighbourhood the child should be born. Just outside the walls of the city, close to the northern gate was Beaumont Palace with its serene views of green meadows beyond which rose the turrets of Oxford Castle from which years ago Henry's mother had escaped on the ice. Here her child should be born.

She had no intention of nursing the child herself and asked her women to find a good woman, with child herself, who could act as wet-nurse to the royal infant.

The woman, clearly in a very advanced stage of pregnancy, was brought to the palace and there she was installed in the royal nursery.

The Queen lay languidly on her bed and bade the woman sit down that she might study her. She was clean, a country woman clearly. Her skin was fresh-looking and she was buxom and quite comely.

"It cannot be long before you are brought to bed," said Eleanor.

"Nay, my lady. I expect it hourly."

"You have no fear of childbirth?"

"Why no, my lady. 'Tis all natural like."

She was not new to breeding and it was for this reason that she had been chosen, for she was known to have good milk and enough for two babies.

The royal child would be fed first and if there was enough over then she might feed her own baby. She understood this and was delighted to do the service asked of her. A stay in the royal palace, the honour of suckling a royal child. Everyone knew a woman was well rewarded for that.

"What is your name?" asked Eleanor.

"It is Hodierna, my lady."

"Well then, you must take good care of yourself for by so doing you will have good milk and only the best will be good enough for my child."

"I know it well, my lady," said Hodierna.

She was brought to bed the very next day and gave birth to a boy. Eleanor herself visited her and admired the child.

He was to be called Alexander.

A few days later a son was born to Eleanor.

He was called Richard and from the first he was more handsome than his brother. His limbs were long and straight and Eleanor loved him dearly.

Hodierna was the best possible foster-mother and she was right when she said she had enough milk for two boys.

As the months passed they grew into two of the finest boys at Court and in time they were very much aware of each other like brothers.

When Henry returned he came to Oxford to see his new son. He admired young Richard, none could help doing that. But it was clear that he had something on his mind.

He had. He had seen Hikenai again and she had reminded him of his promise to do something for their son. He knew he could not delay the matter much longer.

Little Geoffrey would have to be brought to the nursery and while the good foster-mother was there with her little son Alexander, it seemed a good moment to introduce him.

*   *   *

He said to Eleanor when they were in their bedchamber, "There will be an addition to the nursery."

She did not understand him at first. "An addition? We have two sons and a daughter. Is that not enough? Do you want me to spend all my time in the awkward state of pregnancy?"

173

"Nay, nay," he said. "I was not thinking of another for us, though doubtless there will be more. It is a boy in whom I have an interest."

"You have an interest!" Eleanor had sat up. She threw back her long hair and there was bright colour in her cheeks.

"Aye," he answered firmly, "a very special interest."

"Why so?" she demanded.

"I do not intend to be interrogated."

"Perhaps not. But I intend to interrogate."

"You forget, Madam, that you speak to the King."

She had leaped from the bed. She stood facing him, her arms folded across her breasts.

"Are you telling me that you want to bring one of your bastards into *my* nursery?"

"I am telling you Madam that I *shall* bring one of my bastards into *my* nursery."

"I'll not have it."

"The boy will be arriving in a few days."

"He shall not stay."

"He will stay with his half-brothers. That good woman Hodierna will be told that he is to have the same treatment as the others."

"How old is he?"

"Some three years."

"A little younger than William would have been. So . . ." She stared at him incredulously. "You . . . you lecher!"

He laughed at her. "A fine one to talk. A woman who lay with her own uncle."

She lifted her hand to strike him, but he caught it and flung her from him.

"Know this," he said. "I am the master here. You are a subject no less than any other."

"I . . . your subject! What were you but a mere Duke of Normandy! I brought you Aquitaine."

"That is in the past. I am the King of England now."

"And I am the Queen."

"Through my good grace. Remember it. I could have you imprisoned this very night had I wished it."

"How . . . dare you!"

"You will find that the King of England dares much."

"So you were not faithful to me . . . not even at that time . . . in those early days!"

"I was away a long time. How did you expect me to keep

174

from women? She was a woman of light morals. There was nothing more than that."

"And I must have the bastard of a woman of light morals brought up with my children!"

"He is of the King's blood."

"Do you think I will have him in my nursery?"

"Yes, Madam, I do. And I swear to you that should you try to harm him in any way I will take my revenge on you and such will it be that you will wish you had never lived to see the day."

"Do you think I am of a kind to take revenge on babies?"

"Nay I do not. I think you are sensible enough to see reason."

"Henry, I am a ruler in my own right. I will not be treated in this way."

"You will be treated in what manner I think fit."

"I have done much for you . . ."

"And I for you. Did I not marry you . . . a divorced woman twelve years older than myself!"

"I shall hate you for this."

"Do so. We will beget more sons in hate. Come, we will begin now."

She tore herself away from him but he would not release her. He was exultant. The difficult task which he had dreaded was over. She knew there was a child and that that child was coming to her nursery and she accepted this fact just as she accepted him now. He was still irresistible to her.

She would grow out of her romantic fantasies. She would forget the songs that were snug by her troubadours. Life was not like that.

Men such as he was when away from their wives took other women. He had thought she would have been experienced enough to know that. There would be separations in the years to come and other women . . . legions of them. She must learn to accept it and if there was a bastard or two whom he wanted brought up at Court then that bastard should be brought up at Court.

She did accept it. She was too much of a realist to stand against that which was inevitable. But her feeling for him changed from that time. She would no longer consider what was good for him; she would think of her own will and pleasure.

The bastard Geoffrey came to the nursery. He was an engaging little fellow and the King was particularly interested in him and determined that he should not be made to feel inferior to his half-brothers.

As for the Queen she ignored the boy, and for her son Richard there grew up within her a tenderness of which she had not thought herself capable.

*   *   *

The relationship between them having changed they began to see in each other faults which they had not noticed before. To Eleanor Henry seemed often crude in his manners; his style of dress was unimaginative; she disliked his rough hands. Although he could be overbearing where his will was concerned she often thought he lacked the bearing of a King. That was not true exactly. His manner was such as to command immediate obedience. What she objected to was his lack of grace, his simple clothes and the manner in which he rarely sat down to eat but took his food standing as though eating was a habit he had little time for. When she thought of the gracious banquets which had taken place at her father's Court and that of Louis too, she was impatient. His rages too had increased. He made no attempt to control himself in her presence. She had seen him lie on the floor and gnaw the rushes in his fury. There were times then when she thought he would go mad, for his eyes would be wild, his nostrils would flare and he would indeed resemble the lion to which people compared him. It was these violent rages which held so many in awe of him. Yet she had to admit he was greatly respected, and he bound men to him in a manner which was surprising for he thought little of lying or breaking promises. His one idea was to make England great and to hold every bit of land which had come into his possession. He wanted people to regard him as they had his great-grandfather, the mighty Conqueror. There was a difference though. Great William had been singleminded in his conquests. He had married his wife and in spite of long separations had been almost entirely faithful to her. William had been a cold man sexually; Henry was hot. Eleanor knew this and it was a sadness to her that her feelings had changed, for he was still important to her. She could not regret her marriage. She despised herself for having endowed it with an idealism which she should have known it could never possess. She was a romantic; Henry was a lusty earthy man. The quality they shared was a love of power and it had wounded her proud spirit that she should

176

have to accept his infidelity. What hurt most was that while she had been faithfully dreaming of him he had been sporting with harlots, and one in particular he must have thought of with affection, since he brought her child to the royal nursery. How many bastards of his were scattered round the country? she wondered.

She could not hate the child in the nursery, but Henry, to subdue her, made much of the boy. He had made it clear that he was to be treated no differently from Henry or the baby Richard or young Matilda. It would be a different matter when they grew up. Young master Geoffrey would learn the difference then between the heirs of the King and his bastards.

She knew that Henry made much of the boy chiefly to annoy her and refused to let him see how much it did.

Her baby Richard was a great comfort to her. He was going to be handsome. Already he showed signs of his spirit, screaming for what he wanted and charming everyone in the nursery at the same time. Henry ignored the child. Sometimes she thought Richard was aware of it, for whenever his father came near him he yelled in anger.

Henry, too, considered their changed relations. She was a virago, he decided, and all kings should have meek wives who obeyed unquestioningly. Stephen had been lucky with his Matilda, for although she had been a clever woman, quite a strategist it had turned out, and had done so much to further her husband's cause, she had never criticized him and always wished to please him. Had he married my mother, thought Henry, he would have noticed the difference. Henry laughed remembering the fierce quarrels between his father and mother. Whenever they were together there had been conflict. He could remember hearing the shouts of abuse which they had flung at each other. What hatred there had been between those two! His mother had been ten years older than his father. And he was twelve years younger than Eleanor. Was it a pattern in their families—young husbands, older wives, and stormy marriages?

But he could not compare his marriage with that of his parents. Theirs had been one of pure hate and contempt from the start. How his father had ever got his mother with three sons was hard to imagine. But they had done their duty and here he was—thank God the eldest, for he had little respect from his brothers Geoffrey and William.

And his feelings for Eleanor? Well, he did not regret his

177

marriage. She had brought him Aquitaine and she was a Queen to be proud of. No woman ever looked quite as elegant as Eleanor. She knew what clothes she could wear and she knew how to wear them. Wherever she was she caught people's eyes and that was what a Queen should do. The people of England were wary of her as they would be of all foreigners but they liked to look at her and she was well worth looking at.

But she was a proud woman. A meek man would be overawed by her. He thought of poor Louis of France. All those years she had been married to him and had treated him badly and still he had been reluctant to let her go. He laughed to himself to picture her arriving at Antioch and setting eyes on her handsome uncle. And in a short time she was sharing his bed and that of an Infidel it seemed! He had much to hold against her if ever she questioned his behaviour.

Life with Eleanor would henceforth be a battle. He was excited by the prospect, so he could not regret his marriage. Moreover she had brought him Aquitaine. How could he ever regret Aquitaine?

Eleanor was fitted to be a queen in every way providing she had a husband who knew how to subdue her. When she had learned that the King's will was law he would be happy enough in his marriage. They would have more children. She had proved she could get sons and he would not be adverse to a daughter or two. They made such excellent counters in the game of politics. A marriage here and there could cement an alliance far better than any written contract.

But she had to realize that he was the King and that he would be obeyed. She was his Queen and a certain amount of respect was due to her, but what was given her came through his grace, and she must be grateful to him for it.

To expect that of Eleanor was asking a good deal and that was what made the battle between them exciting.

Child-bearing had had its effect on her. Although she did not feed her children herself, fearing to impair her beautiful high firm breasts, the bearing of so many children in so short a time had slightly changed her figure. She had borne him four children and then there were Louis's two girls. A woman who had given birth to six children could scarcely be the sylph she had been when a young girl. She no longer attracted him physically as she had done. The intense desire he had experienced when he first knew her was replaced by a passion which had its roots in the desire to subdue her.

Yet deep within him there was hope for a different sort of relationship. The ideal woman would have been one who adored him, submitted to him, was faithful to him in every way, whose personal egoism was overlaid by her desire to serve him. There were such women. The late King Stephen had found one. To such a woman he would have been kind and tender. He would not have been faithful to her. Had Stephen been faithful to his Matilda? It was a well-known fact that he had not. Yet her feelings had never swerved and she had proved herself a clever woman in her desire to serve her husband. There were very few women in the world like Matilda of Boulogne, and Eleanor was certainly not one of them.

He was glad that Eleanor realized he had no intention of being faithful to her, that he was going to live like a King taking his pleasure where he would and that all his subjects—be they his Queen or his most humble serving-man—must realize that this was the King's way and none should dare question it.

* * *

He could never rest anywhere for long. When he was in the South he must wonder what the people of the North were doing. He had made a habit of travelling about the country without warning which way he was going. This meant that everywhere they must be prepared for him to descend on them at any moment and woe betide any of them who were not carrying out his orders. This habit was applauded by the ordinary people, who had seen the immediate effect it had had on law and order. No robber baron now dared to carry out his cruel tricks. The King would hear of it and his word was law.

England rejoiced. It had a strong King again. Henry was determined to keep his country rejoicing.

With great glee he had discovered that Eleanor was pregnant again. She had deplored the fact.

"What am I then?" she demanded. "An animal whose sole purpose in life is to breed?"

"It is the fate of women," retorted Henry with a smirk.

"I tell you this. I shall have a long rest after this one."

"Three boys would be a fair tally," he conceded.

She hated to see him there—younger than she was, full of health and vigour, off on his travels again, looking for young

179

and beautiful girls who would think it an honour to be seduced by the King and if a child resulted from their dalliance, well, who knew the King might allow it to be brought up in the royal nursery. Hadn't he taken the harlot's Geoffrey and done just that?

She hated him for being free and young.

It was like him to rise early in the morning and only then let it be known that he was ready to start on his peregrinations. What a bustle there was in the castle! Servants would hastily rise from their beds and the grooms, bleary-eyed, would hurry to the stables. The horses themselves, catching the mood, would grow frisky; the cooks and stewards and all the members of the domestic household who travelled with the King quickly gathered together the tools of their trades for the King was on the move and he was impatient with delay.

Eleanor watched from her window. They feared him; yet there was not one of them who would wish to be left behind. His terrible rages made them tremble, but his rough words of friendship enraptured them.

She had to admit grudgingly that he was indeed a King. There he was bawling instructions while they ran frantically round him. There was his bed being taken out. Who would share that with him? she wondered angrily. Fresh straw in case it could not be procured on the way. His platters and his drinking cups. There would not be any great banquets, she thought ruefully. His pleasure lay in the bed rather than the table.

He looked up and saw her at the window. He bowed ironically. No regrets now as there used to be in the old days. Then she would have been down there. She would have begged him to return quickly, to think of her as she would of him. That was changed. She knew him better. He had betrayed himself as the lecher he was. He could not even be faithful in the days when they had been at the height of their passion.

Let him go to his whores and harlots. She was glad to be rid of him.

And he had dared dismiss Bernard de Ventadour. Why? Had he really been jealous as he had pretended to be? There was much that she did not understand about him. Perhaps that was why she could not stop thinking of him.

And now here she was—she, Eleanor of Aquitaine, the elegant lady of good taste and culture, the patron of arts, a woman who must await the pleasure of the King's visits to her bed, which she was beginning to suspect were for the sole purpose of getting children. Was this the romance of which her poets had sung?

There was consolation in her children, and particularly Richard.

He was a wonderful boy and very soon there would be another. It was not a year since his birth and here she was heavy with a child again.

She took Richard in her arms and put his smooth young face against her own.

"The King has gone, Richard," she said.

The child crowed with delight as though he understood.

She laughed aloud and hugged him tightly. In this fine boy she could forget her disillusion with her husband.

Fair Rosamund

Henry made his way to Shropshire. On his accession he had ordered the demolition of any castle which had been erected as a stronghold from which the pillaging of the countryside took place. This had aroused the enmity of many of those who had owned these castles and Henry knew that if he did not continue to have the country patrolled either by himself or his trusted friends these castles would be erected again.

He had heard that this was what was happening in the area of Shropshire and the news had been sent to him by a certain Sir Walter Clifford who himself was having a disagreement with the son of one of the chieftains of Wales.

Henry therefore decided that he would make for Sir Walter's castle in Shropshire and settle this dispute.

When he arrived at the castle he was welcomed by Sir Walter who according to custom came into the courtyard to present him with the traditional goblet of wine, which he himself first tasted to assure the King that it contained no poison, and he himself held the stirrup while the King dismounted.

Then he led the King into the castle hall where the Clifford family were waiting to welcome him. He must forgive their awkwardness, whispered Sir Walter. They were overawed at the prospect of having the King under their roof.

There was the Clifford family, Lady Clifford and her daughters—six of them. Some were married and their husbands stood behind them, but the youngest of them took the King's eyes for she seemed to him the most beautiful girl he had ever seen.

He paused before her and said, "You have a lovely daughter, Sir Walter."

"She will remember your royal compliment all her life, my lord."

"Nor shall I forget such beauty in a hurry. What are you called, maiden?"

"Rosamund, Sire."

"Rosamund," he mused. "The Rose of the world, eh?" Then he passed on, and was conducted to the bedchamber which was hastily being prepared for him.

All the cooks in the castle were set to work for even though the King's eating habits were well known, every one of his hosts would want to produce the best feast of which they were capable. The King would expect it even though he did not wish to over-eat. Every acknowledgement of the honour done to them must be clearly shown.

A banquet was prepared and carried into the great hall. Sir Walter gave up the head of the table to his royal guest as he had done his bedchamber for only the best in the house was good enough for the King.

For once Henry sat down to eat and he was in a more thoughtful mood than was usual. He commanded that Sir Walter's daughter should sit beside him at the table.

She came. He was struck further by the beauty of her fair complexion, and realized he was comparing it with Eleanor's darker one. This girl was indeed rose-like, a little fearful to have caught his interest—which he liked in her—and yet eager to please.

"Why," said Henry fondly, "I never saw a maiden whose looks please me more."

He took her slender white hand and held it in his for a while and then he laid out his own beside hers and laughed comparing them.

"There you see a hand, my child, that holds the strings that lead a nation. A strong hand, Rose of the World, but not so pretty a one as yours eh?"

"It would not be right, Sire, for your hand to be other than it is."

"The right answer," he cried. "You should always think

thus of your King. He is right . . . whatever he is. Is that what you think, my Rose?"

"Yes, Sire. 'Tis true is it not?"

"Your daughter pleases me," said the King to Sir Walter. "She hath a rare grace and beauty."

He kept the girl with him during the evening and when night fell he said to her: "Hast ever had a lover, maiden?"

She blushed charmingly and said that she had not.

"Then this night you shall have one and he shall be the King."

*　　*　　*

He stayed at the castle. Rosamund was enchanting. She had been a virgin but her father had been willing that she should be given to the King. Nor had Rosamund been reluctant; she must rejoice that the King had found her to his liking.

Sir Walter soothed his wife who would have wished their daughter to have been found a husband that she might settle down in respectable matrimony as her sisters had done.

"Nay," said Sir Walter, "Rosamund will bring good to herself and the family. And if there should be a child the King will care for it. To refuse our daughter to the King would anger him. They say his rages are terrible."

"We should have hidden our daughters."

"Nay, wife. Fret not. Naught but good will come of this."

Rosamund was in love with the King. That aura of power had completely bemused her. She was an innocent girl and fearful that she lacked skills to please him, but he told her that her very innocence was at the root of her charm for him.

He found it difficult to tear himself away. He said: "I shall always remember my stay at your father's castle."

"I shall remember it too," she answered.

"You must not think of it sadly," he replied.

"When you are gone I could not be anything but sad."

How charming she was. How different from Eleanor. Was that why he was so enamoured of her? Her great quality was her gentleness, her acceptance of his masculine superiority. She was not without education but she lacked Eleanor's erudition; she adored him and it was very pleasant for one who was surrounded by adulation to sense the complete disinterestedness of this beautiful girl.

"I would I need not go," he said. "I would give a great deal to stay here and dally with you, my sweet Rose."

But the Welsh were rising. He sent out an order that every archer in Shropshire must join his army and he went into battle against Owain Gwynnedd. The fighting was desperate and there were losses on both sides.

He had heard how his grandfather Henry I had often gone to Wales and how he had loved a Welsh Princess Nesta, more it was said than any other of his numerous mistresses. Henry had often gone to Wales to see her, and his Queen was the last to hear of his infatuation with that woman. One of their sons, Henry after his father, was fighting with them now on his side against the Welsh.

During that battle Nesta's son Henry was killed, and Henry the King came very near to losing his life. But for the bravery of one of his loyal soldiers he would have been killed, but the man had stood between him and his assailant and had run his sword through the Welshman's heart before he could attack the King.

This was violent warfare and the King was determined to subdue these Welshmen. Finally he succeeded in driving them back and fortifying several castle strongholds. But he had to remind himself that it was not Wales alone that he must defend. He must return to London for how could he know that while he was engaged in Wales, trouble would not spring up in some other corner of his territories? Thus it had always been since the days of the Conqueror.

But first he would spend a little while with Rosamund. He had been thinking of her when he was not bitterly engaged in the battle. Other women had lost their appeal for him, but desperately he wanted to see this beautiful girl again.

There was great rejoicing in the castle when he arrived, and he exulted to see how pale Rosamund turned when he told the story of his exploits on the battlefield and how but for the bravery of his men—and one in particular—he would not be alive to tell the tale.

That night when Rosamund lay beside him in his bed she told him that she believed she was to have his child.

He was exultant.

"Rosamund," he said, "I love you dearly. I am a man who has known many women but have never loved—or perhaps only once—any as I love you. Think not that ours will be a light relationship and that you will see me no more. I shall come back to you . . . again and again."

She was trembling with delight and he was more charmed with her than ever. She did not beg or plead or ask for favours

185

either for herself or for her child. She was different from other women, he was sure. He thought of the demanding insolence of Hikenai, and of Eleanor's arrogance. This was indeed his Rose of the World.

"I will find a place for you to live," he said, "and I will visit you often. I will be your husband in all but name and you will have our child there. Would you like that?"

"If I could but see you now and then I should live for those times and thank God for them," she answered.

"I shall come whenever I have the opportunity and you may be sure that I shall make many, for I am content with you, Rosamund, and you shall be as my wife to me. Had I not already a wife I would defy all to marry you and your child should be my legitimate son . . . or daughter. But I have a wife, a jealous wife, and I would not wish her to know of your existence, for she is rich and powerful and might do you harm. Have no fear though, I shall protect you. I shall find for you an abode which shall be a secret one and only you and I will know that it is my haven of peace and joy for therein will live my own true wife."

He had not been sure when he had first left her that he would feel as he did now. He made promises easily and often forgot them. But Rosamund was different. He could not forget her. He was as much in love with her as he had been with Eleanor at the beginning of their acquaintance—more so for Rosamund had no rich lands to offer him and he could never quite see Eleanor without the golden shadow of Aquitaine behind her.

He decided that he would find a home for Rosamund near Oxford for he was often in or near that town, and finally he chose Woodstock.

*   *   *

Henry knew that there was constantly going to be trouble in his overseas possessions. If he and Eleanor were in England then there would be trouble in Normandy or Anjou or Maine or even Aquitaine. Subjects did not care that one land should be of more moment to their ruler than another. He was first King of England. That was his greatest title. He must rule England, but he was also Duke of Normandy, Duke of Aquitaine, Count of Anjou and Maine. Those monarchs who had preceded him had had the same difficulties.

Henry therefore looked about him for some means of making

allies who could strengthen his position and there was one man whose support could be of the utmost use to him. This was Louis, the King of France.

He was not sure how the King would feel towards a man who had taken his wife but perhaps since Louis himself was now married he would no longer bear resentment against him. In any case Louis was a King. Petty grievances must not stand in the way of State affairs.

Louis had daughters. Oh, yes, he had two by Eleanor, Marie and Alix, and of course there could be no alliance with them. But he also had a daughter by his second marriage and Henry saw no reason why this girl should not be affianced to his son Henry. At least there could be a betrothal. If he should decide when the children were older that he did not wish the marriage to go forward he would have no compunction in cancelling it. But an alliance now when they were more or less in their cradles—Henry was three, the girl one year—would be beneficial to both him and Louis.

But would Louis see this?

Louis was a man whom he despised—a weakling. Eleanor had told him much about Louis, and if he had been as eager to keep Eleanor as she implied he had been, he must have been very foolish to let her go. Louis would see reason if the case was presented to him in the right manner.

It was difficult for Henry to go to him and put the proposition before him. The man who had displaced him with Eleanor was hardly the one to come along with the proposition. He would send an emissary. He knew the very man. His Chancellor. He respected that man as he respected no other in his kingdom. He trusted Leicester and Richard de Luci, but Becket he admired and had a real affection for. Becket he often thought of as a man of genius. For a delicate matter such as this might prove to be, he was the man.

He would send for Becket and while he was in France he, Henry, would slip down to Woodstock where he was having a bower built in a wood, a haven where he planned to install his fair Rosamund and where their child should be born.

Henry never wasted time. As soon as the idea had come to him he sent for Chancellor Thomas Becket.

The Rise of Becket

It was not only the King who had a growing regard for
Thomas Becket. The Primate Theobald had recognized a
quality in the man from the moment he had come into his
service.

Thomas's origins were unusual. His father, Gilbert, had
belonged to a family of merchants whose home had been in
Rouen but after the Norman invasion, like so many of his
kind, he had seen greater prospects in England and had come
to settle in London.

During Gilbert's childhood he had lived in the village of
Thierceville and one of his childhood playmates had been a
certain Theobald who had always talked of his desire to go
into the Church. This he eventually did, by first entering a
monastery, and later as he rose to become Archbishop of
Canterbury the early friendship had some influence on the
life of Gilbert's son.

Gilbert prospered in the city of London and as he became
one of its leading citizens he kept open house for visiting
noblemen who were pleased to find a night or so's shelter
under his roof. There was no question of the house being an
inn, but favour was given for favour, and the fact that rich
and influential people were often entertained at his house
meant that he was not the loser and reaped rewards for his

hospitality, and with a son and two daughters Gilbert realized how beneficial this could be.

Gilbert himself was a romantic figure. Some years before the birth of his eldest child—his son Thomas—he had, like so many men of his times, decided to make a journey to the Holy Land and had set out with only one servant, a faithful man named Richard who had always served him well. After much tribulation and many hardships they reached their destination, had prayed at the tomb of Christ and feeling purged of their sins prepared to make their way back to England.

The homeward journey was to prove even more adventurous than the outward one and they had not gone very far when the party in which they travelled was surrounded by a company of Saracens, and Gilbert with Richard was taken prisoner.

It was unfortunate for him that he should have fallen into the hands of the Emir Amurath, who was said to be one of the cruellest men of his race. He enjoyed making Christians his slaves but when Gilbert and Richard were brought before him he was immediately struck by Gilbert's appearance. There was a nobility about the man which was apparent to one even as alien as Amurath and he could not help feeling interested in him.

His first impulse was to heap additional humiliations on him but the manner in which Gilbert conducted himself defeated him. Amurath was a lover of beauty of any kind and because of Gilbert's exceptional appearance he did not wish to maim it in any way. For a period he kept him chained in a dungeon and attempted to forget him. Gilbert's dignity had its effect on his jailers and he became friendly with them, learning their language, and because of his determination he did this quickly.

One day the Emir was looking for amusement and suddenly remembered the Christian slave. He doubted he was as handsome and indifferent now as he had been on his arrival. He sent for him.

To his amazement Gilbert could speak his language and the Emir was impressed when he heard that he had learned it from his jailers. Gilbert hastened to explain that his jailers had done nothing but their duty but he had always been quick to pick up the language of those about him and this was what had happened.

The Emir, in spite of his cruelty, was a man of some culture, and did not care how Gilbert had learned to converse in his language. All he cared was that he could. He asked a good many questions as to what his life was like in London and he was interested too in the doctrines of the Christian faith.

So entertained had Amurath been that the next day he sent for Gilbert once more and questioned him at greater length about the manners and customs of the Western world.

Gilbert was delighted to be released from his prison for these conversational exercises which were becoming a habit, and as the Emir was fastidious in his tastes he ordered that Gilbert should bathe and be given fresh robes. This was done, and now it seemed that they met as equals. A friendship was springing up between them and the Emir decided that he would prefer Gilbert not to be taken back to his cell but to be given quarters in his palace.

Gilbert then began to live the life of a Saracen nobleman. He still however felt himself to be a prisoner and never far from his mind was the thought of escape. In his new position he came into contact with other Christians of his party who now worked as slaves in the palace. Many of them were chained about their ankles just long enough to enable them to walk but not enough length to allow them to go far. Others had halters about their necks. The one thought that was in their minds was escape. And Gilbert, in spite of his favoured position, never forgot them and was in constant communication with them in the hope of forming some plan for their release.

The fact that he was so favoured was beneficial to them all, for Gilbert could discover a great deal about the geography of the palace and the most likely means of exit should the opportunity arise.

Moreover the Emir now and then took Gilbert out with him and they would ride side by side, surrounded by a guard, and so Gilbert learned a good deal about the country.

His fellow Christians knew that he was too religious a man to desert them. His recent absolution at the tomb had cleansed him of all sin, and he would not want to incur another even if it were his nature to do so, which they were sure it was not. He joined his fellows often in prayer and the great theme of those prayers, as must be the case with all prisoners, was that Divine guidance which led them to escape.

As the weeks passed the Emir's interest in his captive did not wane. The more fluent Gilbert became the more profound were the discussions, and one day as reward for such lively entertainments the Emir invited Gilbert to dine at his table.

This was to have a momentous effect on Gilbert's life because at the table were members of the Emir's family and among them his young daughter.

The girl was very beautiful; above her yashmak her enormous eyes studied Gilbert. He was different from any man she had ever seen. His fair skin fascinated her; his proud Norman bearing impressed her deeply. She had never seen anyone like him. She curbed her excitement for she knew that it would never do for her father to see it. What would happen she could not imagine—except that it could be disastrous for her and for Gilbert. She listened to his voice which was different from others as was everything else about him; and when the meal was over and the Christian and her father went away to sit and talk as the Emir loved to do, she retired to her apartments which she shared with the other women of the household and could think of nothing but the handsome Christian.

The Emir now made a habit of inviting Gilbert to his table and often his daughter was present. She was now in love with the strange captive, and she was certain that she would never know any happiness without him.

What could she do? She could not tell her father. She had lived the life of a girl of her people which meant that her life had been sheltered. Very soon a husband would be found for her and she would be given to him whether she liked it or not. She was a girl of great determination and she decided that she must learn more of this Christian faith for which these men of the Western world had left their comfortable homes and risked so much. She knew that Gilbert came from a place called London where he had a fine house. He had described it to her father in her presence. Yet he had left it to risk his life and perhaps face torture—for Gilbert had been singularly fortunate in falling into the hands of an enlightened man like Amurath—and all for the Christian faith.

Gilbert often went to pray in a small secluded chamber which the Emir had given him for that purpose; because he had become interested in the Christian religion through their discussions, he had no desire to put any impediment in the way of Gilbert's continuing to worship as he did at home.

Thus Gilbert was allowed an hour's seclusion where he might commune with God.

To his surprise when he entered one day he saw that the

rich arras which hung from the wall moved slightly and from behind it emerged the Emir's daughter.

Gilbert was amazed.

"I did not know any was here," said Gilbert. "I will go at once."

She shook her head. "Stay," she begged.

"It would not be permitted," said Gilbert preparing to depart.

Then she answered: "I would learn more of the Christian faith."

Gilbert looked at this beautiful girl and wanted to save her soul for Christianity.

"What would you know of my faith?" he asked.

"I would know why your face shines when you speak of your God. I would know why you have no fear of my father, why you talk with him and disagree with him as any other of his servants would not dare."

"I trust in my God," he answered. "If it is His will he will protect me. If my time has come I shall go to eternal salvation. That is why I have no fear."

"Tell me of eternal salvation."

He told her as it had been taught to him as a child.

"Could I become a Christian?" she asked.

"You could by believing."

"I could believe," she said.

"You would need instruction."

"You will instruct me?"

He looked round the apartment. "Your father would kill me if he found you here with me."

"But you are afraid."

"No, I am not afraid. Something tells me that it is God's will that I shall save your soul for Him."

"When you come to pray I shall be here," she said. "You will instruct me."

"Then so be it."

They knelt together and he taught her to pray.

And that was a beginning.

Each day when he came to the chamber she was there; she was progressing with her study of his religion. He told her that she must have a Christian name and she was delighted. He called her Mahault, a version of Matilda.

"That was the name of the wife of the greatest Norman who conquered England and brought a prosperity to both

192

that land and to the Normans like myself who now inhabit it," he told her.

She was delighted with her new name. She lived for her meetings with Gilbert. She was a fervent Christian. She took wholeheartedly to the doctrine of loving one's neighbour. Love was better than war. She could see that. People suffered continually for war and as a woman whose great joy in life would be her husband and children, how could she wish to lose them or see them suffer in that senseless preoccupation.

Indeed she was a fervent Christian.

Often Gilbert wondered what his fate would be if the Emir discovered that he had made his daughter into a Christian.

She would ply him with questions. "Christ died on the cross for you, would you die on the cross for him?"

He answered clearly: "I am ready to die for God."

"It is true," she said wonderingly, "for if my father knew that we had been together thus, he might devise a horrible death for you which is even more terrible than the crucifixion. Yet you have instructed me. You have made a Christian of me."

"I have brought you to the light, Mahault," he answered. "And if God wills that the fate which befell his only begotten Son should overtake me, then I trust I shall meet it with fortitude."

In worshipping Gilbert's God the Emir's daughter had come to worship Gilbert also.

She said one day: "The Christian slaves plan to escape. I know it."

"You cannot understand their tongue," replied Gilbert.

"No. But I see it in their eyes. They make their plans. They will attempt to go."

"Do you think they will succeed?"

"If they do not, I tremble for them. Nevertheless they will attempt it." She was fearful suddenly. "Gilbert, what of you? If they should try, would you go with them?"

"They are my people," he answered.

"If you should go, I would wish to go with you," she said.

"How could you do that, Mahault?"

"If the slaves could escape, so could I."

"Nay. You are your father's daughter. This is your home."

"I am a Christian now. My home is across the seas in your London."

"Nay," he said. "Nay that would never do."

"You could take me with you when you go away."

193

"How so?"

"You could marry me. I could be a good Christian and mother to your sons."

"That is not possible. You must not think of such matters."

"I cannot help my thoughts. The slaves are planning to escape. You will go with them and, Gilbert, I want to come too."

"You could never do it."

"Then when you go . . . must we say goodbye?"

"If I were to go, we must indeed."

"I never would," she said firmly. "I will come with you. When the slaves band together and go away from here . . . or try to . . . you will go with them, for you think of your native land and your home is in London. Gilbert, you cannot leave me here because if you did I should die. I could not live without you. You have saved my soul and you must take me with you."

He shook his head but she would not listen to his protests and he said no more of the matter.

There came a time when the long-formed plans were to be put into effect. Gilbert could arrange for horses to be waiting for them in the stables for several of the Christians were working there. They could cut their chains, and together discard their halters and get away . . . with Gilbert's help.

It was dangerous and Gilbert knew that if the attempt failed this would be an end of his pleasant relationship with the Emir. Dire and terrible torments would await them all. But so great was their longing for their native land that there was not a man among them who did not wish to make the attempt.

When he was with Mahault in his sanctuary, Gilbert was tempted to tell her of the plan for she could be of great use to them, but he hesitated. For himself he would have trusted her, but he had the lives of others to consider. He said nothing.

The appointed night came. In the stables the horses were saddled and ready. Gilbert had secreted implements there by which fetters could be cut. None was suspicious, and everything worked so smoothly and according to their plan that Gilbert was certain that God was with them.

Before their escape had been discovered they were miles from the Emir's palace and had reached a part of the country which was occupied by Christians. They joined with them and were able to proceed on the journey back to England.

When she heard that Gilbert had escaped with the other prisoners, Mahault was overcome with grief. True he had never promised to take her with him, but he had certainly cared for her. Had he not risked death and even more than death to save her soul? Had her father given his permission they would have married. But her father would never have consented to his daughter's marrying a Christian. How could he?

But she was a Christian, a fervent Christian, and she vowed she would never be anything else. But now she had lost Gilbert and there was nothing in life she wanted but him.

She longed for death, for that paradise which Gilbert had promised her. It was all that she could hope for.

So ill did she become that the Emir could not understand what ailed her. He was angry with the Christians who had escaped. He missed his discussions with Gilbert. Life had become dull without that man. He plunged into an orgy of pleasure, living the sort of life he had lived before the coming of Gilbert, but he found nothing could give him the same pleasure as he had enjoyed in his discussions with the Christian.

As she lay in her bed, an idea came to Mahault.

Gilbert had escaped. Why should not she? She had listened to his talk at table when he had given a graphic account of the journey he had made from London to the Holy Land. If he could make a journey to her country, why should she not do so to his?

As soon as this idea came to her, her health began to improve. She would lie in bed waiting for the return of her strength while she made her plans. She knew that what she was about to do was hazardous in the extreme; it was a task which no other Saracen girl had ever undertaken. But if she died in the attempt it would be no worse than waiting here in her father's palace until she pined away for lack of any wish to live.

"Faith can work miracles." That had been one of the doctrines of Gilbert's God who was now hers. Why should not faith work a miracle for her?

She grew well quickly; it was amazing what her faith and her belief in the certainty that she would find Gilbert did for her; and there came the day when she was ready.

She had sewn precious jewels into the humblest garments

she could find, for it was not difficult to get these from her servants, and one day she walked out of her father's palace.

The road was not often frequented between the borders of her father's territory and that which was occupied by Christians and taking greatest care to hide herself when any pilgrims did pass, in due course she reached the borders of the Christian country.

Good fortune favoured her for as she was crossing those borders she saw a group of people, and something told her from their looks and manners that they were Gilbert's countrymen and women.

She approached them and again she was lucky for one of them spoke her tongue. She told them the truth. She had become a Christian; she wished to escape to England where she could live according to her faith. But how could she get there?

"You could take ship," she was told.

"How could I do this?"

"Ships leave now and then," was the answer. "We ourselves are awaiting one."

"I could pay for my passage," she told them.

They considered her. Her great determination to succeed shone from her eyes; she begged them to help her. She must go to London, she said, for there lived a man she must find.

At length they agreed to take her. Her passage would be paid for with a sapphire of great beauty and in the meantime she might join their party.

She was not surprised at such amazing luck. She believed that as she had asked for a miracle God would answer her prayers, and it was only natural that her way should be made easy.

The journey was eventful as such journeys invariably were. They narrowly escaped being taken by pirates—which might well have resulted in her being sold into slavery to her own father—and then there was a mighty storm which almost wrecked the ship.

She believed that her shining faith brought her safely through and very soon they landed at Dover.

She knew two words in English: London and Gilbert. The first was of great use because it told everyone where she wanted to go.

She walked from the coast to the city, asking her way with the one word London and finally she was rewarded by her glimpse of London.

She would have been bewildered by the great city if she had not been certain that she was nearing the end of her quest. There was clamour such as she had never seen. In the streets were the market stalls, with goods of all variety displayed to the eyes. Everything that could be imagined was on sale there—bread, meat, clothing, milk, butter and cheeses, usually each with its separate neighbourhood. Milk and butter and cheeses were obtainable in Milk Street, and meat was for sale in Saint Martin le Grand near Saint Paul's Cross. There was Bread Street where the smell of fresh baked bread filled the air. Goldsmiths and silversmiths, clothiers and grocers, they all had their places in these lively streets.

At this time some forty thousand people lived in the city and its environs. People were attracted to the city because of its immense activities and the gayer lives that could be enjoyed there when compared with the quiet of the country. There were many churches, built by the Normans, and the sound of bells was a constant one. It was a bustling, teeming city situated on a river full of craft plying their way up and down; and the stream of the Wallbrook divided the East Cheap from the West.

Everywhere were beggars—some pitiful to behold—and into these streets came the Emir's daughter, certain because of her faith in the Christian God that she would be led to find Gilbert.

She went through the streets calling Gilbert and many took pity on her and gave her a night's shelter; and each day she was sure that she would find the man she had come to seek.

*   *   *

Gilbert had reached London some months earlier. He had resumed his business and as before kept open house for visiting friends. One of these, a Norman knight named Richer de L'Aigle, a man of some culture, owned an estate in the country.

Richer always enjoyed his visits to London, largely because it meant a pleasant evening or two spent with his old friend Gilbert Becket. They would talk into the night and discuss many subjects before Gilbert lighted his old friend to bed with a waxen candle.

Richer had heard of Gilbert's adventures in the Emir's palace and was always interested to talk about them. Gilbert's servant Richard, who had been at his master's side through all that had happened, had also many a tale to tell of those adventures to his fellow-servants.

When Gilbert was telling Richer more details of how he had made the escape which would have seemed impossible, he added that he believed only Divine help had brought them home.

"During that perilous journey," he said, "I made a vow that if I could reach home safely once more I would pay another visit to the Holy Land within ten years."

"So you will be going again. Do not expect the same luck next time."

"I shall wait for God to show me His will," said Gilbert solemnly, "and whatever it may be I shall accept it."

"Still, perhaps it is tempting Providence when you consider you have done it once and come safely through. Think of all those who are lost on the way."

They were talking thus when Richard burst in upon them.

"Master," he stammered. "I have seen . . . I have seen . . ."

"Come Richard, what have you seen?" asked Gilbert.

"A ghost it appears," put in Richer.

"No, masters. I have seen the Emir's daughter."

"What?" cried Gilbert.

"I had heard that a strange woman was in the street. She was calling 'Gilbert'. Just 'Gilbert' again and again. I went to look at her. An apprentice told me she was close by and there she was."

"The Emir's daughter, Richard. You are mistaken."

"Nay, master. I was not, for she saw me and she cried aloud with joy, for she knew me. She remembered me in her father's palace."

Gilbert had risen to his feet.

"You must take me to her."

"She is here, master. She followed me."

Gilbert hurried from the room and there standing in his doorway was Mahault. When she saw him she gave a cry of joy and fell on her knees before him.

He lifted her; he looked into her face and he spoke to her in her own tongue which she had not heard for so long.

"You came . . . so far."

"God guided me," she said simply.

"So . . . you hoped to find me."

"I knew I should, if it were His will and it is."

Richer de L'Aigle looked on at the scene with amazement

as Gilbert called for his servants to prepare hot food. She must be hungry, he said, and she was footsore and weary.

She laughed and wept with happiness. A miracle had brought her across terrifying land and sea to Gilbert.

He considered her. She was beautiful, young and ardent. She loved the Christian faith almost as much as she loved Gilbert. She was a living example of a soul that was saved.

He could not keep her in his house. That was something the proprieties would not allow and Gilbert did not know what he could do with her. There was a good and sober widow who lived close by and to whom he had been able to do some favour. He went to her, told her of his predicament and asked if she would take the strange young woman under her care until something could be settled. This she agreed to do, and Gilbert conducted her to the widow's house where he told her she must wait awhile.

Gilbert had friends in the Church and he decided to ask the advice of some of its members as to what he could do. There was in London at the time a gathering of the Bishops presided over by the Bishop of London, and since the Emir's daughter was an Infidel and would be so until she was baptized, the answer to his predicament could well come from the Church.

Before the Bishops, Gilbert related his adventure, and the Bishop of Chichester rose suddenly and spoke as though he were in a dream. He said: "It is the hand of God and not of man which has brought this woman from so far a country. She will bear a son whose labours and sanctity will turn to the profit of the Church and the glory of God."

These were strange words, for Gilbert had not mentioned the thought of marrying her—although it had entered his head. They sounded like a prophecy. Gilbert was then filled with a desire to marry the Emir's daughter and have a son by her.

"It would be necessary," said the Bishop of London, "for her to be baptized. If she agrees to this then you should marry her."

Gilbert went to Mahault and told her this. Her eyes sparkled with happiness. Most joyfully would she be baptized. She had come to England for this—and to marry Gilbert.

So they were married and very soon she became pregnant. She was certain that she would bear a son who was destined for greatness.

Thus before Thomas was born he had made his impact on the world.

* * *

The daughter of the Emir, now baptized as Mahault, was the most devout of Christians. She was the happiest of women for God had shown her a miracle. She had asked and had been given. She was the wife of Gilbert, a fact which would have seemed impossible while she was in her father's palace. Here it was the most natural thing in the world. Surely a miracle.

And when very soon after the marriage she was pregnant, she was certain that she was going to have a son. The Bishop of Chichester had prophesied this. God had brought her through great difficulties; she had made a journey which many would have said was impossible; she had come to a strange country knowing only two words: "London" and "Gilbert". The first was easy to find; and God had brought her to the second.

She began to have visions. Her son was going to be a great man. It was to bear this son that God had brought her here. She dreamed of him; always she saw him in those dreams surrounded by a soft light. He would be a Christian and his life would be dedicated to God. It seemed likely that he would be a man of the Church and the highest office in the Church was that of an Archbishop.

"I know my son will be an Archbishop," she said.

Gilbert was uneasy. He was no longer a man who could go where he would. He had a wife and soon he would have a child.

She sensed his fears and asked him what ailed him. He told her then that he had made a vow to God that if he arrived home safely, he would visit the Holy Land again and he feared that now he had such responsibilities he would be unable to keep his promise to God.

She smiled at him. "You have made a promise to God," she said, "and that promise must be kept. Do not think of me. If Richard remains with me, as he speaks my tongue, I shall be well enough; and soon I shall speak English, for I must do so since I am to care for my son."

In due course her child was born. It was a boy, as she had known it would be, and when the midwife held him in her arms, Mahault heard a voice say, "It is an Archbishop we are holding."

She could not ask the midwife what she meant by that because she could not make herself understood, but later she asked Gilbert to find out why the woman had made such a remark. The midwife's answer was that she had said no such thing.

*　　*　　*

The boy was called Thomas and he was the delight of his mother's life. She was sure that nothing was too good for him. His education must be of the best. In the meantime since Gilbert had made his promise to God he should keep it without delay for when the boy grew older he would need a father more than he did when he was too young to recognize him.

So Gilbert went off to the Holy Land once more and Mahault devoted herself to looking after her son and learning English.

Her premonitions as to his future greatness continued. One night she dreamed that the nurse had left the baby without a quilt in his cradle and when she reproved her, the nurse replied: "But my lady, he is covered with a beautiful quilt." "Bring it to me here," she had answered, thinking to prove that the nurse was deceiving her. The nurse came with a large quilt of a beautiful crimson cloth. She put it on her mistress's bed and attempted to unfold it, but the more she unfolded the larger it grew, and they took it to the largest room in the house because it was too big to fold in a smaller one. Nor could it be unfolded there so they took it into the street. But they could not unfold it because the more they tried to the bigger the quilt grew, and suddenly it began to unfold itself and covered the street and houses around them, and went on and on, and they knew it had reached the end of the land.

She awoke from this dream with the certainty that it had especial significance, which was that her son Thomas was destined for greatness.

Because she could not be thankful enough to the God of her new religion who had brought her safely to London that she might bear this son, she would have him weighed often and give to the poor a weight of clothes or food equal to that of the boy.

She would talk to him of the need to be good and serve God and how this could best be done by caring for others.

"Always help those poorer than yourself, my little one," she would say. "That is a good way to serve God."

Gilbert returned after three and a half years to find that at the age of four, young Thomas was already showing signs of great intelligence. Gilbert was glad to be home; he would make no more vows. Two trips to the Holy Land should be enough to placate his Maker for he had never been guilty of anything but the most venial sins.

He soon became as certain as Mahault was that there was something special about their son.

In the next few years they had two more children. These were daughters, good bright pleasant girls, but Thomas was apart from them. Sir Richer de L'Aigle had become an even more frequent visitor than he had been in the past. He had been fascinated by the account of Mahault's determination to find Gilbert; he declared he would not have believed it possible for a young woman to find her way with nothing more to guide her than two words. He was of the opinion that only Divine providence could have brought her to Gilbert and his interest in their unusual son grew.

As soon as Thomas was old enough his father put him in the care of the Canons of Merton to whom many well-born people sent the sons they hoped would enter the Church.

"This would be but a beginning," Gilbert confided to his wife. "Afterwards Thomas must attend one of the great seats of learning, but Merton is a good beginning and it would mean that he was not too far from us."

At Merton Thomas was soon surprising his teachers by his ability to learn and so confirming his parents' certainty that he was destined for a great future. It so happened that during harvest time when the great concern was to bring in the corn, the pupils of Merton were sent to their homes to get them out of the way, and during one summer Richer de L'Aigle happened to call on the Beckets. Finding Thomas there, home from school, he suggested that he take him with him to his residence at Pevensey Castle and there instil into him the gracious art of living like a nobleman. Thomas took to the life with as much eagerness as he had taken to learning.

Richer instructed him how to ride like a knight, how to hunt with a falcon and all the accomplishments which could not have been acquired in his London home.

So successful was this stay at Pevensey Castle and so fond

had the young knight grown of Thomas that the invitation was repeated often. Mahault was delighted; she saw the change in her son. He had become fastidious in his dress; he spoke not only like a scholar but like a gentleman and she believed that God had sent Richer de L'Aigle into their lives that Thomas might be groomed to take one of the highest positions in the country.

When Thomas was sufficiently educated to have earned his own living doing clerical work for a merchant of London, he left Merton but his parents had plans for him. The centre of learning was said to be in Paris and no other place would be good enough for Thomas. So to Paris went Thomas.

There he perfected his knowledge of the French language, his great aim being to speak it as a Frenchman; his easy manners—learned at Pevensey Castle—enabled him to mingle with members of high society and he found he had a taste for their company. No one would have guessed that the elegant Thomas was the son of a merchant; and Thomas's great ambition at this time was to play a brilliant part in the world where he gained the respect of men and women and lived in comfort and luxury.

When he returned to London he had the manners of a nobleman although he was educated far beyond most of them; and although she clung to her belief in the dreams and portents which she swore had come to her, even his mother had to admit that Thomas appeared to have no inclination towards the Church. Instead he became interested in business and joined the municipal administration of London. Here his alert mind immediately called attention to him and many rich merchants who were friends of his father sought to get him to join them in the management of their businesses.

Mahault was not dismayed, so certain was she of his destiny. For several years she had suffered during the winter from a persistent cough, and the damp mist of the river after the dry sunny climate of her native land was having an ever-worsening effect upon her health. Strangely enough one of her daughters showed a desire for the religious life and was found a place in a convent at Barking; the other married a London merchant. They were happily settled; the only one not was Thomas. That would come, she was convinced. So great was his destiny that he must have experience of many ways of life before he realized it.

He was twenty when Mahault died. He was with her at the end and on his knees told her of his love and gratitude. She lay smiling at him thinking of the day she had first seen Gilbert and had loved him and his God. She would not have had it otherwise, for she believed that everything that had happened to her had been but a preparation for Thomas.

"God has chosen you, my son," she said, her eyes glowing with prophecy. "I was brought out of my native land that I might give birth to you."

And so convincing was she that Thomas believed her; and afterwards in his most trying moments he would remember the conviction in the eyes of his dying mother and a belief in himself would come to him, a belief which refused to accept failure.

Mahault's death was the first blow. Without her the household was a dull one. Gilbert seemed to lose heart in his business; Thomas was desolate. He no longer took pleasure in following the pursuits he had learned at Pevensey Castle. He knew that he had delighted too much in being on equal terms with the rich and well-born. He could think of little but the loss his mother's passing had made in his life, and he reproached himself that he had not realized what she meant to him until he had lost her.

A fearful disaster struck Gilbert when his house and business premises were burned to the ground. Once a blaze started in the wooden structure there was little hope of stemming it. His losses were great. The shock of this in addition to his wife's death had a deep effect on Gilbert. He had lost too much, and with it the will to rebuild his business. Within a few months he was dead.

Thomas was alone.

He became melancholy. He gave up hunting and staying at the houses of his friends who in the past had delighted in his company. It seemed that he was adopting the life of a recluse when Theobald the Archbishop of Canterbury asked him to visit him.

Theobald, who had played with Gilbert when they lived in their Norman village, had heard of Gilbert's death and wished to renew his acquaintance with Gilbert's son.

They met, and there was an immediate affection between them. Theobald was lonely in his high office and saw in Thomas the son he had never had.

To Theobald, Thomas could talk of his parents and Theobald listened intently. Their minds were in tune. When Thomas visited the Archbishop, Theobald was always loath to let him go and the visits became more and more frequent.

Then one day Theobald said: "Thomas, come into my household. There is much work for you to do. I need someone who will work with me, who will be close to me, whom I can trust."

Thomas hesitated. "Should I be starting out on a career in the Church?" he asked.

"Why should you not? You are fitted for it. Come, Thomas. Think of this."

For some time Thomas considered. Whither was he going? He knew that till now he had been marking time. He thought of his mother's dreams of the Archbishop's quilt and he knew that he must go to Theobald.

So when he was twenty-five years of age Thomas Becket joined the household of the Archbishop of Canterbury.

*   *   *

The Archbishop's palace was a manor house situated at Harrow on the Hill. Here he lived in a state which befitted his position. His power was great. He was more than head of the Church; he had the power to select certain officials of State; and his authority was only second to that of the King. Theobald was rich, for he possessed many castles and manors throughout the country, and from all over the world distinguished men came to visit him.

Thomas, after the years he had spent working in municipal affairs and in a merchant's counting-house, was amazed at the life into which he felt he had been thrust, and he realized that he had much to learn if he were to take his place in it.

Theobald had a special interest in him and was certain that in a few years' time Thomas would be ready for a high office. At the time of his arrival, however, he lacked the learning of the clerics in the Archbishop's household and immediately set about remedying that. His innate elegance, his perfect manners, the purity of his existence and his dedication to learning soon won the admiration of the Archbishop and those who wished him well, but ambitious young men in the Archbishop's household were beginning to regard Thomas with envious eyes.

Why should Thomas Becket be specially favoured by the Archbishop? Who was Thomas Becket? The son of a merchant! And what was that rumour about a Saracen woman? Was this merchant's son, this clerk, going to be put above them? There was no doubt that this young man among all those whom he gathered together in his household in order that they should be prepared to play their part in the Church, was his favourite.

In the evenings when it was too dark to read or study they would gather about the Archbishop's table and there talk of matters temporal and spiritual. The Archbishop was deeply concerned with matters of State and as there had been continual strife in the country since the death of Henry I, politics were discussed at great length; and it was invariably the enormously tall dark-haired man whose comments impressed the company. It was clear to everyone that he was an unusual man. His very appearance set him apart. He was so tall that there was not a man in the palace who came within four inches of him. With his commanding presence he would dominate any scene. No one could have looked less like a man of the Church. His dark eyes inherited from his mother were keen and bright; his big nose was almost hawklike. His frame was spare for he ate very little and consequently he felt the cold and had to wear many garments. His servant Richard who had come with him from his father's house made sure that the little he ate was very nourishing, and he would cook beef and chicken for him. He feared Thomas might become ill, and since he ate so little he must derive the ultimate goodness from what he did.

This was Thomas Becket then, a man who could not fail to be noticed; a man, it was said, of comparatively humble origins whose manners surpassed those of the most nobly born; a man who was aesthetic and fastidious; a man who loved to ride and take part in the pleasures of hawking and yet spent long hours on his knees. He had never been known to cast lustful eyes on any member of the opposite or his own sex.

There was no doubt that Thomas was a very extraordinary man. The Archbishop thought so and watching him closely marked him for promotion, although this would mean setting him above others who were more conventionally suitable.

Among those who were studying with Thomas under the tuition of the Archbishop was a very clever young man named Roger de Pont l'Evêque. He had been the brightest of all Theobald's pupils until Thomas had come. He was destined for the highest posts; he was an expert on canon law and before Thomas had eclipsed him had been a great favourite with the Archbishop.

Roger was both arrogant and sensual, and he hated Thomas not only for his brilliance as a scholar but for the fact that he could not be lured into any adventure which could have discredited him in the eyes of Theobald.

Roger himself had had a very narrow escape. His career as a churchman of high rank might have been irrevocably ruined. The story was that Roger had become enamoured of a very handsome boy whom he had forced to submit to his lust. The boy, Walter, had complained of this and Roger was brought to trial. Roger was a man of power with many influential friends and by means of bribery and threats had won his case against the boy who in his turn was accused of lying and attempting to bring into disrepute a highly respected member of the Church. The bribed judge found that the boy was guilty; his eyes were put out and he was hanged.

Roger had escaped the consequences of his ill-doing and had managed to deceive many—including the Archbishop—into believing in his innocence, but among others he was suspect. He even admitted to a few—in secret—that he had brought disgrace and contempt on the Church.

Roger was the chief of Thomas's enemies, and he determined to get him removed from the Archbishop's palace. But Thomas was fortunate in the fact that Theobald's brother Walter, who was Archdeacon of Canterbury, had a faith in his ability which nothing could shake, and which was even greater than that which Theobald had for him.

Roger, by reason of his undeniable brilliance, was at this time the leading scholar at Harrow and at the head of the line for promotion, which meant that he was closer to the Archbishop than any of the others. By cleverly pointing out the unusual traits in Thomas's character he contrived to convince Theobald that, clever as Thomas might be, he was not of the kind of succeed in the Church.

Theobald considered this and for a time banished Thomas from his palace. The Archbishop's brother Walter, however, took Thomas into his home and kept him there for a while until he could persuade Theobald to take Thomas back. This was an indication of what a powerful enemy Thomas had in Roger, as he was banished on two occasions and was obliged to stay with Walter until the time when Theobald could be persuaded to ask him to return.

When Walter became Bishop of Rochester, Roger received the appointment for which he was waiting and he became Archdeacon of Canterbury.

With Roger in such a post this could have meant the end of Thomas's ambitions, but by this time he was so firmly established in Theobald's regard that nothing could dislodge him. He was then constantly in the company of the Archbishop. When Theobald was at odds with the Crown and was temporarily exiled, Thomas accompanied him to France.

There came the time when King Stephen died and Henry Plantagenet ascended the throne. In the year 1154 Roger became Archbishop of York which meant that the post of Archdeacon of Canterbury was vacant. It seemed to Theobald then that no one could fit this post better than Thomas Becket.

*　　*　　*

That Henry had the makings of a great king was obvious to all, but at the same time he was a man of such violent passion that Theobald felt disturbed. To hold in check such a man was going to be rather like taming a wild horse and it was clear that the King was of a temper to brook no restraint.

It had in the past been almost a habit with kings to quarrel with the Church. Theobald who had now and then been in disagreement with Stephen realized that it would be a very different matter to resist the wishes of Henry.

Theobald discussed the matter with Henry, Bishop of Winchester, brother of King Stephen, and one of the most powerful churchmen in the country.

"The King," said Henry of Winchester, "needs to be held in check and in such a manner that he will not realize that the reins which control him are there. Only the right sort of Chancellor could manage this. We must find the right man. If we do not I see great trouble between the Church and State and we shall find that Henry Plantagenet is not the mild man my brother Stephen was."

"That's true," said Theobald. "What we need is a man who can be a friend to the King, who can persuade him subtly so that he will not know he is persuaded."

"Do you know such a man?" asked Henry of Winchester.

Theobald was thoughtful; then a slow smile spread across his face. "Yes, I think I do. There is my Archdeacon, Thomas Becket."

"Becket," mused the Bishop. "A man of humble origins."

"A man who has risen above his origins. You would not find a man in all England who could please the King better."

"I fancy the King is not over-fond of those of our profession."

208

"Becket is unlike the rest of us. I have often felt I should reprove him for his worldliness and yet I know he is the least worldly of men. He keeps a good table, yes, but that is for others; he himself eats most frugally. His clothes are elegance itself and he keeps his hawks, dogs and horses; but he gives lavishly to the poor. He is the man. He could meet the King on his own level. He could make sport with him and hunt with him; and the King has moments when he likes good conversation; he would have his fill of that with Becket. Becket is the man. A man of the Church who is yet a man of the world."

The Bishop was inclined to be dubious but after he had spent a little time with Thomas he came to the view that the best thing for England and the Church would be to make Thomas Becket its Chancellor.

* * *

Thus at the age of thirty-five Thomas was raised to this high office. He was delighted with his new status, not because of the honours it brought him but because there was so much in the country that he could put right.

For some years now the civil war had been over but during it many men who had lost their castles or humbler homes had been driven to the forest where they became outlaws and robbers. The Chancellor was determined that these men should be hunted down and that the roads might be safe as they had been in the days of William the Conqueror and his son Henry I; he was anxious that the fields should be tilled as they had been before the beginning of the war. He wanted to bring back justice to the courts; he encouraged those who considered themselves ill done by to bring their grievances to him.

Any good man determined to bring justice to England could have done this, but there was something more Thomas could do. He could charm the King. Theobald had told him that it was because it was believed he had the power to do this that he had been chosen for this task. He could be amusing, witty and entertaining; and it was his duty to amuse the King. By becoming an intimate friend of the King he would understand his moods; he could guide him without the King's knowing he was being guided. He was enough of a courtier to be perfectly at home in royal society; he had learned riding, hawking and chess at Pevensey Castle, so he was at ease in the King's circle. None would know that he had not had the same upbringing as any of the King's courtiers and the King himself for that matter. It was for this reason that he had been chosen.

It was remarkably easy.

"Bring this churchman to me," Henry had said, "that I may tell him I'll not have any churchman preach to me."

But when he saw the man he was amazed. That strange quality which commanded the respect of all men was immediately apparent to the King. This tall elegant man who could be witty and amusing, who could ride beside him talking of frivolous Court matters, who could with the same ease plunge into a serious conversation such as enthralled Henry, aroused his interest to such an extent that often when he was at a gathering he would look about him and say: "Where's Becket? Where's my Chancellor?" And when Thomas was brought to him he would laugh at him and say, "Ha, Becket, I missed you. Let us escape and go off together where we can talk."

Theobald and Henry of Winchester watched the growing friendship of the two and congratulated themselves on the wisdom of that plan of theirs to set up Thomas Becket as Chancellor so that he might influence the King.

Henry was delighted. One of Thomas's first acts was to refurbish the King's Palace in the Tower of London.

Henry liked the work that was done there. "Why Becket," he said, "I should have thought as a churchman you would have thought of succouring the poor rather than pampering their King."

"A pampered King is more likely to pamper his poor subjects than one who is so ill housed that his temper is frayed," answered Thomas.

"His temper frays, Becket, well housed or not."

"Since he admits this doubtless time and the help of God will improve it."

"That fellow makes me laugh," said Henry of his Chancellor and he saw more and more of Thomas. He showed clearly that he liked his company.

Thomas had not been a Chancellor a year when Henry declared: "I never thought to make a friend of a churchman, but I swear this man seems to be the best friend I ever had."

He would call on him without warning. He would shout: "Come out, Becket. I'd have speech with you."

Sometimes he sat and drank wine with him. It amused him

that Becket with a sip or two could tell the quality of wine and talk of it, but rarely drank much himself.

Henry liked to plague him while he admired him.

"A churchman," he would say, "yet you live like a king."

"Rather say a king lives like a churchman."

Every day fresh rushes were strewn on his floors; he used green boughs in summer and hay in winter; but it must always be fresh.

"Your cleanliness is greater than your godliness," pointed out the King.

"Why should not the two go hand in hand, Sire?" asked Becket.

"Is it meet for a man of God to display fine gold and silver plate on his table?"

"If he puts them there for love of his friends," answered Becket.

The King would put an arm about the Chancellor's shoulders. "One of these days I will show you for the coxcomb you are," he mocked. "Look at your table; look at your home! Should you not go out into the world with rod and scrip and preach religion?"

"I go out with the rod of my office and preach of justice," replied Thomas.

"Good Thomas, you amuse me and for that I would forgive you all your sins."

"Let us hope, sir, that that other King who alone can pardon our sins is as lenient with you."

And so they grew closer together and hardly a day passed when Becket was not in the company of the King.

The Abbess Bride

While Eleanor was awaiting the birth of her child in the palace and Rosamund was at Woodstock also awaiting the King's child, Henry sent for Becket as he wished to discuss the proposed marriage between his son Henry and the little Princess of France.

He was as usual delighted to see the Chancellor.

"I know not how you will find the French King," said Henry. "As you know the Queen was his wife and she rid herself of him to marry me."

"I know it well," said Becket.

"He was somewhat jealous I believe, and loath to let the Queen go, but the Queen was determined. She's a determined woman as you know also, Chancellor."

"I had gathered so," answered Thomas.

"Now this methinks is a situation which will appeal to your humour as it appeals to mine. My son and the Queen's son Henry shall be the bridegroom of Louis's daughter by his second marriage. Do you think that is not an amusing situation?"

"I think it a very suitable one, my lord, since it will secure alliance with the King of France and little could be more beneficial to you at this time."

"So thought I," said the King. "It is years before the

marriage can take place. My son is three years old. The Princess Marguerite is one. But that will be no impediment to the ceremony as it would be to the consummation. We shall not put the babies to bed together . . . yet."

"I should think not."

"Poor innocents! Still it is the lot of royal children. You should be thankful, Chancellor, that you were not a royal boy or they might have married you when you were in your cradle and that would not have been to your liking, would it."

"I have never had any fancy for the marriage bond."

"Nay, you're a strange man, Becket. You care nothing for women which seems strange to a man like myself who cares very much for them. You know not what you miss. It is a taste which never wearies. It is only that one wishes now and then to change one's partner in the game."

"The Queen would not wish to hear such sentiments expressed."

"You are right, Becket. My Queen is a woman of strong opinions. You will have to mind your step with her . . . as even I do."

"The Queen is one who is accustomed to being obeyed."

"Indeed you speak the truth. I have managed very well during our life together. I always contrive to see that she is either going to have a child or having one. It is a very good way of curbing her desire to rule."

"It is not one which can continue for ever."

"As the Queen tells me. She says when this one is born there must be a respite."

"It is better for her health that this should be so."

"I am expecting a child in another quarter, Becket."

"I grieve to hear it, Sire."

The King burst into loud laughter and slapped Becket on the back.

"You know full well that a king who cannot get heirs is a curse to the nation."

"I know it is well for a king to get legitimate heirs."

"My grandfather used to say that it is well for a king to have children—inside and outside wedlock, for those who are of royal blood will be loyal to it."

"It is not an infallible recipe for loyalty, sir."

"Oh come, Becket, you are determined to reproach me. I won't have it. Do you hear me?"

"I hear very well, my lord."

"Then take heed for if you offend me I could turn you from your office."

"My lord must turn me from it if he will and I shall pray that he finds another to serve him as well as I should."

"I never would, Thomas. I know it and for this I will stomach a little of your preaching. But not too much, man. Remember it."

"I will remember, my lord."

"You have seen my fair Rosamund, Becket. Is she not beautiful? More so in her present state than when I first saw her. It surprises me that my feeling for her does not pall. I love the girl, Becket. You are silent. Why do you stand there with that smug expression on your face? How dare you judge me, Thomas Becket! Are you my keeper?"

"I am your Chancellor, my lord."

"Not for long . . . if I wish it. Remember that, Becket. And if you are going to tell me that I should give up Rosamund I am going to fall into a temper, and you know my tempers, Thomas."

"I know them well, Sire."

"They are not pleasant to behold, I believe."

"There you speak truth, my lord."

"Then it would be well for those around me not to provoke them. I have settled her at Woodstock and I am having a bower built there. A house in the forest . . . surrounded by a maze of which only I shall know the secret. What you think of that?"

"That it is a plan worthy of you, my lord."

The King narrowed his eyes and laughed again.

"You amuse me, Thomas," he said. "You stand in judgement. You reproach me. You disapprove of me, but you amuse me. For some reason I have chosen to make you my friend."

"I am also your Chancellor, Sire," said Becket. "Shall we discuss the mission to France?"

*　　*　　*

For such a mission Thomas could display great magnificence without any feeling of shame. All the scarlet and gold trappings which he so much enjoyed could be brought into play without any feeling of guilt on his part because what he was doing now was for the glory of England. He could not go into

France like a pauper. During his journey he must impress all who beheld him with the might and splendour of England.

A troop of soldiers accompanied the procession, besides butlers and stewards and other servants of the household; there were members of the nobility who were to form part of the embassy, and of his own household he took two hundred horsemen. He had brought dogs and birds as well as twelve packhorses with their grooms, and on the back of each horse sat a long-tailed ape. The procession was followed by wagons which carried Thomas's clothes and others in which were stored the garments of the rest of the party with gifts which would be judicially distributed at the Court of France. And after these were larger wagons one of which was furnished as a chapel for Thomas's use, and another for his bedchamber. In yet another were utensils for cooking so that the party could stop wherever was deemed desirable.

As this magnificent cavalcade—the like of which had never been seen before—passed through France, people came out of their houses to watch it.

"What manner of man can the King of England be?" they asked each other. "He must be the richest man in the world since this man, who is only his Chancellor and servant, travels in such state."

News was brought to Louis that the Chancellor was on his way and that the magnificence of his retinue had startled everyone who had seen it. Determined not to be outdone he gave orders that when the party arrived in Paris no merchant was to sell his goods to any member of the English party. France was to be host to the English and they must have what they would and there should be no question of their paying.

Thomas guessed that this might be the King's wish and in order not to put himself under any obligation which might be detrimental to his mission—he sent his servants out secretly to buy any provisions they would need. He did however accept lodgings at the Temple. There he kept a sumptuous table of which all who came to see him were invited to partake.

In the face of such extravagance the French could only retaliate in kind. They must not be made to look less hospitable, less elegant, less generous than the English.

Louis received Thomas with every honour. How could he refuse the hand of his daughter to the son of a king who came to him in such a manner.

215

He had at first been uneasy. His little daughter Marguerite was but a year old. Poor child, how innocent she was, unaware as yet as to what this mission meant! She would in time go to the English Court there to be brought up as the bride of Henry who would, if all went well, become the King of England with little Marguerite that country's Queen.

Louis still thought of Eleanor and that state of passion to which she had introduced him. He feared he would never forget her and even now he was reminded of how she had left him, and almost immediately her divorce was secured had married Henry Plantagenet whose mistress she had already been.

And now Eleanor's son by another man, and his daughter by another woman . . .

It was an unconventional situation, but such there would always be with a woman like Eleanor. He wondered whether she often thought of him.

But that was a question he could not ask the King's Chancellor. He must agree with his ministers that it was an alliance destined to bring good to both countries. It should ensure peace between them and peace was what the people desired more than anything.

The Chancellor in his magnificence had delighted the people of France. Louis made no objections to the proposed match. In fact he welcomed it.

Thomas was well pleased. This important mission had been achieved with the utmost success.

*   *   *

In the miniature palace close to his own at Woodstock the King visited Rosamund Clifford. He was delighted with the dwelling he had built for her. He called it Rosamund's Bower. It was a fairy house and here she could live secluded while the royal party was in residence at the palace, and he could slip away to be with her with the utmost ease. It had amused him to create a maze of which only he, Rosamund and those who served her, should have the secret. He had not even confided the secret to Thomas. He was not entirely sure of Thomas. He could not understand a man who was not interested in sexual pleasure with women. There were times when he suspected Thomas of indulging in secret what other men talked of openly. He always hoped that one of these days he would catch Thomas. The thought amused him. He often thought what pleasure it would have been for him if he and Thomas could have gone out adventuring together. The fact was there was no man's company he enjoyed more. Thomas's love of extravagance was greater than his own for he was a plain man and hated wearing the garments of royalty. In fact he had, at the Easter church ceremonies, laid his crown on the altar and swore that he would never wear it again.

"There it stands," he had said, "as the Sovereign's symbol. That symbol loses nothing because it stands in a place as well guarded as it is on my head. Let no man mistake me. I am the King. But I do not need a crown to make me so. I stand here, your King by right of birth and on the throne I shall remain, but I can serve my country better by making just laws and defending it from all who would subdue it, by the power of my strong arm and wisdom of mind and these can work better when not hampered by a crown on my head."

There he stood, this man who was neither tall nor short, whose hands were chapped with the wind; his tunic short that he might the easier move about, with his unbounded energy, his fierce temper which was terrifying to behold and his complete kingliness. He was right. He did not need a crown to proclaim him King of England. No man could look at him and doubt it.

And yet he came secretly to Woodstock. In his heart he knew it was due to his tenderness for Rosamund. He wanted no harm to befall her. He wanted to keep her the pure and innocent girl she was—the complete contrast to Eleanor. Perhaps he was a little afraid of Eleanor. He would not admit that fear. Yet she could be a scheming woman and he could not be sure what revenge she would take on him.

It was because of Eleanor that he wished to keep his liaison with Rosamund secret.

He found her feeding the swans on the lake before the little palace.

She stood up with a cry of pleasure when she saw him. She was noticeably pregnant and it occurred to him again that she was even more beautiful than when he had first seen her. There was a serenity about her countenance. She had already the motherly look.

He took her hands and kissed them. "So my Rose is glad to see her King."

She nodded as though her emotion at beholding him were so great she could not trust herself to speak.

Ashamed of his own feelings he touched her stomach jocularly. "And the boy?"

"He fares well. But what if it should be a girl? I trust you will not be displeased."

"Nay, nay," he said, "I'll forgive her if she has one tenth of the charm and beauty of her mother."

Arms about each other they went into the house.

There he stayed for the night. It was idyllic, there to live like a simple man. He did not delude himself into wishing that he had been born to such a life. He was too enamoured of his kingship, but it was pleasant for a spell to live simply under the adoring eyes of a beloved mistress.

Thomas should see me now, he thought. Perhaps he would try to explain his feelings to Thomas.

No, no. Not even Thomas. No one should know how this beautiful innocent girl affected him.

The child would soon be born and she was to have the best attention.

"When I return from France I'll come and see the child," he told her.

The thought of his departure to France always upset her. She visualized all kinds of dangers. She begged of him to take care.

He laughed at her, but tenderly. How could a king take care?

"It's a peaceful mission. I go to see Louis to make terms for the marriage of my son and his daughter. He has already agreed. My good Chancellor got his agreement and I go to seal the alliance and bring the child away with me, for if she is to marry my son she must be brought up in my kingdom."

"Poor child! Poor mother!"

"Ah, Rosamund, be thankful that you are not a royal mother. How much happier you will be with your child in your little bower awaiting the arrival of your lord and master. And I swear to you that he will come to you whenever it is possible for him to do so and this child you carry shall have great honours and never regret, if I can help it, the day the King set eyes on the fairest Rose in all the world."

He left her content with her lot; her only anxiety what dangers he might face across the sea.

What joy to be with one whose love was selfless, who asked nothing, no honours—except perhaps for their child—nothing for herself! She prayed not for herself but for him and the child.

218

He thought: Had she been my wife, I would have been a happier man.

*　　*　　*

How different was Eleanor. He would be going to France and she must perforce stay in England because she was once more with child.

"I promise you," she raved, "there shall be no more of this. Since I married you it has been one child after another."

"You have a fine nursery full, my Queen," said Henry. "There are many queens who have prayed and made their pilgrimages in the hope of getting *one* son. You have two and who knows the next which I have kindly implanted in you may well be another boy. Think of it. Three boys in your nursery!"

"Not to mention the little bastard you have brought to us."

"Young Geoffrey. How fares he?"

"I do not make it my concern to discover."

"You're a jealous woman, Eleanor."

She did not answer. She would never forgive him for that bastard son. While she had been in love with him—and thought constantly of him—he had been sporting with other women and cared so much for this one it seemed that when she produced a child he brought it into the nursery.

"What would I not give to be crossing the sea with you."

"I am flattered that you so much enjoy my company."

"It is not you I wish to be with," she said. "I wish to see my own fair land of Aquitaine."

"That you might sit in the gardens and surround yourself with soft-eyed singers who laud your charms and pretend to be in love with you?"

"Why should they pretend?"

"Because you are no longer young and the bearing of children does not beautify a woman but adds to her years. They would feign to set you up as the Queen of Love. And why? Because you are the Queen of England, that is why."

"Have done," she said. "When this child is born I shall go once more to Aquitaine."

He nodded, smiling derisively at her, but his thoughts were far away in the bower of his Fair Rosamund.

Soon afterwards he left for France.

A message came from his mother. She wished him to call at Nantes where she was staying with his brother Geoffrey.

Matilda met her son with the pleasure she always showed on seeing him. They embraced and she looked at him anxiously.

"How fares it in England?" she wanted to know.

"All is well. I have left the government in capable hands. I have the best man in the world for Chancellor. And Eleanor knows how to rule."

"It was a good marriage," said Matilda.

Henry grimaced. "She's an overbearing woman."

Matilda could find no fault with that. No one could have been more overbearing than herself.

"I wished you to come here," she said, "because of Geoffrey."

"Geoffrey again! Not plotting against me once more?"

"Geoffrey will never plot against you again."

"You are hoping for a miracle."

"Nay, my son. Your brother Geoffrey is grievously sick. I fancy he will never leave his bed again."

"Geoffrey . . . but he is so young!"

"Death strikes down the young as well as the old. You must make sure you lose nothing by his death."

"His *death*! You cannot mean this!"

"You shall see for yourself. I wished to prepare you."

She went with him into the chamber where Geoffrey lay.

"Geoffrey, my son," she said, "your brother is here."

Geoffrey smiled wryly. "The King of England," he muttered.

"I am here," said Henry. He knelt by the bed and looked anxiously into his brother's face. "What ails you, Geoffrey?"

"My time has come. It was a short stay, was it not?"

"Nay, you'll recover."

"Is that a command?"

"You should take it as such."

"You always wanted to command us all. But you cannot command Death, brother."

"You talk nonsense. You will recover."

"I think not. So you rule England now as well as Normandy which was to have been mine."

"I paid you for it, remember?"

220

"I remember your promise to pay me a pension. I don't recall receiving much of it."

"There are many calls on a king's purse."

"I know, I know. And it is of no moment now."

"You had Brittany. You got that by my good graces."

"For which I must be grateful. Were not the dogs grateful for the crumbs which fell from the rich man's table?"

"They were indeed, but I was never a rich man, brother, and you never a dog."

"Not with England and Normandy and . . . what else is it, brother? I'll swear now it will be Brittany."

"Geoffrey, let us be friends."

Geoffrey smiled and held out his hand. "It is always good to be friends with a dying man. Fear not that I should ever seek to haunt you with reproaches, brother. I was always proud to be your brother. You were our mother's favourite. She loved you. You must have had very special qualities to be loved by her." He smiled. "Do you remember how she hated our father?"

Henry bowed his head.

"And he is dead now. And I shall soon follow him. You will go on and on to greater glory, Henry. It was good of you to come to my deathbed. Or did you come for Brittany?"

Henry looked at his brother with sorrowing eyes. He was thinking of how they had played together in their youth; but he was also thinking of Brittany. How could he help it? The Dukes of Normandy had always laid covetous eyes on it. He could bring up the matter when he saw Louis.

He did not talk of these matters to Geoffrey. He tried to soothe him. He talked a little of their boyhood but the continual conflict between their parents had not made that a very happy time.

On a hot July day Geoffrey died. Looking down at the still face of his brother Henry could not believe that he was gone. He felt tears in his eyes and wished that they had been better friends.

But almost immediately came news that Conan of Brittany, the son of the displaced Duke, was marching towards Nantes.

Henry immediately set about gathering together his forces. He left his army to stand against any invaders and went on to Paris where he was determined to get Louis's agreement that he should hold Brittany.

Louis received Henry with all the honours possible. His Queen joined with him. Constance was anxious to see the man whom Louis's first wife had married. She found him bold, a little coarse in some ways, but a man of great strength and she saw at once that he was in complete contrast to Louis.

Unlike Thomas Becket, Henry entered Paris without a great show of magnificence. He had left the best of his army behind to hold Brittany, in any case, and as he was the King of England and Duke of Normandy, ruler over a greater territory than the King of France, he had no need to proclaim what was obvious.

The two men took their measure. It was six years ago that Eleanor had shown her preference by marrying Henry. Louis had recovered from the humiliation now and had a new Queen; as for Henry his passion for Eleanor was fast dying and any cause for resentment against each other seemed to have dwindled away.

They would never be close friends. They were two different types. Louis had arranged special church services which he thought would please his guest. Henry would have preferred to see more of how the people lived, how they reacted to the laws of their land; he would have liked to meet some of the beautiful women of France. But he had come on a mission and it was imperative that he conclude it with satisfaction.

The conferences began. Louis would support Henry in Brittany; he would give the baby Marguerite as her dowry the much disputed Vexin, which was on the borders of Normandy and the Ile de France. This was the buffer state between those two and possession of it meant a certain security for Normandy.

It was a very satisfactory meeting and when Henry left Paris he brought with him the baby Marguerite whom he would take to England to be brought up as his daughter.

Even more satisfactory was the fact that when Conan of Brittany saw the forces of the Duke of Normandy and King of England he changed his mind about standing out against him, and he decided that he must try to make peace. Henry shrewdly agreed to do so and even compromised by making Conan Duke of Brittany, providing he recognized himself as a vassal of the Duke of Normandy and King of England. This Conan agreed to; and at the public ceremony swore that he would serve Henry with his life.

While this was happening Henry received two messages from England.

His wife had given birth to another son. She had called him Geoffrey after the King's dead brother and father.

Henry smiled ruefully. So there would be two Geoffreys in the nursery now. He could picture the elder one being known as Geoffrey the Bastard. That would be as Eleanor wanted it. Was that why she had chosen the same name for her own son?

The other piece of news was that Rosamund had also borne a son. She had called him William.

Henry was pleased. He longed to see his children and most of all he longed to see Rosamund.

*   *   *

Before Henry reached England he received news of another death, which was a little disconcerting. It was not that he cared greatly for the man who had died; but his passing was of some political significance for he was the son of King Stephen. Henry had reason to be grateful to this man, for had he been ambitious he might have laid claim to the throne which as the only surviving son of the late King would have seemed to some a reasonable thing to have done. William however was not ambitious; he had had no desire to build up an army and go to war against Henry Plantagenet. Moreover he was wise enough to realize that the people of England considered Henry the true heir and would have flocked to his support.

William had been very content to stand aside for Henry and become the Count of Boulogne, which title he inherited through his mother and there was no one who could say he had no right to this. Boulogne, however, through its connection with the Crown was a vassal state of England. Henry had been pleased with the state of affairs for Boulogne under William, who was without ambition, had caused him no anxiety, but when William died, Henry realized that it would be necessary to take immediate action to keep Boulogne as it had been, a vassal of England and Normandy.

He had no desire to make war—which was never wise when the matter could be resolved in any other way. And there was another way. Stephen had had also a daughter, Mary, who early in her life had decided on a religious career and was now the Abbess of the Convent of Romsey.

Henry acted promptly. He commanded her to come to him without delay. The startled Abbess protested to the messenger

223

who arrived at Romsey with the King's command, but she was told that this was an order which it would be treason to disobey. She had visions of her convent's being laid to waste, her nuns dispersed, for the King was ruthless enough to take such action, and as the daughter of the late King she was in a precarious position. She knew that William, her recently dead brother, had decided to get out of England for he had felt that it would be unwise for him to stay there as the only legitimate son of the late King when there was a new King on the throne.

Bewildered, the Abbess travelled to Normandy and there she was met by Henry who told her that he had a bridegroom for her and she was to prepare to marry without delay.

"My lord," she cried aghast. "How can I marry? I have taken my religious vows. I am Abbess of Romsey."

"You were," said the King testily. "But you are no longer so."

"How can that be when I have taken my vows? None but the Pope would grant my dispensation."

"Leave that to me," said Henry.

"I am afraid, my lord . . ."

"Afraid," thundered Henry. "You're to marry and that is my command."

"I do not understand. Who would wish to marry me?"

"My cousin Matthew wishes to marry you, Madam, because I have said he should. He knows better than to disobey me."

"But . . . for what purpose? I am not of an age . . ."

"You are of an age to obey your King. When you marry Boulogne shall be yours and Matthew will be the new Count of Boulogne."

Now it was clear. William had died and Henry feared some enemy might take Boulogne. It must be kept in the family.

She said: "I must appeal to the Pope."

Henry narrowed his eyes and the colour flamed into his face.

"Think not that I lack influence in that direction," he said.

He dismissed her and she went immediately to Thomas Becket, who had joined the King's party.

When she told him what had happened he was horrified. The King, who had known what his attitude would be, had said nothing to him. But Thomas was not afraid of offending the King.

"The Pope will stand beside you," Thomas comforted Mary.

"You have taken your vows. They cannot be thrust aside as though they had never been taken just to suit the King's ambitions."

"What must I do?" asked the bewildered Abbess.

"You have told the King you will appeal to the Pope. You must do so without delay."

"Will you help me, my Lord Chancellor?"

"I will dispatch a message to the Pope without delay," said Thomas.

*　*　*

When the King knew what Thomas had done he was furious. He strode into the Chancellor's apartments, his eyes wild, his face scarlet, his tawny hair on end so that he looked more like a raging lion than ever.

"So, Master Becket, you have decided to take the Crown! It is you who rule England and Normandy then?"

Thomas looked at him calmly.

"It is this matter of the Abbess which grieves you, my lord."

"Grieves me! I tell you I am so wild with fury that I myself would hold the burning iron that shall put out those haughty eyes."

"So you have sentenced me without hearing my case."

"I am your King, Becket."

"I know it well, my lord."

"And you fear not to anger me?"

"I fear only to do what I know to be wrong."

"So you are judging us, are you? You, Thomas Becket, clerk of the counting house, would judge your King!"

"It is only God who will do that, my lord."

"You and your piety! You make me sick, Thomas. You are a man and posing always as a saint. One of those days I shall catch you out. How I look forward to that! And if you value your life you will withdraw your request to the Pope on account of Stephen's daughter."

"I have sent her case to the Pope with her consent, my lord."

"Know this. There is no one who gives consent here but the King."

"There is a Higher Power."

"You would serve the Pope then ... rather than your King?"

"I would serve the right, my lord."

225

The King's fury abated a little. It was strange how he found it difficult to keep up a quarrel with Thomas.

"Don't be a fool, Thomas. Would you have me lose Boulogne?"

"If God wills it."

"Have done with this talk of God. I have never known Him go into battle with my grandfather or my great-grandfather."

"They asked help many a time I doubt not."

"His help maybe but they did not sit and wait for Him to make their conquests. If they had, they would have waited a long time. I am not going to lose Boulogne. If I did, what would happen? What if it fell into the hands of some evil lord who knew not how to govern? Nay, Thomas, you're a Chancellor not a priest. Forget your cleric's robes. I can take Boulogne with the utmost ease through this marriage. It will save war and conflict. And all because a nun is asked to relinquish her vows and take a husband."

"It is wrong."

"Have done."

"Nay, my lord, I cannot."

"Send another messenger to the Pope. Tell him that the lady has consented to the marriage. Let it be known that you ask for no barriers to put in the way of this match."

"I cannot do it, my lord."

The King's face was suffused with blood. He took a step towards Thomas, his hand raised to strike him. Thomas stood impassive. For a few seconds Henry seemed as though he would fall on the Chancellor and tear him apart or at least call to his guards to arrest the Chancellor. His eyes wild with rage, looked into Thomas's cool ones, and suddenly he turned and picking up a stool threw it against the wall.

"I am defied," he cried. "Defied by those whom I have befriended. They work against me in secret. By God, I'll be revenged."

Thomas said nothing. He stood there, then with a cry of rage the King threw himself on the floor and seizing a handful of rushes gnawed them in his rage.

Thomas went out and left him.

He had seen Henry in such a rage that he could not control his temper on one or two occasions, but that anger had never been directed against him before.

He waited for what would happen next.

* * *

There was a message from the Pope. He had received news from both the King and the Chancellor concerning the Abbess of Romsey. Alexander was in a very uneasy position. He had been elected at the conclave a very short time before and there had been certain opposition to his taking the Papal crown. As that opposition was backed by the Emperor Barbarossa, he did not feel that the Papal crown was very secure.

He dared not offend Henry Plantagenet who was not only King of England but fast becoming the most powerful man in France. The fact that the King's Chancellor differed from his master and was in the right, was a very special reason for giving the King what he wanted, for the fact that one of his servants was against him and he himself was in the wrong, would make the King doubly angry if the Pope sided against him.

Therefore Alexander granted the dispensation.

When he received it the King roared with gratified laughter. The first thing he did was to send for Thomas Becket.

"Ha!" he cried, when his Chancellor stood before him. "Have you heard from your friend the Pope, Thomas?"

"No, my lord. Perchance it is early yet."

"Not too early for me to have received a reply. He's a wise fellow, Thomas. Wiser than you, my godly Chancellor. I have the dispensation here."

Henry was gratified to see Thomas turn a shade paler.

"It cannot be."

"See for yourself."

"But . . ."

Henry gave his Chancellor an affectionate push.

"How could he do otherwise? His state is not too happy. Why, Thomas, you should study his ways. If you do not, you could mortally offend those who could do you harm. Sometimes it is better to serve them than what you call the right. Oh, you do not believe me? Strange as it may seem I like you for it. But I have the dispensation and our bashful Abbess will soon find herself in the marriage bed and I shall still have control over Boulogne."

Thomas was silent and the King went on: "Come, Thomas, applaud my skill. Was it not a good move, eh?"

Thomas was still silent.

"And what shall I do with my Chancellor who dared to go against my wishes? I could send him to a dungeon. I could put out his eyes. I fancy that would hurt you most. It does most men. To be shut away from the light of the sun, never to see again the green fields. Ah, Thomas, what a fool you were to offend your King."

"You will do with me as you will."

"I am a soft man at times. Are you not my friend? I could have had you killed, and looked on and seen it done with pleasure. But methinks had I done so I should never have known a moment's peace after. It is good to have friends. I know that you are mine and that you do in truth serve only one with greater zeal and that is God or Truth, or Righteousness . . . call it what you will. I like you, Thomas. Know this. If you are my friend, I am yours."

Then the King put his arm through that of Thomas Becket and together they went out of the chamber.

*   *   *

The friendship between them was greater than ever.

When Henry returned to England the two were constantly together and it was noted that Henry found the society of his Chancellor more rewarding than that of any other person. The rift between himself and Eleanor had widened. She had never forgiven him for bringing the bastard Geoffrey into the royal nurseries and he taunted her by making much of the boy. He liked to escape to the domestic peace of Woodstock. His love for Rosamund did not diminish. Perhaps this was due to the fact that she made no demands. She was always gentle and loving, always beautiful. They had their little son, too, and she was pregnant once more. She gave to him the cosy domesticity which kings can so rarely enjoy, and she delighted in keeping her existence a secret; and none but her servants knew that he visited her and they realized that it would go ill with them if through them the secret was divulged.

The King was happy. His kingdom was comparatively peaceful. He was watchful, of course, but then he would always have to be that. For a time he could stay peacefully in England, and he could enjoy the company of his best friend, Thomas Becket.

Sometimes he asked himself why he loved this man. There could not have been one more different. Even in appearance they presented a contrast. Tall and elegant Thomas, the stocky, carelessly dressed King. Thomas's love of fine clothes amused Henry. He teased him about it constantly. Why should he, the all-powerful King who could have chosen the most nobly born in his kingdom to be his companions, care only for the society of this man? Thomas was fifteen years older than he was. An old man! So much that Thomas believed in the King disagreed with; and Thomas would never give way in discussion. The King's temper could wage hot, but Thomas would remain calm and stick to his point. Henry was amused that in spite of Thomas's aesthetic appearance and concern with spiritual matters, at heart he loved luxury. There was no doubt that he did. His clothes betrayed him. He could also be merry at times. Henry liked to play practical jokes on his friend and Thomas responded. The King would sometimes howl with laughter at some of these, even those against himself. There was no one at his Court who could divert him as Thomas Becket could.

They were together constantly. When the King made his frequent peregrinations about the countryside, his Chancellor rode beside him. Sometimes they went off together incognito and sat in taverns and talked with the people. No one recognized the tall dark man with elegant long white hands and his younger freckle-faced, sturdy companion, whose hands were square, and chapped with the weather. An incongruous pair those who met them might have thought, and few were aware that they were the King of England and his Chancellor.

Henry liked nothing better than to score over his Chancellor. He had never forgotten the affair of the Boulogne marriage.

One winter's day when he and the Chancellor were riding through London, with the cold east wind howling through the streets, Henry looked slyly at his friend. Thomas hated the cold. He would wear twice as many clothes as other men, and although he ate sparingly his servant had to prepare beef steaks and chicken for him. His blood was thin, said the King; he was not hardy like the sprig from the Plantagenet tree. Thomas's beautiful white hands were protected by elegant but warm gloves, and even in such a bitter wind which was now buffeting the streets of London the King's hands were free. Gloves, he always declared, hampered him.

Suddenly the King saw a poor old man coming towards them, shivering, his face blue with cold, as he tried to hold his tattered garments about him.

Henry turned to his Chancellor. "Do you see that poor fellow?" he asked.

"Poor man," said Thomas. "He must find this wind trying."

"I can see his flesh through the tatters of his clothes. It would be an act of charity, favourable in the sight of God, to give him a warm cloak."

"It would," agreed Thomas. "And you, my lord, who have need to find favour in the sight of Heaven could win Heaven's approval for such a noble deed."

"Come," said the King. "Dismount."

They did so as the old man approached.

"Hey, my good fellow," said Henry, "do you not find this wind hard to bear?"

The old man nodded. "My lord," he said, "I shall die of the cold if it lasts much longer."

"You need a good warm cloak," said the King. "What would you say if you were given one?"

"You mock me, sir," said the old man attempting to pass on, but the King detained him and turning to Thomas he said: "I see you long to perform this act of charity. Why look what a fine cloak *you* are wearing! It is of rich scarlet cloth and lined with fur. Give it to this poor old man."

"My lord," said Thomas, turning pale, for the thought of riding through the cold streets without his cloak horrified him, "you suffer less from the cold than I do. If you gave him your cloak you would not notice it as I should."

"That is true," said the King. "Therefore it is a more noble act for you to give him *your* cloak." With that he attempted to pull it from Thomas who sought to retain it and in a short time the two of them were fighting together—Thomas to keep his cloak, the King to drag it from him.

Henry was laughing so much that the old man thought they were both mad.

"Come, you good man," said the King. "Come, Saint Thomas Becket. This poor man needs a cloak and you have it. Give it to me. You shall. You shall."

Thomas was no match for the strength of the King and finally Henry had wrested the cloak from him.

"Take it, my good fellow," said Henry to the old man. "It will keep you warm many a day and night. Forget not in your prayers the man who gave it to you for though he was not the owner, it is by his good graces that you have it."

The old man, who could not believe his good fortune and thought that the two noblemen were revellers who might change their minds, wrapped the cloak about him and scuttled off as fast as he could.

Henry's laughter rang through the streets.

"Why Thomas, how blue your nose has become. What an icy wind! You should be thankful that I did not command you to give the poor old man your gloves. What a tragedy if those delicate white digits should have become red and chapped like those of your royal master. Praise be to God, Thomas Becket, I have made a charitable man of you."

Henry thought it a great joke. Thomas riding through the cold streets was less amused.

But the incident was typical of the friendship between them.

The Vacant See

For two years Eleanor had been free of child-bearing. She began to feel young again. Little Richard was nearly three years old—the brightest and most handsome of her children. She always thought of him as her special child. Her preference was obvious, also her dislike of the elder Geoffrey. The Princess Marguerite was in England but Louis had not wished his daughter to be brought up by the woman who had once been his wife. He felt it would have made a situation which could have its dangers. It had been agreed therefore that little Marguerite should be placed in the household of a certain Robert of Newburgh who was known as a virtuous man of the highest character.

Eleanor said goodbye to her children and joined Henry in Normandy. She wished to make a journey to Aquitaine. Whenever she appeared in her native land there was rejoicing. No matter what rumours there were concerning her she was always welcome there. Once more she set up her little court and the troubadours came to her; once more they sang of love and it seemed that Eleanor, no longer young, the mother of six living children, was as desirable as ever.

She thought now and then of Louis who had had three daughters only—and two of them by her. Marie and Alix were betrothed by now, Marie to Henry of Champagne and

Alix to Theobald of Blois. Did they ever think of their mother? And how envious of her and Henry with their fine sons, Louis must have been when his little Marguerite was born. At least that child had strengthened the alliance between France and England, and the bond would be greater when she was in fact married to young Henry.

As she listened to the singing of her minstrels she ruminated that life had been interesting. Henry had disappointed her yet oddly enough she still hankered for him. She often wondered what it was about him that attracted her so much. She so elegant; he quite the reverse. Oh, but he was a man; and his power sat naturally on him. That Angevin temper of his amused her, but her own was a match for it.

Now that she had grown accustomed to the fact that he was unfaithful to her now and then, she had enjoyed their encounters, and looked forward to them. Her only reservation was that they could result in more childbearing. With three healthy sons she had enough, she reckoned. But she was still young enough to bear more.

She was a little jealous of the King's Chancellor for Henry seemed to prefer his company to that of anyone else—even women's. Becket was clever, she conceded that; and he was a good servant, so perhaps she was wrong to resent Henry's devotion to him. A king could not have too many good servants.

She was amused to hear that Louis's wife was pregnant once more. Good for Louis! she thought mockingly. At least he had managed to get her with child twice. She wondered if he was still rather reluctant and preferred to listen to church music instead of the music of love. Not for one moment had she regretted her escape from him.

The life of repose was not for her and whenever she was in Aquitaine she began to think of Toulouse, which had always irritated her because she believed that it should have belonged to her. She had in the past claimed that it came to her through her grandmother Philippa, and she was always hoping that she and Henry would win it back. At this time it was in the possession of Raymond the fifth Count who was a weakling, yet nothing much could be done about it because he had, very shrewdly, married the sister of the King of France.

Oh these marriages! mused Eleanor. How necessary a part of statescraft they were.

Henry came to her when she sat in the gardens with her

233

minstrels. He clapped his hands impatiently implying that he wished them to depart. No one ignored such a signal. The King's temper was well known and something to avoid.

Henry was clearly disturbed. He sprawled down beside Eleanor and said: "I have news. The Queen of France was brought to bed . . ."

"A son," said Eleanor.

"Nay, a daughter."

Eleanor burst out laughing but the King said in a hushed voice: "The Queen of France died giving birth to the child."

They were both silent, thinking of what this would mean. Another daughter for Louis! That was his fourth. Was it that he could not get sons? Eleanor could think complacently of her three healthy boys in the nursery. Poor Louis! What would he do now? He would have to marry again in due course.

The same thought was in Henry's mind.

"He'll wait a while," he said, "and then he'll marry. The marriage of the King of France is of the utmost importance to me."

Henry was casting round in his mind for a wife for the King of France who would be suitable in the eyes of the King of England.

*   *   *

To the astonishment of all, only one month after the death of Queen Constance, Louis married Adela of Blois.

Henry and Eleanor were blank with amazement which quickly turned to apprehension.

"So," cried Henry, "he marries Adela of Blois in most indecent haste and her brother Theobald is betrothed to Louis's daughter. This makes a very strong alliance between the Count of Blois and the King of France."

"Too strong," said Eleanor.

"I like it not," grumbled Henry. "Forget not that the last King of England came from the house of Blois. I like not to see that house too powerful."

"You are thinking that they might bring out a claim to the throne of England?"

"And if they did," replied Henry, "would Louis withhold his support from a house with which he had such a strong alliance?"

"It is a pity that Henry and Marguerite are too young to

marry. Then with his own daughter married to the heir of England, Louis could do nothing but support you."

"Why should they be too young to marry?"

"Henry is six years old. Marguerite not yet three."

"Her marriage portion is the Vexin," Henry reminded his wife. "If the Vexin were in my control Normandy is safe and that would give me an opportunity to turn my attention in other directions."

"But such children!"

"Why not? We shall not put them to bed. But there could be a ceremony. Louis cannot object. He has agreed to the match. I will get them married and with the marriage, the Vexin. Every Duke of Normandy has known the importance of that territory."

"You'd have to get a dispensation from the Pope."

"I got one before for our Abbess's marriage remember. Alexander is very insecure. If I promised him my support for the dispensation do you doubt it would be mine?"

"You are a clever man, Henry."

"My dear wife, I should not long be King of England and Duke of Normandy if I were not!"

She could not help but admire the manner in which he got his will.

Marguerite and Henry were married. It was a quiet ceremony but it took place in the presence of two cardinals, and since it was truly a marriage the dowry could not be withheld. The Vexin was now under Henry's rule and he felt a good deal more easy in his mind regarding the marriage of the King of France with Adela of Blois.

* * *

Urged by Eleanor Henry decided that he was in a position to launch an attack on Toulouse and bring it where Eleanor had long decided it should be—allied with Aquitaine, in the possession of that province's Duke and Duchess.

He had the Vexin to safeguard Normandy; England was well governed by his justiciary the Earl of Leicester, and he sent Chancellor Becket to England to raise a company of knights and bring them into France. He was sure that little effort would be necessary to subdue Raymond of Toulouse. Louis hated war; he would stand aside and all Henry would have to do was take a castle or two to assure Raymond of his strength.

235

Henry had underestimated Louis and it was an unpleasant surprise to learn that the King of France refused to remain aloof. He had a family tie with Raymond who had married his sister; moreover the Count of Toulouse was one of his vassals. It was a fact that Henry Plantagenet was becoming too overbearing—and in consequence it seemed too powerful. Louis was aware that a stop would have to be made to such headlong progress and declared that he would go to the help of his brother-in-law.

Henry was nonplussed. He had no desire to go to war against the King of France; he could see a major engagement developing; it would never do for him to defeat the King of France. Nor would it do for the King of France to defeat him. He could not take over France. There would be endless trouble if he did. He would be fighting in France for the rest of his life.

But what could he do? He had declared war on Raymond of Toulouse. Becket had arrived with his array of knights and the King of Scotland had offered to come to his aid.

Uncertainly he marched to Toulouse and when the walls of the city were in sight news was brought to him that Louis himself was within.

The King called a halt to his armies. He sent for his Chancellor.

"This is a sorry state of affairs, Becket," he said.

"Why so, my lord? It was your wish to make war on Toulouse."

"I know, I know. But the King of France is within that city."

"By being there he declares himself to be an enemy of yours."

"What if I were to kill the King of France?"

"I was thinking, my lord, what if he were to kill you?"

"Bah. He never would. He's no soldier. He'll have no stomach for the fight."

"Stomach enough to place himself at the head of his armies and join Raymond of Toulouse against you."

"I would I had never begun this. Help me out of it, Thomas. Tell me what I can do now."

"The Duke of Normandy is the vassal of the King of France."

"Tell me not what I know already."

"You have sworn to serve him and accept him as your liege lord. How could you then take up arms against him?"

"I can and would if so be I had a mind."

"Yet you have no heart for this because you ask yourself is it a just fight? My lord, in England many of your subjects have sworn allegiance to you. If you break your word to the suzerain of the Duke of Normandy, others might see it as a precedent and act accordingly towards the King of England. Might not those who have sworn allegiance to you break their vows in similar fashion?"

"I see what you mean, Thomas."

"We can abandon this project. We can walk away from the walls of Toulouse."

"And what will be said of that?"

"That the King of England is an honourable man. Since the King of France takes side with Raymond of Toulouse, and as Duke of Normandy Henry Plantagenet has sworn allegiance to him, he abandons what would appear to be certain victory for the sake of his honour."

Henry looked at his Chancellor, narrowed his eyes and burst into his loud laughter.

"You have it, Thomas. You have it, friend. Did I not always know that you would provide me with the right and righteous answer."

* * *

There was a certain amount of puzzlement regarding the King's action. Why had he gathered together an army only to take it to the walls of Toulouse, and then led it away?

Was Henry Plantagenet afraid of the combined forces of Toulouse and France? It was strange for the advantage was all his.

Speculation as to his inability to succeed was dispersed almost immediately for Louis's brother Robert, hungry for power, had seized the opportunity to attack Normandy.

Henry had no scruples here. He went straight into the fight and so trounced Robert that he was soon suing for peace.

Thus Henry's reputation as a man of honour was enhanced with no loss to that as a commander of armies.

It had not been such an unprofitable affair after all. Only Eleanor was frustrated and angry. She had been furious to discover that she was once more pregnant and secretly upbraided herself for allowing this to happen, but she concentrated her reproaches on Henry's failure to take Toulouse.

"It is mine," she declared. "It came to me with my grandfather. You who took England, who took Normandy, could have taken Toulouse."

Henry shrugged his shoulders. "I will take what I want and when I want it," he told her.

"But not Toulouse! You are afraid of the King of France. Afraid of my meek monk Louis!"

"Rant all you wish," said the King. "I shall heed you not."

"Mayhap," retaliated Eleanor, "one of these days my sons will be old enough to fight for their mother."

"A fine thing to say when you may well be carrying one of them now."

"Do not goad me too far, Henry," retorted Eleanor, "or you will regret it."

"You may apply the same to me," he retorted.

Her frustration was intolerable. It was unfair that it should always be the woman's lot to bear the children.

This shall be the last, she promised herself. But had she not said that when Geoffrey was born?

In due course she gave birth to her child in the town of Domfront.

She named her Eleanor after herself.

*　　*　　*

Archbishop Theobald was writing frequently to Thomas.

"You are still Archdeacon of Canterbury yet we never see you here. What of the affairs of the Church? Do you forget them in your secular duties?"

Thomas told the King of the Archbishop's requests for his return.

"Tell the old man I need you with me," replied the King.

"I should doubtless resign my post of Archdeacon."

"Nay. 'Tis better for you to remain in the Church."

"It is long since I was in Canterbury. I should return, for my old friend and patron grows old. In his last letter he calls himself my spiritual father and prophesies that he has not long for this world. He wishes me to go back to Canterbury before he dies."

"You cannot go, Thomas. I need you here. Write to the Archbishop and tell him your King needs his Chancellor. Who brought your name before me when I needed a Chancellor? Theobald Archbishop of Canterbury. So he cannot complain now that I took the man he chose for me, and now I expect him to hold his post."

So Thomas wrote to Theobald and explained to him that he would return as soon as he could leave the King.

Henry smiled secretly. He was determined that Thomas should not have that opportunity. In fact he was wondering how he could bind Thomas more closely to him, for he was enjoying his company more and more. He looked for honours to heap upon him and he decided that he would put his son Henry, the young bridegroom, into his charge.

Already several noblemen had sent their sons into the household of Thomas Becket, where the boys would learn not only book lore but how to behave in a chivalrous and knightly manner. They would learn elegance and courtliness with such a man as Thomas Becket.

"I shall give my boy Henry into your keeping," the King told Thomas. "You will bring him up to be honourable, righteous, and at the same time to behave like a king. You will teach him to love the good things of life and at the same time keep his peace with God. A rare combination, my friend. Sometimes methinks only you know the secret."

"I shall do all in my power to bring up your son as a good Christian Prince," replied Becket.

"Take him to England. Let it be arranged that all the barons and bishops do homage to him. Let England recognize him as their future King."

Before Thomas reached England Theobald was dead and Thomas regretted that he had not disobeyed the King's orders and gone back to say a last farewell to his old friend.

In fairness to himself he could suppress his conscience. He was the King's Chancellor and in this important post had his duties to perform. Theobald would have understood that. Thomas wondered whether at the end Theobald had regretted getting the Chancellorship for him.

He now devoted himself to the task of carrying out the King's orders regarding young Henry. The boy soon became devoted to him and the task was pleasant, but it was not long before there came a message from the King.

Thomas was to join him in Normandy.

*   *   *

The See of Canterbury had been vacant for some months, and the country was without its chief Archbishop. Henry was in no great hurry to fill the post for while it was vacant the vast revenues fell into his coffers.

The winter had been bad and Thomas suffered great discomfort from the cold, and as a result became ill and was forced to rest at St Gervase in Rouen while the royal party went on to Falaise.

One day when he was well enough to sit up he wrapped himself in a loose robe and was playing a game of chess with one of his knights when the Prior of Leicester called to see him.

The Prior expressed astonishment to see him in such unclerical garb. "Why, my lord," he said, "you look more like a falconer than an archdeacon. Yet churchman you are. Your titles even now are formidable. Archdeacon of Canterbury, Dean of Hastings, Provost of Beverley and Canon of Rouen. Nor is that all."

"What mean you by 'nor is that all'?" asked Thomas.

"I speak only of the rumours and what is said to be in the King's mind concerning the Archbishop of Canterbury."

"And what is this then?"

"That he has it in his mind to make you his Archbishop."

Thomas rose unsteadily to his feet.

"Nay, you have heard amiss."

"This is what is said in Court circles. Those who are intimate with the King are saying that he has mentioned your name in this connection."

"It must not be. I know three priests in England whom I would rather see promoted to the Archbishopric than myself."

"Are you not an ambitious man then, Chancellor?"

"My ambition is to do my duty."

"Then could you not please God doubly as head of his Church in England?"

"The King has been my good friend. I know him intimately. I know it would not be good for me to be his Archbishop. I am his Chancellor. As such I can serve him well. It would please me to go on as I am."

"The King holds you in such esteem that he would wish to see you head of the Church."

"If I became Archbishop of Canterbury I should not hold his favour."

"Why should you not?"

"Because the King likes not those who do not agree with him."

"He likes his Chancellor."

"We can disagree in secular matters yes, and do. And in these I should be forced to give way to the King. If I were

240

Archbishop I might be called upon to set aside my duty to God in order to please the King."

"You're a strange man, Thomas Becket."

"I know myself," answered Thomas, "and I know the King. I shall decline his offer of the Archbishopric."

It was difficult to continue with that game of chess. Uneasy thoughts had settled in Thomas's mind and come to stay.

* * *

The King sent for him at his Castle of Falaise.

"Hey, Thomas," he cried. "I trust I see you well. Why, you look thin and wan, man. Be of good cheer. Soon we shall set sail for England. I'll warrant our green fields will make you well again."

The King's eyes were glazed with sentiment. He was thinking of Rosamund in her Bower waiting to see him. It would in truth be good to be home again.

He turned to Thomas and there was deep affection in his eyes.

"I wanted to talk with you, Thomas, about a certain matter. It's months since old Theobald died."

"Almost a year," said Thomas.

"And the See of Canterbury has been vacant all this time. Not that I will complain about that. But it seems we must have an Archbishop there and my thoughts have alighted on the man best suited to fill the part."

"I know of several priests who would fit the role admirably, my lord."

"I know of only one and that makes the selection easy." Henry took a step towards Thomas and laid his hands on his shoulders. "My good friend, it gives me pleasure to reward you for all your services to me. I have decided that you shall be my Archbishop of Canterbury."

"You are gracious, Sire, but I refuse the honour. It is not for me."

"Not for you! What in God's name do you mean? Not for you? It *is* for you. *I* say it's for you."

"My lord, it would not be wise."

"What's this? You and I together. Do we not rule this land, eh? Do I not listen to you and take your advice?"

"When it pleases you to do so," said Thomas.

The King laughed aloud and slapped Thomas on the shoulder.

"True enough, my good friend. The Church has ever been a thorn in the side of our kings. I have often thought to myself, I will never suffer that thorn. And how shall I avoid it? By putting my good friend Thomas at the head of the Church. Have we not been good friends through your Chancellorship?"

"The best," said Thomas.

"I like our friendship, Thomas. That's why I like you with me. I like to go hawking with you. I like to sup at your table. You are as my brother. There, is that not an honour to you? The grandson of great Henry and the great-grandson of greater William chooses you, the son of a merchant, as the best friend he ever had."

"Such condescension is flattering," said Thomas. "I, as a humble merchant's son, am aware of the honour done to me. I value that friendship which you are gracious enough to acknowledge, and it is because I cannot bear to spoil it that I decline the post you offer me."

The King's temper was beginning to rise.

"If my lord will excuse me . . ." began Thomas.

"Nay," roared the King. "I will do no such thing. You will stay here and you will go on your knees and thank me for my munificence in offering you this great post which is what you desired more than anything else, the peak of your ambition, the post on which you set your heart ever since you entered the church."

"May I speak?"

"You may."

"If I take this post it could impair our friendship."

"How so?"

"If we did not agree . . ."

"Are we not now often in disagreement?"

"It is so. But that is in matters of government in which I must perforce give way to you. You are my King and I am your servant. If I became Archbishop of Canterbury there is one whom I must serve before you and that is God."

"A plague on such talk! My ancestors have quarrelled constantly with the Church. There has ever been conflict between them. It is to avoid this that I wish you to be my Archbishop. You and I will have our disagreements but should we ever quarrel seriously?"

"I must repeat that my first allegiance would have to be to God. You are my King and my friend. I would have it remain as it stands now. I beg of you, my lord, to accept my decision."

The King stared at Thomas. "I could force you . . ." he began.

"Nay, that is one thing you could not do," contradicted Thomas.

"Then I must perforce persuade you. Now, your looks do not please me. I like not to see my Chancellor so wan. You shall not travel until you are completely recovered. I must go to England and you shall follow me when you are well."

"You are gracious to me, my lord," said Thomas with some emotion.

"Sometimes I wonder at myself," answered the King. "I have a fondness for you, and I promise you it will not lessen, even when you are my Archbishop."

* * *

Henry went back to England where there were certain matters to occupy him. Leicester and Richard de Luci were good fellows, and it was a fine thing to have such loyal servants; but neither of them pleased him as Thomas did. He missed his company.

When he thought of him he began to laugh. He could never fully understand Thomas. That love of silken garments, those lily-white hands! Whatever he said, Thomas loved luxury. Thomas was a clever fellow, none more clever. Was he capable of putting on a front for everyone to see . . . even his King? Was that pious exterior hiding a sensual man? He couldn't hide that love for the good things of life. His household articles were of the finest. He lived more like a king than the King himself.

How he would love to discover Thomas in some intrigue! Nothing would delight him more. How amusing to discover him . . . say in bed with a woman. How they would laugh together.

Then you and I, Thomas, would go adventuring together, he thought. I can imagine no greater delight.

"My first allegiance is to God." That irked. Thomas, you are human like the rest of us. You want old Theobald's post. You must. And when you have it, you and I will show the Pope of Rome that England can do without the Church, that the King of England is more powerful than any Pope, for all that he's a soldier and a lecher.

If only he could discover Thomas in some awkward situation.

243

He had left Eleanor at Westminster and travelled to Stafford on one of his frequent journeys that his people might see that he cared for their well-being and at the same time made sure of their good conduct. The country was becoming law-abiding again. The roads were safe as they had been in the days of his grandfather. He had abolished the brigandry of the road when no traveller had been safe. These robbers had no wish to lose hands, feet, ears, nose or eyes for the sake of someone's purse; and the King's judgement was relentless. No one could be sure when he would put in an appearance, so there must consequently be no straying from the strict laws which he had laid down.

Some years before the King had enjoyed his visits to Stafford for living there was a young woman of whom he had been quite enamoured. Her name was Avice and she had borne him two sons. She no longer appealed to him. Rosamund had filled his thoughts since he had first discovered her and he had found that no woman satisfied him as she did, so that whenever he had the time to dally it was to Woodstock he went.

Avice might no longer be the slender young girl who had caught his fancy but she was still a very attractive woman—some seemed to think more so in her ripeness than she had been when very young.

The King visited her now and then for old times' sake and had always retained an affection for her.

Now at Stafford he sent for her. She was delighted to come, always hoping that she could regain her old position with him.

He decided to spend the night with her, and when they were together an idea came to him. It so amused him that he could not stop himself laughing.

"Now, Avice," he said, "I want you to do something for me."

"Anything I can do for my lord shall be done," she assured him.

"I want you to see if you can lure my Chancellor into bed with you."

"My lord!" Avice was a little hurt. What greater proof could there be of a lover's indifference than when he suggested she should be turned over to someone else. "You cannot mean Thomas Becket?"

"None other."

"But the man is a cleric is he not?"

"My dear Avice, clerics have been known to enjoy a woman now and then."

"Not this man surely."

"So he would have us believe."

"You think he is deceiving you?"

"I don't know. But I should like to find out. Oh, if I could surprise him in bed with you, Avice, I would reward you well."

"I would not ask for rewards, my lord, to serve you."

"Nay, you are a good wench and pleasant times we have had together—and shall have more I doubt not."

"Yet you would wish me to . . . to entertain this man?"

"I would wish you to prove to me that he is not the virtuous fellow he pretends to be. You are a beautiful woman, Avice. Do this for me and I shall not forget it."

"What would you have me do?"

"He will be coming to Stafford to join the Court. I will send for him. When he arrives I wish you to show friendship to him. Ask him to come and see you. Feign religion if you wish. Visit him at his lodging. My dear Avice, you will know how to go on from there."

"And then?"

"He will be staying in the house of a clerk called Vivien. He has stayed there before. I will speak to Vivien and he will play his part. I want him to surprise you in bed with Becket. Then he will be so over-wrought, knowing you have been my mistress, that he will come at once to me and tell me what has happened. It is a simple enough plot."

"I doubt from what I know of Thomas Becket that it will succeed."

"That is what everyone would say. But you don't know Thomas. I know the man well. I would know him better. You will do this for me, my dear Avice. I shall regard it as a great favour to me."

"I would rather entertain you, my lord."

"So you shall. Do this and I will never forget you."

He studied her appraisingly. She was a very beautiful woman, voluptuous, irresistible.

We shall see, friend Thomas, he thought.

*   *   *

Thomas arrived in Stafford and went straight to the house of Vivien where he had stayed many times before. He was warmly welcomed by the family and taken to his chamber.

He was tired and still feeling weak; moreover he was beset by anxieties. The King would not easily let him refuse the post of Archbishop and Thomas was beginning to think that he would have no alternative but to take it.

It will be the end, he thought. The King and I will be enemies. He will never fall into step and walk beside the Church. There will always be differences of opinion, always conflict. And yet the King was insisting. Although he did not say outright: "I command you to take this post," it was in his mind.

Vivien came to his chamber to say that a message had arrived for him. It was from Mistress Avice of whom he may have heard.

Thomas wrinkled his brow. "I think I have heard the King speak of a lady of that name."

"Very likely," said Vivien, "she was at one time the King's very good friend."

"What can she want of me?"

"She is asking for an audience."

"She may come here."

She came immediately. She was a very beautiful woman. Thomas could understand the attraction she had once had for the King.

She told him that she had sinned greatly during her life and was now eager to repent.

"Men go on pilgrimages to the Holy Land to take part in crusades. What can a woman do?"

"You could go into a convent."

"I fear that would be too easy a way out. You must forgive me for taking up your time but something told me that only a man such as you could give me the advice I need. Will you promise me to think of the matter?"

"The answer is in yourself," said Thomas. "Only you can save your soul."

"Yet such a man as yourself can best advise me. You are a man of God and yet you live at Court. You share much of the King's life. You yourself must have had temptations."

"We have all had temptations," answered Thomas. "We overcome them through prayer. Go away, pray and ask God's help and the answer will come to you."

"Thank you. You have eased my mind considerably. May I come and see you again?"

Thomas said she might and that he would mention her in his prayers.

"That gives me great comfort. How much more readily will your prayers be listened to."

When she had gone Thomas forgot her. He had matters of State to ponder on and he could not help but return to the constant question of the Archbishopric of Cnaterbury.

The next day Avice came again. She found it difficult to pray, she said. Would Thomas teach her?

Thomas, who never turned a supplicant away, said he would pray with her and again advised her to sell her worldly goods and go into a convent.

She used all her wiles, she admitted that she had been the mistress of the King, a fact which aroused Thomas's interest. She came close to him as she talked and the musk smell with which she scented her clothes was pleasant to him. She was a very attractive woman and cleverly skilled in all the arts of seduction. How easily Henry would have succumbed.

He sighed, thinking of the weaknesses of the King, and marvelled that a man so strong, so able a ruler, so determined on getting his will could yet so easily be tempted.

When Avice left Vivien spoke to her. She was smiling as though well pleased with herself.

She must be coming this night, thought the clerk, for the Court was moving on the next day and tonight was the only time it could be.

Thomas returned to his chamber and all was quiet.

It was midnight when the King arrived. He was wrapped in a concealing cloak so that none would guess his identity.

Vivien came to the door holding high a horn lantern. The King stepped into the house.

"The Chancellor is here?" he asked.

"Yes, my lord," said Vivien.

"In his bedchamber," said the King. "I'll warrant he is not alone."

"Go to his room," said the King. "Do not knock on the door. Throw it open and see what you find."

Vivien took the horn lantern and mounted the stairs silently. Gently he opened the door of Thomas's bedchamber. He shone the light of the horn lantern round the room.

The bed was empty!

Vivien felt exultant. The plot had worked. If Thomas's bed was empty then he must be sleeping elsewhere and where? In Avice's bed.

How delighted the King would be.

Henry was standing behind him.

"What?" he whispered.

"He is not here, my lord. He is sleeping elsewhere this night."

"I know where," cried the King and then he stopped short. For kneeling at the bed in a deep sleep, his face pale and drawn in the light from the horn lantern, was Thomas.

The King stared at him for some moments and a great tenderness came over his face.

He put his finger to his lips and with a nod of his head ordered Vivien to proceed downstairs.

"He has fallen asleep over his prayers," he said. "Why did I ever think I could catch a man like Thomas? He can never be caught for this simple reason, that he would never fall into temptation."

* * *

Richard de Luci with the Bishops of Exeter and Chichester called on Thomas.

They talked to him long and earnestly.

They believed that his duty lay clearly before him. He had the King's confidence. Henry would listen to him as to no other man. The Church needed him. The See of Canterbury had remained vacant too long. Clearly it was the duty of Thomas Becket to take the robes of office.

The king had determined that he should; and now the members of the Clergy were in agreement with the King.

Thomas knew that the easy happy friendship with the King must decline. His mode of life must change. Yet the challenge had come and he knew he must take it.

Thomas gave his promise that he would accept the King's offer and became the Archbishop of Canterbury.

The Rising Storm

In his castle of Falaise the King talked with his wife and
mother and the subject of their discourse was the new Archbishop of Canterbury.

Matilda, now showing her age but as fiery as ever, was
repeating what she had said many times before which was to
the effect that her son had made a great mistake when he had
chosen Thomas Becket.

Eleanor shrugged her shoulders. Becket did not greatly
interest her but she did deplore Henry's obsession with the
man which was now spreading to their son Henry. When she
had last met the child he had shown his adoration for the
Archbishop and seemed to look up to him as a divine being. It
was all very tiresome, but better, she thought, that the King
should spend his time with a man like Becket than to be
sporting with all kinds of women.

"Nay, my lady," he replied to his mother. "I could not have
made a better choice. Becket and I understand each other. He
has been a good Chancellor and when the Chancellor and the
Archbishop of Canterbury are one and the same you will see
how easy it is for us to carry out our plans."

"I shall pray that it is so," said Matilda. "But there has
always been trouble between the Kings and the Church. The
Church wants to take power from the State and it is for the

Kings to see that they do not. In appointing this man as head of your Church you have put unlimited power into his hands."

"Becket wielded great power as Chancellor," said the King. "I found him easy to handle then."

"The King and his Chancellor were inseparable," said Eleanor.

"I could never understand this friendship with such a man," put in Matilda. "A merchant's son! It puzzles me."

"Believe me," said Henry, "there is no man in England more cultured."

"It is impossible," snapped Matilda. "You deceive yourself."

"I do not. He is a man of great learning, and has a natural nobility."

"The King loves him as though he were a woman," put in Eleanor scornfully.

Henry threw a venomous glance in her direction. Why did she take sides with his mother against him? Ever since he had put young Geoffrey in the nursery had she manifested this dislike of him.

"I esteem him as a friend," corrected Henry angrily. "There was never any other of my servants who could amuse me as that man did."

"And not content with making him your Chancellor you must give him the chief archbishopric in the kingdom as well."

"My mother, my wife! This is politics. This is statescraft. My Chancellor is my Archbishop. My Chancellor must be loyal to the State and since my Archbishop is also my Chancellor how can he go against that which is beneficial to the State?"

"So this is your idea of bringing the Church into submission to the State," said Matilda. "I hope it works."

"Fear not, mother. It will work."

"Your Archbishop is indeed a worldly man." Eleanor turned to Matilda. "You will know that this man lives in unsurpassed splendour. He maintains seven hundred knights and the trappings of his horses are covered in gold and silver. I heard that he receives the highest in the land."

"And as Chancellor so he should," retorted the King.

"An upstart," said Matilda. "Having been born humble he must continually let people know how noble he has become."

"You, my dear Mother, were born royal but I believe you never allowed any to forget your nobility."

"Oh, but this fellow was quite ostentatious," said Eleanor. "I have heard it said that he lived more splendidly than *you* ever did."

Henry laughed indulgently. "He has a taste for such luxury. As you say he was not born to it but acquired it. Therefore he prized it."

"He has bewitched you," Eleanor told him.

He gave her a glance of distaste. Why did she bait him? She was jealous he knew. So she still had some feeling for him. She had disliked his friendship with Becket almost as much as she hated his love affairs.

She went on to discuss the extravagances of Becket.

"At his banquets there must be every rarity. I heard that he paid seventy-five pounds for a dish of eels."

"One hears this gossip," said the King. "If Thomas was extravagant it was to do me honour. He is my Chancellor and I remember when he went to France in great state it was said that I must indeed be a wealthy man since my Chancellor travelled as he did."

"Clever he may be," said Matilda, "but I warn you. Make sure he is not too clever."

"You will see what a brilliant move this is on my part. This will be an end to the strife between Church and State."

It was only a day or so after that conversation that Henry fell into one of the greatest rages that ever had overtaken him.

A messenger had arrived from Canterbury bringing with him the Great Seal of Office. Henry looked at it in dismay for he began to understand what it meant. There was a letter from Thomas and as the King read it a mist swam before his eyes.

"By God's eyes, Thomas," he muttered between his teeth. "I could kill you for this."

Thomas had written that he must resign his Chancellorship for he could not reconcile his two posts. The Archbishop must be quite apart from the Chancellor. Thomas had a new master. The Church.

Henry's rage almost choked him. This was the very thing his mother had prophesied. This was the implication behind Eleanor's sneers. He had believed in Thomas's love for him; he had thought their friendship more important than anything else. So it had seemed to him. But not to Thomas.

He remembered Thomas's words. It would be the end of their friendship.

Only if the Chancellor and the Archbishop were as one could Henry's battle with the Church be won. If Thomas was going to set himself up on one side while he was on the other there would be conflict between them.

His grandfather had fought with the Church. Was he to do the same . . . with Thomas?

And he had thought himself so clever. He was going to avoid that. He was going to put his friend into the Church so that the Church would be subservient to the State—so that the King would rule and none gainsay him. Henry Plantagenet had planned to have no Pope over him.

And this man . . . who called himself his friend, to whom he had given so much . . . had betrayed him. He had accepted the Archbishopric and resigned from the Chancellorship.

"By God, Thomas," he said, "if you wish there to be war between us, then war there shall be. And I shall be the victor. Make no mistake about that."

Then the violence of his rage overcame him. He beat his fist against the wall and it was Thomas's face he saw there. He kicked the stool around the chamber and it was Thomas he kicked.

None dared approach him until his rage abated. They all knew how violent the King's temper could be.

*　　*　　*

Eleanor and Henry took their farewell of Matilda and travelled to Barfleur. The King had declared he would spend Christmas at Westminster.

His anger against Thomas had had time to cool. He reasoned with himself. Thomas had reluctantly taken the Archbishopric and he had in some measure forced it upon him. Therefore he must not complain if Thomas resigned the Chancellorship. It was disappointing but he might have known that Thomas would do exactly as he had done. He was after all a cleric.

There will be battles between us, thought Henry. Well, there have always been battles of a kind. It will be stimulating, amusing. I long to see Thomas again.

Eleanor said: "I'll dare swear your Archbishop is trembling in his shoes as he awaits your arrival."

"That is something Thomas would never do."

"If he has heard what a mighty rage you were in when you

heard he had resigned the Chancellorship, he will surely not expect you to greet him lovingly."

"He is a man of great integrity. He would always do what he believed to be right."

"So he is forgiven? How you love that man! I'll warrant you can scarcely wait to enjoy his sparkling discourse. And only a short while ago you were cursing him. What a fickle man you are, Henry!"

"Nay," answered Henry, "rather say I am constant, although I may be enraged for a time that passes."

"Your servants know it. All they must do is anger you, keep out of your way and then return to be forgiven."

"You know that is not true," he said and closed the conversation.

Do not think, she mused, that I may be thrust aside for a while and then taken back. You may be in a position to subjugate others but not Eleanor of Aquitaine. I shall never forget that you placed your bastard into my nurseries to be brought up with my sons. Richard was now six. She had watched his manner with his father. He was all for his mother, and would be more so. And Richard was the most beautiful and most promising of their children. Henry the eldest had already gone to Becket and clearly doted on the man. Little Geoffrey was too young to show a preference. Henry could have the adulation of his little bastard and be content with that, but when the time came it was his legitimate children who would inherit their parents' possessions. Richard should be Duke of Aquitaine; on that she had decided. He could already sing charmingly and loved to play the lute.

At Barfleur they waited for the wind to abate. It would be folly to set to sea in such weather. But day after day it raged and it became apparent that they could not be in Westminster for Christmas.

There were festivities at Cherbourg, but it was not the same. Eleanor would have liked to be with her children on Christmas Day. She had planned an entertainment for them with minstrels and dancers and she knew that young Richard would have enjoyed that and shone too above the rest of them. He would have made bastard Geoffrey seem an oaf.

It was not until nearing the end of January that they set sail.

When they reached Southampton Thomas Becket and their son Henry were waiting there to greet them. Henry, eight years old, had grown since they last saw him. He knelt before them and his father laid his hand on his head. He was pleased with his son's progress. There was nothing gauche about the boy. That was due to Thomas.

And Thomas? He and the King looked at each other steadily. Thomas was clearly uncertain what to expect. Then the King burst out laughing.

"Well, my Chancellor that was and my Archbishop that is, how fare you?"

And all was well between them.

On the journey to London the King rode side by side with his Archbishop and every now and then the King's laughter rang out. There was a contented gleam in his eyes. There was no one who could amuse him like Thomas.

As they neared the end of the ride he referred to his anger when he had received the news of Thomas's resignation.

"I guessed it would be so," said Thomas.

"Yet you dared provoke it."

"It was inevitable. I knew I could not remain Chancellor. That was why I did not wish to become Archbishop in the first place. I was certain that it would impair our friendship."

"There will be battles between us, Thomas. But by God's eyes, I'd rather have battles with you than docility from any other man."

"Nay," answered Thomas, "harmony is best."

"See," retorted the King. "You disagree with me already."

Thomas smiled ruefully as he gazed at the darkening sky over Westminster.

* * *

Summer had come. The King had ridden to Woodstock and there had found many an opportunity to slip away to Rosamund. She was delighted to have him with her after his long absence abroad. The children had grown and danced round him to see what gifts he had brought them while Rosamund reproved them gently. What did gifts matter, she demanded, when they had their dear father with them?

"I would that I could come to you more often, Rosamund," he told her. "Here I find a peace which elsewhere is denied me."

The fact that he kept his liaison with her a secret apart from one or two who must inevitably know of it—gave it a touch of romance which he had never known with any of his other mistresses.

"Has anyone come to the house?" he always asked her.

One or two people had, she told him. They had wandered through the maze of trees and by chance arrived there. They had been strangers who had not associated her with the King.

He was always a little uneasy that Eleanor might discover Rosamund's Bower. And if she did? Then perforce she must suffer it. But he feared her in a way. She was no ordinary woman. There was a power about her, he had to admit. She still fascinated him as she had in the beginning of their relationship and it was because of Eleanor that he felt a need to keep Rosamund's existence a secret.

He could not stay long or he would be missed and speculation would be rife.

There was to be a meeting of the Great Council and he had summoned this to Woodstock in order that he might enjoy a brief respite with Rosamund. Now he reluctantly said farewell to her and went back to take part in it.

Here a difference arose between the King and Thomas. It was not a matter of great moment, but it was a sign of what was to come, like the rumble of distant thunder of an approaching storm.

The problem of raising taxes was always a pressing one. Henry was not extravagant in his personal life; but he needed a constant supply of money to keep his armies in readiness, that he might go into action if need be at home in England and most certainly he would have at some time to maintain his overseas possessions.

It was the custom throughout the country to pay a tax which was quite small to the Sheriff of the district. This had been in existence before the Norman conquest and Henry proposed that this tax instead of being paid to the Sheriffs should come to the national exchequer.

There was an outcry among the landowners. The Sheriffs were appointed by the King whom they paid handsomely for their appointments. Because of these taxes collected from every man who owned land in their area they grew rich very quickly.

Thomas said that if the tax was paid into the Exchequer the Sheriffs would demand it be paid to them also, so that any man who owned land would in effect be paying a double tax.

255

He had a great following and he did not think he would have any difficulty in making the King see his point.

Henry, however, aware of the sly comments of the Queen who had hinted that he was ready to be guided by his Archbishop, decided that he would not give way in this issue.

Thomas's vast lands in the See of Canterbury gave him a big interest in the matter, and he spoke in favour of the landowners.

"Saving your pleasure, my Lord King," he told Henry at the Council, "we will not pay these monies as a tax."

How dared Thomas defy him! How dared he stand up before the Council and deliberately state that he would not do what the King demanded!

"By God's eyes," cried the King, using the oath he favoured when his anger was mounting that it might be a warning to any who heard it not to provoke him further, "they shall be paid as a tax and entered in the King's books."

"Out of reverence for the same eyes," replied Thomas, "they will not be paid on my land, and not a penny from any land which, by law, belongs to the Church."

Here—even on such a small matter—was the conflict between Church and State showing itself.

Henry knew that he had lost. The Church had its laws outside the State.

Eleanor affected to be amused by the outcome.

"It would seem your clever Archbiship has more power than the King."

"It is this matter of the law of the Church against the law of the State," he grumbled.

"It is time that was changed," said Eleanor. "Is the King the ruler of his country or is the Archbishop of Canterbury?"

She did not help to soothe his resentment.

*   *   *

It was inevitable that another cause for friction should arise. This took place very soon after the affair of the Sheriff's tax.

If a member of the Church committed a crime he was tried not by the King's court of law but by a court set up by the Church. This was a matter which had long rankled among the high officials of the State. It was said that the courts set up by the Church were too lenient with their members, and that a much less harsh punishment was meted out to offenders than was the case in the secular court.

The case of Philip de Brois was an example.

This man was a Canon who had been accused of murdering a soldier. This had taken place some time before, when Theobald was Archbishop and the diocesan court which had tried him had found him not guilty and acquitted him.

The matter was not allowed to rest. From time to time the King's travelling judges visited various parts of the country in order to try and pass sentence on those who had committed crimes. It was this order instituted by Henry which had brought considerable law and order to the country and made the roads safe for travellers.

Several men who were convinced of the guilt of Philip de Brois captured him and brought him before the King's Judge Simon Fitz-Peter.

De Brois, believing his case to have been settled, defied the court. As a Canon, he said, the King's justiciary had no power over him and he demanded his release. He quoted the law and was released.

When the matter was reported to Henry he was furious.

"The King's justice has been insulted," he cried. "I'll not allow this to pass. That man shall be taken and brought to trial and his judge shall be my justiciary Simon Fitz-Peter. We shall see how he fares then."

News of what was happening was then brought to Thomas at Canterbury. He was still saddened by the matter of the Sheriff's tax. These conflicts between himself and the King he had foreseen, and now there was this matter of the accused Canon.

He was convinced that the law of the Church must stand, even though it angered the King. They had argued about it in the old days, but good humouredly Now it was a matter of putting their beliefs into practice.

The King had always said: "The State should be supreme."

And Thomas: "In all matters but where it infringes on the law of the Church."

"Is the Pope then ruler of England?" Henry had demanded.

"The Pope is head of the Church wherever it may be."

Thomas knew how that rankled! Henry was not the first King to seek to throw off the restraint.

"Philip de Brois cannot be tried by the King's justiciary," declared Thomas. "But since the King demands another trial he shall be tried in my own court at Canterbury."

The King was powerless. He knew that Thomas had the law of the Church on his side and until that was altered he must give way.

The second time in a few months! This was what came of making Thomas Becket Archbishop of Canterbury.

At the court of Canterbury Philip de Brois was again acquitted of murder but for his comtempt of the King's court he was sentenced to be flogged. He also had to forfeit two years of his salary from the Church.

"So," cried the King, "the Archbishop of Canterbury allows his clerics to murder as they will."

"In the Archbishop of Canterbury's court Philip de Brois was acquitted of murder," was Thomas's answer.

"One law for the churchman, one for the layman," cried the King. "By God, I'll have justice in my land."

He was however a little appeased by the sentence which had been passed on Philip de Brois. At least it showed that the Church had some respect for the King's court.

But the rift was growing.

The King, urged on by his wife and mother, determined to take his battle against the Church a step further.

He called together a Council at Westminster and at this declared that if a cleric was guilty of a crime he should be given over to the King's officers to be punished. He demanded that the Bishops support him on this point for he was determined to maintain law and order in the land. The force with which he addressed the company gave no doubt of the determination with which he backed up his demands; and everyone knew that this was a direct stab at Thomas Becket.

The Archbishop of York, that Roger de Pont l'Evêque who during their sojourn in Theobald's household had hated Thomas because he was jealous of him, saw an opportunity of doing considerable harm to the man who had now risen to the highest peak of power in the church.

Roger had watched the rise of Thomas; he had gnashed his teeth over the stories of the King's love for that man; he had heard how they had roamed the country together, behaving as some said like two schoolboys, how they shared games and jokes and behaved like brothers. It was very galling to a man of Roger's ambition to see Thomas Becket rise so high.

He saw now a chance of contributing to his fall, for if the King had once loved Becket, he was at this time irritated by his recent behaviour.

The members of the Church met to discuss the King's

ultimatum and the three chief of them were Roger of York, Hilary of Chichester and Gilbert Foliot of London. Right or wrong, Roger had decided that he would stand against the Archbishop. He persuaded the Bishops that they must do this, for the King was too strong for them.

Thomas summoned them to Canterbury.

"You are foolish!" he cried. "What means this? It is the Church's ruling that a man cannot be punished twice for the same crime. The liberty of the Church is involved in this."

"Of what use the liberty of the Church, if the Church itself should perish?"

"You are bewitched," cried Thomas. "Are we to add sin to sin? It is when the Church is in trouble and not merely in times of peace that a Bishop should dare to do his duty. In the old days men gave their blood for the Church and now they must be prepared to die if need be in defence of the Church's liberty. By God, I swear that it is not safe for us to leave that form which we have received from our fathers. We cannot expose anyone to death for we are not allowed to take part in any trial of life and death, and if we were to pass a man of the Church over to the secular court they could sentence him to death."

Roger had to admit the power of the man and he could not persuade the others to stand out against him.

Henry plunged into another of his violent rages.

"I will have obedience," he shouted. "I will not allow these clerics to defy me because of their cloth. I will have them swear, man by man, that they obey royal customs in all things."

He sent for the Bishops, including the one he called their master—Thomas Becket, Archbishop of Canterbury.

When they were gathered together he raged before them in such a manner as to strike terror into all their hearts—except that of Thomas. He had seen those rages before.

Oh Henry, he thought, how far we have grown apart. I knew it was the end of our friendship when I became your Archbishop.

Henry was saddened too. How different it used to be, Thomas! he thought. You were my friend when you were my Chancellor. Everything you did was for my good. You loved me; you served me well. And now you set yourself against me. You have another master, your Church. I'll get you back, Thomas. I'll force you back.

"I will not speak to you collectively," declared the King, "but separately."

He was gleeful. That was clever. Singly he could strike terror into their miserable hearts.

One by one the Bishops gave way; Roger cynically, his eyes on future advancement at the time when Thomas was disgraced and sent into exile, or whatever fate the King had reserved for him, for then his place would be vacant and the King would give it to one who knew where his advantage lay.

Thomas could have wept with sorrow. The Bishops had betrayed the Church. Of course he knew how violent Henry could be when he was fighting for his own way. He could understand what veiled threats were uttered; he knew exactly how those defaulting Bishops would make peace with their consciences.

And then Thomas?

"So you will not swear to serve your King?" demanded Henry.

"I will give him all earthly honour saving my order," answered Thomas.

The King might rave and rant but he would not swerve from that. Thomas remained adamant, and finally the King strode out in great anger.

In his private chamber he sent for his secretary.

"Write to the Archbishop of Canterbury," he commanded. "Say that any posts, honours and land which came into his possession when he was Chancellor of this realm are to be resigned to me without delay."

The secretary complied and the King felt a little eased. That would show Thomas what it meant to defy his master. Thomas loved his luxurious houses; he loved all the pomp that went with them. Very well, he should do without them.

Thomas immediately complied with the King's demands.

"That is settled then," said Henry.

*   *   *

The King made it clear that he had not done with this matter, but meanwhile another had arisen which gave him great cause for annoyance.

His brother Geoffrey was dead but his younger brother William still lived and Henry was eager to make provision for him. A young brother roaming the kingdom of England or the dukedom of Normandy could come to mischief.

He had often discussed this matter with his mother and they had decided that when an opportunity occurred for William to marry advantageously, he should take it.

The opportunity came. King Stephen's son William had died in the service of Henry. His widow, the Countess of Warenne, was a very rich woman. Here was William's chance, decided Henry.

He called William to him and told him of his plans; William decided that he must first see the lady and become acquainted with her before she knew that a match had been suggested between them.

Henry was nothing loath to a little romantic behaviour and when William came to him and told him that he loved the Countess of Warenne deeply, Henry was delighted.

"The marriage should not be delayed," said the King, "for the sooner the Warenne estates are securely in the family the better."

Opposition came from a quarter from which Henry was now becoming accustomed to getting it.

The Archbishop of Canterbury pointed out that William Plantagenet and William of Blois had been second cousins; therefore the marriage of a widow of one to the other was not legal.

Henry cursed the meddlesome Archbishop but in view of the fact that his own wife had obtained a divorce on the grounds of consanguinity with Louis of France, he could not demur.

He kept the Countess's estates in the family by marrying her off to one of his illegitimate half-brothers, but he was very angry.

So was his brother William. He declared he would no longer stay in a country which was ruled by an Archbishop, and went to join his mother in Normandy.

Matilda and he agreed about the character of Thomas Becket, and Matilda whipped up William's resentment to fury. Henry had been a fool, as she had always said, to favour the man. He should have known that to pick a Chancellor out of the gutter was folly. She had over the years exaggerated Becket's lowly origins. It had always been a characteristic of hers to make the facts fit her case. Thomas Becket would ruin the country she was sure. Henry should send him into exile and the sooner he appointed another Primate the better.

She would not let the matter rest. She discussed it day after day with her son until it seemed to him that he had lost everything that made life worth living. When he caught a cold his spirits were so low that he could not throw it off and it affected his chest.

In the draughty castle he grew very ill and in his delirium he talked of the Countess of Warenne and how he no longer wished to live because he had been unable to marry her.

When he died Matilda, wild with grief, proclaimed that Thomas Becket had killed her son.

She wrote at once to Henry.

"Your brother is dead. Life was no longer worth living for him when he lost the woman he loved. Your Archbishop has done this."

When the news reached Henry he was stunned.

William was but a young man—younger than he was! And he was dead! Was it possible to die of love? His mother declared it was. "If he had been allowed to marry the woman he loved this would never have happened to him," she insisted.

Nor would it, thought Henry. His wife would have cared for him for she loved him. But Thomas Becket would not permit the marriage to take place, and now my brother William is dead!

You have a lot to answer for, Thomas Becket, and this is something I shall never forget nor forgive.

The King's Triumph

Henry could not stop thinking of Becket. Sometimes he would awake from a dream in which they had been the friends they used to be when they were King and Chancellor together. No one could amuse him as Becket had done. He could find little pleasure in the company of others. Even at Woodstock he would find himself thinking of Becket.

The man seemed determined to plague him. What had happened to him? He had grown serious—the churchman had completely superseded the gay reveller, for Becket *had* been gay. How he had loved to sit at his table and look at the fine plate he possessed and the magnificent livery of his servants! If he himself ate frugally and drank little it had not mattered. It had been part of the eccentricity of the man which Henry had found so attractive.

Was there a way, he wondered, in which they could be reconciled? If only Becket would give way to his wishes the whole Church would follow him. As for the Pope, he was not in too happy a position and could make little trouble. Henry could reform the Church in his country and Alexander could not afford to raise a voice against him.

He decided to see Thomas and he sent a command for him to meet him at Northampton.

When the King arrived with his great retinue he sent a

message to Thomas to stay where he was, for it would be impossible for the town to accommodate two great parties such as theirs would be.

And I doubt not, thought the King angrily, that your party is as grand and as great as mine for you were ever a lover of ostentation, my Archbishop.

They met in a field and Thomas rode his horse to meet that of the King. For a moment they remained looking at each other, and the knowledge of the great friendship which had once been theirs swept over them both so that it was an emotional moment.

Then the King said: "Dismount. We will walk and talk."

This they did and the King took Thomas's arm as he said, "I marvel that you have forgotten all the favour I have shown you. I wonder how you could be so ungrateful as to oppose me in everything."

"My lord, I am not ungrateful for favours received from you alone nor from God through you. I would never resist your will as long as it is also the will of God. You are my lord. But God is your Lord and mine also and it would be good for neither of us if I should leave his will for yours. One day we shall both stand before him to be judged."

The King made an impatient movement but Thomas would not be silenced. He went on: "St Peter says we must obey God rather than man. And although I would obey the wishes of my King whenever it was possible I could not do so if they went against my duty to God."

"Pray do not preach me sermons," retorted Henry. "I have not come here for that."

"I do not intend to preach, my lord, only to tell you what is my mind concerning these matters."

"And what think you is in my mind? Is the King to be tutored by one of his rustics?"

"You refer to my humble birth. It is true I am not royal. St Peter was not royal either but God gave him the keys of Heaven and made him the head of the Catholic Church."

"That is true," said the King. "But then he died for his Lord."

"I will die for my Lord when the time comes."

"You have risen high and you think that because of this which has come to you through my goodness you are of such importance that you may defy me. Do not trust too much in my friendship."

"I trust in the Lord," said Thomas soberly, "for foolish is the man who puts his trust in men."

"Enough of this, Thomas. We are almost in agreement. I just wish you to swear to serve your King."

"So will I, but only when serving him does not conflict with the will of God."

"Only when . . . ! I will not have conditions. Swear to serve your King."

"I could not . . . without that condition."

"I have tried to reason with you, but you will not be reasoned with. Because of the friendship I once felt for you and could feel again, I have met you here. I wished to speak to you in person. I am offering to accept you again, Thomas, that things may be as they once were before between us. I have been fond of you. I miss you. Do you remember how amusing life was when we were together? Come Thomas. All you have to do is say a few words. Say them, Thomas, and all will be well."

"I cannot say what you wish, my lord, for as I see it to do so would be to deny my God."

"A plague on your sermons and a plague on you, Becket. I have raised you up. So could I put you back. Think of that, rustic. And remember you stand against the King."

With that he turned and left Thomas.

* * *

There was only one thing to be done and that was to appeal to the Pope. In France news of the conflict between King and Archbishop had already been received. Louis sent letters of encouragement to Thomas and hinted that if he should find it impossible to go on living in England there would be a welcome for him in France.

The position of the Pope was not a very happy one. The Emperor of Germany had joined forces with his rival and had forced Alexander to leave Italy. He was now residing uneasily in France. He was afraid to offend Henry as he had been on other occasions. At the same time he believed that Thomas was in the right.

But it came to his ears that Henry Plantagenet had uttered threats against him and because of his very precarious position he could not face any opposition from that quarter. Wanting to applaud Becket he must yet placate the King, who had already written his account of the matter.

The Pope would understand, wrote Henry, that a King could not tolerate what appeared to be disobedience in any of his subjects be they priests or merchants. All he wished was a statement from the Archbishop to the effect that he would serve his King in all ways, and this he must have for the sake of his kingly dignity. Neither the Pope nor the Archbishop must think for one moment that he would take advantage of this. He wanted to see a strong Church. He knew full well that it was their religious beliefs that kept men virtuous. Did they think he wanted a nation of thieves and robbers and irreligious men? Not he! But a King could not have it be known that some of his subjects believed they could defy him; ay, and had boasted of it in public.

The Pope wrote to Thomas to the effect that he believed there should be moderation and submission for thus he was sure that Thomas could avert great trouble which would bring no good to the Church. He commanded Thomas to submit to the King for, he added, he believed the King would accept nothing else and this was not the time for the Church to quarrel with the King of England.

When he received this letter, Thomas was astonished and depressed. He must obey the Pope.

He discovered that the King was at Woodstock, and there in his palace Henry agreed to see him.

Henry was in a good mood. He invariably was at Woodstock, and when he heard that Thomas was asking for an audience he received him at once.

"Well, Thomas?"

"My lord. I have heard from His Holiness."

"And what instructions have you had from him?" asked the King.

"He tells me that I must do as you wish. I must agree to serve you wholeheartedly."

"Ah," said the King. "So our little trouble is over. You have decided to pay me the homage due to your King?"

"The Pope had sent his command."

"He had wisdom enough for that," said Henry with a laugh.

"I cannot disobey him."

"But you don't agree with him?" cried Henry.

"I think I was right in what I did."

"But you will now withdraw. That is better. You will swear absolute allegiance to your King."

"I do," said Thomas, "for I am instructed by the Pope that

this assurance is only to preserve your dignity and you will not put into action any reforms regarding the Church."

"You have sworn, Thomas."

"Yes, my lord."

"That is good. You have sworn to me in private, but because you declared your disobedience in public, in public must you swear your allegiance. Farewell Thomas. We shall meet soon. I shall summon you to Clarendon where you may make your oath of submission publicly."

*   *   *

No sooner had Thomas received the King's summons to Clarendon than he began to question what he had done.

The Pope was in a difficult position; he had advised him to submit to Henry because he feared the King's antagonism. Thomas should never have taken his advice. He knew Henry well. Who should know him better? During the years when he had been his Chancellor and they had roamed the countryside together he had become familiar with every twist and turn of that violent nature. When Henry had made up his mind to have something, he was going to have it. He would lie, cheat, fight, threaten to do anything to obtain it. He had no scruples and now it was clear that he had made a vow that he was going to subdue his one-time friend and Chancellor. He had to show Thomas that he was his superior. It had always been so in their games and practical jokes. Henry liked a good adversary that he might glean more glory in victory.

His promises that he had no wish to interfere with the Church meant nothing. Of course he wanted to interfere with the Church. He wanted to bring it to heel as he did his dogs. He was going to make the Church serve the State. He might pay lip service to the Pope, but everyone in the kingdom be they Bishops or Archbishops must learn that he was the master.

And Thomas had privately agreed to accept his rule in all matters—because a weak Pope had been afraid to order him to do otherwise.

Thomas spent hours on his knees in prayer. His hair shirt tortured him, even more than it would most men for his poor circulation made his skin extra sensitive. Yet he did this penance in the hope that he might expiate his sins and win God's help. He thought of his pride when Richer de L'Aigle

267

had taken him to Pevensey, and the joy he had found in living the life of a nobleman. He thought of his rich garments, his cloaks lined with fur, his velvet doublets, the delight he had taken in being the King's constant companion. Earthly vanity that had been. Was he being asked to pay for it now?

As soon as he had become Archbishop of Canterbury he had changed. His love of luxury had abated for he had seen the folly of it. He remembered how he had turned his face from Canterbury, how he had tried so hard not to take the post, for he knew it would be an end to the merry life.

And now his feet were firmly placed on a path which he must follow, for it was his destiny.

He trusted that God would show him what to do at Clarendon for he knew what happened there was going to affect his future for good or ill.

In the great hall, Henry was seated in the centre of the dais and on his left hand was his son, young Henry, aged nine years old.

The boy's eyes lit up at the sight of Thomas and the Archbishop's heart warmed to him. There was one who loved him. He did not meet the King's eyes but he knew that the elder Henry watched him covertly.

As Primate he took the place on the right hand of the King—the second most important post in the kingdom. There were the Bishops all assembled and among them the Archbishop of York, Roger de Pont l'Evêque. Roger could not hide his satisfaction. He would be remembering the old days in the household of Theobald when a certain young man—not of noble birth—had joined the young men there and won the old Archbishop's affection as none of the others had done. Roger had done his best to appease his envy by getting Thomas expelled; he had succeeded in this on two occasions but when Thomas had been recalled he was in higher favour than ever. How envious Roger must have been when he heard of the King's friendship with the man he hated! People used to say in those days: The King loves the Chancellor more than any other living being.

And now here was triumph, for everyone in that hall knew that they had been assembled to witness the public humiliation of the King's one-time beloved friend.

Yet Thomas had his sympathizers there—mellow men, men of integrity. One was Henry of Winchester, brother of King Stephen, a man who had once had great ambitions, but who had long discarded them realizing their emptiness. He knew the nature of the King and that of Thomas too. The Earl of Leicester and Robert of Luci were good honest men who served the King well. They would not go against Henry but they did not wish to see such a man as Thomas Becket humiliated. They understood his scruples and applauded them and would rather that it had not been necessary to call this meeting.

If Thomas knew the King, the King knew Thomas. He was well aware that Thomas had given him his verbal promise because as a churchman he had believed he must obey the Pope. It was a slip, Thomas, thought the King exultantly. Your poor weak Pope trembled for his own skin, and you fell into the trap. And now you regret it. And you can well refuse to take the oath in public. And I know you well. I know your eloquence. I know that you could sway a multitude to your way of thinking. Look around the hall, Thomas. See the armed men I have had stationed here. Others see them. They will know for what purpose they are here. There is not a man in this hall who would dare offend his King, Thomas. Except perhaps you. Consider the folly of it, Thomas.

He himself opened the meeting.

The Archbishop of Canterbury, he said, had come to swear before them all that he would unconditionally serve his King.

Thomas rose from his seat.

"My lord," he said. "I will swear to serve my King when that service does not conflict with my duty to the Church."

The King's face was scarlet, his eyes blazed and every man in the hall save Thomas trembled. Thomas felt only exultation, for he had done what he believed was right. He had feared that in that assembly he might have quailed, but he had come through safely, and he felt he was sustained by God.

Henry's fury broke forth. So great was his rage that he was incoherent. He could only fling abuse at his Archbishop. Thomas remained calm and pale as though he did not hear the King.

Nor did he. He was thinking, I have taken the first step. Whatever happens to me I must accept. If it is death then it will soon be over and I shall have died for God and the Church.

The King suddenly strode out of the hall. His son took a trembling look at Thomas and followed him. Thomas caught the cynical eye of the Archbishop of York, who in those seconds could not disguise his pleasure.

Thomas made his way to his lodging that he might meditate and pray for strength to go on as he had begun. It was not long before Joceline, Bishop of Salisbury and Roger, Bishop of Worcester called on him.

"Come in, my friends," said Thomas.

They came in and regarded him with fearful eyes.

"We implore you, my lord," said the Bishop of Salisbury, "to make your peace with the King."

"I do not wish to be at war with the King," answered Thomas.

"He will kill us all if you do not take the oath, my lord."

"Then we must die. It will not be the first time that men have died for the Church of God. Countless hosts of saints have taught us by word and example: God's will be done."

"You have seen the King's mood. You saw the armed men who filled the hall."

"I saw them," said Thomas. "Pray for courage. It may be that our hour has come. If so, our only fear must be that we may lack the courage to face it. Pray for that courage. God will not fail you."

They went away sorrowing and in great fear.

Then came the Earl of Leicester and the King's uncle, the Earl of Cornwall.

"The King considers himself to have been insulted," said Leicester. "He declares he will be avenged."

"Then avenged he must be."

"You have only to swear that you will give absolute obedience to the King."

"I am a man of the Church."

"The King declares that you have promised him in private to serve him."

"I told him that the Pope had advised me to."

"We advise you too, my lord. We are your friends. We deplore this quarrel between you and the King."

"I know you to be my good friends and I thank you for it. I know you to be wise men. It is easy for you to swear to serve the King absolutely because you have not given your allegiance to the Church. I have told the King that I will obey him in all temporal matters. It is only when his will conflicts with that of Holy Church that I must disobey him and follow my true Master."

"The King is in an ugly mood."

"I know those moods well. Many times have I witnessed them."

"Never before were they directed in earnest against you."

"I know that the King is a man who will not be crossed. He will have what he wants and if he wants my blood I doubt not that he will have it."

"He does not want your blood, only your obedience."

"But if I cannot give him what he asks?"

"We fear, my lord, that we may be called upon to do you to death. That would to us be a crime, but we must perforce commit it if it is the King's command that we should."

"Ah, gentlemen, that is a matter for your consciences."

"If you would but swear . . ."

"Nay, my lords. That is something I cannot do. Leave me now. Go to the quiet of your chambers and pray that when your hour of decision comes God will enable you to do what is right."

Thomas was still on his knees when there was yet another visitor. This was the Grand Master of the English Templars, Richard of Hastings, and with him came another of the Templars, Hostes of Boulogne.

These were holy men and Thomas trusted them. They were in the King's confidence and assured Thomas that they knew his mind and that he had talked to them of his true feelings.

"The King has a deep affection for you still, my lord Archbishop," said Richard of Hastings. "He wishes us to be his mediators. He says you will readily understand the position in which by the stubbornness of your determination and the violence of his temper you have been placed. This matter has gone so far that he cannot retreat. It would seem weak in a king, who having shown what he says he is determined to have, to accept something less. He has sworn to us that he wishes only to have your oath in public and if you will give it he will not tamper with the laws of the Church."

"Is this indeed so?" asked Thomas.

"He has sworn it is so."

"He does not always keep his promises."

"He has asked what good would come to the realm if he had an open quarrel with the Church. What harm would come if he quarrelled with his Primate so as to make a rift between the State and the Church? The King wants a reconciliation with you. If you will but return to the hall and give him what he wants you need have no fear. The King has given his word. But you must swear in public to take the oath of absolute obedience to the Crown."

"You have indeed come from the King?"

271

"We have indeed."

"And he has sworn that he will keep to his promises not to interfere in Church matters?"

"He has sworn."

"Then I will send for my Bishops and tell them that on your advice and assurances I can make this oath in public."

*　　*　　*

Thomas returned to the hall. The Archbishop of York watched him cynically while the others looked as though a great burden had fallen from their shoulders.

The King was almost merry. His eyes were kindly and full of affection as he turned to his Archbishop of Canterbury.

Thomas rose to his feet and swore to the assembly that he would obey the customs of the realm in good faith.

"You have all heard what the Archbishop has promised me on his own part," cried the King in a loud voice. "Now it only remains that at his bidding the other Bishops should do the same."

"I will that they satisfy your honour as I have done," said Thomas.

All the Bishops rose and made their promise. Only Joceline Bishop of Salisbury hesitated and looked at Thomas.

"What ails you, my lord Bishop of Salisbury?" roared the King.

"You are sure, my lord," asked the Bishop looking at Thomas, "that it is right for me to take this oath?"

"By God's eyes," cried the King, "that man is ever against me."

His eyes narrowed and he had turned to one of his armed soldiers.

Thomas said quickly: "You should take the oath, my lord, as we all have done." And forthwith Joceline of Salisbury took the oath.

"Now," cried the King, "everyone here has heard the promises the Archbishops and Bishops have made that the laws and customs of my kingdom shall be observed. In order that there may be no further dispute on the subject, let my grandfather Henry's laws be committed to writing."

The meeting ended in triumph for the King.

Flight from England

In the great hall of the justiciary Richard de Luci read out the clauses of the code which was known as the Constitution of Clarendon, and Thomas realized at once that he had been duped. Henry had had no more compunction in lying to the Templars than he had to him. He had been ready to promise anything to gain his point. Sometimes Thomas thought that this was not so much a quarrel between Church and State as a conflict between Thomas Becket and Henry II of England. It was like one of the games they had played in the past, only this time it was in deadly earnest.

When the Clerk read out that clerics were to be tried on all accusations by the King's justiciary, Thomas could not forbear crying out: "This is against the laws of the Church. Christ is judged anew before Pilate." Another clause stated that no one must leave the kingdom without the King's consent.

"The kingdom will become a prison," said Thomas. "What of those who wish to go on holy pilgrimages? What of those members of the Church who were summoned by the Pope to attend a council? Would they not be obliged to obey the Pope even if the King refused permission?"

There was worse to follow. There should be no appeals to the Pope without the King's consent.

"How could an Archbishop agree to this?" demanded Thomas. "When he receives the pallium he takes an oath not to hinder appeals to the Pope."

As Thomas protested the King sat glowering at him and when the reading was over he stood up and in a voice of thunder cried: "Now shall the members of the clergy sign and seal these constitutions and the Archbishop of Canterbury shall do so first."

Thomas looked at his Bishops, some of whom hung their heads in shame while others, more bold, looked at him appealingly. To sign and seal such a document was to deny their duty. The Bishop of Salisbury murmured that if they signed it they would be guilty of perjury.

The King looked on. His armed guard was standing alert. One word from him and there would be a bloody massacre.

"God help me," prayed Thomas.

Then he said in a clear voice: "We need time to study this document. I am sure the King in his grace will give us a few hours to discuss it together in private."

He picked up a copy—there were three—and the Archbishop of York took another.

He mounted his horse and with his small company about him, he rode to Winchester. He despised himself. He had gone too far along the road to placating the King. He should never have taken the oath in public; he should never have agreed to it in private. He should have led his weaker brethren. He should have defied the King, inviting death. What mattered it if he were done to death? All that mattered was that he should be faithful to God and the Church.

He could hear the members of his suite discussing the Constitutions.

"What could he have done?" asked one. "If he had defied the King more openly it would have been the end for us all."

"Yet has he not endangered the liberties of the Church?" asked another.

His standard-bearer, a Welshman of an impetuous nature, cried out suddenly, "Iniquity rages through the land. No one is safe who loves the truth. Now that the chief has fallen, who will stand?"

"To whom do you refer?" asked Thomas.

"To you," answered the Welshman. "You, my lord, who have betrayed your conscience and your fame and the Church. You have acted in a manner which is hateful to God and

274

against justice. You have joined with the ministers of Satan to overthrow the Church."

"Oh God of Heaven, you are right," cried Thomas. "I have brought the Church into slavery. I came not from the cloister but from the Court, not from the school of Christ but from Caesar's service. I have been proud and vain. I have been foolish. I see that I have been deserted by God and am only fit to be cast out of the Holy See."

His Archdeacon rode up beside him.

"My lord," he said, "if you have fallen low, rise up bravely. Be cautious and strong and the Lord will help you. Did he not make David great and was he not an adulterer and a murderer? Did not Peter deny him thrice and was he not the founder of His Church? You have been Saul and now you are Paul. You know what you must do. The Lord will help you do it."

"You are right, my friend," said Thomas. "I will start again. God will be beside me and never again will I fall so low. I will die for the Church if need be."

*   *   *

There seemed to be only one thing Thomas could do. He must see the Pope. He must tell him everything that had happened and ask what he must do next. The King's edict was that no one should leave the country without his consent. Even so he must get away. The King had ignored him but he would not continue to do so. Thomas knew that Henry was trying to shift the power from Canterbury to York for he was aware that in Roger there was a man of immense ambition as well as an enemy of Thomas Bocket

Thomas disguised himself as a wandering monk and with a few members of his suite rode to Romney where he had arranged that a boat should be waiting for him.

He reached the coast without mishap but so violent a wind had blown up that he was forced to abandon the project.

He could not remain at Romney but must return to Canterbury, and this he did. But he intended to try again in a clement season, and one day when the weather was mild he set out again.

His servants, believing that he had now reached France, were afraid to stay in his palace and with the exception of one cleric and his boy servant, they left.

They talked awhile of the sad fate of the Archbishop and

how the man, who many had said had ruled the King, for when he was Chancellor the King had loved him dearly, was now fallen so low, the lower for having risen so high.

"Ah, my boy, it is a lesson to us all," said the cleric. "Now go and make sure the doors are shut and bolted that we may sleep safely this night. In the morning we must depart for it will not be long before the King's men arrive. They will take away all the worldly goods of the Archbishop for the King would despoil him not only of his office but of his goods as well."

The boy took a lantern and went to do his master's bidding, and as he came into the courtyard in order to close the outer door he saw a figure slumped against the wall. He held the lantern high and peered. Then he let out a shriek and ran to his master.

"I have seen a ghost," he cried. "The Archbishop is dead and has come to haunt the place."

The cleric took the lantern and went to see for himself.

He found no ghost but Thomas himself.

"My lord," he said, "you are back then?"

"The sailors who were to take the boat across to France recognized me," said Thomas. "They would not sail, so fearful were they of the King's wrath. I see that God does not wish me to escape."

*   *   *

If this were so then he must try other methods. It occurred to him that if he could see Henry, if he could talk reasonably, if he could remind him of their past friendship they might yet come to an understanding.

He asked for a meeting and somewhat to his surprise the King, who was at Woodstock, agreed to see him.

Henry was in a mellow mood. He had spent a few days in the company of Rosamund and their two children, and these sojourns always had a softening effect on him.

When Henry saw Thomas he noticed how wan he had become.

"You've aged," he said. "You are not the merry reveller you once were."

"Nor are you, my lord King, the friend who joined in our fun."

"We have had our differences," answered Henry, "and alas

they persist. Why did you attempt to leave the country? Is there not room here for us both?"

Thomas looked at the King sadly but Henry would not meet his gaze.

The King went on: "Why have you asked for this audience? What have you to say to me?"

"I had hoped, my lord, that you might have something to say to me."

"There is much I would say to you, but first there is one thing that you must say to me. Have you come to your senses, Becket?"

"If you mean by that have I come to sign and seal the Constitutions I can only say Nay."

"Then go," cried the King. "There is nothing else I want to hear from you."

"I had hoped for the sake of the past . . ."

"By God's eyes, man, will you obey my orders or will you not? Go! Get from my sight. I will hear one thing from you and one only."

Thomas came sorrowing away.

*   *   *

The Queen had followed the conflict between Becket and Henry with some interest. It amused her to recall how great their friendship had been and how there was a time when Henry preferred that man's company to anyone else's. It was strange to think that she had been jealous of Becket. Who would be jealous of him now? Poor broken old man. If she were not so pleased by his downfall she could be sorry for him.

She was forty-two years of age now—still a beautiful woman, still able to attract men, or so her troubadours implied. They still sang songs to her and she did not feel that they flattered her overmuch.

Since her marriage with Henry she had not wanted any other man, which was strange when she considered how he angered her; but then perhaps it was because he did anger her that she found his company so stimulating.

Now when they talked together of Becket, she did not say to him as his mother had done, "I told you so." She let him pour out his disappointment in that man and fed his anger against him. It brought them nearer together.

She often wondered how many mistresses he had scattered

277

about the country. As long as there were several of them it was not really important. The only thing she would not tolerate was if there was one who specially took his fancy.

But no! She was sure this was not so. And the fact that she could talk to him of the exigencies of Thomas Becket certainly brought them closer together.

They were passionate lovers at this time, almost as they had been in the early days of their marriage. It was intriguing that his hatred of Becket was driving him into her bed.

He would lie awake sometimes and talk about him. He would tell her little incidents from the past which she had never heard before. How he had often tried to tempt Becket to indiscretions with women and never succeeded.

"You didn't try hard enough," she told him.

"But I did. I even sought to trap him. But not he. I don't believe he ever slept with a woman in his life."

"What sort of man is he?"

"Oh, manly enough. He can ride and hawk with the best. He is skilled in all the arts of chivalry."

"And where could a rustic learn such things?"

"He was always an appealing fellow. Some knight taught him these things when he was quite a boy."

"He is a schemer. He wormed his way into Theobald's good graces. I believe the Archbishop of York could tell you some stories."

"I never liked that fellow. Though he'd be loyal to me rather than to Thomas. He's ambitious. I thought Thomas was, but he's changed."

"You should not allow him to flout you."

"He is Archbishop of Canterbury. He would have to resign of his own volition."

"You should make it impossible for him to cling to office."

"How so?"

"Is it beyond your powers? You know a good deal of how he lived when he was constantly in your company. There must have been something you could bring against him."

The King's eyes shone. "I will do it," he said. "I will find something from Roger of York, and John the Marshall will surely contrive something."

"Then do this, for I do assure you that that man is determined to plague you and while he is Archbishop of Canterbury you will not be true King of England. Could you bear now to hear of something other than the affairs of your Thomas Becket? Then listen to me. I am pregnant again."

The King expressed his pleasure. He would welcome an addition to the nursery. A girl or a boy. He would not mind which.

All the same his mind was still on Thomas Becket.

* * *

As Eleanor said it was easy. John the Marshall some time before had claimed the manor of Pagham which was one of the archiepiscopal estates. The case which had been tried in the Archbishop's court had been decided in Thomas's favour. Now he could have the case re-tried in the King's court and accordingly a summons to attend was sent to the Archbishop.

After his meeting with the King, Thomas had grown so sick at heart that he had become ill and had had to take to his bed. He was therefore unable to obey the summons and sent four of his knights to the Court in his place.

This gave John the Marshall a chance. To ignore a summons to Court showed a contempt of it and this was a crime.

Thomas was ordered to appear before a council at Northampton to answer the accusation. When he approached Northampton a rider met him with the news that the lodgings which were always at his disposal in that town had been given by the King to another member of the council; he must therefore find his own shelter.

Thomas saw then that the King was determined to humiliate him, but fortunately he could go to the Saint Andrew's Monastery. Still hoping to bring about a reconciliation, Thomas went to the castle to pay his respects to the King. Henry was at Mass when he arrived and Thomas was obliged to wait in the anteroom for the service to be over. When it was Henry emerged, and as Thomas went forward ready to kiss his hand if it were extended to him for this purpose, the King walked past him as though he did not see him.

This was indeed the end, thought Thomas. The King would neither receive nor listen to him. He was clearly bent on his destruction, and if Thomas would preserve his life he must get out of the country.

When the Council sat, Thomas was called to account for having held the King's Court in contempt. He explained that he had been ill and had sent his knights to stand in for him. This was not accepted and a fine of ß500 was imposed.

Then came another list of charges. ß300 was demanded for

it was said he had received this as the warden of the castles of Berkhamstead and Eye. Thomas replied that he had spent this and more in repairs to the King's palace of the Tower of London and far from having profited from any money he had received, he had spent far more in the King's service.

Thomas's heart was heavy for he saw that the King was determined to ruin him. He had cast back in his mind to the days of their friendship when the King had given him money that he might live in a manner similar to his own. Now he demanded that this money should be paid back. Moreover Thomas had received revenues from several bishoprics and abbeys and the sum mention was some 40,000 marks.

It was no use. Thomas could not fight against such injustice. When he came out of the council chamber that day he believed the end was near.

*   *   *

The next day he was back. His Archdeacon Herbert had said to him: "My lord, we do not know what this day will bring forth, but forget not that you have the power to excommunicate all those who stand against you."

William FitzStephen, one of his faithful Canons, replied: "Our lord would not do that. The Holy Apostles did not do it when they were taken. My lord will pray for them I doubt not and forgive them."

Thomas laid his hand on FitzStephen's shoulder and blessed him.

Thomas was allowed to retire to an inner chamber and there to discuss with his Bishops what action he should take against the charges which were being brought; and finally in great impatience the King sent some of his barons to enquire whether Thomas Becket was prepared to give an account of the money he had spent during his Chancellorship.

Thomas replied with dignity that he was ready to obey the King in all things saving God's obedience. He was not bound he said to give an account of his Chancellorship and had been summoned to the court to answer the charges brought by John the Marshall and none other.

"I would remind you," he said, "that when I was chosen to become Archbishop, before my consecration I was delivered over by the King to the Church of Canterbury, free from all secular claims. I place my person and the Church of Canterbury under the protection of God and the Pope."

When the King heard what Thomas had said his fury was obvious and one of his knights reminded him that his great-grandfather, William the Conqueror, had known how to tame clerics. Had he not imprisoned Odo, Bishop of Bayeux, who was his own brother?

In the inner chamber, hearing of the King's wrath, the Bishops believed that the Archbishop would be imprisoned and doubtless have his eyes put out. They feared too that they who had been with Thomas and had listened to him and stood beside him would suffer a like fate.

It was the Earl of Leicester, a man of principle who clearly had no liking for his task, who came into the chamber.

"The King will have you deliver up your accounts or hear your sentence," he told Thomas.

"Hear me first," replied Thomas. "You, my lord Leicester, know full well that I had no wish to become the Archbishop of Canterbury and that it was the King who willed it. It was for love of him rather than for love of God that I gave way, which is why today both God and the King have deserted me. You know that when the post was given me I was declared free of all secular obligations."

"I know it," answered Leicester. "I would not pass judgement on you."

"Then I am not your prisoner."

"Nay, my lord."

"Then I shall go from here. I shall appeal to the Pope."

Thomas then rode and passed out of the chamber. As he went he stumbled over some faggots and almost fell. At that moment a sneer arose in the company and the King's bastard brother who was standing by called, "There goes a traitor."

Thomas surveyed him in such a manner that the man quailed before him.

"If I were a soldier," said Thomas, "with my own hands I should prove you false."

He mounted his horse and rode to the monastery of Saint Andrew's. There he retired to his private chapel and spent a long time on his knees, and when he went to the refectory he found that of the forty knights who had accompanied him to Northampton only six remained.

"Your table is depleted," he said sadly, but many poor people came into the monastery and begged to be allowed to gaze on the face of the man whom they were calling the saviour of the Church, and they were Thomas's guests at that meal.

When it was over Thomas asked that his bed should be

placed behind the high altar. Before he retired to it he called one of his servants to him. This was Roger de Brai, a man whom he knew he could trust to serve him with his life.

"Roger," he said, "my life is in danger. It may be this night the King will send his guards to take me."

A look of horror crossed Roger's face. He could visualize the fate which could await the Archbishop. Incarceration in a dungeon, his eyes perhaps gouged out. Left to live out a dark and wretched existence, for the King might have qualms about murdering the Archbishop of Canterbury.

"I think it is God's will that I should not be taken," said Thomas. "If I were, the fight would be over. Roger of York would fall in with the King's wishes. Henry is already trying to set York over Canterbury. This must not be. I am going to get away to France . . . if it is God's will. The King of France will be my friend and I can reach the Pope."

"What would you have me do, my lord?"

"Tell Robert de Cave and Scailman to be ready to leave with me. I can trust them as I trust you. Then saddle four horses and have them ready. These horses must not come from my stables. Take them to the monastery gate and the three of you wait there as though holding the horses for someone who is visiting the monastery. I will join you there."

"It is a rough night, my lord."

"I know it. I can hear the wind and rain, Roger. But it is tonight or not at all."

Roger went away to do his bidding and Thomas went to his bed behind the high altar. He was conducted there by Herbert his Archdeacon, and when they were alone Thomas embraced him and told him what he had planned.

"It is the only way," agreed Herbert. "You must attempt to escape tonight. Tomorrow might be too late. The King's mood is very ugly. I wondered you were not arrested in the council chamber."

"I know Henry. His courage deserted him at the last moment. He wants control of the Church but he is afraid of God's wrath. That mood will not last for before anything is his determination to have his own way. My dear good friend, I wish you to lose no time in going to Canterbury. Collect what valuables you can carry and then cross the sea. Wait for me there if you should arrive first which may well be. Go to the Monastery of Saint Bertin near Saint Omer. I trust ere long that we shall meet there. Now be gone. We must lose no time."

The Archdeacon kissed the hands of his Archbishop, asked for his blessing and was gone.

*   *   *

The church was quiet. The monastery slumbered. Thomas rose from his bed and took off his stole. He put on his black cappa, and taking only his pallium and his archiepiscopal seal set out.

Roger with the two lay brothers, Robert and Scailman, was waiting with the horses.

They went through the unguarded gate of the town and rode on to Grantham where they rested for a while. After that they reached Lincoln.

It was a long and tortuous journey and every minute they feared discovery, for so far had they to travel that the King's men might have caught them in any town where they paused to rest.

But Thomas had loyal supporters throughout the country. Many people knew that this was a struggle between the Church and the State and that the King sought to set himself in sole judgement over them. They knew that Thomas Becket was a good man. He had given much to the poor; he was a man of God who had dared defy the King. They were already looking upon him as a saint. There were few who would not feel honoured to give him shelter in their houses, and Thomas was determined to protect them by denying his identity whenever it was questioned. Thus he came to the fen country and finally to the village of Eastry close to Sandwich and but eight miles from Canterbury.

They stayed for a while in the house of a priest who found a boat for them and kept them in his house until the time came when it appeared they could make the crossing with safety.

The boat was small, the sea was rough, but they could wait no longer.

"We will place ourselves in God's hands," said Thomas. "If it is His will that we live then we shall and if the sea takes us then that is His will too."

They set off; the little boat was tossed cruelly on the waves but miraculously it seemed to keep afloat and the very violence of the wind blew the boat across the water. They landed on the sands at Oie, not far from Gravelines.

"Thank God," cried Roger, but Thomas was not sure that they were out of danger yet.

He was right because they discovered that they were in the territory which belonged to the Earl of Boulogne. This was that Matthew who had married the Abbess of Romsey, the match which Thomas had opposed. Matthew had borne him a grudge for this, for although the marriage had gone through it was only due to the King's cunning that it had and Thomas had done all in his power to prevent it.

"We dare not risk falling into the hands of the Earl of Boulogne," said Thomas. "He would send me back to the King."

So it was no use hoping for comfort. They must continue their arduous journey on foot as though they were four itinerant lay brothers. Until they had left the realm of the Earl of Boulogne they would not be safe, and there were many alarms during the journey, for the news had spread that the Archbishop of Canterbury had landed and people looked out for him.

He almost betrayed himself on one occasion when the three footsore travellers came upon a party of young men out hawking. In a careless moment Thomas showed his interest and knowledge of the hawk on the wrist of the leader of the party.

"How should a travelling lay brother know of such things?" asked the young man. "By my faith, I believe you to be the Archbishop of Canterbury."

Scailman, who was quicker witted than Roger or Robert, said quickly, "You must be a simpleton if you imagine the Archbishop of Canterbury would travel in this manner."

" 'Tis true," said the young man. "I remember when he came here as the Chancellor of England. Never had such magnificence been seen."

They passed on while the young man was telling his companions of the brilliantly caparisoned horses and the reputed extravagances of the Archbishop of Canterbury.

"We must take greater care," said Scailman.

"I must take heed that I do not fall into the trap of betraying myself," answered Thomas. "But for your quick wits, Brother Scailman, that could have been an awkward moment."

How thankful he was to see the towers of Clairmarais, a monastery close to Saint Omer. There he was given a great welcome and a messenger was sent to Saint Bertin where Herbert had already arrived.

They embraced each other, delighted that they had completed the most hazardous part of their journey. But there was no time for delay. Thomas should rest awhile at Saint Bertin and then they must make their way to Soissons.

"Once we are there," said Herbert, "we can make sure of the protection of the King of France."

Within a few days they had reached that sanctuary.

Rosamund's Bower

There was great rejoicing in France for Louis's wife had given birth to a son. A male heir for France when it had been despaired of. Louis was delighted; all over France the bells rang out and the news was proclaimed through the streets of Paris. He had feared that he could beget only daughters.

Henry heard the news with despondency. His son Henry was married to Marguerite of France and he had hoped that on the death of Louis, since the French King had then no male heir, young Henry might take the crown. He would after all have a certain claim through his wife and with the King of England and Duke of Normandy behind him, his power would be great.

Alas, fate had decided against him.

Eleanor shared his chagrin and she herself very shortly afterwards gave birth to a daughter. They called her Joanna.

The birth of his son seemed to add a new dimension to Louis's character. He cast off much of his meekness. He had a son to plan for now. This showed immediately in his reception of Thomas Becket to whom he accorded a very warm welcome.

"It is one of the royal dignities of France to protect fugitives, especially men of the Church, from their persecutors," he said. He would do everything in his power to help Thomas reach the Pope.

Henry's feelings were incomprehensible even to himself. He was half pleased that Thomas had escaped. He could have arrested him in the council chamber. Why had he not done so? he asked himself many times. Because he did not want Thomas's blood on his hands. The man exasperated him beyond endurance; he set the hot blood rushing to his head; and yet at the same time he could not entirely suppress a tenderness for him. Often memories of the old days would come crowding into his mind. What fun they had had! No one had ever amused him quite as much as Thomas. What a fool the man was! If only he had been ready to do what the King wished, their friendship would have gone on and on to enrich both their lives.

He sent his envoys to the Court of France with gifts for Louis and congratulations, which Louis knew were false, on the birth of his son.

They had come, they said, to speak of the late Archbishop of Canterbury.

Louis with surprising spirit answered that he had not known that Thomas Becket was the *late* Archbishop of Canterbury. "I am a King even as the King of England is," he went on, "yet I have not the power to depose the least of my clerics."

They realized then that Louis was not going to be helpful and that Thomas had indeed found a sanctuary with him.

They asked him if he would write to the Pope putting the King of England's grievances to him. They reminded him that during the conflict between England and France the Archbishop had worked assiduously against France.

"It was his duty," said Louis. "Had he been my subject he would have worked so for me."

There was nothing Henry could do now to prevent the case of Thomas Becket being put before the Pope, and he made sure that his side of the case should be well represented; that old enemy of Thomas's, Roger, Archbishop of York, was among his emissaries.

The friends Thomas could send, headed by Herbert, were humble in comparison; they had no rich gifts to bring to the Pope. The Pope in his Papal Court at Sens received them with affection however and was deeply moved when he heard of the suffering of Thomas Becket.

"He is alive still," he said. "Then I rejoice. He can still while in the flesh claim the privilege of martyrdom."

The next day the Pope called a meeting and the King's embassy and those who came from Thomas were present.

Carefully the Pope listened to both sides of the story and later sent for Thomas.

When he was received by the Pope and his cardinals, Thomas showed them the constitutions he had brought from Clarendon. The Pope read them with horror and Thomas confessed his sin in that he had promised to obey the King and that only when he had been called to make the promise in public had he realized that the King had no intention of keeping his word. After that he had determined to stand out against Henry no matter what happened.

"Your fault was great," said the Pope, "but you have done your best to atone for it. You have fallen from grace, but, my son, you have risen stronger than you were before. I will not give you a penance. You have already expiated your sin in all that you have suffered."

Thomas was determined that they should know the complete truth.

"Much evil has fallen on the Church on my account," he said. "I was thrust into my post by the King's favour, by the design of men, not God. I give into your hands, Holy Father, the burden which I no longer have the strength to bear."

He tried to put the archiepiscopal ring into the Pope's hands, but the Pope would not take it.

"Your work for Holy Church has atoned for all that has happened to you," he said. "You will receive the See of Canterbury fresh from my hands. Rest assured that we here shall maintain you in your cause because it is the Church's cause. You should retire, my son, to some refuge where you can meditate and regain your strength. I will send you to a monastery where you must learn to subdue the flesh. You have lived in great comfort and luxury and I wish you to learn to live with privation and poverty."

Thomas declared his burning desire to do so and it was arranged that he should for a while live at the Cistercian monastery of Pontigny which was in Burgundy.

*　　*　　*

Eleanor was once more pregnant and a few days after Christmas in the year 1166 another son was born to her. They called him John.

Soon after the birth of this son Eleanor began to wonder why the King's visits to Woodstock always raised his spirits. There was a lilt in his voice when he mentioned the place.

What, she asked herself, was so special about Woodstock? A pleasant enough place it was true, but the King had many pleasant castles and palaces. She determined to find out.

When Henry was at Woodstock she joined him there and she noticed that he disappeared for long spells at a time, and that when she asked any of her servants where he might be, she could get no satisfactory answer.

She decided she would watch him very closely herself and all the time they were at Woodstock she did this. One afternoon she was rewarded for her diligence. Looking from her window she saw the King emerging from the palace, and hastening from her room she left by a door other than the one which he had used, and so before he had gone very far she came face to face with him.

"A pleasant day," she said, "on which to take a walk."

"Oh yes, indeed," he answered somewhat shiftily she thought, and was about to say that she would accompany him when she noticed attached to his spur a ball of silk.

She was about to ask him how he had come by this when she changed her mind.

She said that she was going into the palace and would see him later. He seemed relieved and kissed her hand and as she passed him facing towards the palace she contrived to bend swiftly and pick up the ball of silk.

He passed on and she saw to her amazement that a piece of the silk was still caught in his spur and that the ball unravelled as he went.

She was very amused because if she could follow the King at some distance she would know exactly which turn he had taken in the maze of trees by following the thread.

It was an amusing incident and if he discovered her they would laugh about her shadowing him through the maze of trees.

Then it suddenly occurred to her. He had been visiting someone earlier. It must be a woman. From whom else should he have picked up a ball of silk.

A sudden anger filled her. Another light of love. He should

not have them so near the royal palaces. She would tell him so if she discovered who his new mistress was.

He was deep in the thicket, and still he was going purposefully on. She realized suddenly that the end attached to his spur had come off and he was no longer leading her. Carefully she let the end of her silk fall to the ground and followed the trail it had left. There was no sign of Henry.

She would leave the silk where it lay and retrace her steps to the Palace. When the opportunity arose she would explore the maze and see if she could discover where Henry had gone.

She was very thoughtful when he returned to the Palace for there was about him a look of contentment which she had noticed before.

The next day Henry was called away to Westminster and she declared her intention of staying behind at Woodstock for a while. Immediately she decided to explore the maze. This she did and found that the thread of silk was still there. She followed it through the paths so that she knew she was going the way the King had gone. Then the silk stopped but she could see that the trees were thinning.

It did not take her long to find the dwelling-house.

It was beautiful—a miniature palace. In the garden sat a woman; she was embroidering and in a little basket beside her lay balls of silk of the same size and colour as that which had attached itself to the King's spur.

Two young boys were playing a ball game on the grass and every now and then the woman would look at them.

There was something about the appearance of those boys which made Eleanor tremble with anger.

The woman suddenly seemed to be aware that she was watched for she looked up and encountered the intent eyes of the Queen fixed on her. She rose to her feet. Her embroidery fell to the floor. The two boys stopped playing and watched.

Eleanor went to the woman and said:

"Who are you?"

The woman answered: "Should I not ask that of you who come to my house?"

"Ask if you will. I am the Queen."

The woman turned pale. She stepped back a pace or two and glanced furtively to right and left as if looking for a way of escape.

Eleanor took her by the arm. "You had better tell me," she said.

"I am Rosamund Clifford."

The elder of the boys came up and said in a high-pitched voice: "Don't hurt my mother please."

"You are the King's mistress," said Eleanor.

Rosamund answered, "Please . . . not before the children." Then she turned to the boys and said: "Go into the house."

"Mother, we cannot leave you with this woman."

Eleanor burst out laughing. "I am your Queen. You must obey me. Go into the house. I have something to say to your mother."

"Yes, go," said Rosamund.

They went and the two women faced each other.

"How long has it been going on?" demanded Eleanor.

"For . . . for some time."

"And both of those boys are his?"

Rosamund nodded.

"I will kill him," said Eleanor. "I will kill you both. So it was to see you . . . and it has been going on for years, and that is why he comes so much to Woodstock." She took Rosamund by the shoulders and shook her. "You insignificant creature. What does he see in you? Is it simply that you do his bidding? You would never say no to him, never disagree, never be anything but what he wanted!" She continued to shake Rosamund. "You little fool. How long do you think it will last . . ."

She stopped. It had lasted for years. There might be other women but he kept Rosamund. He would not have kept Eleanor if it had not been necessary for him to do so. She was jealous; she was furiously jealous of this pink and white beauty, mild as milk and sweet as honey.

"Do not think that I shall allow this to go on," she said.

"The King wills it," answered Rosamund with a show of spirit.

"And I will that it should end."

"I have told him that it should never have been . . ."

"And yet when he comes here you receive him warmly. You cannot wait to take him to your bed. I know your kind. Do not think you deceive me. And he has got two boys on you has he not! And promised you all kinds of honours for them I'll swear! You shall say goodbye to him for you will not see him more, I promise you."

"You have spoken to the King?"

"Not yet. He knows not that I have discovered you. He is careful to hide you here, is he not? Why? Because he is afraid his wife will discover you."

"He thought it wiser for me to remain in seclusion . . ."

"I'll warrant he did. But I found you. One of your silly little balls of silk led me here. But I have found you now . . . and this will be the end, I tell you. I'll not allow it. And what will become of you, think you, when the King has tired of you? 'Twere better then that you had never been born. Why did you lose your virtue to such a man? You should have married as good women do and brought children to your lawful husband. Now what will become of you? The best thing you can do is throw yourself down from the tower of your house. Why don't you do that?"

Rosamund stared at her in horror.

"Yes. I wish to see you do it now."

"I could not."

"It is best for you. You are a harlot. It is better you were dead. I will bring you poison and you shall drink it. Or I will bring you a dagger and you can pierce your heart with it."

Rosamund thought the Queen was mad. There was such a wildness in her eyes.

"Wait . . . wait," begged Rosamund. "Wait until the King returns. If you killed me he would never forgive you."

"Do you think I want his forgiveness! He is a hard man. A selfish man. A man who will have his way. Go into your house. Think of your sins. I should repent if I were you, and the only way you can receive forgiveness is to go and sin no more. Tomorrow I will come again and by then you will have decided what you are going to do. Tonight say your prayers, ask forgiveness for your harlotry, and tomorrow be prepared to die."

Eleanor threw Rosamund from her and ran back through the maze of trees. A madness was on her.

She hated him. Why should she care so fiercely that he had deceived her? Why did it matter so much? It mattered because this was the woman he wanted. She knew how gladly he would have set Eleanor aside for her.

Back at the Palace she shut herself into her bedchamber. She lay on her bed and stared at the ceiling.

She hated Henry and she loved him.

I am ageing and she is young, she thought. Once he cared for me, but now he sees me as an old woman. Did they not shake their heads over us because I am nearly twelve years older than he is? When we were younger it did not seem to matter. I had so much to offer. Would he have wanted me if it were not for Aquitaine? Would he? As much as he now wanted Rosamund Clifford?

For all those years he had gone to her. She could tell the age of the liaison by the age of the boys. And he went to see them and was happy there—happier than he was in his royal palaces!

I will kill her, she thought. I will take to her a phial of poison and force her to drink it. When he comes to see her he will find a corpse.

She shall not live to mock me.

*   *   *

Fortunately for Rosamund Henry returned to Woodstock the next day. Eleanor came to him while he was preparing to leave, as she knew now, for that little house in which he had installed his mistress.

"So you came back early. Were you so eager to make love to Rosamund Clifford?"

He stopped short to stare at her. Caught! she thought with grim satisfaction. She saw the redness come into his eyes. He was now going to fly into one of his notorious tempers because she had found him out.

"What know you of Rosamund Clifford?" he asked.

"Oh, not as much as you, I admit. But I did discover the lady's bower."

"Who took you there?"

"You, my lord, with your little skein of silk."

"What nonsense is this!"

"No nonsense. The pretty lady's skein of silk was attached to your spur. I found it and trailed you there . . . or almost. Yesterday I paid a call on her. She did not welcome me as eagerly as she must welcome you."

"You *went* there!"

"What a haven! And two fine boys too! Henry, what a man you are for getting boys on harlots! I declare your reputation will soon be that of your grandfather and mine."

"So you have discovered this."

"Yes, indeed. You are found out."

"Know this. I will do as I will."

"We all know that, my King. But while you may do as you will with low-born maidens, you may not with the Queen of England and Duchess of Aquitaine."

Henry laughed but it was not pleasant laughter.

"You should know me well enough by now to realize that I will not be told what I must do by those two."

293

"Neither of them will tolerate a mistress here in the Palace even though she is hidden in a maze. You fool Henry, did you think you could keep the woman's existence a secret from me for ever?"

"I did not and I care not.",

"Yet you did not wish me to know."

"I thought it kinder to you not to know."

"Do you think I want your kindness? Do you think I shall fret because you have a mistress or two?"

"Nay, you are too wise. You know full well that if I want a woman I will have her."

"How long has this one been your mistress?"

"Suffice it that she is."

"You have a special fondness for this one, eh?"

"I have."

"She is as a wife to you, is she?"

"She is."

"And you would to God she were."

He looked at her steadily. "I would to God she were."

She struck at him; he caught her hand and threw her from him.

"You she-wolf," he said.

"And you are the lion. Henry the Lion, King of the Forest. But forget not the she-wolf has her fangs."

"If she dares show them to me or mine they will be torn from her. Doubt that not. And know this. If you harm Rosamund Clifford I will kill you."

"All Aquitaine would revolt against you if you dared."

"Do I care for Aquitaine? I will subdue Aquitaine as I have all my territories. Do you forget that I am the King and master of you all ... every one of you. Don't be a fool, Eleanor. You are the Queen. Does that not suffice? You have borne my heirs. We have a nursery full of them. Four fine boys. Henry will be King to follow me—*your* son. Is that not enough?"

"No. It is not enough. I will not have you sport with your mistress a stone's throw from the Palace. She must go. Get rid of her."

"I'd liefer get rid of you."

"If you go back to that woman I never want to share your bed again."

"So be it," he said. "You are no longer young. There are others who please me far more."

She struck out at him as she had done before but he seized
294

her and threw her on the bed. In the old days, there would have been a rising of sexual passion on such occasions. Not now. There was now hatred for her. It was clear to her that the two youngest children, Joanna and John, had come into being through custom or the need of a king to get as many children as he could to ensure the succession.

Suddenly she felt defeated. She was an ageing woman. She had lived an adventurous life; she had had her lovers, but that was over now.

She still had power though. She was still ruler of Aquitaine. In that fair land her troubadours still sang to her beauty.

She had a great desire then to be there.

"I am going to Aquitaine," she said.

"Your people are ever glad to have you with them," answered the King. "It is well that you should go. They grow restive when their Duchess is not among them."

"I will take Richard with me and young Marguerite."

Her anger had left her. He would be free to dally with Rosamund Clifford. Perhaps now he need not keep her in her secret house—unless the lady was coy.

Eleanor had discovered the secret of Woodstock and it had brought to her some understanding of herself. The King was tired of her. He no longer loved her. She was merely the mother of his children and the ruler of Aquitaine. Let her go. He would be free of her. Let him alone that he might give himself to those two passions which consumed him—his love for Rosamund Clifford and his battle with Thomas Becket.

*   *   *

As she knew she would, Eleanor found her children at their books. Matilda, the eldest daughter, was a year older than Richard who with his fair good looks and elegant figure was her favourite. It was not only his charm and good looks which made him so, but the fact that his father seemed to dislike him. Why? Because Richard more than the others resented the intrusion into their circle of the bastard Geoffrey—and Henry knew that more than anything on earth Eleanor loved this son.

She loved his brother Geoffrey too, and when she came into their quarters and called his name there was never any confusion because of that other. She never spoke to him if she could help it and if she was ever obliged to she never looked at him when she spoke and never called him by a name.

295

Richard called him Geoffrey the Bastard. There had been many a fight between them. She suspected that the sly little bastard complained to his father about the unkindness of Richard.

Her son Geoffrey was beautiful. Strangely enough he had inherited the looks of his grandfather of the same name, Geoffrey of Anjou who had been known as Geoffrey the Fair. There was little Eleanor, too young as yet to show much character, adoring Richard because he was by his very nature the leader.

Joanna and baby John were too young to join the schoolroom but John was already showing signs of having inherited the famous Angevin temper. Rarely, she was sure, had a child screamed so much when he was displeased as Master John.

As she watched them in those few seconds before they were aware of her, she was overwhelmed by her emotions. She had always been fond of children. Even her two daughters by Louis had been important to her during their early life. It was difficult for a Queen who had so many calls upon her time to be as much with her children as a humbler mother might have been—and in the days of her marriage to Louis she had craved adventure because she had been so bored with her marriage.

She had never been bored with Henry. Now that she hated him, for she was sure she did, he could still arouse in her an emotion which was far from boredom. She was of a nature to prefer hatred to ennui.

Richard looked up and saw her. The pleasure in his eyes compensated her for the King's contempt of her. Henry might find her ageing, no longer an inspiration to love, but Richard loved her with a love which did not depend on years. He was her beloved son; there was an understanding between them. They were allies against the King, for Richard was fully aware that for some reason his father did not like him.

Richard rose from the table and ran to her. He knelt and kissed her hands.

"Mother," he said, raising his beautiful eyes to hers.

"My dearest boy," she answered, and her son Geoffrey was already clamouring for attention.

She thought: They love me. They truly love me. Is it like this when the King comes to their schoolroom?

Geoffrey the Bastard stood up and bowed stiffly. She looked past him as though she were unaware of his existence.

296

Another child had come into the room. This was Marguerite, the little French Princess, who was married to Henry and was now being brought up in the royal household.

Marguerite curtseyed to the Queen and greeted her in her pretty accent.

Eleanor drew them all about her and asked questions about their lessons. They answered eagerly, but Richard was the cleverest she noticed with satisfaction.

"We are going to Aquitaine," she said. "That is my own country."

"Are we all going?" asked Richard.

"As yet I am unsure, but one thing I know. You, my son, will go with me."

Richard laughed aloud to show his pleasure.

"That pleases you, my boy?" she asked ruffling his fair curly hair.

He nodded. "But if they had not let me go . . ." *They* meant his father . . . "I should have followed you."

"How would you have done that?"

"I would have ridden to the sea and got into the boat and then I would have ridden on to Aquitaine."

"You will be an adventurer, my son."

Then she told them about Aquitaine and how the troubadours came to the Court and sang beautiful songs, for Aquitaine was the home of the troubadours.

"Listen, Marguerite," commanded Richard. "Does not my mother tell beautiful stories? Is she not better than your old Becket?"

"What is this talk of Becket?" asked the Queen.

"Marguerite always talks of him. She says that she and Henry cried when he went. Marguerite loved him . . . so did Henry. They said they loved him better than anyone, better than our father . . . better than you . . . That was wicked wasn't it, my lady, for he is a wicked man."

"You listen to gossip," said the Queen. "You will not mention this man. He was wicked because he offended the King. That is an end of him."

"Is he dead?" asked Richard, at which Marguerite burst into tears.

"He is not dead," said the Queen to pacify Marguerite. "But he is not to be spoken of. Now I will sing you a song from Aquitaine and you will understand then how happy we shall be there."

And there with Richard leaning against her knee and Geoffrey looking at her with wondering eyes, and Matilda and Marguerite sitting on their small stools at her feet, she thought: Here is my future, in these beautiful sons and particularly Richard. What care I for you, Henry Plantagenet, when I have my sons? I will bind them to me and they shall be truly mine. They will hate those who do not treat me well—even though that be you, King Henry.

* * *

When Eleanor left England the King was relieved. He decided now that he would live openly with Rosamund and brought her out of seclusion. She was a great solace to him but he was a worried man. He thought constantly of Thomas Becket, and try as he might he could not get the man out of his mind. Thomas would be living now in poverty in his monastery. Thomas who had loved luxury and needed comforts. Henry remembered how cold Thomas had been when the wind blew and how he had laughed at him for his weakness. But Thomas was by no means weak. He had a strong spirit and was of the stuff that martyrs are made.

There was not room for us both in England, thought Henry.

He could not long enjoy his solitude in England, peaceful as everything was there. Fresh trouble had broken out in Brittany which meant crossing the seas again. He said a fond farewell to Rosamund and left.

"The fate of all our kings, since my ancestor William the Conqueror took this land and added it to his estates of Normandy," he mused.

In September news came to him that his mother, still known as the Empress Matilda, was grievously sick at Rouen; and before he could get to her side she was dead.

That saddened him. There had been affection between them, and she had loved him as dearly as she was capable of loving anyone. Now that she was dead he thought of all she had done for him; how, when she had known that the English crown could not be hers she had schemed for it to be his. He had been her favourite. Her brothers—now both dead—had been nowhere with her.

In a way she reminded him of Eleanor—both strong women, both brought up with the idea that they would be rulers. It was a mistake to bring up women so. Matilda's married life had been stormy from the start. At least he and Eleanor had started by loving each other.

As mothers he compared the two women. Eleanor seemed to be developing an obsession concerning that young cub Richard. And I never took to him—mine though he undoubtedly is. He's his mother's boy. Ready to defend her against any—including me. A fine sportsman. It did a man good to look at such a boy and know he was his son. But he could not like him—not as he could young Geoffrey, the whore's son. Strange, he had begun by making much of the boy because Eleanor hated to have him in her nurseries, and it had grown from that. And Henry, his first born since they had lost William, Henry was a fine boy. Charming and handsome. A son to be proud of. There was an estrangement between them now for the boy had been put under the tutelage of Becket, and the man had somehow weaned him from his natural affections and taken them himself. Thus when there had been a quarrel between Becket and the King, the boy would take the side of his tutor rather than his father.

Becket. It all came back to Becket.

* * *

The King had been thinking about his eldest son and some time before it had occurred to him that if young Henry were crowned King of England during his father's lifetime there could be no doubt of the succession.

Some of his ministers thought that it would be unwise to have two crowned Kings.

"My own son!" cried Henry. "What should I fear from him?"

True, young Henry was but a boy, but that would not always be so.

The more he thought of the idea the more he liked it. It would bind young Henry to him. Surely he would be grateful to a father who had done so much for him. Surely that would wean his allegiance from Becket.

Then again his ministers reminded him, it was a law that a king must be crowned by the Archbishop of Canterbury, and as the Archbishop was in exile who could perform this important ceremony?

There was Roger, Archbishop of York, and the King's servant. But the Archbishop of York was not the primate, though the King had done everything in his power to make him so.

In the privacy of his apartments he thought: What if I made my peace with Thomas? Then he could come back and crown young Henry. He had to admit that he wanted Thomas back. He wanted to renew the fight. He couldn't help it. The man had been close to him. Young Henry mourned for Thomas and so in a way did his father.

Fortunately for Henry, Pope Alexander was a man of devious ways and when such a man was in difficulties, as Alexander undoubtedly was, it was not an insuperable task to make him agree to something which was outside his rights.

In a weak moment Alexander agreed that the coronation of young Henry should be performed by Roger Archbishop of York.

Knowing that having been forced by Henry to make such a concession Alexander would immediately attempt to rescind it, Henry put preparations for the coronation into progress.

He sent word to Eleanor that Henry, who had joined her and the other children in Aquitaine, was to be brought to Caen with his wife, young Marguerite, and wait there until he sent for him.

Eleanor had written to the King telling him that Marguerite had declared that the coronation could be no coronation unless it was performed by the Archbishop of Canterbury, and this so angered the King that when he sent for his son he commanded that he come alone. If Marguerite thought she must be crowned by her beloved Becket she should have no coronation at all.

Meanwhile messengers had arrived from the Pope who, afraid of what he had done, sent letters to cancel his previous promise.

Henry took the letters and promptly burned them. He gave the impression that he had not received them. He had the ports watched and all travellers searched so anxious was he that no edict should reach his Bishops from the Pope. One however did get through. This was a nun who had been sent by Thomas and she carried a letter to Roger of York.

She arrived and found her way to Roger on the day before that fixed for the coronation. He read it. Thomas forbade him! The Pope forbade him! Roger had come to his present position through obeying the King, not Thomas and the Pope.

The day dawned and young Henry, aged sixteen and reckoned to be the most handsome prince in the world, was crowned by Roger de Pont l'Evêque, as King of England.

The King watched with complacence.

He had yet again proved that he could do without an Archbishop of Canterbury, and he had secured the succession—so he believed.

He himself was thirty-seven years of age and constantly engaged in battle as he was he might meet his death at any time.

All was well. England would have a King to follow him, if by mischance he were to meet his end.

Traitor's Meadow

There was one who was not pleased by the coronation and that was the King of France. It was the custom for kings of France to have their eldest sons crowned before their deaths and so make a new king who could step right on to the throne when the old man died. But what of his daughter? Was she not the wife of young Henry? Why was she not crowned?

Louis then began to make attacks on the Vexin for he said that if Henry did not regard her as young Henry's wife and Queen, he saw no reason why he should have her dowry.

Henry decided that it was easier to crown Marguerite and make peace with Louis than to stand out against the crowning and have to make war. One thing he could not do was lose the Vexin.

While he was in France the Archbishop of Rouen visited him, and the reason for his visit was to tell him that the Pope wished him to make his peace with Thomas Becket. It was an impossible situation. For several years England's Archbishop had been in exile and this displeased the Pope. Becket would be happy to return to his post. It was for the King to invite him to. If he did not the Pope had hinted that he would have no alternative but to excommunicate the King of England.

Henry pretended to consider the matter. To see Thomas again! He had to admit that the idea was not displeasing. On the contrary it filled him with an excitement he could not understand.

He was in excellent spirits when he met Louis to take leave from him before returning to England.

"Tomorrow," he said, "that thief of yours shall have his peace and a good one too."

"By the saints of France, what thief pray?" asked Louis.

"That Archbishop of Canterbury of ours," answered Henry.

"I wish he were ours as well as yours," replied the King of France. "You will please God and man if you make a good peace with him, and I shall be ever more grateful to you."

*　　*　　*

It was dawn and the meeting was to take place in a green field which was called Traitor's Meadow.

The King of France, although he was stationed near by, had declared that he would not be present at the meeting for he realized that it would be an emotional encounter.

Henry surrounded by a few of his knights rode ahead of his party into the meadow, and there he waited until he saw approaching from the opposite direction the well-known figure and two of his friends riding on either side of him.

Oh God, thought Henry, is this he? He who used to look so fine on his horse in his magnificent cloak lined with fur. The years have ill-used him.

He spurred his horse that he might ride ahead and greet his old friend.

Thomas did the same and in that field they faced each other.

"Thomas," said Henry, his voice shaken with emotion.

"My lord King."

Henry dismounted and Thomas did the same. Then the King held out his arms and they embraced.

"Thomas, it has been so long since we met."

"It is five years," replied Thomas. "A long time for a man to be away from his home."

"I have thought of you often and the days we used to spend together. I doubt I ever laughed as much as I did with you. Why did you plague me so? Why could you not have been as I wished?"

"Because I was your Archbishop, my lord, and I owed my allegiance first to God and then to you."

"I wanted you to have the highest honour. You knew that."

303

"It was an honour that should have come to me through my service to God, not through your favour."

"By God's eyes, what troubles we have made for ourselves! My son Henry talks of you fondly. You bewitched him, Thomas."

"I am glad that he did not lose his love for me."

"Nay. 'Tis hard to do that. You will come back to England, Thomas. Canterbury has been too long without its Archbishop. Your lands shall be restored to you."

Thomas smiled but sadly. He knew Henry so well. How often in the past had his emotion extracted promises from him which in cooler moments he had not kept. Yet it was pleasant to be with this man, this Henry, for had they not loved each other well?

"I have often thought," said the King, "that I would take the cross to the Holy Land. If I did, Thomas, I would leave my son Henry in your care."

"He is almost a man now with a will of his own."

"Yet he would be guided by you and this would I do if I were to leave on a crusade."

Leave on a crusade! Leave England! Leave Normandy, Anjou, Aquitaine! These were the meaning of life to him. He would never leave them. But he liked to dream. He wished to show Thomas that he loved him, so he let himself indulge in this fancy.

"I could not undertake a secular office," said Thomas. "But if you so desired I would give my advice to the young King."

"Thomas, you shall return. We will forget our differences. Come back to us soon."

"My lord is good," said Thomas. "There are certain Bishops who have offended against the Church. None but the Archbishop of Canterbury should have crowned the young King. Those Churchmen who agreed to this should be called to task for doing so."

The King's affability was a little strained at this.

"I believed that as King of England I was entitled to have my son crowned wherever and by whomsoever I wished. You will remember how my grandfather and great-grandfather were crowned."

"My lord, when the Conqueror was crowned by Aldred of York the throne of Canterbury was virtually vacant. Stigand had not at that time received the pall from a legitimate Pope. As for your grandfather Henry I, when he was crowned Anselm the Archbishop was in exile. The Bishop of Hereford crowned him as Anselm's representative and as soon as Anselm returned he was requested to perform a new coronation."

" 'Tis true," said Henry. "And you shall perform a coronation for my son and this time his wife shall be with him for the King of France was sorely vexed because his daughter was not crowned with Henry."

Thomas knelt then at the King's feet; Henry leaned forward and lifted him.

Then he embraced him.

This was indeed a reconciliation.

Murder

Six years before he had escaped from the town of Sandwich and now he came back to it. His servants had set up the cross of Canterbury on the prow and as the little boat came in the people came down to the shore to welcome him. Many of them waded in the water battling for the honour of helping him ashore. On that strand many knelt and asked for his blessing.

One man shouted: "Blessed is he that cometh in the name of the Lord." And some of them shouted: "Hosanna."

As he took the road to Canterbury people fell in behind him. They cried out: "He is back among us. God has blessed us and given him back to us."

In the city of Canterbury itself they set all the bells ringing; people dressed themselves in their finest garments; they filled the streets; they cried to each other that all was well with Canterbury for Thomas Becket was back.

Thomas walked into the Cathedral. The joy of being in his own church was unsurpassed. He sat on the throne and one by one his monks came to receive the kiss of peace and the people who had crowded into the Cathedral looked on with awe.

Some whispered to the others: "All is well now. He is back."

*   *   *

There were many who were deeply disturbed by his return; those who had helped to destroy him, those who had taken part in the coronation of young Henry, those who had believed their ambitions would be furthered if he were out of the way. And chief of these was Roger, Archbishop of York.

"How long will he last?" he asked his friends. "Has he not laid strictures on us because we officiated at the ceremony of coronation. I have the King behind me. I will empty my coffers . . . I will spend eight—nay ten thousand pounds—to put down this man. Let us to Normandy where the King is and there we will tell him of how Thomas Becket conducts himself as soon as he has returned to England."

Smarting under the threat of excommunication the Bishops agreed with him and they set out for Normandy.

Thomas meanwhile was discovering that the King had not kept his promise to return his estates, and had even taken revenge on his family. His sisters had been forced to go into exile. Mary who had become a nun had gone to a French convent, and Matilda and her family had also gone to France where the Abbot of Clairmarais had given them refuge.

How deep had Henry's feeling been? Had he really meant his promise of friendship?

Roger of York was a powerful man and he had been Thomas's enemy from the day when they had been together in Theobald's household. He now knew that Thomas's rise could only be his fall, and he had meant what he said when he had boasted that he would spend his fortune on ruining him.

He was an influence in the Church; he had won the King's favour by showing him that he had no scruples and was bent on reaching his ambition which was to be head of the Church in England.

Before he left for Normandy he went to Woodstock to see the young Henry.

Henry was proud of his Crown and his attitude had changed since his coronation. He was apt to be critical of his father and wise men said that it was folly for one king to crown his successor while he still lived. The boy King was undoubtedly a little arrogant; he was surrounded by sycophants, and when Roger came with that unctuous manner which he knew so well how to use and flattered the young boy, he could influence him.

"Becket is on his way to see you, I doubt not," he told him. "I'll warrant you will have little time for the old hypocrite."

Henry was puzzled. "I liked him well," he said. "He tutored me, you know."

"Ah, my lord. That was when you were a young boy and could be easily deceived. How quickly you learned to see the truth. I'll swear that you see this more quickly even than your noble father."

"It may be so," said Henry solemnly.

"I said to my Bishops, 'Our lord, the young King, will see right through the old fellow when he comes trying to wheedle something out of him.' "

"Why should he wheedle?"

"Because, dear lord, you are who you are: our King."

Henry smiled. "I could not help but like the fellow . . ."

"Until you saw that he was a troublemaker. You saw it ere your father did, I warrant."

Henry was silent. He supposed that Thomas was a troublemaker. His father and the Archbishop had quarrelled.

"You know he has excommunicated those of us who took part in your coronation?"

"Why so?"

"Because he did not believe you should be crowned."

"And why should he presume to do that?"

"Because he *is* presumption. He was against the coronation. There should be one king at a time, he says."

"Does he indeed! Then he will have to be taught otherwise."

"I knew you would think that, my lord. He has insulted you by his protests against the coronation. I'll warrant you'll not lose an opportunity of insulting him."

Henry was thoughtful.

* * *

Thomas was travelling to Woodstock. What pleasure it would give him to embrace his pupil. He would see young Marguerite too. He had loved the pair of them dearly; and they had been eager to learn from him.

First he could pass through London and when he reached that city, his reception was as heartening as that which he had received in Canterbury.

The Bishop of Winchester received him in his Palace of Southwark and caused the bells to be rung for he was as good a friend as Roger of York was bad an enemy.

"It warms my heart to see you back," he said. "And see

what a welcome the people of London give you. You will overcome your enemies."

When Thomas went into the streets people came to him and knelt on the cobbles for his blessing, but there was one distressing incident when a mad woman who called herself a prophetess ran amok through the crowd. "Beware of the knife, Archbishop," she kept crying. "Beware of the knife."

They hustled her away and Thomas went on his progress. But that night his dreams were disturbed and in them he heard the old woman's cry: "Beware of the knife."

* * *

When he approached Woodstock, his good friend Abbot Simon of Saint Albans, who had travelled from his monastery to greet the Archbishop, said that he would go as messenger to the young King and tell him of the approach of his old friend and counsellor.

It saddened him when Simon returned with the news that the young King refused to see him, and that he had been told by one of Henry's knights that there would be no welcome for Thomas Becket at Woodstock.

So he travelled back to Canterbury.

It was Christmas time and on Christmas Day at High Mass his text was "On earth peace to men of good will."

He was full of foreboding.

Young Henry had been turned against him, and how could he know what was in the mind of his father?

* * *

Henry was at Bayeux when Roger of York and some of the excommunicated Bishops arrived to see him

The first thing he asked was: "How fares the Archbishop of Canterbury?"

"As he always did, my lord," said Roger of York. "He is roaming the country and seeking to turn many of your subjects against you."

"How has he done that?" demanded the King.

"He has only to appear and the people shout for him. He poses as the martyr who has suffered greatly because of the King's ill will."

"And his ill will towards me? What of that?"

"He does not mention that, my lord. He poses as a saint.

Many say he is. The people follow him wherever he goes. They kneel before him and they think that if he gives them his blessing their sins are forgiven them and they are sure of their place in Heaven. He declares the young King is no king for he should never have been crowned."

"He has preached this?"

"Assuredly so, my lord. He has cursed all those who took part in the coronation. He will excommunicate them he says."

"Then he will excommunicate me," said the King.

"He has said *all*, my lord, and that would assuredly include you. He gathers multitudes wherever he goes. He is marching through England calling on the people to turn out the young King."

"By God's eyes," said the King, "he has deceived me again. He is against me and mine."

The rage was beginning to show in his eyes; he tore at his hair and pulled at the stuff of his doublet.

He shouted to Roger and his companions: "What would you have me do, eh? How would you have me act?"

"It is not for us to advise you, my lord," answered Roger. "That is for your barons, but as long as Thomas Becket lives you will not have good days, nor a peaceful kingdom and quiet times."

Henry clenched his fists and those standing near him took a pace backwards for they could see that his wrath would burst forth at any moment and would be terrible.

"A fellow who has eaten my bread has lifted up his heel against me. A fellow who first broke into my court on a lame horse with a cloak for a saddle swaggers on my throne while you, the companions of my fortunes, look on."

He glared at the company and his gaze rested on a certain knight named Reginald FitzUrse. The man trembled before the wrath of the King.

"A curse upon all the false varlets I have maintained!" spat out Henry. "They have left me long exposed to the insolence of this low-born cleric and have not attempted to relieve me of him."

He strode angrily to the door, and eagerly they fell back to let him pass.

When he had gone there was a deep silence in the room.

* * *

Reginald FitzUrse, a man of some ambition, asked three of his friends to come to his chamber where they might talk in secret. These three were William de Tracy, Hugh de Morville and Richard Brito.

When they were there and he was sure of secrecy, FitzUrse said: "It was a command from the King. He looked straight at me when he said those words. He is commanding me to kill Thomas Becket."

"I believe that to be so," replied Hugh de Morville. "I believe he would reward well those who rid him of the troublesome priest."

"I have asked you here that we might share this honour of doing service to the King. He will not forget us, depend upon it."

"The Archbishop is at Canterbury surrounded by his friends."

"That should not deter us."

"What should we do then?"

"First we go to Canterbury and there we will make our plans."

"Then," said Richard Brito, "why do we not set out without delay?"

"We will leave this night for Canterbury," answered Reginald FitzUrse.

Within a few hours they were on their way to the coast to take ship for England.

*   *   *

On the 28th of December the four knights came to Saltwood Castle and there they rested. They had collected a party of men known to be enemies of the Archbishop, those who thought they could profit by pleasing the King and there they conferred together. They would incite the people to march on the Archbishop's palace.

They soon discovered that this was impossible as the people were fervently on the side of the Archbishop and nowhere more than in his own district.

They therefore marched on alone.

Thomas was at refectory talking with some of the monks and clerics as was his custom. They had been trying to urge him to escape, for they were well aware that the King's knights were in the neighbourhood endeavouring to inflame the people against him.

He had awakened that morning with a presentiment of disaster and had said that he believed his end was very near.

Those who loved him implored him to leave. They were but six miles or so from Sandwich; a boat could be procured. The King of France would offer him hospitality.

"Nay," said Thomas. "Not again. I know the time has come and it is God's will that I stay to meet my fate."

While they sat there his Seneschal came in to announce the arrival of four knights.

They stood before him looking at him insolently. He knew them all by name for they had served him when he had been the Chancellor.

"God help you," said FitzUrse and his voice was exultant.

"Have you come here to pray for me then?" asked Thomas.

"We come with a message from the King. Will you hear it now or in private?"

"At your pleasure," answered Thomas.

"Nay, at yours."

Thomas saw that they were all unarmed, yet he read murder in their eyes and he thought: The King has sent them to kill me.

"It shall be at your pleasure," he said, for he had no will to stop their designs. Rather did he welcome them, so certain was he that his martyrdom was at hand.

"You have offended the King," said FitzUrse. "You have broken your agreement with him. You have threatened excommunication of the King's friends and roamed the country rallying people that they might act against the King. Our Lord the King commands that you go at once to his young son, King Henry, and swear fealty to him and make atonement for your crimes against our great King, Henry II."

"There is no man—saving young Henry's own father—who loves him more than I. I have none but warm and loyal feelings for him. The welcome given me by my friends has been mistaken for disloyal demonstrations against the King and I am ready to prove this in any court. Any excommunication is decreed by the Pope. As for those who have taken part in the coronation of the King's son I have no jurisdiction over the Archbishop of York, but if the Bishops of London and Salisbury who shared in that ceremony ask pardon and stand trial for their actions they will be absolved. I have had the King's leave to punish those who invade my office."

"You accuse the King of treachery when you say he allowed you to suspend those who took part in a coronation ordered by himself," said FitzUrse.

"I do not charge the King with treachery, but you know of our agreement."

"From whom do you hold your Archbishopric?" demanded FitzUrse.

"From God and the Pope."

"And not from the King?"

"By no means. We must render to the King that which is the King's and to God the things that are God's."

The knights were nonplussed and hated him the more for confounding them.

Thomas said softly: "You cannot be more ready to strike than I am to suffer. Understand this. I did not return to fly again."

The knights looked at each other in bewilderment. FitzUrse, the leader, cursed himself for having no weapon at hand and for a moment wondered whether he would snatch the crozier and batter the Archbishop to death with that.

Then he turned and hurried from Thomas's presence, the others following him.

Thomas's friends were terrified. They knew that the four knights were bent on murder.

"I wish to go into the Cathedral to pray," said Thomas; and it occurred to several of the monks that he had the air of a bridegroom going to his marriage.

He left the palace with a very few of his monks. Terror had invaded the place, and it occurred to Thomas that his enemies would kill him before he could reach the Cathedral.

He came in by the north transept and as he did so the four knights appeared at the far end of the cloister. Thomas moved towards the altar and in the gloom was not seen by the knights; but the monks who had accompanied him ran to shelter in various parts of the Cathedral. Only one cleric, Edward Grim, remained beside him.

They shouted: "Where is the traitor, Becket?"

"Here," cried Thomas. "No traitor but a priest of God. If you seek me you have found me. What do you wish of me?"

So calm was he that Morville and Tracy were suddenly afraid for they knew they were in the presence of a great man.

Tracy called: "Fly, or you are a dead man."

"I do not fear your swords," answered Thomas. "I welcome death for the sake of the Lord and the freedom of the Church."

Aware that the others were wavering, FitzUrse cried: "You are our prisoner. You will come with us."

"I will not," answered Thomas.

FitzUrse stretched out to seize his pall. "Do not touch me, pander," said the Archbishop.

This enraged FitzUrse who waved his sword over the Archbishop's head.

Thomas knew that the moment had come. He murmured: "Unto Thy hands, oh Lord . . ." as FitzUrse shouted: "Strike!"

Tracy lifted his sword and the faithful Edward Grim tried to ward off the blow. His arm was severed from his body and he fell fainting to the ground. The sword came down in Thomas's head and cut off the tonsured part of his crown.

FitzUrse came in and delivered another blow which sent Thomas to his knees. Brito struck out with his sword and Thomas fell dying to the floor.

FitzUrse cried: "The deed is done. Let us be off, comrades. This traitor will never rise again."

*　　*　　*

His body lay on the stones and Osbert, his chamberlain, came and wept over him. Then he cut off a piece of his surplice and covered his master's face.

The soldiers were ransacking the palace and the monks were in hiding. It was as though a terrible darkness had fallen over the cathedral; and when it was quiet and the ravagers had gone, and the news of what had happened had spread through the town, people came to the spot where he lay and they wept and knelt and called him, "Thomas the Saint and Martyr."

The monks collected his scattered brains and put them in a basin as holy relics, and they found that beneath his robes he wore a long hair shirt which was alive with vermin and which must have tormented him sorely.

All night they knelt beside him, and in the morning because they had heard that his enemies were coming to take his body and give it to the dogs, they took him to the crypt and they buried him before the altars of Saint John the Baptist and Saint Augustine the Apostle of England; and from that day it was said miracles were performed at the shrine of Thomas Becket.

The King's Remorse

When the news was brought to the King he was filled with remorse and a certain terror.

"I have done this," he said. "I am the murderer of Thomas Becket."

He shut himself in his bedchamber and wished to see no one. There he thought of all they had been to each other in the days of their friendship and how there was not a man he loved as he had loved Thomas Becket.

And he had killed him.

They were calling him a martyr. They were calling him a saint. They said that at his shrine miracles were performed. The whole of Christendom was shocked by the murder and the whole of Christendom said: "Who has done this wicked deed?"

It was FitzUrse and the others. Nay, it was the King. Had he not cursed them for not ridding himself of the man?

All his life the memory of Thomas Becket would be with him. He might do a public penance but he would never forget.

Thomas lay dead, his brains had been scattered on the stones. And his body they said was inflamed with the bites of the vermin who at his will had infested his hair shirt. Thomas, who had loved silk next to his skin and had hated the cold winds to blow on him! He was dead—killed by his one-time friend.

There was not room for the two of us in England, thought Henry, because I wanted to be supreme ruler not only of State but of Church. And because of this he lies dead and I am to blame. I am the murderer who killed the martyr.

But he was a King; he had his life to lead; his country to govern.

His son Henry, whom he had crowned, he now knew unwisely, was eager to take his place. Thomas had been against the crowning. It was never wise to set up a new king while the old one still reigned.

His wife Eleanor hated him. His son Richard had turned against him.

Where could he go for comfort? To Rosamund? She would give him solace, but he could not talk to her of his troubles. She would never understand them. She would agree with everything he said, and that was not what he wanted.

What was Eleanor doing? How long before she roused his sons against him? He was unhappy. He was afraid, for he was a lonely man and his soul was stained with the blood of one he had loved.

BIBLIOGRAPHY

Abbott, Edwin A.	*St Thomas of Canterbury*
Appleby, John T.	*Henry II* *The Vanquished King*
Aubrey, William Hickman Smith	*The National and Domestic History of England*
Dark, Sidney	*St Thomas of Canterbury*
Demimuid, Monsignor	*Saint Thomas à Becket*
Duggan, Alfred	*Thomas Becket of Canterbury*
FitzStephen, William, his clerk, with contemporary sources translated by George Greenaway	*The Life and Death of Thomas Becket*
Guizot, M. Translated by Robert Black	*History of France*
Henderson, A. E.	*Canterbury Cathedral Then and Now*
Hope, Mrs	*The Life of St Thomas Becket of Canterbury*
Hutton, the Rev. William Holden (arranged by)	*Thomas of Canterbury. An account of his Life and Fame from Contemporary Biographers and other Chroniclers*
Hutton, the Rev. William Holden	*Thomas Becket*
Knowles, M.D.	*Archbishop Thomas Becket, Character Study*
Morris, John	*The Life and Martyrdom of St Thomas à Becket*
Pernoud, Régine. Translated by Peter Wiles	*Eleanor of Aquitaine*

Robertson, James Craigie	*Becket, Archbishop of Canterbury*
Rosenberg, Melrich V.	*Eleanor of Aquitaine, Queen of the Troubadours and the Courts of Love*
Salzmann, L. F.	*Henry II*
Speaight, R.	*Thomas Becket*
Stephens, Sir Leslie and Lee, Sir Sydney (Edited by)	*The Dictionary of National Biography*
Strickland, Agnes	*Lives of the Queens of England*
Thompson, Robert Anchor	*Thomas Becket*
Wade, John	*British History*

Get Your
Coventry Romances
Home Subscription NOW

And Get These
4 Best-Selling Novels
FREE:

LACEY
by Claudette Williams

THE ROMANTIC WIDOW
by Mollie Chappell

HELENE
by Leonora Blythe

THE HEARTBREAK TRIANGLE
by Nora Hampton